W9-BXU-738

Renewal

Renewal

A Novel

by

RUSSELL SHAW

GARNET BOOKS SAN FRANCISCO

Cover by Marcia Ryan

For Garnet Books
A Division of Ignatius Press

ISBN 0-89870-109-0
Library of Congress catalogue number 86-81998
Printed in the United States of America

There may even be a moral in it; history teaches us our lessons, more often than not, obliquely. Not what happened, but the meaning of what happened, concerns us. At what sources do they feed, these torrents which threaten, once and again, to carry off our peaceful countryside in ruin?

Ronald A. Knox, *Enthusiasm*

I

For a long time everyone had known that Wernersburgh was in for a shaking-up when Bishop Frisch retired, but there was sharp disagreement on whether that was a good thing or not. The conservatives were frankly worried, while for the liberals Frisch couldn't leave the scene too soon. Neither party really grasped how radical the change would be; but the Bishop himself claimed to know. It was 1970: anything could happen in the Catholic Church—and most things did. "Après nous le déluge", Frisch often told cronies, just stopping short of predicting tumbrels and the guillotine.

One wet Wednesday morning in September, he seemed ready to predict them, too. The Apostolic Delegate had written, saying the Holy Father had accepted the obligatory resignation, which Frisch had tendered on turning seventy-five a few weeks earlier; the news would be announced the following Tuesday; his successor would be named soon after; he was to serve as Apostolic Administrator until Wernersburgh's new bishop was appointed. Glowering, Frisch intoned, "Après nous le déluge". As if in confirmation, rain rattled against the windows of his office on the chancery's second floor. Standing on the other side of the big desk, Hugh Boylan, Auxiliary Bishop and Vicar General of the diocese, cleared his throat doubtfully.

"You think I'm exaggerating, Hughie?" The old man snorted. "Wait and see."

"I'm nervous too, Peter, but . . . " Bishop Boylan groped for consolation and, typically, located it in Rome: "The Vatican must see the need for continuity." He was a big man, heavy and bald and slightly pop-eyed, who pursed his lips to look judicious. Pursing them now, he resembled a kewpie-doll with toothache.

Bent and carapodic, Bishop Frisch sat crouched like an immemorial crustacean over the cluttered desk. "The Vatican . . . continuity", he repeated drily. "Rome dozed off ten years ago, and it's still asleep. Meanwhile they've been scheming to put a liberal in my place. Got their man, too."

Boylan eyed him in alarm. "You know who it is?"

Frisch sighed. "Ambrose Farquhar."

"Farquhar? They wouldn't!"

"They have. He was Gatti's candidate, and the Archbishop got his way. It's in the bag for Farquhar—the Delegate told me so himself." He said it with morose satisfaction.

His dumpling cheeks gone suddenly pale, Hugh Boylan slumped sacklike into the chair beside the desk. "If Archbishop Gatti likes him so well, why doesn't he keep him in New Antwerp?"

Bishop Frisch considered that a fatuous question, but he answered it in deference to Boylan's state of shock. "Farquhar has been Gatti's Auxiliary for five years. Time for him to move up."

"I've been *your* Auxiliary for seven years!"

"If I could do anything for you, Hughie, God knows I would. As matters stand . . . ", Frisch shrugged. "Talk to the Archbishop. He's calling the shots these days."

"But why send Ambrose Farquhar *here?*"

"Because this diocese has been a bone in Gatti's throat for a long time, and he can count on Farquhar to do a thorough housecleaning." Rising painfully—it was one of his gouty days—Frisch hobbled to the large window. Beside it hung an autographed color photo in profile of Pius XII at prayer. He stood watching the rump of the morning rush hour traffic churn sullenly through the rain toward the downtown business district. "A nice day for my funeral."

Bishop Boylan was still trying to take it all in. Unlike some he could have named—unlike even Frisch—he wasn't an especially political bishop. He knew all there was to know about the diocese of Wernersburgh ("comprising", in the words of the Catholic Directory, "the counties of Polk, Suffolk, Garfield, Arthur, Sunflower, and Merrifield in the southwestern part of the state"), but he was largely ignorant of the great ecclesiastical machine outside its borders. Even his outburst to Frisch—"I've been *your* Auxiliary for seven years"—signaled no craving for anything grander than his present position of modest eminence and responsibility in this cozy corner of the Church. It wasn't ambition that filled him now but apprehension at the thought of serving under Ambrose Farquhar.

Farquhar's career was exemplary of its kind: marked out early by Archbishop Gatti of New Antwerp as a protégé, he'd served successively as the great man's secretary, Assistant Chancellor, and, currently, Auxiliary Bishop and Vicar General. On paper it was a *curriculum vitae* very much like Hugh Boylan's own. But the resemblance was superficial. Boylan sought no personal fame, but Farquhar had made quite a name for himself—firebrand and creative innovator in one version, hatchet man and dangerous radical in another. He was Archbishop Gatti's man in either case, and to Boylan, schooled by Frisch, that made him bad news.

Frisch and Gatti, to get at the root of the matter, had known each other too long and too well for either's good. They'd been rival students at the North American College in Rome in the early 1920s, then for two decades pursued parallel careers in the great archdiocese of New Antwerp, which sprawled so uncouthly in the northeastern quarter of the state. Both were Auxiliaries when the archdiocese last became open, both were considered in the running for the job, and Gatti got it. Six months later Frisch got Wernersburgh as his consolation prize. And then—"Just to make things worse", he'd explained to friends in private—came the Second Vatican Council and its aftermath.

Traumatized by Vatican II (in Frisch's account) and seeking to expiate the rigid orthodoxy of his earlier years, Archbishop Gatti had given himself and his archdiocese relentlessly over to what he chose to call "renewal". That meant the multiplication of bureaucracies (disaffected priests dubbed the New Antwerp chancery "the Pentagon"); endless consultative processes, in which a small number of clerical and lay activists traded clichés on church affairs, and iron-fisted coercion of conservatives—all accompanied by self-congratulating rhetoric about the New Church that was supposedly emerging from the ascetical, doctrinal, catechetical, and liturgical shambles.

Was that an unfair picture? Not as Hugh Boylan saw things. True, Gatti enjoyed enormous prestige outside his archdiocese. But that, Boylan believed, was only because most news of what was happening in New Antwerp was filtered through the liberal Catholic establishment now controlling most instruments of communication in the Church. Insiders told a different story: Gatti, an autocrat behind a democratic facade, was pursuing policies that would eventually destroy the Catholic Church in New Antwerp and replace it with a monstrous new bastard sect, neither authentically Catholic nor honestly Protestant.

In all this Ambrose Farquhar was at least his Archbishop's agent and possibly a good deal more. Many held that Farquhar was the instigator of much of the mischief, egging on Gatti to even more outrageous experiments while assuring him that the data of disaster—massive defections by priests and nuns, a drying up of new vocations, the sullen silence of the dismayed laity (punctuated by occasional angry outbursts at the latest outrage perpetrated or condoned by the "Pentagon")—were the necessary growing pains of the New Church. Something had certainly been tossed into the dustbin of history in New Antwerp, and Farquhar had helped toss it there; but while Farquhar and Archbishop Gatti might believe it was only the sloughed-off skin of the old ("Tridentine") ecclesiastical structure, Hugh Boylan felt sure it was the bludgeoned corpse of the true Church.

The worst of Frisch's shocking news was that everything he and Frisch had striven to do here in Wernersburgh—and by and large had succeeded in doing—now stood to be undone. Certainly the diocese had its problems: pockets of dissidence among the priests, with a defection now and then; uppity nuns engaged in constant agitation; fewer vocations than were needed; and an undertone of grumbling among lay liberals, who professed to find Catholic life here excruciatingly dull and hankered after the dazzling calamities of New Antwerp. But for the most part, Frisch and he had managed the impossible. In the five turbulent years since the end of Vatican II they'd kept the diocese a bastion of sound doctrine, maintained liturgical discipline (or at least driven abuses underground), held the clergy and religious in check, sustained the docile lay majority with sound preaching and lawfully administered sacraments, and they had run a seminary which, if not precisely thriving, had at least not degenerated, as many others had, into an ecclesiastical frat house before expiring for want of students.

Perhaps Wernersburgh *was* a little dull, but dullness in defense of orthodoxy was a badge of honor in Boylan's book. Peter

Frisch had his critics (*he* did, too, for that matter), but they were captious and unavailing—and, more to the point, attracted more attention outside the diocese than at home. There was, for example, a bothersome young priest, Arthur Kucharski, whose articles in the notorious *National Catholic Recorder* often rankled. But within the diocese all was placid—certainly on the surface and, so far as Boylan could tell, pretty far beneath it too. Whatever people's private opinions and practices might be, birth control was a non-issue as a matter for public discussion, while priestly celibacy was taken for granted, liturgical aberrations were invisible, and no heresy was heard in the pulpits and classrooms of Wernersburgh (except for the two local Catholic colleges, St. Bruno's and Maryheights, about which Frisch could do little except fume).

These days the only direct challenge to this generally orderly scene came from the city's daily newspaper, the *Globe-Herald,* which served as mouthpiece for the disorganized, muzzled dissidents of the diocese. But even the *Globe-Herald* didn't greatly worry Frisch and Boylan. They had a fierce journalistic guard dog of their own: the diocesan paper, the *Catholic Truth,* as vigorous in defending good order as the *Globe-Herald* in attacking it. If Wernersburgh wasn't paradise, it came as close as the Auxiliary Bishop could reasonably hope at a time when the Church elsewhere—New Antwerp being indisputably the most horrible example—was going down the tubes. And to sacrifice all *this* . . .

"As long as I've been around, I still don't understand how such things can happen in the Church." Turning from the window, Peter Frisch limped back to the desk and sat down wearily. Once more he studied the Delegate's letter. "Is the system so culpably stupid that it can only crank out mistakes, or is it all part of a plan? Consider this, Hughie: the Pope and the curia were secretly kidnapped years ago and replaced by

Marxist-Masonic look-alikes. That would explain a lot, wouldn't it?"

Boylan failed to see the humor of it. "You said Rome went to sleep ten years ago. That's a good enough explanation for me."

"And probably the correct one. At least it holds out hope."

"Of what?"

"Rome might wake up. The harm already done will cripple the Church for years. But so far it isn't final and irrevocable. There's time to turn things around."

"So many people already hurt. . . . "

"That's the damnable thing", Bishop Frisch agreed with sudden passion. "People get hurt. What's the first responsibility of a bishop? The care of souls! And what becomes of the *people* of this diocese now? Doesn't anybody see the connection between sound doctrine and discipline and the salvation of souls?"

"You did, Peter", Boylan said huskily. The line on Frisch was that he lacked human feeling, but his Auxiliary believed differently: orthodoxy was the service his mind rendered to his heart; doctrine and discipline were good for people.

Bishop Frisch sighed. "At least I knew there was a connection. But fashions in bishops change. We're expected to be *pastoral* today." He pronounced the word with distaste, like a man naming a nasty disease. "Do you know what pastoral means? Forming bad consciences—telling people they haven't sinned when they have, or excusing their sins without insisting they give them up. It means risking people's damnation, but doing it gently—with guitars and the kiss of peace."

Talk like that frightened Boylan. He asked, "What will happen to the chancery staff?"

"How much housecleaning? I can't tell you, but Farquhar will want his own team."

"Think of Justin Walsh!" Bishop Boylan exclaimed.

"Being a layman—"

"And being editor of the *Catholic Truth*—he's terribly vulnerable."

"You can be sure Farquhar has his eye on the paper already."

"Do you think he'll fire Justin?"

"He'll do whatever he must to make the paper his", Frisch said, "and probably talk all the while about how he wants it to be open and independent. Of course the *Catholic Truth*'s been that for years, precisely because I could count on Justin to think as I do. If Farquhar is smart, he'll handle it the same way—find an editor he trusts and give him his head."

"I'll try to protect Justin", the Auxiliary Bishop promised.

"And what about yourself, Hughie?" Frisch demanded. "Who's going to look out for you?" In his grief the old man was heaping coals on his own head. Boylan was shaken at seeing Peter Frisch, of all people, come to this.

"I guess I can look out for myself", he said, meaning it as a bold affirmation. But it sounded tentative and weak. Trying to recoup, he added, "Maybe I'll get a diocese of my own."

"I wanted you to have *this* one. Now . . . I don't know." Two previous Auxiliaries had been promoted to Ordinary, but that was when Frisch enjoyed the powers of patronage. They'd declined dramatically in recent years, as Frisch grew more conservative—or other bishops more liberal—and became increasingly isolated within the hierarchy. There was nothing he could do for Boylan now, and both men knew it.

It had grown darker outside as the clouds closed in and the rain fell more heavily. Summer was over. The office was dark too, its only source of illumination a thick-shaded lamp on Frisch's monolith of a desk. "If you could have anything in the world you wanted, Hughie," the old man said quietly, "what would it be?"

"That you were twenty years younger."

Peter Frisch bowed his head. Rain pelted the streaming window panes. Gradually Boylan became aware of another sound, intimate and frightening: Frisch was crying. Indecision petrified the Auxiliary—should he pretend he didn't hear, offer consolation, or what? Nothing in his experience told him what to do; and that, he reflected wretchedly, was how everything would emphatically be from now on.

Bishop Frisch's retirement was announced in Rome, Washington, and Wernersburgh on Tuesday of the following week. Greeted with indifference in the first two places, the news caused strong feelings in the third: among liberals relief, as at the lifting of a siege; among conservatives regret and apprehension. Would the Pope name a successor of like views (in which case Hugh Boylan's chances were rated excellent) or would he opt for change by appointing a progressive? Frisch and Boylan knew but kept it to themselves; others guessed with every appearance of certitude.

By Thursday morning Bishop Boylan had decided to share the secret with Justin Walsh. It wasn't merely that they were old friends; the editor had a right, as Boylan saw it, to early warning, so that he could give plenty of time to mending his fences—or burning his bridges, as the case might be.

He sought out Justin in his sixth floor office, a sunny room filled with overflowing book shelves and filing cases, its walls (where wall could be seen) crammed with photos, citations, scrolls, and other memorabilia of two decades' service. Wearing a bright blue pullover sweater and smoking a large pipe, Justin Walsh was reading one of the first copies of that week's issue of the *Catholic Truth* to arrive from the printer. As usual he was enjoying the product of his labors.

"Good issue!" he exclaimed to Boylan as he entered. "I

wanted something special for Bishop Frisch, and this is. Look!" He thrust the paper on the Auxiliary, his blue eyes candidly searching for signs that his enthusiasm was shared. At fifty-five Justin had a bristling shock of prematurely white hair and was starting to grow stocky, but he had a child's capacity for excitement and showed his feelings just as easily.

Boylan did his best to rise to the occasion. "It looks good, Justin." Occupying the top center of page one was a large color portrait of Frisch, the one he'd had taken five years ago, presciently observing that he wouldn't have to bother again about *that.* To the right was a story on the retirement, to the left an account of Frisch's career and, beneath, a long editorial of appreciation, plainly Justin's work. Flipping through the pages, he glimpsed more in the same vein: sidebars on the history of the diocese, highlights of the Frisch years, and a center spread of photos from the files. The *Catholic Truth* had gone all-out.

"He deserves the best", Justin said warmly. "This diocese owes him everything. I want people to remember that."

Boylan smiled wanly. "People have short memories."

"The *Globe-Herald* would like them to. You saw this morning's paper?" Unearthing it from the clutter on his desk, Justin read scowling from the first page. " 'Speculation Starts on Frisch Successor.' That means they're impatient to hustle him out."

Boylan had read the story. Written by Gwyneth Harley, the *Globe-Herald* religion writer and a longtime nemesis of the chancery, it said the obvious, but said it with a certain flair that he'd learned to associate with Harley: if the Vatican wanted a conservative in the job, Boylan's own chances were excellent; if not, various names were mentioned. Ambrose Farquhar's wasn't among them. Even for Gwyneth Harley, it seemed, that was too improbable to mention.

Justin was grinning expectantly. "What need is there to speculate? It's obvious who'll get the job."

The Auxiliary cleared his throat uneasily. "Mind if I shut the door?" Surprised, Justin shook his head. "There's something I want to tell you—in strict confidence. You're entitled to know, but nobody else." Boylan took a deep breath. "Ambrose Farquhar is getting the job."

"Farquhar?" Justin was thunderstruck. "What the hell . . . ?"

Boylan raised a hand to stop him. "Our loyalty to the Church is being tested."

"Is Ambrose Farquhar the Church?" Puffing clouds of smoke, Justin flushed with distress—for Boylan and himself.

"He's the Holy Father's choice."

The editor looked disgusted. "We both know the Holy Father doesn't know him from Adam. In fact, the Holy Father probably couldn't find Wernersburgh itself on a map." He brooded, shaking his big head in dismay. "I absolutely do not understand this."

"The Church only asks that we accept it, Justin," Bishop Boylan said sententiously, "not that we understand it."

"You want this to be a matter of faith, but if *my* faith depended on the notion that the Church makes only good personnel choices, I'd have lost faith a long time ago."

Justin's jaw was starting to jut, a good sign he was settling down to argue. Boylan rose quickly and said, "Try to make the best of it. Don't start with a prejudice against the man. It isn't worthy of you."

Justin blinked and seemed chastened. "Sorry." Impulsively he rose and extended his hand. "I just wish it were you. But count on me. . . . I'll do the best I can for the sake of the Church."

Of course he would. Hadn't he always? Perhaps this new state of affairs really would prove workable. Such thoughts were still on Justin's mind that night as he maneuvered his elderly Pontiac homeward through rain-clogged traffic along gleaming streets. The facts, as he saw them, were these: he was a conservative, lay Catholic editor and Farquhar, by all accounts, a very liberal bishop—one who (according to Justin's files) had said he'd be "the first to ordain a woman if Rome would give permission", who'd repeatedly urged "compassion" and "pastoral sensitivity" (code words in Justin's book for toleration verging on approval) toward divorced and remarried Catholics, homosexuals, practitioners of birth control, and most other violators of the Church's moral code on sex and marriage, who'd never lost an opportunity to lend his name to any trendy social cause (from Chicano rights to acid rain and Vietnam) that caught his attention. Not quite Justin's cup of tea.

Ponderously but firmly, nevertheless, Justin had made up his mind: he wouldn't let himself be forced out nor would he resign. Perhaps, as shepherd of a conservative flock, Farquhar would move toward the center; perhaps Justin himself would have a role to play in fostering that desirable evolution; perhaps—well, any number of perhapses. The point was that he refused to panic. He'd wait things out. Hugh Boylan was right, after all: this was a test of loyalty to the Church, no less. That put everything in a different light.

Lying atop the stack of mail on the hall table when he got home was a fundraising appeal from St. Bruno's College. Justin tossed it aside contemptuously. In his view his old school had become a hotbed of antiwar protest, pot smoking, sex, and bad theology. It was one of the situations in the diocese Frisch hadn't been able to do much about, and it rankled.

Eleanor was scraping carrots in the kitchen. She and Justin brushed cheeks. "Have a good day, dear?" Jonathan was watching "Star Trek" on the TV in the breakfast nook. "Hi, Jon", his grandfather called. The pale, blond little boy waved but kept his eyes on the screen. He was seven years old, and Mr. Spock fascinated him.

"I have news", Justin informed his wife portentuously. "Let's go into the living room."

She gave him a curious look and, drying her hands on her apron, followed him. Dropping into his favorite chair, he announced, "They've chosen a successor to Bishop Frisch."

"Who is it?"

"Ambrose Farquhar."

"Really?" Eleanor waited for some clue to how he expected her to react. No student of church politics, she barely recognized Farquhar's name and attached no special significance to it.

"Auxiliary Bishop in New Antwerp", Justin said curtly. "I guess it will work out."

"I'm *sure* it will, dear", she agreed, her gentle face relaxing. Evidently she'd concluded that optimism was the note he wanted her to strike; but hearing it struck so artlessly, Justin was annoyed.

A clattering came from the front hall, a gust of cold air, and their daughter Megan breezed in wearing her white trench coat. Taller than her mother, almost as tall as her father, she had Eleanor's features but Justin's blue eyes and hair as dark as his had once been. Like him too, she exuded energy, but her nervous restlessness was distinctly her own.

"Did you watch the show tonight?" Megan was a producer with the "Evening News" on Channel 6. As an old newspaperman, Justin scorned television news. Eleanor seldom watched it either, although with her that had more to do with lack of interest than with disapproval.

"It was lovely, dear", she murmured, deceiving neither Megan nor her father.

"You, Daddy?"

"I was driving home at the time. Why?"

"Because we did a feature on the Frisch years, that's why. I'm sorry you missed it."

"I can imagine your line", Justin growled.

Megan smiled indulgently. "Unlike the *Catholic Half-Truth,* we're objective. What you take for slanting are facts you won't acknowledge." It was an old argument. Megan enjoyed it, but Justin took it seriously.

"Your father got some news today", Eleanor said mildly, "about our new bishop."

"Ellie . . . ", he began in a cut-it-out-tone. It was too late: Megan gave him a sharp look over her newly lighted cigarette.

"So they've made the choice already! Who is it?"

"This is confidential, Megan. The announcement won't come for several weeks."

"I'm a professional, Daddy. We're talking off the record. Now—who?"

Reluctantly he said, "Ambrose Farquhar."

She whistled through her teeth. "My God! *He'll* shake up Wernersburgh."

"That's what passes for objectivity on the 'Evening News', I suppose."

"Everybody knows Frisch put the diocese in a time capsule twenty years ago. When Farquhar opens it, he'll find the pre-Vatican II Church preserved on ice."

"*Your* commitment to the Church doesn't entitle you to criticize."

"I'd better get dinner ready", Eleanor interrupted uneasily, rising. "Will you stay, Megan?"

"I had a bite at work."

"Let me give Jon something at least. He must be starved, poor boy."

Megan checked her watch and frowned. "Close to seven! Thanks, Mother. It'll save me the trouble of cooking."

Nodding, Eleanor left the room. Megan stubbed out the cigarette and took her mother's place on the sofa facing Justin. Each was itching to set the other straight.

"I suppose," she began, "Farquhar's appointment will cause problems for you?"

"Why should it?"

"You don't seriously expect to hit it off with him?"

"Why not?"

Megan laughed. "Come off it."

He said, "I intend to do everything in my power to make things work well. No doubt there will be changes."

"If Farquhar deserves his reputation, it will be a revolution."

"I suppose you'd welcome one."

"I keep telling you that I don't think of myself as Catholic anymore. What happens in the diocese doesn't concern me personally. I look at it with— "

"—detachment", Justin interrupted scornfully. "But you're raising Jonathan a Catholic, aren't you? Don't tell me your religion means nothing to you."

"I'd have to raise him something, even if it were only atheist. I make Mother happy this way."

"You don't mention me, I notice."

"You've got Vinnie. Having a priest in the family should be enough for you."

"I care about Jonathan too."

"I thought your concern had never extended beyond my not having an abortion."

Justin blinked and shook his head, like a man who has been punched. "Thank you", he said with dignity.

"I'm sorry." Megan appeared flustered. "That slipped out. It's been a long day, and I'm tired."

"Of course you aren't totally mistaken", he went on doggedly, unwilling to let it drop. "Leaving Jonathan aside—I have more feeling for him than you imagine—I don't condone what you did. I didn't then, and I don't now."

"You've always made that clear."

"And your claim to be disinterested where the Church is concerned doesn't deceive me either. You want to justify yourself, and you think a new bishop will help somehow."

"I hope he'll help those who feel a need for it. Sorry, Daddy, but I'm not one of them. The Church can do whatever it damn well pleases and it won't make one particle of difference to how I live."

Father and daughter confronted each other angrily, just as they'd been doing for years. Eleanor, returning, found them in this attitude. "You've been fighting again", she said in a tone of sorrowful reproach.

"Nonsense", Justin said. "I discuss things, but I do not fight."

Megan gave a harsh laugh. "As you, Mother, are better situated than anyone to verify."

Eleanor sighed. She told Megan, "Jon is just finishing up."

"Good." She rose. "I think we overstayed our welcome."

"Megan. . . . "

She fixed him with a hard look. "Yes?"

"You judge me very harshly."

"Since when does *my* judgment matter to you?" Turning angrily on her heel, she left.

Justin's eyes met Eleanor's. "Is dinner ready?" he asked.

But when it was, he had little appetite and only picked at his Salisbury steak. Eleanor, always a light eater, skimmed a volume of John of the Cross and served Justin, making only cursory inroads on her own plate. Over coffee she took off her reading glasses and said, "I wish you and Megan wouldn't quarrel."

"*I* don't quarrel."

"She has a hard life, Justin. Harder than we realize—working and trying to raise a child alone. We have to be sympathetic."

"I *am.* And as for you—God knows, you do plenty for Megan. I can't imagine another mother who'd do as much. Unfortunately, Megan isn't very grateful."

"She is, dear, in her own way."

"Megan's way . . . ", he considered it ruefully. "Don't expect me either to understand it or approve it, Ellie."

Justin brooded. After a while Eleanor said quietly, "Is it true there's a problem with the new bishop?"

He started and frowned. "That's only Megan talking," he said defensively. The reply satisfied neither of them, but neither said any more.

After dinner, pleading work to do, Justin went upstairs to the spare bedroom, formerly Megan's, which he now used as a study. But instead of working, he sat at his desk staring at the photograph of Vinnie on the wall. Thank God, *something* had gone right. His son was barely a year and a half away from ordination; at least no one could take that from him. Justin studied the young man's features, patterned on his own, with satisfaction: Vinnie was everything Megan wasn't—loyal to Justin's beliefs and values, loyal to Justin himself. The only trouble was, having Vinnie for a son couldn't make up for having Megan for a daughter.

She'd gotten pregnant eight years ago during her senior year in college. Jonathan's father was presumably known to her, but not to Justin and Eleanor. Ellie preached and practiced unqualified forgiveness, and in his better moods he conceded that was right—for her. But forgiving shouldn't mean condoning, and it damn well shouldn't mean seeming to approve. A lot of people in the Church had gone that way, he reflected bitterly. It wasn't a big step from forgiving sin to excusing it,

Justin held, and from excusing to denying that there was any sin: people made mistakes, they damaged relationships and weakened community, they even failed to realize their potential for self-fulfillment. But did they *sin?* Personal sin had seemingly dropped out of the scheme of things overnight, leaving behind it as the only recognized species of wrongdoing something called "social sin"—a form of misdemeanor apparently peculiar to the United States' involvement in Vietnam and to the multinational corporations doing business in South Africa. "If Dante were alive today", Justin had once demanded in an editorial, "would he populate hell with multinationals?"

It was all part of what they called "renewal"—as if to say the Church was, all the Justin Walshes of the world to the contrary notwithstanding, slowly but surely recovering its health after a bad spell. An execrable attitude, one he'd never agree with. But the chilling question facing him now was how Bishop Ambrose Farquhar felt about it all. Justin thought: God help this diocese and me.

Ambrose Farquhar would have been deeply troubled if he'd known how much apprehension his appointment was causing in Wernersburgh. He did not expect the transition to be absolutely trouble-free, but, heart brimming with good will toward his new flock, he hadn't a clue that reciprocal benevolence didn't await him in every sheepfold. Archbishop Gatti tried to warn him, but Farquhar's euphoria kept getting in the way.

"Peter Frisch spent twenty-five years shaping Wernersburgh in his own image", Gatti explained patiently. "You'll have your work cut out for you, Ambrose, just getting people to accept you."

Broad-faced and boyishly earnest, Bishop Farquhar smiled. To him the task didn't sound all that difficult. Once the new reality sank in on the people, wouldn't they naturally be pleased?

Not wanting the Archbishop to suppose his pearls were taken lightly though, he asked politely, "What should I do?"

"Avoid being isolated from the diocese. Believe me, the chancery crowd will try to isolate you, either because they think they're protecting you or because they know they'll lose power if you go over their heads. Find key people who are on your side from the start. The media are crucial. If they become hostile, you've got two strikes against you."

"I like journalists."

"I know you do. But Wernersburgh isn't New Antwerp. Look at the diocesan paper—you're familiar with the *Catholic Truth?*"

Farquhar winced. "I've been reading it lately."

Archbishop Gatti nodded. "Then you know the problem *there.* Locate some friendly journalists. They'll be useful to you."

Opportunity to act on that advice came sooner than either expected. Bishops' appointments are closely held secrets; the few people who know of them in advance are scrupulous about confidentiality. How then does it happen that they're often common knowledge long before they're announced? That, too, is a secret, and even more closely held. One morning Gwyneth Harley of the Wernersburgh *Globe-Herald* phoned Ambrose Farquhar. "I want to drive up to New Antwerp next week and meet you, Bishop. Strictly off the record. Call it getting acquainted."

"Is it worth your time?"

"Obviously."

He gave in readily. This was better than if he'd tried to arrange it. "Come ahead", he told her.

They sat a week later in a German restaurant. Bishop Farquhar sipped a draft beer, while Gwyneth traced patterns with her fingernail in the moisture on a glass of white wine. In her late thirties, she had a high, narrow forehead and shrewd gray eyes that took in everything.

"I guess we need to be clear at the start . . . ", he was saying. "This really isn't an interview."

Raising her hands as if to demonstrate that there was nothing up the sleeves of her severe, gray pin-striped suit, she protested, "No notebook, no recorder. I'm not even going to speculate in print about whether you'll be named. It's as I told you on the phone—I want to get to know you. You may be in Wernersburgh for a long time, and I may be writing about you for as long as you're there. We both benefit from talking."

"I haven't gotten final word on the appointment", he demurred.

She grinned. "This chat is still worth the price of dinner to me. What do they do well here?"

"The schnitzel is excellent."

"Sounds fine." She put aside the menu. "You have a reputation as a liberal. Do you deserve it?"

"Try me."

"What about women priests?"

"I've said I'd be happy to perform the first ordination after Rome gives approval."

"Not before?"

"No way."

"What are the chances Rome will approve?"

"It will happen some day. A change like this comes slowly. It's important to keep up the pressure and not to get discouraged."

"I believe you mean that." She looked at him with greater interest.

Farquhar suspected he'd struck pay dirt. "Of course I do. The Church has been bad on women's issues for a long time. Not intentionally, perhaps, but because she took for granted the cultural prejudices of the times. Religious people are always tempted to call prejudice God's will, and we've often succumbed. But the difference, Gwyneth, is that the Church, unlike a lot of other institutions, *wants* to do what's right and eventually gets around to doing it. My duty—the duty of any Catholic—is to help the Church clarify its thinking." This was part of a talk he gave occasionally; it had pleased audiences before, and it evidently pleased this audience now.

The waiter took their orders. Gwyneth lit a cigarette. "What about celibacy for priests?"

"I believe in it strongly as an option, but it shouldn't be mandatory. I chose celibacy, but there's no reason why a priest shouldn't have the opportunity to choose marriage."

"Despite the present law?"

"Oh, the law will have to be changed first", Bishop Farquhar said. "I don't advocate breaking the law."

"Some break it. Others quit the priesthood."

"That shows the law needs changing."

"Rome doesn't favor that either."

"But it acknowledges we're dealing with something that can be changed. I think it's certain to come."

"Certain?"

"As the number of priests declines. The Holy Spirit usually moves the Church in that way. It takes a crisis for us to make a change that was needed all along."

Dinner came. The schnitzel was excellent. While they ate, Gwyneth moved on to social issues. The Bishop produced for her approval his faultless views on such matters as race, ecology, Vietnam, Nixon, and the Third World. "But seriously," she objected after a while, "what do you imagine the Church can do about these things?"

"Be a prophetic voice, as it was at Vatican II. Nothing changes without prophets."

"Prophecy isn't fashionable in Wernersburgh, Bishop."

"The diocese hasn't had a prophet lately."

"I'll check the files when I get home. . . . How about ecumenism?"

"We've got to move ahead. We're being much too timid. We keep *saying* the right things, but it doesn't go beyond lip service. People expect action."

"Such as?"

"The goal is unity. Why aren't we uniting?"

She looked skeptical. "I suppose there are non-Catholics who could swallow the Church, but they can't swallow the Pope, too."

Bishop Farquhar was enjoying himself by now. Eyes sparkling, he said, "We assume there's only one kind of communion with Rome, all or nothing. But why not think of it in degrees? Why can't there be a level of communion that is less than total, yet entirely real? Think of concentric circles—all are perfect circles around the same point, but some happen to be closer to the point than others."

"Divorce and remarriage?"

"Indissolubility of marriage is another beautiful ideal. But can everyone realize it? Maybe some marriages *do* die. Let's be open to the possibility and not do anything to compound the misery of people in such cases."

"Would you admit Catholics who've divorced and remarried to the sacraments?"

"The discipline of the Church won't allow me. But a bishop can't know everything that's happening in his diocese, can he?"

They ordered coffee. Sipping hers and regarding him with a long look of appraisal, Gwyneth said, "You're going to be quite a novelty in Wernersburgh."

Farquhar said, "What can I expect?"

"Shock at first. Most Catholics think every bishop is like Frisch. Even among those who know better, quite a few think every bishop *ought* to be. You'll take getting used to."

"What about the priests?"

"They'll have to be coaxed out of their shells. Same with the nuns. There are a few parishes that are alive and a number of people who in their hearts think as you do. The Catholic colleges, St. Bruno's and Maryheights, are pockets of resistance. But most of what's good in the diocese has been underground so far."

"And Bishop Boylan?"

"He hasn't had an idea in twenty years without Frisch's approval. Good luck with him." She smiled grimly.

"Are you a Catholic, Gwyneth?"

She hesitated, and he thought for a moment she might not answer. Instead, she said, "Not a Frisch Catholic."

He laughed. "That's clear."

"And not yet a Farquhar Catholic. I like what I've heard this evening, but I want to see what you do when you take over."

"So do I", he acknowledged. "Tell me about the *Catholic Truth.*"

She considered that with professional judiciousness. "It's well edited. Justin Walsh knows his business. But ideologically he's somewhere to the right of Frisch."

Farquhar nodded. "I've been reading the paper lately."

"Then you've seen me and the *Globe-Herald* skewered there. That's something Walsh does regularly—screaming 'anti-Catholic' whenever we run something critical of Frisch. As a tactic, it's been effective over the years."

"You don't care much for Walsh?"

"I respect his ability. Maybe even his integrity—at least, according to his lights. But he's a large part of what's wrong with the diocese—a large part of the problem facing you." She stubbed out her cigarette decisively. "Justin Walsh is one of your biggest problems, Ambrose. I hope you find the solution."

The next night after work Gwyneth was eating dinner in a Wernersburgh restaurant with Fritz Jacoby, the *Globe-Herald*'s editorial page editor, with whom she'd been living for the last two years. They lingered over coffee, in no rush to drive back to the apartment, while she told him about her conversation with Ambrose Farquhar. Jacoby, a hairy man with a curly beard, smoked his pipe and grunted now and then as she spoke.

"There's one thing I'd like to ask you", he said at last.

"What's that?"

"Frisch, Farquhar—what difference does it make? If Catholics want to do something their own way, why don't they just do it? The bishop can't lock anybody up."

Her gray eyes snapped angrily. "You don't understand Catholics."

Jacoby nodded amiably. "I don't even understand you. What's your stake in all this?"

"I'm a reporter", Gwyneth said in a frosty tone. "Farquhar is going to be a hell of a good story."

"Maybe, but don't get *too* close to it—that's my advice." He stretched. "I'm feeling horny."

"Pig."

"Catholic prude." He grinned. "I think you've got the Church in your genes."

"We all do—Catholics. You really don't understand a thing."

"My bad luck, I guess", Jacoby drawled. "It sure looks like a lot of fun."

II

Megan was concentrating on not speeding. Having reluctantly taken time off from work for a conference with Jon's teacher, she was tempted to push the Volkswagen beetle and catch a few of the traffic lights she kept missing. But the police were conscientious in this part of town, and she didn't want a hassle or a ticket; instead she fumed. Bursts of chilly autumn rain spattered on the hood and the wipers dragged grimy snail tracks across the windshield. The all-news radio station was reporting that a presidential commission had concluded that the killings at Kent State were "unwarranted". The bland, bureaucratic word infuriated Megan, and, snarling, "Stupid bastards!" at the radio, she angrily flicked it off. Lighting her third cigarette in a row, she braked to a halt as yet another light turned from yellow to red.

Megan drummed her fingers on the steering wheel as she waited, observing with disapproval that her nails were ragged again: she had a habit of chewing them. For the most part she was exceedingly careful about appearance, but fingernails were a chink in her armor. The idea did not please her. She was vulnerable to Jon, but she wanted no other exceptions. Stop biting your nails, she commanded herself, gunning the engine as the light went green.

She wasn't looking forward to this conference with Mrs.

Brickfield. She'd heard it before from other teachers and heard it again on the phone the other night from this one: Jon was a bright boy, no troublemaker, but he seemed bored and didn't fit in easily with the other children. Megan's unspoken answer was: So what? Jon *was* bright, which accounted for the boredom, and as for not being on easy terms with other kids, that also was due to his being smarter than most. If the school can't handle intelligent children, she thought, why the hell doesn't it say so instead of trying to make the parents feel guilty?

Parking up the street from the Millard Fillmore School in that feisty mood, she made her way to the second grade prepared to concede nothing. The tiled corridor smelled of disinfectant, stale lunches, and damp clothes. Jon was loitering by the classroom door.

"She's waiting for you", he informed his mother.

Kissing him, Megan said, "Put on your windbreaker and go out on the playground if it isn't raining. I'll be along in a few minutes." Still irritated, she glanced at her watch and said, "I'm not late."

"I think she's really down on us", Jon confided, slipping on the windbreaker.

Megan gave him a mock frown. "Buzz off, pal. I don't need your advice."

Shrugging, he sidled away, only pausing to fire "Don't say I didn't warn you" over his shoulder as he disappeared through the doors to the stair well. Shaking her head, Megan rapped on the frosted glass window and entered the classroom.

Mrs. Brickfield sat at her desk correcting papers. Younger than Megan had expected—indeed, not much older than Megan herself—she had bleached hair and a look of syrupy earnestness. She wore a white blouse with a fussy, pleated front, a light blue skirt, and sensible shoes. Megan disliked her even more than she'd expected.

Smiling, Mrs. Brickfield rose. "Mrs. Walsh? I'm Helen Brickfield."

Megan noted the "Mrs." without correcting it. The teacher had made the same mistake on the phone. "I'm pleased to meet you, Mrs. Brickfield."

"Sorry I can't offer you a proper seat." Miniature desk-and-chair combinations were grouped in clusters about the room; the only full-sized chair stood behind the teacher's desk. Having vacated it to greet her visitor, Mrs. Brickfield obviously didn't intend to relinquish it for good.

"I'm comfortable standing."

The teacher resumed her seat. "It was good of you to find time to come. You work, don't you?"

"At Channel 6. I'm a producer with the 'Evening News'."

"It must be very interesting."

"It is."

"I considered going into communications myself when I was in college. Before I chose teaching, I mean."

"A lot of people do." The classroom smelled as stale as the hall. A row of cardboard jack-o'-lanterns colored in orange crayon and taped above the blackboard grinned mockingly down at Megan. "Excuse me," she said, "but I'm expected back at work."

"Then, about Jon. . . . "

"Yes, about Jon."

"He's a bright little boy, and I do so much enjoy having him in class."

"I'm glad to hear it."

"It's not as if he couldn't do the work or had a behavioral problem. There's so much of that these days, you know."

"I suppose so."

"Nevertheless . . . I get the feeling that things could be so much *better* for him. Do you know what I mean, Mrs. Walsh?"

"Not exactly."

"I believe he's bored."

"He probably is."

"And then . . . he doesn't really seem to relate closely to his peers. He's pleasant enough; he's accepted by the others. But I don't believe he has any real friends. Does he have friends in your neighborhood?"

"None to speak of." They lived in a condominium in a development where there were few children Jon's age. Anyway, Jon was seldom there; he spent weekday afternoons at his grandmother's, while on weekends Megan often took him to the studio or, if she wasn't working, tried to make up for the rest of the week by taking him to museums and the zoo. She had no mental image of him playing with other children; it wasn't something he did or seemed very interested in doing. Megan explained all this grudgingly to the teacher, who listened sympathetically, as if learning of a family tragedy.

"And does your husband spend much time with him?"

"I'm not married", Megan said coldly. "Nor divorced, nor widowed. Nor do I live with anybody. Have you got the picture now?"

Mrs. Brickfield wasn't flustered. "I thought that might be the case", she said calmly. "What threw me off was Jon. He talks about his father all the time."

"He talks about his father?" Megan faltered. That was something she hadn't expected.

"Very convincingly, too." She sighed. "This class is atypical. The incidence of intact, two-parent families is unusually high. I suppose Jon feels he has to compete. When the other children talk about their fathers, he talks about his. He's really quite good at it—very credible, very natural. He even had me believing him, despite what the school records say. I'm sorry about the confusion."

"Jon has never set eyes on his father", Megan said weakly.

"I'm sure it's not uncommon. Except that in this class—well, it is."

"Are you trying to tell me something?"

"We're both trying to understand Jon better."

"I mean, what would you suggest—shall I install a man in the apartment so that Jon won't have to lie to the other kids?"

"That isn't the point, Mrs. Walsh."

"For God's sake, I'm not *Mrs.*"

"Sorry." The teacher reached beside her on the floor for a large canvas carrying bag, which she set on the desk. Plainly she was ready to call it a day.

"I mean, what do you suggest, Mrs. Brickfield? You asked me to come here. What would you like me to do about Jon?"

She turned a smile of sweet sadness on Megan. "If you want to know the truth," she said, "I think he's lonely. But I haven't got a solution."

"Then why ask to see me?"

Mrs. Brickfield paused in her packing. "I have your son in class five hours a day, five days a week. I like him. And he isn't happy. I wanted to tell you that because you're his mother. What you do about it is up to you."

"Oh, balls!" Megan turned and walked angrily out of the room, hurried down the long, stale corridor, clattered down the stairs to the first floor, and burst out the front door. She paused there, gulping the damp air and letting her anger subside, then walked more slowly around the building to the playground in the rear. It was misting. Jon squatted beside a jungle gym watching a fat starling stroll pompously across the wet asphalt.

"Put your hood up", she told him, at the same time doing it for him and brushing rain drops from his hair. The boy rose and slewed a small stone at the starling, which fluttered aside and flew away.

"She wants to zap me", Jon said.

"Brickfield? Why's that?"

He shrugged. "I dunno. Maybe she hates kids."

Shivering a little, Megan turned up her coat collar, "Are you happy here?"

"Sure." He glanced guardedly at her. "She say I wasn't?"

"She said you don't have many friends."

"I've got all I want."

"There are so few kids where we live . . . would you like to ask somebody from your class over on Sunday?"

"No." He seemed alarmed. Megan saw why: having invented an imaginary father, he wouldn't want to be shown up as a liar. She grimaced.

"I guess it's kind of hard on you—just the two of us."

"You do fine", he said stubbornly.

"Sure I do. But Brickfield thinks I can't cover all the bases."

The boy made a face, too. "She thinks she's a shrink", he pronounced disgustedly.

Megan laughed. "You're right. Come on, I have to drop you off at your grandmother's and get back to the station." After the show they'd planned a going-away party for Jerry Wertz, the news director for the last five years, who was moving to a station in Chicago. Megan liked Jerry and wanted to be there.

Driving through the thickening late afternoon traffic with Jon beside her, she decided he was right. As a do-gooder, Mrs. Brickfield had to invent problems for people who had none. She and Jon had encountered the type before—people who oozed sympathy on sight and couldn't accept the fact that their life suited them. From such encounters Megan had learned to resist benefactions whose price was moral indebtedness.

In fact, she reflected, she'd been doing that from the very start—from the moment, that is, when, driving home from the upstate university after graduation, she'd told her parents she was pregnant. Her father was stunned, then furious: "Who did it?"

She sits tight-lipped and defiant in the back seat. "What's the difference?"

"Don't provoke me. I want to know whether marriage is in the picture or not."

"It's not."

"But, Megan", Eleanor chimes in from the front seat, "have you discussed the possibility . . . with him?"

"Mother, forget it."

Justin demands, "Do you even know who the father is?"

She draws in her breath sharply in a gasp of pain and indignation. "Thanks a million."

"Damn!" Slamming his fist on the seat beside him, he tells Eleanor, "This is what comes of sending her away to school."

"The university didn't get me pregnant", Megan remarks coldly.

He sputters. Eleanor says sadly, "You shouldn't joke about it, dear."

"I suppose you've been to confession?" he asks.

"No."

"We'll get that taken care of as soon as we get home."

She shakes her head in despair of him. "Forget that, too."

"Don't be stupid", he snaps. "It's bad enough to make a mistake but worse to persist in it."

"It might make you feel good to hustle me off to confession," she tells him, "but it won't do a thing for me. Literally nothing. I don't believe in it, Daddy—sorry, but I don't. And you know better than anybody that there's no point in my receiving a sacrament I don't believe in."

His jaw jutting, he says, "I see we have a great deal to discuss."

"Oh, God!" She casts her eyes heavenward.

But Justin is persistent. "You'll get in touch with Catholic Charities about adoption, I presume?"

"No."

"Obviously you haven't thought that through either."

"I'm going to keep the baby."

He explodes again, "That's a ridiculous idea!"

"Justin . . . ", Eleanor begins.

"If I'm going to have him adopted, I might as well have him aborted", Megan says furiously. "There's hardly any difference."

"That's nonsense."

"Not to me. As far as *I'm* concerned, the difference is just in how and when I get rid of him. Only I'm not going to do that. I'm keeping him. No abortion, no adoption. Got the picture?" Her voice quavers, and suddenly she is on the brink of tears.

Eleanor turns and extends her hand over the back of the seat. Megan clutches it and sobs.

No one speaks after that for a long time. The only sounds are the engine and Megan crying. Finally, taking a deep breath, Justin says in a low voice, "Are you going to live at home?"

She hesitates until she is sure she is in control again. Then she says, "Until after the baby is born. If you're willing."

"Of course we are, Megan", Eleanor says.

"How about you, Daddy?"

"If it's acceptable to your mother. . . . "

"I don't mean permanently, understand. I'll get a job and get out as soon as I can. Just give me a few months."

"But I want you to get this straightened out with the Church . . . with God", he insists.

"Is that the price of a room—a good confession?"

"Do you imagine you don't need it?"

"Please don't quarrel again", Eleanor begs them.

Megan smiles grimly. "I'm not interested in quarreling. But

I'll tell you both something—I've made up my mind that from now on *I'll* decide what I need and what I don't."

"Everything on your terms—is that it?"

"Everything that concerns *me*", she agrees.

Letting Jonathan and herself into the house, Megan found a grocery bag of fresh vegetables—lettuce and cabbage and carrots were visible—on the floor in the front hall, evidently abandoned by her mother. That was typical; Eleanor tended to forget what didn't interest her, and housekeeping fell more or less into that category. Megan picked up the bag and carried it into the kitchen, followed by Jon. "Here we are", she announced cheerfully to her mother.

Eleanor sat in the breakfast nook reading. She looked up vaguely with a smile. "You're hardly late at all."

"Mrs. Brickfield hates me", Jon told his grandmother matter-of-factly.

"I'm sure she doesn't, dear. Do you want something to eat?"

Eleanor busied herself getting him a snack. Picking up the book her mother had left facedown on the table, Megan found it was *The Introduction to the Devout Life.* She read: "If nothing obliges you to go abroad into company or to receive company at home, remain within yourself and entertain yourself with your own heart. If company visits you or if any just cause invites you into company, go as about God's work, Philothea, and visit your neighbour with a benevolent heart and good intention."

"The Better Homes and Gardens Guide to Mysticism", Megan remarked, dropping the book with good-humored contempt.

Eleanor was not dismayed. "You ought to read it", she said mildly.

"I looked into it in college."

"Seriously, I mean."

"One of these days."

Jon settled down with cookies and milk in front of the television set. The two women drifted into the living room. "Shall I give him dinner later?"

"I guess so. I have to stay late at the station."

"They ask a lot of you."

"I *want* to do it, Mother."

"I hope so. What did Mrs. Brickfield have to say?"

Glancing at her watch, Megan lit a cigarette. "She's a well-meaning bitch. She thinks I don't provide a proper home for Jon."

Eleanor's eyes widened in surprise. "She said that?"

"As much as. No playmates. No father. . . . Fathers are big in the second grade this year. Jon feels left out."

"I see."

Megan looked suspiciously at her mother. "I suppose you agree with her?"

"He *could* be happier", Eleanor said.

"Who couldn't?"

"It's a joy to have him here, but sometimes I wonder how he feels about it. Isn't it dull for a child to spend so much time with older people?"

"Do you want me to hire a baby-sitter, Mother?"

"You know that isn't my point."

"Yes." Megan frowned. "You're saying what Brickfield said. 'Give him a real home—mother, father, siblings, dogs, cats, guppies, the works! Especially *father.*' That's the message, right?"

"I've never understood why you didn't marry."

"There's too much else I'd rather do."

"Marriage, family, home—that's all I wanted at your age."

"Has it made you happy?"

Eleanor considered. "Yes."

"Congratulations", Megan said. "And congratulations to Daddy. He was lucky."

Eleanor shook her head ruefully. "Don't be hard on your father. He's a good man, and he loves us."

"In his way." She crushed out her cigarette. "But I shouldn't pick on him now, of all times."

Anxiety flickered in Eleanor's hazel eyes. "You mean . . . the new bishop."

"Daddy will have to adapt like everybody else. You may not always agree, but you go along with the person in charge. He's been spoiled."

"His principles make it hard for him to compromise."

"I call it spoiled."

"Not by you at least", Eleanor said loyally.

"You needn't keep reminding me."

"I'm sorry, Megan. I know you do your best."

"And you agree with Brickfield that my best is pretty piss poor. Tell me", she taunted, "what would Francis de Sales say?"

Eleanor gave her a rather calculating look. " 'The first purgation that must be made is that of sin.' "

"Damn!" she howled. "Under the skin you're just like Daddy, aren't you?"

"You know I'm not going to preach. But please don't criticize your father."

"Because he can't *help* preaching?" Furious, Megan headed for the door, then paused and added over her shoulder, "He ought to be grateful to me. I introduced him to the real world. That will be helpful, now that he's going to get another big dose of it."

The party was perking along nicely on the set of the "Evening News", but Megan was starting to worry. Cissy Malone, the blonde who did the weather, was starting to look tight. As far as Megan was concerned, Cissy could get as plastered as she liked later, but she had to make it through the late news show first.

Sidling up to the weather lady as she helped herself to another Scotch and soda at the cloth-covered table full of liquor and mixers and ice, Megan said, "Not now, Cissy."

Cissy gave her a glassy stare. "What do you mean by that?"

"I mean you can't go on the air if you're drunk."

Cissy put her glass down in disgust. "You're a stinker, Megan."

"Somebody has to be. Anyway, I'm doing you a favor. Have a Coke."

Jerry Wertz had been watching with approval. "Well done", he told her in a low voice as she turned away from the bar and encountered him. They moved off together out of earshot of Cissy.

"It's a pain playing nursemaid", Megan complained.

Jerry smiled. He was a tall, thin man, with a nice smile that crinkled his long face agreeably. "As you said to Cissy—somebody's got to do it. It's only one of the things you do well."

"Likewise, Jerry."

"If you ever want to make a change, look me up in Chicago."

It caught her by surprise. "Are you serious?"

"Of course I am. You know, Megan, you underrate yourself professionally."

"I haven't heard you say that very often."

He laughed. "I can afford to say it now that I'm leaving."

Megan said reflectively, "Wernersburgh is home to me. And it would be tough to move on account of Jon. And anyway, I like the station. Even old Cissy."

"It's just a thought", Jerry said casually. "File it for future reference, if the time ever comes."

"I'll do that", she told him, and thought no more about it.

III

Ambrose Farquhar's appointment as sixth bishop of Wernersburgh was announced before Halloween. For once both the *Catholic Truth* and the *Globe-Herald* hailed the same event, but their reasons were vastly different. Led by Gwyneth Harley's pro-Farquhar stories, the daily saw his choice as the repudiation of Peter Frisch. The *Catholic Truth* proclaimed that Farquhar had been named to Wernersburgh to continue Frisch's policies. Those who knew anything about it held that in taking that line Justin Walsh had blundered badly and merely made an ass of himself.

"It's one thing to try to influence events and another to misrepresent them", Megan lectured him.

Justin fumed. "Who says it isn't the liberals who are wrong on this one?"

"Wait and see what Farquhar does, Daddy", she advised him.

Justin wasn't one to do that. He'd always liked to dig into a story and anticipate events, and now he had a greater than ordinary personal stake in the events in question. All Saints' Day found him making the long drive to New Antwerp. An occasional dry snowflake fluttered randomly into the windshield, but otherwise the corpse gray sky was as unproductive as the lifeless fields that fell away monotonously on either side of the highway.

His mind drifted as he drove. He'd had his favorite recurring dream the night before and for a while relished the agreeable emotions it evoked. In the dream he sat in a corner of a large, well-lighted room where scarlet-clad cardinals at a long table hung upon the reading of an editorial from the *Catholic Truth.* No one addressed him, but no one needed to; his heart swelled with pride.

Real life was less glamorous, but he had no serious complaints. At least, he'd had none up to now. Bishop Frisch, while allowing him a free hand with the paper, had given him ample indications of esteem. Some jokers in the chancery even called him the "First Lay Bishop of Wernersburgh". He couldn't help being gratified. Marked out early for an ecclesiastical career by his mother, he'd given no clear sign of pursuing one for many years. Thus he'd been making up for lost time for a long while now. He felt he owed it to his mother.

Kevin Walsh, his father, had been a moderately successful attorney with Irish good looks who died young, leaving his widow and six-year-old son meagerly provided for. But Mary Walsh coped. As a daughter of one of Wernersburgh's prominent old German Catholic families, she not only looked to the Church in her hour of need but naturally looked high. In particular, she looked to her older brother, Monsignor Henry Reicher, one of the diocese's most distinguished pastors and a confidant of the Bishop of Wernersburgh, Cornelius Weiss. Within three months the young widow was Weiss's private secretary. She was to occupy that position for the next quarter century, until his death and her retirement in 1946.

Mary Walsh became a diocesan institution in her own right in those years; a power behind the episcopal throne whose influence, though exaggerated by some either out of ignorance or envy, still caused blustering senior pastors to address her with extreme respect and young priests to blush and stammer when she called them to account for breaches of protocol or procedure. Bishop Weiss, a taciturn, reclusive man more easy with documents than with human beings, relied on her to shield him from distasteful encounters; those wanting to do business with the Bishop learned to present their case to Mrs. Walsh, then wait for her to descend from the mountain with a reply.

As her power grew, so did her estimation of the system she served. It was a natural step to wanting Justin to become a priest. She'd had a longtime crush on the priesthood anyway, and now she set out to pass it on to her son, speaking so often and with such assurance of the great goal she had in view for him that his vocation was taken for granted by her friends.

At first, Justin had no problem with that. He wasn't a rebellious child, he liked pleasing his mother, and the prestige of the priesthood was attractive to him. Uncle Henry, polished, self-assured, commanding deference on all sides, was an awesome figure, and the thought that he, too, was destined for such a role swelled his pride. The priesthood, in young Justin's view, resembled a high-toned club, whose senior members (remarkable personages like Bishop Weiss and his splendid uncle) were scarcely visible to mere mortals, while even those at its lowest level (junior curates) shone with glory from on high.

Perhaps, nevertheless, his mother overdid it. Her harping on the priesthood's superiority to every other way of life eventually nourished a worm of doubt in the boy's mind: Was he worthy? The question became acute when concupiscence flared in adolescence, and it led him to defer the announcement Mary Walsh was anticipating. Tension grew heavy between them as Justin's graduation from St. Bruno's Prep. approached. Unable to stand it any longer, she confronted him one day.

"Justin, we've got to make plans for next year", she said firmly at dinner.

He nodded unhappily, knowing that meant: What about the seminary? "I've been thinking about it, Mother."

"And what are your thoughts?" She was a strong-featured woman with carefully waved silver hair and a commanding manner. Respecting her immensely, he'd never imagined circumstances in which he would directly, deliberately disappoint her. "Thinking is fine, but we're coming to the point where action is required."

"I just haven't made up my mind." Looking up, he caught her shrewd glance across the table. He knew she suspected he was weighing the diocesan priesthood against the Companions of Christ, the religious who conducted St. Bruno's Prep, and attributed his delay to that. Although she strongly preferred the secular clergy, Justin supposed she would tolerate the Companions. But his uncertainty lay much deeper: Did he want to be a priest at all? His anxiety shot up now as she said, "I know you want to make your decision carefully, dear, but you *do* have to decide. Perhaps it would help if you discussed things with your Uncle Henry."

That of course would *not* help. Knowing they'd reached a critical moment, Justin said desperately, "Maybe I really *have* decided."

She brightened. "You make me very happy."

"I want to go to St. Bruno's next year."

The smile faded: St. Bruno's was the Companions' college in Wernersburgh. "I thought you had something else in view."

"You mean the seminary?"

"Of course."

Justin stopped scraping at the lemon sherbet and put down his spoon. The time had come to speak his mind. "I'm not sure I want to be a priest."

Her jaw—a Reicher jaw, like Justin's—set grimly. "That is a foolish thing to say."

But he'd learned stubbornness from her. "I just haven't made up my mind yet."

She stared hard at him, fingering the strand of pearls around her neck. "I suppose I can't blame you for acting your age, Justin, but I admit I'm disappointed—I thought you were more mature."

"I need more time", he protested. "What's the hurry? A couple of years won't make any difference."

She pounced on that. "You mean you might enter the seminary before you graduate from St. Bruno's?"

Relieved, he said, "It could happen."

He could almost read her mind: it wasn't what she wanted, but neither was it what she'd begun to fear; it might be as much as she could hope for now. "All right", she announced decisively at last. "I suppose you must have the time you need."

Justin entered St. Bruno's College still in good faith, assuming that in due course he really would sprout a vocation. Hadn't he as much as promised his mother that he would? But all that changed when he met Eleanor Schneider in his sophomore year—she was then a freshman at Maryheights—and they fell in love. Overnight his calling to the priesthood was exposed as the figment of his mother's imagination it had always been.

Mary Walsh took it hard, but ultimately she took it. To Justin's great surprise, his Uncle Henry played a crucial role in that. One Sunday afternoon his mother poured out her complaints bitterly to her brother over tea in their living room, while Justin sat red-faced and silent in an armchair, expecting reprimands from his uncle when she finished. Monsignor Reicher, ramrod straight, white-haired and regal, sipped tea throughout his sister's lamentation. "I ask you, Henry," she concluded, "how can I convince him that this is only infatuation? He wants to throw his future away, and I can't make him understand."

Setting down his cup, Uncle Henry turned and studied Justin. "And how do you feel about it?" he asked in his resonant voice.

"I want to marry Eleanor", he confessed.

His mother snorted, but Uncle Henry kept his attention fixed on Justin. "Does she want to marry you?"

"I haven't asked her."

The priest nodded gravely. "I suggest you do that eventually," he said. "Since marriage is incompatible with ordination, her answer would seem to have a bearing on whether you do or don't become a priest." Did he detect the slightest hint of a smile on his uncle's lips? If so, it vanished in an instant as he turned back to his sister. "Mary, cultivate detachment in this matter. Wishing him a vocation won't get him one. The priesthood is a glorious way of life for those who belong there, but it's hell on earth for those who don't. You wouldn't want *that* on your conscience, I'm sure."

That was the turning point. As if his uncle had pronounced an absolution, he was suddenly free of an enormous burden. And with that sealing off of the vocational cul-de-sac into which his mother had been urging him, everything else seemed to follow easily: marriage to Eleanor, a newspaper career, and at length even service to the diocese. His mother had been dead three years and Uncle Henry eight when Boylan approached him about editing the *Catholic Truth;* he knew at once that accepting the job would bring those relationships to term. Having found his vocation, he was at peace.

Now things were changing again. Uneasy about Bishop Farquhar's appointment, he nevertheless wanted it to go well. He needed to live out his own vocation to the end. It didn't seem as if he were asking a great deal—except to him. Mary Walsh's son had found his niche in the diocese of Wernersburgh; it was essential that the new bishop let him keep it.

Some interviews take fire while others merely smoke and fizzle. Justin's with Bishop Farquhar was of the second kind. Sitting in the Bishop's office in the brassy, modern New Antwerp chancery, he asked predictable questions and got predictable replies: Farquhar was grateful to the Holy Father, delighted to be coming to Wernersburgh, honored to be Peter Frisch's successor, and appreciated all he'd learned from Archbishop Gatti and the priests and people of New Antwerp. On specific issues he was general and bland. He supported the Church's teaching on all matters, considered himself a moderate on social questions, believed in consultation and dialogue, but held that, finally, it was the bishop's job to formulate and express the consensus.

Did he plan any changes?

Fixing Justin with a searching look, Farquhar gave the only interesting answer of the interview: "Change is inevitable. The renewal of the Church must go forward according to the spirit of Vatican II. I believe that's why the Holy Father is sending me to Wernersburgh, and I intend to see that it happens there."

Against the preceding blandness, that clipped and intensely spoken reply was startling, as if a chef had unexpectedly set a *flambé* concoction blazing on the table after hamburger, mashed potatoes, and green beans. Apprehensively Justin asked, "What changes do you have in mind?"

"My mind is open, Justin. I've got a lot to learn about Wernersburgh. I need to do a lot of listening. What changes would *you* make?"

The editor hesitated, then said boldly, "None. The diocese is solid as a rock, thanks be to God and Bishop Frisch. You're inheriting a healthy operation. If you want my advice, Bishop, the job is mainly to keep it running as smoothly as it has been."

Farquhar regarded him still more closely, nodding in what Justin hoped was agreement. "You wouldn't change a thing?"

"Nothing", Justin said emphatically, believing he was having an effect.

"Interesting." The Bishop went on nodding. "Very."

Ambrose Farquhar's installation in early December was an ecclesiastical extravanganza whose like Wernersburgh hadn't witnessed in years. Bishop Frisch and Bishop Boylan directed the arrangements, and, however they might have felt at heart, they'd clearly concluded that protocol—and possibly faith itself—obliged the diocese to welcome its new shepherd with a kind of pious carnival. Farquhar tried from a distance to discourage excess and actually succeeded in pruning it a little, but the installation ritual itself was a pageant of baroque opulence. Jammed to overflowing, dark and ancient Holy Comforter Cathedral suddenly blazed with television lights, like an octogenarian grande dame decked out in diamonds. The Apostolic Delegate presided, a suave Italian polished to a high gloss in the practice of diplomacy, while Archbishop Gatti, florid and ebullient, was evidently celebrating a personal triumph. Gorgeously vested, some thirty bishops marched to bray of trumpet and thunderous organ down the cathedral's nave, thus giving visible testimony to episcopal solidarity. Frisch and Boylan progressed side by side—not too rapidly, for the old man's sake—their faces eloquent, to those who understood such things, by their studied expressionlessness. As for Bishop Farquhar, radiant as a bride, he looked young, vigorous, and full of holy zeal.

Justin Walsh, standing in a crowded pew near the sanctuary with Eleanor beside him, watched his new bishop pass with mixed emotions: triumphalistic satisfaction at so grand a celebration of apostolicity, a twinge of anxiety lest this particular member of the apostolic college be a little less than Athanasius or Augustine. These were strange times. A few days earlier a man with a knife had tried to assassinate Pope Paul VI in the Philippines. In Justin's mind the incident somehow summed up a lot that was happening in the Church these days. What was a pope doing in the Philippines in the first place, and why should someone try to kill him? The old order passes; but what *was* the new?

Bishop Farquhar's homily was unexceptionable—all that is, except for one passage that made people like Justin uneasily aware that, whoever he might turn out to be, he wouldn't resemble Peter Frisch. Exalted, awash in light in the high, marble pulpit, Farquhar pronounced:

"What is a bishop called to be today? Many things, of course—pastor, administrator, fund-raiser, teacher, leader, standup comic and tragedian, a holder of innumerable hands and binder-up of wounds beyond counting. But especially a bishop is summoned to the thankless calling of prophet—speaker of hard truths exhorting the Church to accept its future.

"Its future, mind you, not its past or present. The Church can't waste time dreaming of a glorious yesterday or contemplating a complacent now. Time passes. Questions mature into challenges, then become crises. The worst response is not to respond because, locked in the past, we'd rather think of what has been than shape what is to be.

"A bishop can't let that happen. And I make you this pledge, my sisters and brothers in the Church of Wernersburgh: with your help, I won't permit it. A time of renewal, change, and movement forward in our pilgrimage is now at hand. Together let us discern the Spirit's working in the signs of our times. Join me, your bishop and brother, in giving prophetic utterance to a shared vision of our future as Church."

Eleanor whispered, "What is he talking about?"

"God only knows", Justin said aloud, drawing a few stares.

But he and others had some notion. Comparing notes at the reception later in the ballroom of the Sasser Hotel, Justin and Bishop Boylan stood on the sidelines sipping punch and watching Farquhar, exhausted but game, still greeting well-wishers in an endless reception line.

"What did you think of his sermon?"

Boylan gave him a guarded look. "What did *you* think?"

"I didn't like that business about leading us all into the future—as if we'd never get there without him."

"He *is* the future of the diocese now."

Justin frowned. "I'm not sure his vision of the future and mine are the same."

"Pray they don't conflict", Boylan murmured, his words muted by the din. "Well, Mrs. Hebblethwaite," (gushed to a fur-bedecked old female tugboat churning toward him with gushing uppermost in mind) "such a joy to see you on this memorable occasion!"

IV

There was no chance that Bishop Farquhar's vision of the future would conflict with Monsignor Oscar Dudley's, for Monsignor Dudley was determined that, whatever the Bishop's vision might be, he was going to share it. Dudley was no fool: he knew his chancery critics would call him an opportunist, but their notion of loyalty was primitive, a survival of days when liege lords, fiefdoms, and oaths of fealty were in vogue. Chivalry had died with Christendom, and loyalty now adopted an abstract, bureaucratic mode: one was loyal to structures and processes. Peter Frisch might go and Ambrose Farquhar come; the system stayed. Oscar Dudley stayed with it.

Chancellor of the diocese of Wernersburgh for five years, Vice Chancellor for four years before that, Monsignor Dudley at forty was pink-faced, plump, and prematurely bald, with rimless glasses and a prissy manner. But he was no mere figure of fun, as captious pastors, uppity priests, and assorted other troublemakers learned in due course. Behind the spinsterish facade lay a shrewd, unsentimental mind, an enormous capacity for work, and a firm will that Oscar Dudley and those he served should always come out on top. Not liking him, Bishop Frisch found him merely indispensable.

"He keeps the machinery running", he'd once told Hugh Boylan when the Auxiliary Bishop, echoing others, complained of Dudley's arrogance. "I couldn't get along without him, Hughie, and neither could you if you were in charge. But don't think I'm fond of him. Efficient, hardworking, conscientious, and bloodless—that's Oscar. He works for me because I'm bishop, and he'll work for anybody else who'll have him in the future. People like that are flexible. They're good at making gas ovens as well as cathedrals."

Ambrose Farquhar, gentler than Frisch, hadn't seen Dudley in that light until now. Coming into a strange environment, he was simply glad to find someone as competent and accommodating as the Chancellor on hand to help him. Soon Dudley was his closest confidant and advisor, as well as chief executor of his program—just the roles he himself had played with Archbishop Gatti.

Farquhar and Dudley sat one morning in December in the Bishop's office. It was Frisch's old office, already refurnished and now awaiting repainting; the wall by the windows displayed a telltale rectangle of lighter hue where Pius XII at prayer had formerly hung. They were discussing what the Chancellor had already learned were Farquhar's two full-blown obsessions: the seminary and the newspaper.

"From everything I've been able to determine, Oscar," the Bishop was saying, "this diocese has a classic Tridentine seminary. Isn't that the case?" He'd spent a day there the week before and had been going on like this ever since.

Monsignor Dudley nodded. "St. John's is a museum piece."

"Filled with fossils."

Dudley thought of his own years at St. John's as a period of light and order, prayer, discipline, and grace. But time distorted everything; even then the place had probably been out of date. More recently, in any case, its conservatism had become notorious. Reaching into a file in his lap the Chancellor extracted a letter and handed it over with a modest smile. "As you asked,

Bishop, Monsignor Caldron has submitted his resignation as rector."

Farquhar beamed approval. "Let's find him a good job."

"Several pastors are retiring this year."

"Give me a list, with notes on the parishes."

Dudley was planning to do that. They might not know it yet, but at least some of his colleagues in the chancery were also on their way to new jobs. Farquhar had hinted that there might be a surprise in store even for Bishop Boylan. The question of soon-to-be-available pastorates thus became urgent, along with whether assignment to a particular one would be construed as reward or punishment. Such matters were the Chancellor's meat.

"And then, Oscar, who replaces Caldron as rector? *That* is the question."

Indeed it was, and Dudley already had the answer. But he'd learned from Frisch, and was having it confirmed by Farquhar, that people in authority grow nervous when subordinates solve problems prematurely—before, that is, the superiors can position themselves to take credit. Therefore he pretended to be stumped.

"It's difficult these days to know what to look for in a rector", he said, tapping his cheek thoughtfully with his gold pen.

"A good administrator and a competent scholar," Bishop Farquhar said decisively, "but above all a model for the students—a model of the contemporary priesthood. A man fully committed to the *aggiornamento.*"

"It's possible", the Chancellor said carefully, "that the man we want is at hand."

Farquhar looked interested. "Who?"

"Ronald Lackner."

The Bishop pondered that, nodding. "He certainly makes a favorable impression."

"Ron's been teaching systematic at St. John's for over ten years. We were classmates."

Dudley's friend had studied in Rome after ordination and earned a doctorate there. "Ron got rave notices, but he never contracted *romanita*", the Chancellor explained. "In fact, he's a bit of an iconoclast at heart." Seeing that the Bishop looked pleased, he went on with mounting confidence. "Parish work for a year or two after coming home, then Frisch assigned him to the seminary. I have to admit—the Bishop recognized talent, and there wasn't anyone around who could hold a candle to Ron. He's been out there ever since. Respected by the faculty, popular with the students, and known and liked by all the younger clergy of the diocese."

"But can the man I want be at St. John's *now?* Remember, Oscar, I want someone who will *change* the place."

"The seminary faculty is like the chancery staff. We've all had to be loyal—that goes without saying—but it doesn't follow that we all agreed with Bishop Frisch. The fact is that you have a Ronald Lackner at St. John's, just as here you have . . . well, me." For Oscar Dudley, it was a bold verbal stroke, which he delivered with some apprehension. But its impact was plainly positive.

"You give me cause for hope", Bishop Farquhar said warmly. "Ask Lackner to come by. You can't imagine how important it is to me to put the rectorship in good hands as soon as possible."

Monsignor Dudley nodded gravely and made a note on his yellow pad.

"Now, as for the *Catholic Truth*. . . . " Taking a copy of the paper from the desk, the Bishop sighed. "Even more urgent than the seminary. If I let this go on week after week, people will conclude that I like it. No, Oscar, something must be done quickly." Flipping pages, he paused to cite choice examples: " 'Monsignor O'Shaughnessy's Question Box'—not a hint of

Vatican II in it. A family column that's nothing more than a weekly tirade against birth control. And these editorials—'Already ankle deep in a noxious tide of pornography, Americans today face the question: Will we plug the dikes of decency or be swept away by a rising flood of filth?' " Throwing down the paper, he threw up his hands in despair.

Monsignor Dudley clucked sympathetically. "Embarrassing."

"The paper is a catechetical tool. Imagine how *this* paper is forming people! Something must be done."

"Change editors, I suppose?" He wasn't hostile to Justin Walsh, but he wasn't friendly either. The Chancellor took the same attitude toward him that he took toward most people: when a man outlived his usefulness, you got rid of him.

But Farquhar objected, "He's had the job for years. I can't just put him out on the street."

The Chancellor nodded agreement, thinking of the list of open parishes he was to prepare. "It's easier to deal with priests."

"Not that we shouldn't welcome the laity as collaborators in the renewal. . . . "

"But they're hard to get rid of when the time comes." After a moment he added, "Of course there is another solution. Name a priest as editor *over* Walsh."

Farquhar considered that gravely. "Do you think he'd take it?"

Dudley shrugged. "Suppose he resigned . . . it would be clear that it was his choice, not yours."

The Bishop looked thoughtful. "And as for a suitable priest—have you anyone to suggest, Oscar?"

"As a matter of fact, Bishop, a name does occur to me."

Arthur Kucharski was pecking out an article in the sitting room of his two-room suite, second floor rear of St. Brendan's cavernous rectory. This was another in a series he'd been writing for the *National Catholic Recorder* called "Diary of a Suburban Priest"; he used the pen name Father Veritas.

Dropping his hands from the keyboard of the boxy old Royal, he scanned the sheet of paper.

> Priests are products of their culture and mirror it to perfection. With his personal stereo, color TV and Oldsmobile, his golf days, rectory happy hours and Florida vacations, the suburban priest reflects his affluent parishioners in everything but sex—and to tell the truth, differences are breaking down there, too.
>
> Result? The suburban priest is radically incapable of speaking a prophetic word to his world. How can you criticize credibly what you're immersed in, part of? The German clergy were too German to be harsh with Hitler; most of us are too materially comfortable to get mad at Mammon. No eunuchs for the kingdom, we, but mere *castrati* of an affluent society.

Not bad. The series had gone nicely up to now; he expected a good reception for this latest article. The pen name had saved him hassles with Bishop Frisch, but everyone important to him knew who Father Veritas was.

Arthur went back to work, typing steadily. He liked to work in the afternoon, just when Monsignor DiNolfo, the pastor, was napping next door: occasionally he even managed to provoke some pounding on the wall. Tall, blond, and moustached, he hunched over the typewriter and composed.

> Priests as prophets: our job is consciousness-raising. But who will raise the consciousness of priests? Even the clerical lifestyle, which should detach us from our surroundings, give us distance and a sense of perspective perversely has the opposite effect.
>
> Celibacy. A celibate is best situated to criticize the sexual *mores* of the culture, no? But it doesn't work that way in

practice. In matters of sex, clerical celibates relate to the culture like poor kids pressing their noses against a toy store window on Christmas Eve. They aren't criticizing—they're envying!

The telephone rang. Arthur snatched it up impatiently. "Yah?"

"Father Kucharski, this is Oscar Dudley at the chancery."

"Yah." He wasn't enthused; younger priests were no fonder of the Chancellor than Boylan's friends were.

"Bishop Farquhar wants to see you. Can you make it at eleven tomorrow?"

Arthur scowled. Trouble. A bawling out about Father Veritas. And Farquhar was supposed to be a liberal! "Just let me have it over the phone, Monsignor."

"I beg your pardon?"

"It would save everybody time if you told me now what he wants."

There was a pause. Then Dudley said, "He'd like to talk with you about becoming editor of the *Catholic Truth.*"

Arthur's blue eyes widened with astonishment. "You're putting me on."

"Not at all."

He shook his head. Then whistled through his teeth. This was hard to take in. "What does Bishop Farquhar know about me?"

"Whatever I've told him, Arthur."

"Editor?"

"I'm not offering you the job. That's up to the Bishop. And he'll *only* do it if you're the man he wants. Can we count on seeing you tomorrow?"

His head was swimming. "I guess", he muttered. "But what do *you* know about me then? Like, we're not exactly close friends."

"I know you studied journalism at the state university before entering the seminary. I know you've practiced journalism since ordination. At least, I *believe* that's correct, isn't it? I assure you, I didn't pick your name from a hat."

Arthur was sure of that: no priest in Wernersburgh would suppose anything that ingenuous of the Chancellor. But had somebody given Dudley an earful about him? "All the same", he finished, "I guess you know about me mainly from hearsay."

"I've followed your work with interest for a long time. With admiration, I might say. You *may* be what the Bishop is looking for."

That Dudley followed his work with admiration was as strange a notion as any yet. Dudley had several times been the instrument for conveying Bishop Frisch's displeasure about the *National Catholic Recorder;* he'd expressed no regret in doing so.

"The *Catholic Truth* has an editor", Arthur objected.

"Bishop Farquhar wants someone more in sympathy with him."

"Will he give the new man a free hand?"

"That's his intention, certainly. . . . May we count on seeing you tomorrow, Arthur?"

"One last question. Has he read my stuff?"

"He thinks highly of your work."

Arthur glowed. "You said eleven? I'll be there."

Hanging up, he leaned back and lighted a menthol cigarette. Next door Monsignor DiNolfo was blowing his nose with stentorian trumpetings, but Arthur took no notice. The editorship of the *Catholic Truth* was within his grasp! The thought tickled him: nasty Arthur, perennial malcontent and troublemaker, a power in the diocese! What would his friends say? What would DiNolfo say? He laughed out loud. Who *was* this

Ambrose Farquhar anyway? The sheer arbitrariness of the Church dazzled him. Careers were made and broken, lives uprooted, on a bishop's whim. It had the careless bravura—astonishing midair leaps and tumbles, with occasional ghastly falls from the heights—that only an institution supposing itself under divine protection would dare cultivate. In such ways—refracted, crabbed, and partial—did faith manifest itself to Arthur Kucharski.

"He may have suited New Antwerp, but on the whole he won't suit Wernersburgh", said Dr. Walter Caldron. Meager, chickennecked, sallow, bald pate ringed by a thin fringe of white hair, he was in a more acerbic mood than usual tonight, for Bishop Farquhar was on his mind, and the Doctor wasn't pleased to have him there.

"Give him time, Walter. We mustn't leap to conclusions", said Judge Stanley Gorman in his most judicious manner. A bulky, florid man with bushy, gray eyebrows and silver hair, he was enjoying both the conversation and his second Scotch and soda.

They turned to Justin. "What do you think?"

The editor sipped bourbon. Still wanting to give Farquhar the benefit of the doubt, he was finding that increasingly difficult these days. "I don't know him well yet", he said, seeking refuge in unaccustomed diplomacy.

Dr. Caldron sniffed. "Don't criticize the boss, eh?" He turned again to Judge Gorman. "There's already enough evidence on the record to indict if not to convict, Stanley."

Dressed in tuxedoes like the other Knights of Mount Olivet who crowded the dark-panelled room on the Sasser Hotel's mezzanine, the three men stood talking near the holly decked bar. Soon they would file next door for a filet mignon dinner. This was the annual pre-Christmas function of the Order, and from time immemorial the Sasser, Wernersburgh's finest, had been its site. The Knights of Mount Olivet were like that—they'd sooner not meet at all than meet at the Holiday Inn.

The Knights, in other words, had a clear sense of who they were: the authentic lay leaders of the diocese—lawyers, doctors, successful businessmen and bankers—who could be counted on to organize and carry through fund-raising campaigns, serve on boards, provide professional counsel, make introductions and referrals, and in general give indispensable assistance in easing the diocese through worldly reefs and shoals. Bishop Frisch had made astute use of the group; as men accustomed to getting the most out of things, the Knights recognized and appreciated that. Frisch had been one of them. Bishop Farquhar—that remained to be seen.

Although wealth wasn't required to join the Knights of Mount Olivet, it helped. On that score Justin was an odd man out; but he more than qualified for conservatism and loyalty to the Church. Inducted ten years earlier into the Sovereign Military Order of Olivet, he regarded membership as a cherished element of his identity.

"What don't you like about Bishop Farquhar's performance, Walter?" Justin asked the doctor warily.

Caldron took a sip of sherry. "His treatment of Bishop Boylan for one thing", he said tartly. "Hasn't Boylan been put on the shelf?"

It was true. Boylan's fall and Oscar Dudley's rise were the talk of the chancery—and now, it appeared, the talk of the diocese as well. These things worried Justin deeply, but he wasn't yet at the point of acknowledging his anxiety to others. Defensively he said, "A bishop is entitled to get his advice where he wants it."

Doctor Caldron sniffed. "All the same, it's shabby treatment of Boylan. . . . Hello, Jack, how are you?" He turned to greet his brother, Monsignor John Caldron, who was approaching with a martini on the rocks in hand. Although the seminary rector was five years older than his brother, he strikingly resembled him, except for being twenty pounds heavier and rather more cheerful. He'd been chaplain of the local chapter of the Knights of Mount Olivet for as long as Justin could recall.

"Gentlemen", Monsignor Caldron said, shaking hands affably all around. "You seemed to be having a rather intense discussion."

"About changes in the diocese", Judge Gorman told him.

"Changes." Monsignor Caldron nodded significantly. "They *are* beginning, aren't they?"

"Here's another one for you", Gorman affirmed. "No offense, Justin, but not even the *Catholic Truth* has been itself lately."

Justin bristled. "How's that, Stanley?"

"The last few issues have been awfully bland."

"Pulling punches to please the Bishop?" Doctor Caldron asked.

Justin scowled. He'd been negotiating a mine field blindfolded, and he knew it showed in the paper. "Bishop Farquhar hasn't given me any orders", he snapped.

Monsignor Caldron picked up on that. "Perhaps you're getting a message anyway, Justin. A lot of us are. Stanley is right—there's something wishy-washy about the paper these days."

"I'm not aware of any difference", he insisted angrily.

"Everyone else is", Doctor Caldron said, making a face and pecking his beak nose into his sherry.

"Speak of the devil", Judge Gorman said heartily as Bishop Farquhar, trailed by Monsignor Dudley and Bishop Boylan, entered the room. Separating himself from the group, the judge went to greet Farquhar effusively in his capacity as Grand Commander of the local chapter.

"I'm surprised he came", Doctor Caldron remarked.

"Bishop Frisch always came", his brother pointed out.

"That's why I'm surprised to see this one."

Farquhar worked the room earnestly, shaking hands like a man doing his duty. Dudley hovered beside him, but Bishop Boylan detached himself quickly and, getting a Scotch on the rocks at the bar, joined Justin and the Caldrons.

"Isn't Bishop Frisch coming?" the doctor demanded.

"He's cut back his schedule a lot, Walter", Boylan said.

Caldron sniffed. "What a shame."

"Anyway Bishop Farquhar made it."

"Evidently."

"And yourself of course, Hughie", Monsignor Caldron observed pleasantly. "The episcopacy hasn't abandoned us, Walter."

"Auxiliary bishops don't count for much", Boylan observed.

"All bishops are equal," Doctor Caldron said, "but some bishops. . . ."

Bishop Farquhar, Monsignor Dudley, and Judge Gorman reached the little group, which expanded to receive them. "We were just saying how generous it is of you to be with us, Bishop", Monsignor Caldron told him.

"I want to meet with every organization in the diocese", Farquhar said seriously. "I'm trying to squeeze everybody in, but it isn't easy."

"The Bishop is constantly on the go," Monsignor Dudley remarked, "but at least tonight we didn't have any schedule conflicts."

"Lucky for us", Doctor Caldron said mildly. "The Knights of Mount Olivet would have hated losing you to the divorced and remarried Catholics, Bishop."

Farquhar was innocent of irony. "Actually, I'm meeting with the divorced and remarried next week."

Boylan winced. "Of course, Bishop," he brought out in a choked voice, "the Knights of Mount Olivet are special."

"Special?"

Boylan gave up. "Monsignor Dudley can explain."

But Justin, fuming, decided to try. "Present in this room, Bishop, is the cream of Catholic lay leadership in the diocese."

Smiling dubiously, Bishop Farquhar looked around him at the slightly smashed men in tuxedoes who filled the noisy room. He said, "There aren't any women."

Justin flushed. "No."

"Nor any Blacks or Hispanics."

"Race isn't a criterion of membership."

Judge Gorman looked upset. "I assure you, Bishop, that the Knights of Mount Olivet are one hundred percent committed to integration. I wouldn't be a member otherwise. But this isn't the kind of organization whose membership can be manipulated to be socially and racially representative. There's no reason why every group in the world should be required to fit that . . . that. . . . "

"Procrustean bed", Doctor Caldron said. He seemed to be growing more cheerful as the others grew more disturbed.

"Nevertheless, Judge Gorman," the Bishop objected, "a *church* organization— "

"Have you met Congressman Treadwell, Bishop?" Monsignor Dudley started to draw him away. For a moment Farquhar hesitated as if he wanted to pursue his point, but then he gave in, delivering only a parting shot: "A church organization has to be *prophetic.*" And he was off to the next knot of Knights, with Dudley at his side and Gorman trailing behind.

Bishop Boylan, Monsignor Caldron, and Justin avoided one another's eyes. But Doctor Caldron was buoyant. "Prophetic?" he hummed. "Isn't that something now? We're to have a prophetic diocese. And we've got our very own prophet to lead the whole shebang. Wernersburgh—the New Jerusalem. Who'd have thought it?"

"Shut up, Walter", his brother said casually, checking his watch. "Thank God, it's time for dinner."

Having thronged the bar for refills to see them through the meal, the Knights straggled next door, where they arranged themselves at round tables. Justin sat with the Caldron brothers and Bishop Boylan.

"Tell me," the doctor said to no one in particular, "do you think the diocese will survive him?"

"Walter . . . ", the Monsignor began.

"Be fair, Walter", Boylan urged.

"Give him time", Justin added doggedly.

"He has all the time he wants, whether I give it to him or not." Doctor Caldron grinned knowingly at Justin. "You have my sympathy."

To everyone's relief he dropped the subject then. Dinner went by uneventfully, and by the time coffee and brandy were on the table and a cigar was in his hand, even Justin felt cheerful again. Seated at the head table, Stanley Gorman surveyed the room, tapped his water glass with a spoon, and rose to scattered hand-clapping. "Brother Knights. . . . "

The judge did it well, with the easy manner of a man comfortable with himself and his audience. The formal introductions—Bishop Boylan, Monsignor Caldron, Monsignor Dudley—he handled with relaxed good humor. Last on the list came Bishop Farquhar.

"We're fortunate to have our new Bishop with us so soon after his installation, at a time when his schedule is extremely crowded and he is much in demand. I believe", Gorman beamed toward Farquhar seated beside him, "we can take his presence as a sign of his special interest in and affection for the Knights of Mount Olivet." Polite applause: the Knights didn't doubt that they merited all the esteem they received. Addressing Farquhar, the Judge said, "Your Excellency, would you say a few words?"

The Knights rose as their Bishop did, standing and clapping at their places. After a few moments they subsided, leaving Farquhar looking out over the room with a bemused expression.

"I certainly feel affection for you," he began conversationally, "but as for interest in your organization—I suppose that depends on what the organization does, and I haven't got a really clear picture yet."

Nervous laughter greeted that. It wasn't precisely what the Knights were accustomed to hear. Like the others, Justin listened closely.

"Don't think I haven't got some notion of why the Knights of Mount Olivet exist. I know you mean to serve the Church, and no doubt you do that in your own way. But I've been routinely telling every group I talk to—so don't think I'm singling you out—that the time has come to ask yourselves what the Church *really* needs today and how well you're meeting that need. You might be surprised." Bishop Farquhar paused and smiled at the Knights. A deathly silence had fallen over them; they looked as if a lunatic were explaining where he's hidden the bomb.

"As a group you are men of influence—lawyers, doctors, businessmen, community leaders, that sort of thing. That means you can do the diocese favors. You know whom to talk to, how to open doors, how to get things done. And you're generous with your money. Influence and money—those are the forms your service to the Church takes. I suppose my predecessor had many reasons to be grateful to you."

"And he knew it", someone at the back of the room remarked audibly.

"So do I", Bishop Farquhar said, unflustered. "I don't disparage it. I only suggest that you take a fresh look at who you are and what you're doing. Not because there's necessarily something wrong with the past, but because the past is done with. You should be thinking about the present and the future."

Some time earlier Doctor Caldron had leaned back and closed his eyes while a beatific smile lighted his meager features. Opening his eyes now, he stared hard at Farquhar, then winked at Justin. "He thinks we're idiots", the doctor observed jovially.

Justin nodded grimly.

The Bishop was warming to his theme. "Let's suppose you *are* men of influence. What does that imply for the Knights of Mount Olivet today? Start with your ecclesial context—the Church's preferential option for the poor. I don't have to tell you what that means."

"But you will", Monsignor Caldron muttered.

" . . . the poor, the oppressed, the needy, and the voiceless—they're the people toward whom and on whose behalf the Church is called to extend its ministry today. And they are the ones on whose behalf the Knights of Mount Olivet, exercising *their* ministry of service within the Church, are called to use their influence."

Over the years, Justin knew, both corporately and individually the Knights had been responsible for innumerable benefactions—mountains of Christmas baskets, armies of orphans dispatched to summer camps, scholarships without number enabling needy students to attend St. Bruno's College and Maryheights. And of course there was the seminary, recipient of lavish aid from the Order. But this, plainly, wasn't what Bishop Farquhar had in mind. He wanted political clout for welfare mothers, economic muscle for Chicano migrants, power of all kinds for those whom the Knights' charity had, up to now, only helped sustain. Given the Knights' mentality, it wouldn't fly. Stanley Gorman was a conscientious law and order judge whom repeat offenders trembled to encounter in a courtroom; Walter Caldron's engagement with the social agenda was limited to denouncing socialized medicine; otherwise he served a wealthy clientele by implanting pacemakers with exquisite skill. While begrudging Bishop Farquhar no preferential options of his own, they and their brother Knights had no intention of sharing them.

"And let us broaden our horizons as to who the 'poor' and the 'oppressed' really are today", he was saying, "and of how the Church should serve them."

Doctor Caldron nodded agreeably. "Perhaps he's going to mention cardiologists."

"Let me give you an example. Judge Gorman was telling me over dinner about your program for giving baskets of food to the poor at Christmas. Very commendable, I'm sure. But consider that the poor in Wernersburgh include a significant number of workers and their families who suffer from unemployment and underemployment brought about by the policies of businesses and banks on whose boards some of you sit. Deliver the Christmas baskets—certainly. But do more: change the policies and practices that keep the objects of your charity poor!"

Groans greeted that. Judge Gorman held his head in his hands. Bishop Farquhar frowned.

"I'm sorry if you don't like to hear that", he said. "But we must be honest. 'Let him who is without sin cast the first stone.' I admit that the institutional Church, too, has sinned—sinned repeatedly—against justice in her own policies and practices. But I promise you, in Wernersburgh, at least, that's going to change."

Farquhar looked pugnaciously around the room, but no one said anything. The Knights were too stunned to make a peep. Justin only wanted the embarrassment to end, and he supposed the rest felt the same way. As if sensing this and agreeing, the Bishop launched now into his peroration.

"We have a new agenda. The *aggiornamento* is here. Renewal is the name of the game. The Church of Wernersburgh faces new challenges and tasks. For many years the Knights of Mount Olivet stood at my predecessor's side, supporting him as he went about his duties. I hope you'll continue to stand at my side as I go about mine.

"Make no mistake—neither you nor I can live in the past. Perhaps some things I've said have shocked you. 'Who is this crazy bishop?' Well, if I *am* a little crazy, it's with impatience to see the Church renewed—a beacon of hope for the hopeless, an advocate for the powerless and oppressed, a liberator of those in chains, and always a prophet to the smug, the self-satisfied, the consumers of conventional wisdom.

"Do the Knights of Mount Olivet feel as I do? That's for you to say. You have a choice, gentlemen, between renewal, relevance, and the future on the one hand and stagnation, irrelevance, and the past on the other. If anything I've said has helped bring you closer to facing that choice, my time has been well spent. God bless you all."

Bishop Farquhar hesitated for a moment, but there was no applause. He sat down amid stony silence.

Slowly and reluctantly, clearing his throat while he searched for words, Judge Gorman rose to respond on behalf of the Order, as custom obliged him to do. Clasping the back of his chair, he stood for a moment, head bowed, then began to speak in a low voice. Justin had to strain at first to catch his words.

" . . . grateful to you, Bishop, for your candor. You deserve a candid reply." Gorman paused, glanced around, then resumed more confidently. "Every man here has faults, but none of us is totally insensitive. We see the same suffering and injustice you do. For the most part, we haven't caused it, but you're right—we can do *something* about it, and generally we do what we can. Of course we know Christmas baskets aren't the answer. Sorry, though, I guess some of us like Christmas baskets. They're part of the season. Maybe they even help to humanize things a little. But they certainly aren't the answer. Believe me, most of us are looking for the answer, each in his own way, his own line of work, as opportunities arise.

"The problem some of us would have with what you've said, Bishop, is that it assumes there's only one way—*your* way. You speak of being advocates for the oppressed, and I see the point. But by profession I'm not an advocate—I'm a judge. I expect the Church to recognize and respect that. Every man in this room would say the same about what he does.

"You can be sure, Bishop Farquhar, that the Knights of Mount Olivet welcome you to Wernersburgh. We thought the world of Bishop Frisch, we're prepared to think the same of you. We're honored by your invitation to stand at your side. But you also have to stand by us. The Knights aren't perfect, Bishop, but this is an organization whose members do try to apply their values in areas where they aren't always very welcome today. Maybe you could call that renewal. Anyway it's hard work. We seek the Church's encouragement and support. We seek yours. I hope we'll have it, whether or not we all buy into your agenda for us."

Flushed and embarrassed, Gorman sat down. Several men applauded loudly. The moment for prayer having come, Bishop Boylan did the honors with a hurried Hail Mary. The Knights scattered with every sign of relief.

"An evening to remember", Doctor Caldron remarked to Justin.

The editor's jaw was set like granite. "I'd rather forget it."

"Are you going to write this up for the *Catholic Truth?*"

"It was off the record. Thank God."

Boylan stopped him on the way out. "Let me buy you a cup of coffee."

They went downstairs to the coffee shop. Plastic wreaths hung on the walls and strings of colored lights blinked on and off above the counter. Taking a booth, they were awash in piped-in carols.

"What did you make of all that?" the Bishop asked.

"Do you think he was trying to outrage people or does that just come naturally to him?"

Boylan pursed his lips. "He's an intelligent man. I suppose it was deliberate. He meant to shake you up."

"He did a good job." Justin dumped sugar and cream liberally into the steaming coffee and stirred it angrily. "He alienated everybody."

"Including you?" Bishop Boylan sighed. He said, "We don't have many opportunities to talk at the office, and there's something I need to tell you."

His tone made Justin look up apprehensively. "Yes?"

"You'd better keep your eyes open . . . as far as your job is concerned, I mean."

"He's going to *fire* me?"

"I don't think so. But he wants to get control of the paper. I suppose that will be at your expense."

"That says a lot about him."

"About both of you. Be careful, Justin. Try not to upset him. That's as much as I can tell you."

"I'd be more grateful if I knew what to do about it. We both heard him just now. How can *I* please a man who thinks like that? Why should I *want* to please him?"

"Is that your integrity talking—or your stubbornness?"

Justin said, "It's the better part of both."

V

Planted like God's sentinel upon an isolated hilltop, St. John Vianney Seminary commanded a sweeping view of the valley falling away in motley planes of Turner gray and watery brown toward the horizon: small farms, woodland, itinerant creeks glazed with icy patches, all powdered with a sparse coating of new snow. Above Justin and Vincent, the leaden January sky swelled heavily earthward. Pausing to take in the view from the steps leading to the main entrance, they stood for a few moments breathing halos of steam in the damp, cold air, then resumed their walk along the crunching gravel path that circled the sprawling building like a stony scapular.

The seminary was a huge structure of gray stone hewed from a nearby quarry and reassembled in the form of a battlemented Victorian castle. A rambling porch trimmed with curlicued green woodwork gave the building something of the look of a summer resort or sanitarium from the McKinley years, but that was the only humanizing concession; otherwise St. John's was rigorously somber, a stone sermon on detachment, duty, and dying to self.

Had there been any eavesdroppers, the gnashing of gravel beneath their shoes would have masked their conversation, but no one except Justin and Vincent was out on this raw Saturday afternoon.

"... came out here again last Thursday to visit with us and spent the evening", Vincent was saying agitatedly. "I think he means well, but his ideas are pretty strange."

Justin gave him a gloomy look. "For instance?"

"We had a kind of bull session after dinner," the young man explained, "and somebody asked the inevitable question—about celibacy, I mean."

"What did Bishop Farquhar say?"

"That it's the current discipline of the Church, but he thinks it might be on its way out in the long run. 'That makes it pretty tough on you fellows'—I'm quoting now—'but experiencing in your own lives how the Church puts people through the wringer should make you more compassionate priests.' He actually said that, Dad!"

Vincent, hatless, wore a black windbreaker and gray woolen scarf. Taller by two or three inches, he had Justin's features but in a blunter version, as if with repetition nature grew careless about details—a heavy, almost granitic chin, wide and expressive mouth, and broad, coarse nose. But his complexion was unusually fine—fair, so smooth one wondered whether even yet he shaved, and mottled in this biting air with wine-colored splotches; while his wide-set hazel eyes had Eleanor's vulnerability and candor.

"Did the other men like him?" Justin asked.

"As a person? Sure. But as a bishop—for his ideas, I mean—that's hard to say. Not everybody here thinks alike", he finished apologetically.

"Maybe not, but Bishop Frisch and Monsignor Caldron have done a great job of keeping this seminary orthodox at a time when most others aren't."

That was true. Although St. John's was down to a hundred and twenty-five students (it had been built for three hundred), that was a respectable number these days. And the fact that it included nearly a hundred men from other dioceses testified to the seminary's good reputation with bishops who appreciated eternal verities and a tight regimen and, like Frisch, still wanted their priests trained in both.

Reaching the back of the building, they struck off downhill along a service road that ran past a grove of evergreens sheltering outdoor stations of the cross. Beyond the trees one glimpsed the red brick outlines of the college-level seminary, its hillside site appropriately subservient to the theologate crowning the hill.

Justin had driven the twenty miles out to the seminary that afternoon for two reasons: to see Vincent and also to drop off Eleanor with Father Paul Drake, the archdiocesan archivist and her spiritual director. As always, it gratified him to see how closely Vincent's thinking mirrored his own. He was like that: a loving, serious, docile son who listened to his father and accepted what he told him. Vincent's soundness was a great consolation to him.

"Are you sure that Monsignor Caldron is leaving?" Justin asked now.

"That's what he keeps telling people."

"Any idea yet who his successor will be?"

Vincent winced. "I was afraid you'd ask. It looks like Father Lackner."

"Lackner!" Justin groaned. "I might have known."

"He and Bishop Farquhar spent a lot of time together when the Bishop was here. Everyone says it's settled."

"Lackner was Frisch's biggest mistake at St. John's. He should never even have been assigned to the seminary. And to make him rector! How do the students feel about *this?*"

"Some think it's terrific", the young man admitted.

"God help us if *they* become priests!"

Coming abreast of the evergreen grove, they turned off the

road by unspoken assent and trudged across a field. At the far side they passed through a screen of trees and entered the circle where the stations were. The mosaic scenes of Christ's agony were sheltered in rude boxes of weathered wood nailed to tree trunks. Pausing before Jesus' first fall, Justin contemplated the figure crushed beneath an enormous cross.

"We've been lucky for a long time", he said. "Bishop Frisch kept a lot of things from happening here that happened everywhere else. Now it's our turn."

Vincent was still thinking of the seminary. "Personally, I can accept Father Lackner as a rector", he said. "After all, I'll be ordained in just a year."

Justin smiled at that. Evidence of his son's unquenchable vocation always boosted his spirits. It seemed the necessary completion of some important pattern in his own life, a generous gesture closing the gap. And it restored the balance which Megan's terrible defection had upset.

"That's what matters, Vinnie", he agreed. "Get yourself ordained and don't worry about the rest of this. It will work out."

"I worry about you", Vincent said earnestly.

Justin forced himself to laugh. "What are you talking about?"

"How long will Bishop Farquhar let you go on editing the *Catholic Truth?*"

"Why not forever? If he doesn't bother me, I won't bother him."

"Aren't you concerned?"

Justin felt helpless. What could he do if Farquhar did move against him? In a low, angry voice he snapped, "Of course I am", and with that turned back to the road. "Come on. Your mother will be through soon, and you've got studies to attend to." Briskly he began slicing through the cold, humid air, beating his gloved hands together in a swimming stroke. For a moment Vincent hung back, watching him with a troubled look; then, nodding to the small image of God in pain, he followed his father across the shallow snow.

"Arthur, you can't imagine how pleased I am to hear you say that!" Monsignor Dudley threw back his head and laughed in triumph, his gold-rimmed glasses catching the light and flaming brazenly like twin shields flaunted. Things were going his way.

Arthur Kucharski grinned a little nervously. "I think you knew two weeks ago that I was hooked."

"But you kept us dangling, didn't you? Tell me," Dudley leaned forward confidentially, "if you wanted the job, why did you do that?"

Arthur shrugged. "Most things seem hardly worth having once you get them. For two weeks I've been asking myself whether it will be like that with the *Catholic Truth.*"

"And you decided it won't."

"It's worth finding out."

Dudley laughed again, less heartily. "You're an original, Arthur. I wonder what you'll make of the paper."

"So do I."

"I must tell the Bishop the news." Rising, he hurried out of the office. Left alone in the Saturday afternoon stillness, Arthur reflected that the Chancellor was receiving his reward: his master's approval. Presently Dudley returned smirking and said, "He's free now."

They went down a corridor, through a secretary's cramped cubicle, and into Farquhar's spacious office. The Bishop rose from a modern desk of blond wood, removing half-glasses and slipping them into his breast pocket as he strode forward with a warm smile. To Arthur's surprise he was wearing a red cardigan sweater and a red and white checked sport shirt; he and Dudley were in clerical black.

"I'm delighted with your decision, Arthur", Farquhar said, grasping his hand enthusiastically.

"I'm looking forward to getting started, Bishop."

"Come—let's talk."

Bishop Farquhar led the way to a sofa and chairs, where China cups and a silver thermos of coffee were waiting. From previous visits Arthur was familiar with the routine. "Mind if I smoke?" he asked casually, helping himself to coffee.

"Go right ahead." Farquhar was still beaming. "What finally made up your mind?"

He looked up from pouring, and his eyes met the Bishop's. "Your promise that I'd have a free hand."

"I wouldn't want it otherwise."

"That's our style these days", Dudley chimed in.

"I want to believe that. But working for the system makes me nervous."

A smile danced across Bishop Farquhar's boyish face, exploding paired networks of sympathetic wrinkles at the corners of his eyes. "We're very much alike in that", he said, and Arthur knew he could do no wrong.

Cocking his head skeptically, he observed, "Bishops *are* the system."

"I've been bucking the system for years", Farquhar replied, still smiling. "From the inside, of course. But what does it matter—inside, outside? What counts is whether you want to serve the system or change it. I'm for changing it, and I think you are, too."

Arthur sipped his coffee. Outside it looked like snow. He felt warm and contented. "My appointment isn't going to make everybody happy, Bishop. Plenty of people in this diocese think I'm bad news."

"I'm not trying to please that crowd but shake them up. Let them grumble."

"What really sold me", Arthur went on, "was that session you had with the Knights of Mount Olivet. You must have really let them have it."

The Bishop looked surprised. "How did you hear about that?" He glanced uncertainly at Monsignor Dudley.

Arthur grinned. "They couldn't wait to go out and start bitching. I've got some of those guys in my parish. Can't stand them. Walter Caldron for one—ugh! They've been gumming up the diocese for years."

"The Knights of Mount Olivet mean well," Bishop Farquhar pronounced, "but they don't understand renewal. It's my job to bring them along."

Dudley had been drumming his fingers on the arm of his chair. He said, "Perhaps we need to make something clear to Arthur."

They looked at him in surprise. "What?" asked the Bishop.

"The Knights' dinner was a closed affair. The Bishop's remarks were private and off the record. I assume we won't be reading about the incident in the *Catholic Truth.*"

"I'm sure that won't happen, Oscar", Bishop Farquhar exclaimed. "That isn't what Arthur has in mind for the paper."

Arthur looked blankly from one to the other. "It's a pretty good story", he protested.

"No story", Dudley told him softly.

"Where I want you to use all your creativity", Farquhar went on as if nothing had happened, "is in exposing the diocese to the renewal. Stir people up, get them thinking! Feel yourself challenged by it, Arthur."

He wanted the editorship too much to argue. "No story", he agreed to Dudley.

They chatted on, Farquhar sketching grandiose visions of the role the newspaper would play in building a new church in

Wernersburgh while Arthur listened, aflame with eagerness for glory. In a pause in the conversation, Dudley asked, "Have you considered how you're going to handle Justin Walsh?"

"Don't you think he'll quit? It would make things a lot easier."

"He's in his fifties. His roots are in Wernersburgh. I can't imagine where he'd go or what he'd do."

Bishop Farquhar added earnestly, "I hope he adjusts. Our task, Arthur, is to persuade such people that the possibilities of Catholicism weren't exhausted by the ghetto experience of their youth. Fear of the unknown holds them back. We must help them conquer fear and be at home with uncertainty."

"Is there anything else I should know about him?" Arthur asked.

Dudley began ticking items off on his plump fingers. "A devout layman—exemplary in many respects. . . . His son is in the seminary."

The Bishop looked surprised. "I didn't know that."

"Third year theology. Unfortunately, he's as conservative as his father. He could be troublesome."

"Other children?" Arthur asked.

"His daughter works at one of the television stations. I believe", Dudley added delicately, "that there's something odd about her situation. She has a child, but it appears she isn't married."

"Divorced?"

"I suppose."

"That must be a sore point for Justin."

Bishop Farquhar said, "You'd think such experiences would teach a man compassion, but I find none in the *Catholic Truth*'s editorials."

"Ideology and compassion don't mix, Bishop," Monsignor Dudley said.

"Anything else?" Arthur asked.

"Your appointment won't be announced for several weeks", Dudley told him. "We're trying to put together a number of things in an orderly way. Please keep it to yourself until then."

"The question", Farquhar said thoughtfully, "is whether you can bring Justin Walsh along with you. Try, Arthur. If the paper's to be an instrument of renewal, Justin himself may be a test case. Will you make the effort?"

Embarrassed, Arthur said, "Sure. But if it doesn't work, will I have your support to do what's necessary?"

Farquhar glanced at Dudley. The chancellor's Buddha-like expression seemed to strengthen him. "I pray it doesn't come to that, Arthur. But, yes—you'll have my full support in dealing with Justin Walsh."

She'd made her confession earlier, and now they were only chatting, as they often did, enjoying each other's company over cups of herb tea while a kettle hissed on the hot plate in the corner.

"Bishop Farquhar visited us last week", Father Drake remarked.

"Justin is always speaking of him. Does he really have horns, Father?"

"Calf horns perhaps," he said mildly, "but the way he combs his hair makes it hard to tell. He's awfully sincere and painfully naive. The diocese may be in for a difficult time while he learns his job." He sighed. "Dear me. It's a considerable leap from Peter Frisch to Ambrose Farquhar. I'm glad my leaping days are over, Eleanor."

Paul Drake seemed oblivious to the stupefying waves of heat rising from the loudly knocking radiator. He wore an old black sweater, frayed at the wrists, but even so his small hands, clutching the crook of a black cane, looked blue and icy cold.

Sombre illumination of the snow-threatened late afternoon seeped into the basement office through a recessed window just under the high ceiling, while a heavy-shaded gooseneck lamp spilled golden light over the desk top, accentuating the deep shadows elsewhere in the book-filled room.

Father Drake was in his early seventies, Eleanor knew, but he could have passed for older: the stroke five years ago had aged him badly. All the same, given its severity, his recovery had been surprisingly good. There was the cane, of course, and the left side of his face did not work well (he'd learned to keep the right side turned toward visitors); neither did his left arm, which he manipulated mainly with his right hand—a handicap that had obliged him to stop offering Mass in public. But his speech was largely unimpaired, only rarely did he grope for a word that wouldn't come, and his mind seemed as clear as ever.

For many years Father Drake had taught history at St. John's college seminary, down the hill, and at Maryheights, where he also served as chaplain. It was there that Eleanor had first come to know him as a teacher and advisor. Since the stroke that put an end to his teaching, he'd lived at the seminary in semi-retirement, puttering in the diocesan archives and giving spiritual direction to seminarians, priests, and a few lay people like Eleanor who knew him from his active years. In that select circle he was regarded as a wise man and perhaps a holy one.

"Justin suffers a great deal", she told him now.

"Do you suffer with him?"

"I would suffer *for* him, but I don't think I'm capable of suffering *with* him. But I am terribly sorry for him, if that's what you mean."

"He may be in for worse."

"Megan says the Bishop will take the paper away from him."

"I imagine so."

Eleanor caught her breath. "That will be very cruel."

"Not as the Bishop sees it. He has policies to pursue. Justin's in the way."

"Then the Church is cruel to permit such things."

The old priest nodded slowly. "Of course. The Church has an atrocious record when it comes to rewarding her servants. At least those who are loyal. When there's a change in course, they're always the first to be . . . "

"Sacrificed." Eleanor finished for him, wincing. "That's hideous."

He made a small deprecating gesture with his good hand. "Many saints have been made that way."

"Haven't others been unmade?"

"Perhaps. But, people rationalize—they blame the Church for their bad will. 'If the Church were not so hard, I wouldn't have sinned.' But if the Church were ever so much softer than she is, they'd still find ways of sinning."

"Does that apply in Justin's case?"

"I'm not *his* director, Eleanor."

"Then tell me, what sin have *I* committed?"

"Possibly none. But when the blow falls on Justin, you'll be tested, too."

"My loyalty to the Church?"

"No, to Justin. You're generous elsewhere—to Megan, Vincent, your grandson. Even to God. But I think Justin needs more. . . . "

"He's very self-sufficient, Father."

"But now he's going to be badly hurt."

"And I must suffer *with* him?"

"If you can . . . if he'll let you. Try him at least."

They were saying goodbye outside the car. Snow had begun to fall, and big wet flakes clustered thickly in Vincent's dark hair. Eleanor reached up to brush them away, and he ducked, laughing. "I *can* take care of myself, Mom."

"Go in now before you catch pneumonia", she exclaimed, laughing back.

Justin watched with a frown. Abruptly he told Vincent, "Try not to worry about things."

The smile faded from Vincent's face. "You too, Dad."

"Concentrate on your work. The goal is ordination." He glanced toward the ghostly mass of the seminary, growing indistinct as the light failed and the snow fell more heavily. "You've got less than a year and a half. This place can take care of itself after that."

Eleanor looked questioningly from one to the other. "What's *this* all about?"

"No need to worry", Justin repeated mechanically, opening the car door for her. "We've got to get going."

Kissing Vincent, she climbed in. Father and son trudged around to the driver's side. "Don't worry about me either," Justin muttered gruffly, "I can take care of myself."

"It seems so unfair. . . . "

"I chose to work for the Church when it looked like an attractive thing to do. If that choice meant anything, I have to stand by it now, when the consequences aren't so attractive." He thrust out his hand. "God bless."

They pulled away waving, while Vincent waved back in the gathering darkness and the snow.

The wipers made a thunk-thunk sound against the impacted ice at either end of their short arc. The heater radiated smothering waves of warm air. Clots of snow danced ecstatically toward them in the headlights, then abruptly vanished into the darkness on either side. Justin was an excellent driver, the highway still fairly clear, and Eleanor found the scene more atmospheric than alarming.

On the radio the news concerned three priests and a nun who'd been indicted on charges of conspiring to blow up the heating systems of several federal buildings in Washington, D.C., and to kidnap Henry Kissinger. Having stood as much as he could, Justin switched it off with a curse. "They're mad. My God, they're absolutely insane!"

She nodded. "It doesn't sound very sensible."

"*Sensible?* These people are overgrown children. And they're dangerous. Priests and nuns . . . what in God's name do they suppose they're doing?"

Wanting to distract him, she wanted also to do what Father Drake had told her. "You and Vinnie were very solemn", she observed.

"Bishop Farquhar visited the seminary again last week", Justin answered grimly. "He's going to name Ronald Lackner the new rector."

"I don't know him."

"He's the sort of person you'd expect Farquhar to choose. Imagine, Ellie—St. John Vianney is going to have its first Modernist rector."

She sighed. "Perhaps you should do what you told Vinnie—not worry, I mean."

He glanced sharply over at her. "He's got to concentrate on getting ordained, but I'm already in the thick of things."

Eleanor stared unhappily at the darkness and the snow. "What will happen at the *Catholic Truth?*" she asked. "Is it true they're planning to take the paper away from you?"

"Is that what Drake thinks?"

"Yes. . . . *Will* it happen?"

"Bishop Boylan thinks so, too."

Shivering despite the heat, she turned up the collar of her coat. "Justin, why wait for it? Why not just leave?"

"And go where? I'm fifty-five. I've been editing a religious newspaper for twenty years. Who needs me?"

"Couldn't the Knights of Mount Olivet help you find something?"

He bridled at the suggestion. "The Knights aren't an employment agency."

I'm treading on sacred ground, she reminded herself; but she persisted mildly. "It seems a pity just to wait for trouble to come."

"There's something else you overlook", he said reluctantly. "As long as I'm at the *Catholic Truth,* it's harder for them to have things entirely their way."

"Them?"

"Farquhar and whoever he brings in as editor."

Again she sighed. Justin was naturally combative: imminent misfortune simply dictated a new mode of battle, and for all she knew, he'd enjoy defeat as much as victory. These were things Father Drake hadn't taken into account.

"Can't you just leave the diocese to the Bishop?"

"Why not leave it to those lunatics who want to kidnap Kissinger? That isn't my style, Ellie. Besides, it's as much my Church as theirs . . . or Farquhar's."

"He's a bishop."

"And I'm only a layman? But I'm as obliged to do what I can for the Church—as a layman—as he is to do what he can as a bishop. I may be able to do less, but that doesn't make my duty any less."

She could tell he was pleased with his answer; she might very well read it as an editorial in a future issue of the *Catholic Truth.* Father Drake told me to suffer with him, she thought, but suppose he isn't suffering? Wait, I suppose, until he does.

Staring out at the dancing snow, she said, "Have it your way, Justin", and added in silence: For however long you can, poor dear.

VI

The wind rose in late February, and there was a sense of change in the air. It was just then that Bishop Farquhar's first clergy appointment list appeared, dispelling any lingering notions that he might maintain the status quo. Father Ronald Lackner was named rector of St. John Vianney Seminary, succeeding Monsignor John Caldron, who got a choice pastorate; several longtime stalwarts of the chancery were sent out to pasture in parishes, and younger men were appointed in their places. Confirming what had long been known by insiders, Bishop Boylan was appointed to the new post of "Exurban Vicar"; it seemed to have something to do with parishes in the rural counties to the west of the city. In an accompanying statement Farquhar spoke warmly of his intention to share pastoral responsibilities with the Auxiliary Bishop. Succeeding him as Vicar General of the diocese was Monsignor Oscar Dudley.

"What does it all mean?" Justin asked.

"It means", Bishop Boylan sighed, "that he's putting his stamp on things."

Sitting at his desk, the editor was holding that week's *Catholic Truth,* which announced the appointments with fanfare appropriate to the Second Coming. He threw down the paper in disgust. "That's what I was afraid of!"

"It was bound to happen", Boylan said resignedly. "He has no need for me around the chancery. Dudley's his man."

"And Lackner at the seminary!"

The Bishop shook his head. "I admit that's disturbing."

"I feel ashamed", Justin exclaimed, "printing this drivel without explaining what's really going on."

Bishop Boylan smiled faintly. "Ah, Justin, how can you explain it anyway?"

As the new shape of things began to emerge, however, conflicting explanations were hazarded. The clergy and the more sophisticated laity had recognized from the start that Bishop Farquhar was a far cry from his predecessor; his encounters with various groups—the Knights of Mount Olivet weren't alone—made that clear. Now that his actual program was emerging, it evoked strong, mixed reactions. People who believed that the diocese had been cut off from the Vatican II renewal by Frisch, welcomed Farquhar's moves and cried for more; those who held that Wernersburgh had been all but miraculously preserved from the turmoil and collapse occurring everywhere else in the Church were in despair.

Quite a few people of the first sort were ready and eager to take matters into their own hands, confident that, with the new mood at the top, they'd either be supported or—better yet, in some respects—officially ignored. Strange liturgies, hitherto subterranean and scattered, began now to crop up publicly and unabashed, and in St. Philomena's parish the pastor and his two assistants made a splash by dressing up in rented clown suits to concelebrate Mass—an event duly recorded by the *Globe-Herald* and TV news but predictably ignored by the *Catholic Truth.*

That was small potatoes though: the new tolerance seemingly extended to dissenting views counted for a lot more. Gwyneth Harley wrote a series on the state of Catholic opinion in the diocese, and priests and laity alike obliged her by deploring the Church's obstinacy on matters like birth control, divorce, and clerical celibacy. Ronald Lackner supplied a quote that was cited jubilantly for weeks afterward in certain priestly circles: "The Church elsewhere has come of age since Vatican II. In Wernersburgh we're just getting started. A lot of people are likely to be hurt: cleaning out the intellectual rubbish of bad teaching and the emotional debris of repressive pastoral practice upsets those who think such things are the essence of Catholicism. But it will make for a healthier Church in the long run. If you want to know what infallibility really means, it's the Church's ability to confront its mistakes and sooner or later correct them. The Spirit is moving us to do that now in Wernersburgh, and thank God we've got a bishop who agrees with him—or her."

Change was in the air, and its odor had strange effects. The President of Maryheights College, Sister M. Josepha, informed the world that she was quitting religious life after nearly thirty years and becoming plain Clare O'Donoghue; the Sisters of Dolorous Humility, proprietors of her venerable institution, dithered for a few days and then announced that she'd be kept on as President, while they turned over control of the college to a lay board and abandoned their corporate identification with it. Maryheights had gone secular in the twinkling of an eye. Asked by reporters for his assessment of these startling developments, Bishop Farquhar thanked the sisters for half a century of service to the diocese and expressed hope that Maryheights (henceforth to be known as Wernersburgh Community College) would remain a source of "value-oriented education"—a remark taken to mean that he was uneasy with schools that were *too* Catholic.

The diocese was still absorbing all this when the rash of priestly defections hit. Priests in Wernersburgh had left the priesthood before, but departures had been relatively rare—

Peter Frisch prided himself on that. Now they suddenly came in clusters, as if an impacted backlog were surging forward. They followed no pattern: some were men who'd been ordained only a year or two, others had been priests for a quarter of a century; some sought laicization, others—metaphorically and in a few instances literally—just walked out the rectory door one day and never came back.

A few disclosed romantic entanglements. In one widely remarked case, the pastor of a large and affluent parish, a man of fifty-seven, eloped with the nun who was principal of the parish school. The *Globe-Herald* tracked them down in New Antwerp, where they assured Gwyneth Harley that they were happy, unrepentant, and disillusioned with the Church for not receiving them with open arms. "We're still Catholics," the former pastor explained, "but we'll be a long time getting over the emotional mauling we suffered from the Church. The pressures to hang on and conform are enormous. I'm just glad we saw the light when we did." To which Bishop Farquhar, when asked, had no response.

Others did. Doctor Walter Caldron met Justin on the street one blustery day and drew him into the entrance of an office building to talk. His nose a scalded red, his eyes brimming with tears from the boisterous wind's buffeting, the Doctor demanded, "I suppose Farquhar's pleased with the way things are going?"

"He doesn't tell me how he feels, Walter."

"It's marvelous to see his grand plan for the diocese unfold. Priests and nuns running off together, crackpot liturgies everywhere you look, Catholic schools collapsing. And loyalty punished! What happened to my brother was typical of Farquhar's notion of renewal."

Justin winced. "I regret it deeply."

Sniffing furiously, Caldron tugged down his homburg against

the wind. "I suppose I shouldn't blame *you,* Justin. I suppose you deserve sympathy."

"I get along."

"It must be awful for you."

"Does the paper look that way?"

Caldron laughed. It was not a pleasant laugh. "The paper is a joke. Bland as custard. You know that."

"I didn't realize you were so strong on diagnosis, Walter."

The doctor laid a gloved hand on his arm. "Sorry, Justin. *I* can joke about it, but it's *your* cross. If I can do anything. . . . "

"I can't think what."

The conversation left Justin rattled. Blandness *was* his goal in the *Catholic Truth* these days; editing the paper had become an exercise in omission. The alternative was to acknowledge what was happening in the diocese and fight it. And that would be suicidal. He'd made up his mind to hang on, survive until better days came. But when would they? With all his other advantages, Bishop Farquhar also enjoyed the advantage of youth; better days for Justin might mean retirement. The thought depressed him.

Meanwhile, as Caldron said, the paper was a joke. Justin had trouble meeting the eyes of Ferdy Ruffin and Nancy Lattimore, who together with him comprised the senior editorial staff. They'd both served loyally for years, but now the paper's public eclipse made them doubt the value of their work.

One Thursday morning they were holding their weekly editorial meeting in Justin's office. Ferdy, short, dour, and bald, smoked a large cigar, while Nancy, tall and voluble, strode about holding forth. She wore spinsterhood with resentful pride, like a dowdy hat she dared others to make fun of.

". . . time we got some reactions to what's happening at Maryheights. There's a story there that we're missing."

"We've had a lot of stories on Maryheights", Justin said.

"All you did was rewrite handouts. Let's find out what the students and parents and alumnae really think about the sellout."

From a fog of cigar smoke Ferdy asked, "Alumnae like you, Nance?"

She glowered at him. "There are people with a stake in that school who haven't had a say about what the nuns have done. The *Catholic Truth* owes them a hearing."

Ferdy nodded, tipping cigar ash delicately into an ashtray on Justin's desk. "I buy that. What do you say, Justin?"

He stared at the desk top. "The story is stale."

"Justin!" Nancy's eyes were wide with astonishment.

"That's how I see it."

"I'll do the story on my own time and submit it."

"It won't get published."

"Why the hell not?" she demanded furiously. "Don't tell me it's news judgment. Your mind is made up."

Justin said, "Ask Monsignor Dudley."

"What's he got to do with it?"

"He gave me the word last week. No more about Maryheights. 'The Bishop wants to spare the sisters further embarrassment.' "

Nancy gave a little gasp of outrage. Ferdy said acidly, "How kind of him!"

"If you think this is easy for me. . . . "

"Sorry, Justin. Nobody thinks that."

"I guess it doesn't help", Nancy reflected, "for us to fight among ourselves."

"Like most banal remarks," Ferdy said, "that one is true."

Justin chuckled and the crisis had passed. Even so, the strain was beginning to tell. The editorial conferences were increasingly disagreeable experiences, weekly reminders of their new vulnerability and impotence.

Gnawing a hangnail, Nancy demanded now, "Why don't Farquhar and Dudley just put out the paper themselves?"

"They're too busy screwing up the diocese", Ferdy said. "They need somebody else to screw up the paper for them."

The phone rang. Justin answered. "Now? . . . All right, I'll be down in a minute." He hung up. "That was Dudley. Bishop Farquhar wants to see me."

The other two exchanged apprehensive glances. "What about?" Nancy asked.

Rising, Justin shrugged. "Call the police if I'm not back in thirty minutes."

It required an effort to joke. He hadn't had a private interview with Farquhar since the Bishop had arrived in Wernersburgh, and this sudden summons seemed ominous. Justin was afraid he knew what lay behind it.

The Bishop was smiling and solicitous—nervous, in fact. "Let's be comfortable", he said, drawing Justin to the sofa and chairs in the far corner of his office. "Can I offer you coffee, Justin?"

He shook his head, looking about him like a first-time visitor. Farquhar's changes caught him by surprise. He had the sensation of a man returning to his old home and finding it occupied by strangers: it was the *same* place, no doubt, but also disorientingly different. He couldn't help saying, "You've changed the office."

"I like a bright room", Bishop Farquhar explained. "It was heavy before. And this—" he gestured at their comfortable chairs and the low table with its cups and saucers and silver thermos of coffee. "There are a lot of conversations which shouldn't take place at a desk." Leaning back, fingers laced, he regarded Justin thoughtfully. "We haven't had many opportunities to talk. It's been a busy time for me. So many people to meet. So much to do."

Justin said firmly, "Bishop Frisch left the diocese in very sound shape." His eyes met Farquhar's.

"In some respects you're right. Financially, we're pretty solid. I'm grateful for that. Not every new bishop is so lucky."

"Frisch kept the diocese solid across the board."

Smiling, the Bishop shook his head. "Not quite. The renewal of the Church is years behind schedule here. Thank God, we're getting under way."

Justin thought of the recent rash of bizarre events—the defections, the weird liturgies, the revolution at Maryheights, the humiliation of Bishop Boylan, Monsignor Caldron, and other good priests. "If what's been happening lately is renewal, Bishop, a lot of people could do without it."

"It's painful at first", Farquhar acknowledged. "That's because it was deferred so long. There are times in the life of the Church, just as in the lives of individuals, when changes are natural. Later, it's more difficult. That's what we're experiencing now in Wernersburgh." He helped himself to a cup of coffee, adding cream and sugar generously. "I can't interest you?"

"No."

Again the Bishop gave him a thoughtful look. "I hope you understand", he said, "that although we may disagree about a number of things, I'm grateful to you for your loyalty to the Church."

"That excludes a lot from your gratitude."

Farquhar ignored that. "Even where we disagree, it isn't necessarily unhealthy. The *Catholic Truth* ought to be a forum for a variety of opinions and points of view. You and I needn't see eye to eye on everything."

"I'm sorry, Bishop," Justin said, "but I don't think of the paper as you do. The people who read the *Catholic Truth* already are bombarded with opinions and values hostile to faith. The *Catholic Truth* shouldn't worsen their confusion. It should give the Church's view of things as clearly and consistently as it can." This had been his Catholic Press Month editorial last year; he hadn't dreamed then that he'd soon be using it as his own *apologia.*

Farquhar said, "That assumes there's only one Catholic point of view and that you know what it is. The Church is bigger than you imagine, and its mind is made up on fewer things than you suppose. Since the Council, Catholics have been re-exploring the richness of their own tradition. You underrate them in thinking they can't handle it."

Justin flushed. "No one ever complained that the *Catholic Truth* wasn't challenging. At least, not until recently."

"I appreciate the effort you've been making to please me. It must go against the grain. But the results aren't very exciting, and you know that as well as I. So how do we . . . take the *Catholic Truth* out of its straitjacket?"

The Bishop paused, but Justin only frowned in reply. Farquhar went on.

"I've thought about it a lot, and I believe I've found the solution. I wouldn't want to lose you, Justin, but it isn't fair to ask you to carry the whole burden—especially since the paper must move in directions you won't welcome. We have to bring in someone who can launch the new initiatives and take the criticism if things go wrong."

"Who?"

"Do you know Father Arthur Kucharski?"

Justin's jaw jutted. "I know *of* him."

"I've named him editor of the *Catholic Truth.* The appointment is effective immediately. He'll call you this afternoon and be in the office Monday. You're to remain in your present position, but from now on you report to him. It's for the best in the long run—for you and everybody else. I've taken you very much into consideration in reaching this decision,

Justin, and I count on having you with us for many years to come."

Bishop Farquhar stopped and smiled, relieved at having said it. Stunned, Justin rose blindly.

"Do you have any questions?" the Bishop asked.

Justin shook his head. "You've told me everything I need to know."

When he returned to his office, Nancy and Ferdy straggled in without being summoned. Nancy demanded nervously, "What happened?"

Slumping behind the desk, he said, "He's naming a new editor."

"How awful! Who?"

"Arthur Kucharski."

"Oh, my God!"

Ferdy said, "What happens to you, Justin?"

"I can stay on." He smiled grimly. "Farquhar has my best interests at heart. Nothing has changed—except that I report to Kucharski. We all do."

"Why is he doing this?"

"Because he wants the *Catholic Truth* to be his kind of paper. I won't give him that, so he's bringing in someone who will."

"Kucharski has been attacking the Church in the *National Catholic Recorder* for years."

"I suppose Farquhar is aware of that."

"What does Kucharski know about editing a newspaper?"

"What difference does it make? We're to teach him."

"You speak of Farquhar's kind of paper", Ferdy said. "What's that?"

"He says he wants a variety of viewpoints."

"But this is a *Catholic* newspaper," Nancy objected.

"Bishop Farquhar holds that there's no such thing as *the* Catholic viewpoint", Justin said. "There are various opinions entertained by various Catholics. The job of the *Catholic Truth* is to air them all."

Ferdy lighted a cigar and puffed angrily. "That expresses a viewpoint in itself. 'What is truth?' "

Justin shook his head sadly. "We shouldn't jump to conclusions."

"Haven't you concluded the same thing?"

He hesitated, then pronounced distinctly, "I am trying not to conclude anything right now. I don't understand Farquhar, and I don't know what it will be like working for Kucharski. I think I'd better suspend judgment until I find out. I'd advise you two to do the same."

Nancy regarded him fiercely. "Are you talking about suspending judgment, Justin, or closing our eyes?"

He chuckled harshly. "We're all going into this with eyes wide open. God knows what we're going to learn."

But it was Ferdy, wreathed in smoke, who had the last word. "Nothing we care to, I'm sure."

"How did he take it?" Monsignor Dudley was asking just then.

Bishop Farquhar looked troubled. "Not too well, I think."

Dudley said hopefully, "He resigned?"

"No, Oscar, and I don't want him to."

"I hope you're not taking too idealistic a view of that question, Bishop."

"Justin Walsh is a test case", Farquhar announced. "He represents a whole generation of Catholics who believe as he does—good people at heart, but terribly narrow in their views. *We* made them that way, and we have to change them. Let's be patient."

"Some are beyond change", Dudley said.

"I hope you're wrong."

"And Justin Walsh—"

But Farquhar cut him short, repeating, "Let's be patient."

VII

Shadows lengthened as the light began to fail. Eleanor sat in her bedroom, her thoughts somewhere between reverie and prayer. As she grew older, the past became an increasingly hospitable environment, hardly less accessible than the present and in many respects more interesting, while the future was merely an insubstantiable hypothesis. Time wasn't a totally permeable medium, of course, but she felt the really interesting part of her life had already been lived and was available to examination.

Justin is quite different, she reflected. He lives in the present as confidently and unselfconsciously as a child. That was typical of how he organized his entire life, operating by categories as clearcut as primary colors: so much (time, discourse, emotion) for her, so much for the family, so much (a great deal) for his work, and so much more (a very great deal) for religion. (She thought "religion", not "God", for she assumed that was the correct way of putting it in Justin's case. He cared deeply, passionately, for the institutions, creeds, rituals, and trappings of faith, but there were no grounds for supposing that faith had for him an interpersonal dimension—that it had ever occurred to him to stand in God's presence and simply wait.)

He's always been the same, she thought, memory traveling back. They'd met at one of the spit-and-polish mixers that the girls of Maryheights were allowed to give during the fall for the boys from St. Bruno's. The thinking was that the young gentlemen and ladies would mingle decorously under the watchful eyes of faculty chaperones, thus launching a year of chaste dating and virginal courtship and leading, in many cases, to happy Catholic marriages and wholesome Catholic homes. The system worked surprisingly well, especially by comparison with the lurid customs of a later time. Indeed, it baffled Eleanor how young people these days *did* manage their sexual pairings-off, having been bombarded from their earliest years by every possible inducement to promiscuity and polymorphous lust that a sophisticated and irreligious age could devise. Thirty-five years earlier, sublimation had been the only recourse for a pious young Catholic; today, it seemed, the goal was to tame concupiscence by working it to death, as one might exhaust a hound by running it.

A small hired band thumps away at glutinous romantic favorites of the day in a corner of Maryheights' immaculate gymnasium. The dance has only just begun, the St. Bruno's boys are still clumped on one side of the room, laughing boisterously to build their confidence, while the girls, tense enough to to shriek, giggle and scream among themselves and feign indifference to their guests.

Eleanor is a freshman, and this is the first of these dances she will attend. She senses the nervousness of her friends but finds herself surveying the scene with ironic detachment. It doesn't occur to her to interpret what she is witnessing in terms of sexual tension, yet she understands it even if she lacks language to express it. Years later it will occur to her that she was a surprisingly cool customer then, given her youth and sheltered upbringing; but the convent-bred, Catholic schoolgirl of the day, though naive about many things, was schooled to be shrewd about the emotional life.

"Would you like to dance?"

The boy stands beside her grinning self-confidently. She takes him in with a glance: moderately tall and decidedly broad-shouldered, a square ruddy face and a rather amazing mass of bristly, jet black hair. She likes his smile, isn't sure about the rest.

Eleanor nods. They step out onto the dance floor.

"Has anyone told you that you're the prettiest girl in the room?"

She can't help laughing. "Has anyone told you that you have the corniest line in the room?"

He laughs back. "Lots of people. My name's Justin Walsh. I'm a sophomore at St. Bruno's."

"I'm Eleanor Schneider. I'm a freshman."

"I thought so. I didn't see you around last year."

"You know absolutely everybody at Maryheights?"

"Everybody worth knowing."

"That sounds as if we're here for your approval."

Justin guides her expertly. The floor is starting to fill up. "I approve", he says. "Do you like Maryheights?"

"I think so."

"Only *think* so?"

"I've just been here a few weeks. The work is awfully hard."

"The solution is to relax when you can. That reminds me—what are you doing Friday?"

"I'll have to check and see."

"Don't bother. You're going out with me, Eleanor."

Banality is the midwife to the greater part of life. They were married a month after Eleanor's graduation and spent a week in Montreal on their honeymoon. A year later Megan was born. In early 1942, Justin left his job as a reporter at the *Globe-Herald* and enlisted in the army. Eleanor and Megan moved in with Eleanor's parents. Justin spent a quiet war writing propaganda in Washington and London. Returning after three years, he doffed his first lieutenant's bars and resumed his job at the newspaper. Vincent was born in 1946. Their lives settled back into the rut marked out for them.

She and Justin had lived in reasonable contentment with each other for the last quarter of a century. Friends sometimes marveled that she could bear so readily with his assertiveness and need to dominate, but they presented no problems for her. She handled him by sticking quietly to her guns, minding whatever she had to mind, and not disputing him. He adjusted. He wasn't an ungenerous man, and he loved her. His need was satisfied by giving her directions; that done, he seldom noticed whether she carried them out. For her part, Eleanor had no objection to being told what to do, provided she could then do as she liked.

Now, though, the terms of their relationship were shifting, as Justin's world came crashing down around him. It was strange to think of him needing her help—there was little precedent for that. Had Megan's pregnancy marked an exception? Perhaps; but if so, he hadn't let on, and she, preoccupied with Megan, hadn't considered him. Now, as Father Drake pointed out, it was different: Justin himself had been struck down. Searching the past, she found nothing that told her what to do.

Often lately she'd examined the problem in her prayer. Prayer was Eleanor's medium of choice: not so much something she did, as an atmosphere she lived in. She could no more have said when she began to pray than when she began to breathe, for even as a child she'd never felt really alone; and, ultimately, was prayer anything else than adverting to the fact that one wasn't? As for asking *for* things—like the knack for helping Justin in his trouble—that was easy: you brought a matter forward, placed it in the context, so to speak. Words were superfluous. The point was simply to acknowledge absolute dependence. Therefore in prayer she merely set her relationship with Justin within that other relationship, which was the substance of prayer itself. And, although the answer she sought hadn't yet come, she was neither surprised nor troubled. Grace builds on nature; she had yet to nurture a natural capacity for helping him.

The front door opened and closed. Eleanor started. Glancing at the Baby Ben alarm clock on the desk, she saw that it was after six. She'd been daydreaming, and here was Justin home and dinner to be prepared! Rising, she hurried downstairs.

He stood in the closet fumbling with his overcoat. A metal hanger clattered to the floor; he stooped for it with a grunt, then abandoned the effort and turned to face her. Seeing him in the backlighting from the small lamp on the hall table, she knew at that instant what he would look like when he was eighty. It wasn't so much his features which betrayed him as his posture. Normally Justin carried himself aggressively—shoulders back, chin out, challenging the world—but now he seemed to have fallen in on himself: the sleeves of his jacket overlapped his wrists, his collar was too large for his neck, and his trousers were baggy around his withered shanks. Eleanor was aghast.

"They've named a new editor", he said dully.

"Oh, Justin! I'm sorry."

He shambled past her into the living room. She followed, switching on a lamp as he dropped into his easy chair.

"Let me fix you a drink."

He nodded. "Yes."

Escaping to the kitchen, she prepared a stiff bourbon and water. Jon was glued to the TV. "Grandpa is home", she informed him.

He didn't look around. "When is my mom coming?"

"In a little while, dear."

"I want to finish this show."

Nodding, she went back to the living room with the drink. Justin took a long swallow. "It's Arthur Kucharski", he said.

Eleanor sat down on the sofa. "I don't believe I know him."

"*Father* Arthur Kucharski", Justin said with heavy irony. "Writes for liberal rags under a pen name."

All this was significant to him, but it meant nothing special to her. "Is he an older man?"

"He's a punk", Justin pronounced carefully. "A troublemaker from the day he was ordained. And now Farquhar has named him *editor!* It's inconceivable."

"Perhaps the Bishop doesn't know—"

"He knows exactly what he's getting. *Exactly*", he repeated, as if it gave him pleasure. He drank deeply. "This is the kind of man he wants to run his paper."

"What about you?"

"I can hang around. But Kucharski's in charge."

"Would it help if you talked to the Bishop?"

"I *did*", he retorted angrily. "We had our first conversation since he took over. He laid it all out for me—how he sees the paper, what Kucharski's to do, where I fit in. He knows what he's doing. I thought I was dealing with a reasonable man. Instead, Farquhar turns out to be . . . ", he groped for the right word " . . . an enthusiast."

"But perhaps Father Kucharski is a decent person."

"Goddammit!" Justin exploded at that, and spilled his drink as a result. Mopping furiously at his trousers with a handkerchief, he went on. "I gave him the benefit of the doubt as you told me to do, Ellie. It will all work out, you said. How right you were! It *has* worked out—a bloody rotten disaster. Now you tell me the same thing about Kucharski, without even knowing him. Am I the only person in the world you're prepared to think badly of?"

Offended, she said, "That isn't fair, Justin."

"Another of those warm, intimate domestic scenes?" It was Megan; she stood grinning in the hall doorway.

"We didn't hear you come in, dear."

"That's because Daddy was making so much noise."

"Ha", Justin growled. "Just what I need—the wisdom of show biz."

"I know you want me to stay," Megan said, regarding him ironically, "but Jon and I really have to be going."

Justin stopped her, rising. "Wait", he commanded. "I'll get him. I'm going that way anyhow." He lumbered past her toward the kitchen, bearing his empty glass.

When he was gone, Megan whistled softly between her teeth. "What's wrong with *him?*"

Eleanor spread her hands helplessly. "The Bishop is putting someone else in charge of the paper."

"That's a crock all right," Megan agreed, "but everybody saw it coming. Who's the new man?"

"A priest named Arthur Kucharski."

"Kucharski?"

"Your father doesn't like him. He's terribly upset about the choice. It *does* seem strange", she added reflectively, "when you think about it."

Megan looked queer. "Uh-huh."

"You disagree?"

"I think you're right, Mother. It's a strange choice."

Wearing his windbreaker and flushed with indignation, Jonathan burst into the room, trailed by Justin with a fresh drink. "He won't let me finish my show", the boy protested to the two women.

"A brainless, suggestive situation comedy", Justin said darkly. "Why do you two allow him to watch that garbage?"

"Sorry, Jon", Megan explained. "You're toe-to-toe with the

Torquemada of Wernersburgh in his own living room. Nobody wins at that game."

"I'm merely trying to impress on the child that there are such things as moral standards."

"You needn't worry, Daddy. The idea is getting through to him even without you."

"I can't imagine from what source."

Megan bridled. "What's that supposed to mean?"

"Both of you, please stop", Eleanor exclaimed, rising in alarm.

"No—let him say what he means." Megan's eyes snapped with anger.

Justin laughed bitterly. "You *know* what I mean." Settling heavily into his chair, he took a sip of bourbon.

"Pretend I'm dumb. Tell me."

"I have reason to worry about how Jonathan is raised. Nothing in your situation suggests you have a strong grasp of moral principles."

"You're unspeakable."

"The truth hurts."

"Thank God you won't be preaching that crap in your miserable newspaper any more."

Father and daughter confronted each other speechless with anger. Appalled, Eleanor implored, "Megan, go home."

"Gladly." Snatching her son's hand, she said, "Come on, Jon, we aren't welcome here", and swept out, slamming the front door behind them.

Eleanor felt shaken and ill. Turning to Justin, she demanded, "How could you do that?"

He seemed about to make an angry retort, then caught himself and rubbed his eyes instead. "I don't know", he admitted, looking at her in confusion.

She sank down on the sofa. "Justin, forgive her."

"I can't." He drank deeply.

"And forgive Bishop Farquhar. And this man Kucharski. Please."

"That's lovely, Ellie. Lovely and puerile."

"It's what God asks of you."

"I'm doing a lot in not going out in the street and complaining about Farquhar to everyone I meet. I'm doing a *very* great deal in allowing Megan and her bastard to have access to my home. I—"

"Justin, for heaven's sake!"

Again he rubbed his eyes. "I take that back," he said thickly. "Not feeling too well. A difficult day. Also, drinking on an empty stomach . . . not a good idea."

Reaching toward him, she said, "Justin, I know you've been hurt, but don't make it harder for yourself." The words sounded painfully artificial to her, and she felt herself blushing.

"'sall right, Ellie. I know you mean well." He rose unsteadily. "And I'll make it. Really. Just now though I think I will have another drink." Walking with exaggerated care, he left the room.

Eleanor looked hopelessly after him. God, she thought, how *shall* I help him? She had to face the fact that after thirty years she didn't know.

"How is he taking it?" Vincent asked. He sat cradling the receiver at the desk in the telephone room, a sparsely furnished cubicle on the first floor of the seminary where the students made their calls. It was Friday afternoon; earlier that day he'd gotten Eleanor's message to phone her as soon as he could.

Her voice was filled with anxiety. "Not well. He went to work today, but he's terribly depressed. Along with everything else, he and Megan got into another fight last night."

"Count on Megan", Vincent commented.

"You can't really blame her—"

"You *always* say that, Mom."

"Somebody has to. . . . Vinnie, is this man Kucharski as bad as your father says?"

"He isn't the sort of person Dad will work with comfortably."

"Why would Bishop Farquhar choose him?"

Vincent frowned. "The Bishop is making a lot of funny choices."

Eleanor sighed. "I'm almost sorry I called you."

"Of course you should have called. Tell Dad . . . ", he hesitated, searching for the right words but not finding them "to hang in there." He felt strange offering encouragement to his father, but most things had turned topsy-turvy lately. "He's hurting now, but he'll feel better as time passes. And maybe it will even work out. Maybe Kucharski's not so bad."

"It's a terrible blow for him. We have to help."

"You're trying, Mom."

"Your father has never been the sort of man who needed help."

He winced. "I know."

"Work hard, Vinnie. He's terribly proud that you're going to be a priest. That's the most important thing *you* can do for him."

"Sure. I understand."

Hanging up, Vincent sat scowling out the window. Shadow and sunlight dappled the bare fields in the valley below as hasty clouds scudded across the late afternoon sky. He found it hard to take all this in, hard even to know how he should feel. Accustomed to respecting authority, he was repelled by the rebelliousness of his contemporaries, and St. John's had reinforced him in this. Thus his father's shabby treatment, coming on top of his own fears about the new direction at the seminary, not only angered him but made him uneasy with his anger. For

Bishop Farquhar was at the root of what was happening, and to be angry at a *bishop* was something Vincent's code didn't permit him without guilt.

His immediate solution was to be angry at Megan and—he realized, to some extent—even at his mother. The news that Megan had quarreled with his father—at such a time!—was enough to set him off: he could imagine her provocative attitude in the face of Justin's troubles; imagine, too, Eleanor's insistence on making excuses for her against all reason. Vincent shook his head disgustedly. "Poor Dad", he murmured, rising and leaving the room.

Confused and dejected, he walked slowly down the long, dim corridor toward the stairs. A voice from behind caught him by surprise.

"Got a minute, Vinnie?" Father Ronald Lackner strode long-legged and grinning toward him.

Vincent waited politely but not enthusiastically. "Yes, Father."

"Let's go up to my room."

Vincent followed as Lackner trotted up the steps and sped down another corridor toward the faculty wing. He'd been expecting this encounter. Lackner's appointment as rector hadn't been announced yet, but already he had been making gestures that showed that he meant to take full command. Among these was a series of one-on-one interviews with the third-year men. Father Lackner said he wanted to know them better and get their suggestions; those who'd had the treatment called it "sizing us up". Lackner was invariably cordial, they affirmed, but there was a veiled hint that they'd have to measure up to his standards, or else find themselves in unspecified difficulty.

There was sentiment that these initiatives were premature and wanting in good taste: Monsignor Caldron, after all, was still in charge. Some even said Lackner seemed too hungry for the job, an unnecessary craving, now that the job was assured him. But Lackner paid no heed. He was reported to have confided to friends that the place needed drastic renewing, Farquhar was insisting on it, and in view of the Bishop's expectations he couldn't begin too soon. Vincent found that unsettling: life at the seminary might soon become rather complicated.

All this flashed through his mind as he followed Father Lackner. So did the thought that the timing of this interview could hardly be worse. In view of all his mother had just told him, he would have preferred to be alone. But a priest, he reflected, didn't have the luxury of setting his own schedule. Crossing himself behind Lackner's back, he followed the rector-to-be into his sitting room and took the chair pointed out to him.

Large, high-ceilinged, lined with sagging bookshelves, the room was furnished with comfortable, shabby odds and ends—deep chairs shaped and worn by years of sitting, nondescript large tables littered with books and journals, numerous big table lamps with shades askew, and a battered wooden desk. Tall windows whose irregular panes had a slightly distorting effect looked out upon a panoramic view of the valley to the east, now starting to grow dim as the sun rushed unseen to extinction on the building's far side.

The tall priest dropped into an easy chair across from Vincent. A lanky, balding man in his early forties, with a beak nose and shrewd gray eyes, Lackner wore an unbuttoned black sweater and a red and white checked shirt. "I hope I'm not taking you away from anything pressing."

"No, Father."

"I've been trying to talk to you fellows individually over the last couple of weeks. Our relationship is going to change soon." He chuckled lightly. "I guess you know that Bishop Farquhar has decided to name me rector when Monsignor Caldron steps down?"

"Yes, Father."

"So I think it's important that I get to know you all a little better and find out what's on your minds. Especially you, Vinnie. You're one of the leaders in the class, you know. You carry a lot of weight with the others."

Vincent was flustered. "I don't know. . . . "

"Of course you do. It's all to your credit." Lackner leaned back smiling slightly and studied Vincent in silence, perfectly at ease in the face of the young man's uneasiness. That was his way; he was notorious for employing the same trick in class, fixing a dull student with a long stare and silent smile while the object of this attention squirmed uncomfortably.

Vincent didn't squirm. They had never clashed violently in class, but neither had they hit it off, and at least once they had come to the brink of trouble. Lackner had a knack for hinting things without saying them, which kept him out of trouble with the authorities but angered Vincent. The Council of Trent was a particular problem.

He had it in for Trent, as if what had happened there four centuries earlier were a personal affront, an eruption of dogmatic absolutism aimed at him. He left no doubt that he considered the Council an obstacle to progress, much of whose work would have to be undone if the renewal of the Church were to proceed. Yet he never flatly said so. Instead he said, "It is necessary to interpret the teaching of Trent in its historical context. Trent was the Church's attempt to respond to the needs of those times. It can hardly be taken as the Church's response to the needs of our times."

Having heard this often before, Vincent had spent a good deal of time puzzling over it. One day he had his question ready. "Are you saying, Father, that the teaching of Trent served a purpose in its day but doesn't serve any now?"

Lackner smiled patronizingly. "It serves the purpose of explaining part of the process by which we got where we are. Historically, Trent was of enormous importance."

"But wouldn't you say Trent *settled* some things—doctrinal questions, I mean—once and for all?"

Vincent found himself the target of Lackner's famous stare. Uneasy silence settled over the classroom, but he didn't wilt. He hung on grimly, waiting for an answer. And at last it was Lackner who gave way. "Don't be too quick", he said testily, "to suppose that questions are settled. You box yourself in that way, Mr. Walsh. Of course, some people *want* to be boxed in—it makes life much simpler—but that's not something I'd commend to you."

"Just the same, Father, didn't Trent teach some things that are binding?"

Lackner shrugged. "If it makes you feel better, let's say it did. No doubt it did. I don't want to waste the whole period on *that* question." Having said that, he resumed his lecture.

"You had him on the ropes, Vinnie", his friend Fred Connery remarked after class.

"He didn't want to answer me", Vincent replied, proud and indignant at the same time.

But he hadn't made a crusade of it. He and Lackner coexisted for the rest of the year, if not amicably, at least without flare-ups. Was Lackner a little more careful? Possibly, Vincent thought. If so, it had been worth the trouble.

"Do you have any suggestions for improvement here?" Father Lackner asked now. "Any changes you'd like to see?"

Vincent pondered. "None that occur to me, Father."

"This is a very conservative seminary, Vinnie."

"It's what I'm used to", Vincent confessed humbly. "Anyway, I'm getting a good formation for the priesthood here. I wouldn't want to spend my life in a seminary, but for my money St. John's is swell."

"Some of us *do* spend our lives in seminaries, however."

"I didn't mean—"

Lackner laughed. "I know exactly what you mean. And you're right. A seminary isn't the place to pass a lifetime for most priests. But it's crucial for what it does. That's why those of us who make a career of it must keep looking for ways to improve. Frankly," he added, "you're a bit too complacent about the old place, Vinnie. St. John's has been standing still while other seminaries have been moving ahead. I intend that *we* start moving, too."

The young man received the news without enthusiasm. "Yes, Father."

"Take the faculty. Good men, of course, but a little behind the times in many cases. We'd all benefit from some fresh ideas. . . . You've heard of Bruce Poirier, I suppose?"

Vincent had. Poirier was a moral theologian who'd fought publicly with bishops in several parts of the country during the last few years.

"A friend of mine", Lackner said proudly. "We're going to have him as a visiting professor at St. John's. What do you think of that?"

Vincent thought nothing of it that he cared to share with Lackner. "I guess it's fine, Father."

"That's just one example of what I hope to do. There's a lot going on out there, Vinnie, and I want to expose you men to it all. You'll be better priests for the experience."

"I suppose so."

"Who's your spiritual director?"

"Father Drake."

Lackner frowned unconsciously. "You hit it off with him? You feel it's profitable?"

"Yes."

"Father Drake is an excellent priest of course, but a little. . . . " He cleared his throat. "The stroke slowed him down", he said.

"He's very generous with his time."

"He has lots to be generous with. . . . Well, no need to do anything about that immediately. Just be aware that when you feel like a change, there are other men here who'd be glad to take you on."

Vincent stirred uneasily. He cared a lot about his relationship with Father Drake, and this open bid to give it up shocked him. Resistance, however, could only be passive. "Thank you", he said.

"One other matter. I hope things work out for your father."

Vincent started. Had Lackner overheard his conversation with his mother just now? But that wasn't possible. Putting the thought aside resolutely, he said, "You've heard about the situation, Father?"

"Everything."

"Even the appointment of a new editor?"

"Arthur Kucharski. I learned that a few days ago."

"My father only heard about it yesterday."

"Never underestimate the clerical grapevine, Vinnie." Lackner grinned. "Let me offer you a piece of advice. Naturally your sympathies lie with your dad. But don't get too involved emotionally. As a priest you'll have to take the good of the diocese into account too."

Vincent's anger was mounting. "He got a raw deal."

"Of course *you* think that. But not everybody would agree."

"He's been editor of the *Catholic Truth* for twenty years!"

"Times change. It's time for somebody else to have a crack at it."

"The paper has been his whole life."

"He hasn't *lost* his job", Lackner said, annoyed at being contradicted. "I doubt that he's going to suffer anything."

"Except humiliation."

"That's up to him."

"I don't see how."

Father Lackner regarded him with visible irritation. "I'll lay it on the line for you", he suddenly snapped. "For years your father treated the *Catholic Truth* as if it were his private property. Sure, Bishop Frisch let him do it, but not everybody liked it. *I* didn't like it, and I'm not the only one. I'm sure it's hard on him now, but what Bishop Farquhar has done is best for the newspaper and the diocese. I applaud it. And I advise you not to get your nose out of joint on account of it."

"You applaud Father Kucharski?"

"He'll liven up the paper."

"And you'll liven up the seminary?"

They glared at each other. "Keep your cool, Vinnie", the priest said. "You've got a good record here. Don't spoil it."

Vincent swallowed hard. "I don't plan to."

"Flexibility", Lackner said, relaxing. "Acquire flexibility. Times change. Bishops change. Editors change . . . and rectors, too. You've got to change along with the rest. The Church is being renewed. Don't resist it, or you may get hurt."

"I understand."

The light was growing dim; Vincent had a hard time making out his expression. "Do you?" Lackner asked. "We'll see."

VIII

When other priests accused Arthur Kucharski of being disillusioned with the priesthood, he had a glib response: he'd never been illusioned. Strictly speaking, though, that wasn't true. Although he'd played the role of clerical malcontent throughout much of his priestly career, it had not always been that way. The Second Vatican Council marked for him a period of real religious enthusiasm. He'd thought of himself then as an Xavier Rynne Catholic, for that pseudonymous writer's accounts in *The New Yorker* of what was transpiring in Rome opened new vistas to the young seminarian, suggesting that ordination would be the religious equivalent of investing in a growth industry.

Growing up Catholic in New Antwerp, the son of devout Polish parents, a student in Catholic schools, Arthur had been indelibly impressed by the aura that surrounded the priesthood. Catholics had an acute awareness of the human foibles of their clergy, but side by side with that they showed deferential respect to priests, whom they saw as possessing arcane knowledge and awesome powers. The prestige of the priesthood wasn't lost upon the gangly schoolboy, a milkman's son whose parents still spoke Polish around the house and concealed neither their disappointment that his two older brothers hadn't sprouted vocations nor their ardent hope that young Arthur would.

Even so, he'd been in no rush to make up his mind and commit himself to a way of life involving hardships as well as prerogatives. One milestone came and went with his graduation from grade school (St. Stanislaus Kostka's). His parents hoped he'd opt for the minor seminary, but fall found him in the Christian Brothers' high school. Four years passed; his mother said the rosary every day and his father made visits to the Blessed Sacrament while following his route, both of them praying that Arthur would be called. But he wasn't. Instead he headed off to the state university to study journalism. His parents grieved, but Arthur kept his own counsel. The priesthood lay at the back of his mind for future reference, like a gift shirt tucked away in the back of a drawer to be taken out on another occasion and reinspected for fit, color, and general suitability: out of season now, it might be just right later.

In the next four years, however, there were many times when nothing seemed less likely to him. It was the complications of his private life, relationships he found easier to terminate than pursue, that eventually brought the old idea back to life. He had, too, a brief but intense religious interlude late in his senior year, when the Mass and prayer seemed appealing again, and the desire to make some dramatic gesture for God, to perform some startling act of immolation, consumed him. It didn't last of course, but it tipped the balance at the time.

Arthur felt rather smug about his decision, but that soon wore off in the seminary. He'd chosen St. John Vianney's and the diocese of Wernersburgh in which to pursue his vocation for the excellent reason that he wanted to get out of New Antwerp. His parents were too close for comfort there, and so was a girl named Tanya Stein. He'd gotten involved with her at the university, and he didn't care to run into her again, now or later. In retrospect, though, it wasn't clear that he'd chosen well. Things were already starting to come unglued in many seminaries in the early '60s, but Bishop Frisch, scenting chaos, had cracked down early at St. John's. At his urging, every hint of intellectual heterodoxy or behavioral laxness was snuffed out by Monsignor Caldron at its first appearance. Rigidity, formality, and decorum were the norm. Arthur grew restive under this regimen, yet he stayed, increasingly grim and furious, sustained by the expectation that nothing would be able to withstand the forces of change unleashed by Vatican II: the future belonged to those who, like himself, were bold enough to ride the wave of renewal.

He looked forward to ordination as a liberating experience. Leaving behind the constraints of the seminary, he expected to begin carving out for himself the kind of priestly career he'd long anticipated. Disappointment came early. His first assignment was to an uptown parish, Holy Comforter, whose grandfatherly pastor and affluent, sophisticated parishioners patronized the young priest intolerably. Father Arthur was cosseted, humored, coaxed, and teased like a toddler—denied responsibility and treated with indulgence. Even his gestures of rebellion—angry sermons against complacency and wealth—were received by his congregation with the tolerant indifference they'd have shown toward a child's tantrums. "Father Arthur", they said with knowing smiles much more than with words, "wants to shock us. Never mind. He's a little wet behind the ears. Give us time—ten years or maybe fifteen—and we'll make him a priest in our own image."

At this stage in his life, alternating between rage and despair, Arthur rediscovered journalism. The bitter homilies, which Sunday after Sunday evoked blank apathy from his parishioners, began to serve as grist for essays in the pages of liberal journals like the *National Catholic Recorder.* Before long, without exactly seeking it, Arthur Kucharski had a small but growing reputation, especially among the closet-liberal clergy of Wernersburgh, whose protest against Peter Frisch's reactionary policies expressed itself mainly in surreptitious reading of publications like the *Recorder.*

Such priests weren't Arthur's only local audience, however; he also had readers in the chancery. One day Monsignor Oscar Dudley summoned him to an interview, and Arthur went, chip on shoulder, expecting the worst and determined to give as good—or bad—as he got.

"You've been writing a lot lately", the Chancellor said.

"I like to write."

"Do you have time for it—I mean, in relation to your duties?" Dudley's glasses flashed as he bobbed his head from side to side interrogatively.

"I hold up my end around the parish. Not that there's much to do. Have you ever seen a parish for zombies, Monsignor? That's Holy Comforter."

"It's one of the finest parishes in the diocese."

"That's a matter of taste."

Monsignor Dudley cleared his throat. "Bishop Frisch has read some of your articles."

"Has he?"

"He wondered why you weren't publishing in the *Catholic Truth* instead."

Arthur guffawed. "The *Catholic Truth* and I aren't on the same wavelength."

"It would be a more suitable outlet for your talents."

"Are you telling me Bishop Frisch wants me to stop publishing?"

"Not at all." Dudley looked pained. "But since you have a flair for writing, you should make what you write more directly accessible to the diocese. Also, perhaps you might take a more positive approach. There's a certain negativism in your writing that is disturbing in a young priest."

"I might sound more positive if you'd transfer me out of Holy Comforter."

The Chancellor gave him a blank look. "What do you imagine would suit you?"

"I don't want to be chaplain to the bourgeosie. I want a ministry with a challenge."

It was 1967: Harvey Cox and *The Secular City* were the rage in religious circles, along with civil rights, the war on poverty, and Vietnam. Dudley said dryly, "The inner city, I suppose?"

"That would suit me."

"I'll make a note of it."

Clergy appointments came out two months later. He was transferred from Holy Comforter to St. Brendan's, a notoriously stodgy parish in an upper middle-class suburb, whose pastor, Monsignor Ralph DiNolfo, was a near-legendary embodiment of clerical *dolce vita:* a new Buick every year, long golfing vacations in the winter, and an indolent, princely routine around the parish. Arthur phoned Dudley in a rage and demanded an interview with Bishop Frisch. Rather to his surprise, he got one.

Arthur's attitude toward the Bishop was more respectful than either of them fully understood. Rebelling against what Frisch represented, he nevertheless held the man in an awe dating back to seminary days. Frisch stood for certitude and authority, and Arthur was drawn to both even while he rejected them. Facing Frisch across his desk, he was simultaneously querulous and deferential.

"I was expecting something *different* from Holy Comforter, Bishop", he explained.

Chin cupped in hand, the old man stared coldly at Arthur.

"No two parishes are the same, Father", he said.

"You'll find much to interest you at St. Brendan's if you look."

"Monsignor Dudley and I discussed this weeks ago. He knew I was hoping for something else."

"The inner city? Dudley told me. Half the young priests in Wernersburgh imagine they'd like to work in the inner city. Very commendable, I'm sure, but most of you couldn't take it. And we wouldn't have rectories to accommodate all of you, supposing there were something for you to do there."

"Am I being punished, Bishop?"

"For what?"

"For my articles in the *Catholic Recorder.*"

Bishop Frisch frowned. "I know of your writing, Father, I admit that. I haven't forbidden it, and I'm not planning to. On the other hand, I must say I don't like to have such negative things in print under the name of one of my priests."

"Then I *am* being punished."

He brushed that aside. "The carping tone, the cynicism—" he said, warming to his theme. "That isn't healthy in a priest. You sound as if you were restive under authority and wished to substitute your judgment for that of superiors. Nothing uncommon about *that* these days, unfortunately. But let me give you a piece of advice. Leaving aside any higher consideration, it's not the way to be happy in the priesthood."

"I'd be happy if I had a more challenging ministry than working in parishes like Holy Comforter and St. Brendan's."

"We need priests in those places just as much as others. There are souls in St. Brendan's as well as in the inner city. Take a less self-indulgent view of your priesthood. If you want to grandstand, I won't prevent your doing it in the pages of the *Catholic Recorder,* but neither will I abet it by giving you an assignment that gratifies your romantic view of yourself. Learn to be a priest by doing what you're told wherever you're told to do it. That's the key to it, Father."

The words stung. Grandstanding: that was an ugly accusation, but Arthur couldn't entirely deny it. In that moment Veritas was born. The writing would continue, for it was increasingly important to him; but the mortification of a pen name would be his bribe to conscience.

Why hadn't he simply left the priesthood? The possibility occurred to him—indeed, there were times when it obsessed him—and the widespread exodus of priests was already underway outside Wernersburgh and soon would reach massive proportions. What formerly had been regarded with horror, hushed up, spoken of (if at all) elliptically and in whispers, like a case of leprosy in the family, was now broadcast everywhere and not infrequently defended. So why shouldn't Arthur Kucharski, fuming over his battered Smith-Corona and wishing Ralph DiNolfo a rich assortment of vile fates, take the same route?

To a surprising degree the answer had to do with Bishop Frisch—Frisch and stubbornness. Arthur believed that the Bishop expected him to quit, perhaps even wanted him to; therefore he wouldn't. Which raised an interesting question: Could spite be the mortar of a vocation? He'd never come across anything remotely hinting that, but possibly he was now demonstrating the thesis in his own right. More than that though: as an idealist, he was stubbornly loyal to the vision of the Church of Vatican II that he'd formerly glimpsed or imagined. That Church was painfully emerging in other dioceses, he believed, and the same thing would happen sooner or later in Wernersburgh. He aimed to hang on, nurture the vision, and, as "Veritas", be a voice from underground proclaiming that its day would come. It wasn't the ministry he would have chosen, but it seemed one he could accept.

Humanae Vitae came close to breaking him. Appearing in the hysterical summer of 1968, Paul VI's reaffirmation of contraception's intrinsic evil turned the previous stream of priestly departures into a flood. How bishops chose to handle the matter seemed to make little difference: where they insisted, like Frisch, on adherence to the encyclical, dissenters left in protest; where they winked at dissent, malcontents denounced the system as a hypocritical sham no more worth fighting than serving. Defections were the outcome in either case.

Arthur regarded *Humanae Vitae* with angry contempt, yet he somehow stayed in place, sustained by spiteful stubbornness, quixotic attachment to what he called the spirit of Vatican II, and especially the outlet provided by Veritas. In a widely noted article at the time he wrote:

> Why do I stay? God knows, the inducements to leave are plentiful: a bishop who imagines he attended Trent, not Vatican II, a pastor who hasn't read a book or had a new idea in twenty years, and a crowd of "faithful" who see me as a kind of witch doctor of the middle class, warding off bad luck by white magic while blessing the spiritual hollowness of their lives. Add to that the pastoral and doctrinal calamity of *Humanae Vitae,* and I needn't search for reasons to quit.
>
> But I stay. Because under all the cultural debris and human pain of the present moment I discern a new Church struggling to be born. Because the future of that new Church will be shaped by those who are tough enough to endure the pettiness of the present. Because, just as much as quitting in protest, staying in protest is a relevant way of serving God's people today and bringing tomorrow's Church closer to reality.

That brought a quick phone call from Oscar Dudley. "I must insist that you avoid personalities, Father."

"What personalities? I didn't name anybody."

"Avoid personalities", Dudley repeated firmly. "Everybody

knows who Veritas is. You haven't been very discreet, and now you're on terribly thin ice."

"I get the message", Arthur said, and hung up the phone.

That was as close as he'd come to an open break with the chancery. He knew now that he could provoke one whenever he wished, and the knowledge was sufficient.

He found priestly work neither unbearable nor exciting. The Catholics of St. Brendan's were very much like those of Holy Comforter: educated, affluent, middle-aged, deferential, unreachable. Only rarely did he encounter an exception, but it was the exceptions who brought him such satisfaction as he found in his ministry: like-minded, alienated enthusiasts, they looked to him as a kind of chaplain to their random, underground movement. He gave such people an increasing amount of his attention, celebrating ad-libbed liturgies on innumerable dining room tables, then socializing, counseling, bitching, and scheming into the wee hours. Naturally he had increasingly less time for his uncongenial parishioners, but, as Arthur explained it to himself, that was their fault.

On balance, then, he found the situation tolerable. He wasn't filled, but he did get a certain amount of nourishment from his gnawing resentment. Besides, he could read a calendar as well as anybody, and Frisch's retirement was drawing steadily closer. In the meantime Veritas provided an outlet for his anger while winning him growing semipublic recognition among his fellow priests. He found to his surprise that he was actually looked up to by a segment of the local clergy—those who were younger, more eager for change, and therefore more angry at Frisch and the system. Even DiNolfo began to treat Arthur with apprehensive respect; having been pricked once by Veritas's pen, he apparently wanted to avoid worse in the future.

Arthur's hopes soared at the news that Frisch was finally

stepping down and Ambrose Farquhar would succeed him. There was no telling what the transition would mean for him personally, but he felt confident it would mean something good. Even so, nothing quite as good as the editorship of the *Catholic Truth* had occurred to him. Dudley's first call stunned him. But native canniness kept him from leaping at the offer: it was better to play hard to get. And that seemed to pay off. Farquhar promised him the sun and the moon—total support and absolute autonomy. He'd learned at the very start of course that Farquhar had his own way of exerting pressure, but Arthur was prepared to blink at that. He was hooked, he ached for the job, and, if the truth were told, he'd have taken it on almost any terms. Arthur Kucharski, milkman's son, renegade and troublemaker, marginalized priestly dissident and voice of the underground Church, had been waiting in the wings for a long time; at last he was being called to center stage.

"Since you're the editor," Justin growled, "you might as well take this office. It's the biggest."

Arthur shook his head. "This is yours. There's a vacant office down the hall that will suit me fine."

It was Father Kucharski's first morning. Things were not going well with Justin Walsh. Looking about him in hopes of hitting on a new topic, the priest observed the wall full of plaques, scrolls, and photographs. "That's a pretty impressive record."

"I've been in the business a long time", Justin acknowledged.

"I know I've got plenty to learn", Kucharski conceded. "I studied journalism in school, but nothing takes the place of experience."

"You've kept up your writing anyway, Father."

Arthur laughed. "That must be one of the worst kept secrets in the diocese. You're right, I can't pretend to be a total novice, and I'm not shy about sharing my ideas. I count on you to do the same, Justin."

"What's your opinion of the *Catholic Truth?*"

"Technically it's a good paper. But there's a new ball game in Wernersburgh now. The diocese is changing, and the paper has to change, too."

"In what way?"

"To reflect the pluralism of the Church."

"Bishop Farquhar said the same thing."

"He and I think alike."

Justin ran his fingers through his bristly white mane of hair, then drummed them on the desk top. "I'm going to level with you, Father. I don't like having you in charge, but I'm willing to try to make it work."

"Fair enough."

"We're going to have to get a couple of things clear, though."

"That suits me."

"How do you see your role here?"

Lighting a cigarette, Arthur grinned. "I'm not interested in the day-to-day stuff. I want to decide in general terms what's going into each issue, then let you put it together. And of course I'll write the editorials."

Justin's drum beat on the desk top accelerated. "That doesn't leave me a lot to do", he said far down in his throat.

Arthur exhaled smoke. "It depends on how you look at it. As a way of dividing up the work, I think it's fair."

"What does fairness have to do with any of this?"

"Give it a chance."

"I said I would", Justin told him fiercely. "Unlike you—a priest, I mean—I can't afford to quit."

"Don't think this new arrangement reflects a lack of appreciation for the past. I know what you've done—"

"You haven't any notion. I started here twenty years ago. How old were you then?"

"Fourteen. What difference—"

"Do you know how I got this job?"

"I can't say I do."

"The paper was a miserable rag. Bishop Frisch wanted something better. That's right—*Frisch.* He understood that the diocese needed a first-rate newspaper. So he and Boylan recruited me to give it one. I didn't come to them, they came to me."

"Swell. I believe you."

"I didn't *need* this job", Justin said. "I was doing fine at the *Globe-Herald.* But I liked the idea of editing the *Catholic Truth.* It was my service to the Church. I thought it would be a short-term assignment, but I got hooked. I fell in love with what I was doing, and I stayed. Hell, I stayed too long."

"I've told you repeatedly, we can make this work if *you* want it to."

"You must think I'm pretty dumb, Father, to feel as I do about working for the Church. It's the priests' Church, isn't it? The rest of us can visit, but the clergy are the hosts, and we have to clear out when you tell us."

Arthur felt a headache coming on. He said wearily, "Nobody's asked you to leave."

"But I have no right to stay either."

Too tired and too annoyed to argue the point, he said, "Put it that way if you like. You work for the bishop of Wernersburgh, and he's decided on some changes. You can be a sorehead about it if you want, but this happens a million times a day in a million different jobs that have nothing to do with the Church."

"Take it or leave it?"

"Exactly."

"Oh, I'll take it, Father. I haven't any choice. But I do insist on one thing. . . ." Reaching under the desk and hauling out a large cardboard box, Justin stepped to the wall and began removing the framed scrolls and photographs. "This office is yours."

Arthur did not stir. "That isn't necessary", he said coldly.

Tokens of Justin's former triumphs went clattering into the box. He didn't look around. "It's entirely necessary, Father, if we're going to do this right."

For all that, Arthur later had to admit, Justin was a professional. Having installed himself in the small office at the end of the hall, he settled in and brought Ferdy Ruffin and Nancy Lattimore along with him. Things worked as Arthur wanted: he gave general directions, stories were assigned and written under Justin's supervision, the *Catholic Truth* came out each week on time.

The changes began at once: as Arthur said, he wasn't shy about his opinions. He started with the paper's syndicated features, dropping the conservative columnists whom Justin favored and replacing them with more provocative writers who suited his taste. In short order, the *Catholic Truth*'s Op Ed page was clamoring with controversy and liberal advocacy.

Gratifying to Arthur, the flow of letters to the editor picked up at once. Most expressed shock and indignation. "Has our diocesan newspaper fallen into the hands of liberal leftists who've undermined the Church in other dioceses?" demanded an angry scrawl signed Walter Caldron, M.D. "Here's a vote for sending your propaganda sheet packing and bringing back the *Catholic Truth* we've all known for years!" Chuckling, Arthur decided to run Doctor Caldron's diatribe at the head of that week's expanded and revivified letters column, now one of the paper's liveliest features.

As he'd told Justin he would, Arthur also took over the writing of the editorials. By the end of March he felt confident enough to proclaim unabashedly the new philosophy guiding the *Catholic Truth*.

A Catholic newspaper in this postconciliar age doesn't exist to give answers but to ask questions. The Church has suffered too long from the mentality that thinks that everything worth discussing was settled at the Council of Trent (with just a little mopping up on the matter of papal infallibility reserved for Vatican I). During the past century that view brought Catholic thought and Catholic life to an increasingly sterile dead end.

Vatican II changed all that. Recognizing the signs of the times, the Council took a questioning approach. It began a process, pointed a way. The challenge for the Church now is to forge ahead fearlessly, not looking back with regret to the days of seeming security, when every question had a clear catechism answer, but embracing uncertainty in the confidence that the Spirit is still with God's pilgrim people.

The *Catholic Truth* intends to be that kind of newspaper for that kind of Church. Readers looking for the "Catholic" line on every issue should be warned: we haven't got it. But those who want to join the post-Vatican II Church in "catholic" dialogue and question-raising will feel at home in these pages from now on. The Church is on pilgrimage. We aim to be a paper for those making the trip.

"You're good at rhetoric", Justin said drily after the editorial ran.

"It's more than just rhetoric for me."

He sniffed. "Maybe that's the problem."

Elsewhere there was much satisfaction with the paper's evolution. Arthur didn't see a lot of Bishop Farquhar, but Monsignor Dudley was frequently in touch, and he conveyed steady encouragement to press ahead. "Of course the Bishop gets complaints," he explained one day in Kucharski's office, "mainly from conservative pastors who liked the paper exactly as it was. But he expected that, and he wants it. If you weren't upsetting them, he'd be worried."

Arthur, collarless and in shirtsleeves, leaned back. "So would

I", he confirmed. "Know what DiNolfo said to me? 'You've managed to give me a problem in conscience about selling the diocesan paper in the back of my church.' I couldn't compose a neater tribute."

Dudley smiled blandly. "They've simply got to make the transition. If they can."

"Of course, if there were enough pastors like DiNolfo, they could cause the paper money trouble."

"Don't worry, Arthur, the quota system has been in place for years, and it will stay in place." Both knew what that meant: pastors were required to pay for subscriptions equivalent to forty percent of their registered parishioners; whether or not they got the money back in their parishes was their problem. The system gave the paper an automatic subsidy while leaving the diocese itself comfortably in the clear. In the Frisch years, with Justin Walsh as editor, most pastors had cooperated willingly enough; but already it had occurred to Arthur that this mightn't be the case in the future.

"You'll hold their feet to the fire?" he pressed Dudley.

"If that's what it takes. Bishop Farquhar has promised you his support, and I assure you that you'll have it when you need it." Wiping his glasses with a crisp white handkerchief, the new Vicar General held them up to the light for inspection. "There's a matter I'd like your advice on, Arthur."

"Yes?"

"The Bishop is very sensitive to the potential of communications. Having gotten the *Catholic Truth* moving in the right direction, he'd like to find someone who can handle public relations for the diocese—be his spokesperson, deal with the media. Frisch didn't care about that, of course. His attitude was always, 'Damn the press.' But Bishop Farquhar sees it differently. He believes an open approach can help move the diocese forward."

"He's right."

"Do you have any ideas who might do the job? He wants an experienced communicator."

Arthur said, "Gwyneth Harley."

"You know her?"

"Very well."

"An unusual suggestion. She was anathema to Bishop Frisch. Still . . . do you think she'd be interested?"

"I won't know unless I ask her."

Monsignor Dudley rose to go. "Let me check on that."

A short time later Arthur's phone rang. It was Dudley. "Go ahead," he said, "talk to her. And, Arthur—the Bishop thinks it's a terrific idea."

"Of course I couldn't commit myself without knowing a lot more", Gwyneth said.

"Naturally", he agreed.

"And I couldn't take the job on a permanent basis", she added. "A year's leave of absence is the most I could spare—supposing the paper would let me have it. I can get a lot started for Farquhar in that time, but someone else will have to pick up where I leave off. Would he be interested in an arrangement like that, Arthur?"

"There's a good chance", he said judiciously.

They sat over drinks in a downtown restaurant. Arthur wore a blue blazer and tie. As he'd told Dudley, he knew Gwyneth Harley well. She was one of the little band of alienated Catholics whom he'd served as a kind of unofficial chaplain. She reciprocated by encouraging him to pursue his journalistic career in the face of opposition from the chancery. They were good friends.

Even so, since speaking to Dudley, Arthur had begun to wonder if he'd gone too far in suggesting her, since she might very reasonably feel she was better off where she was. He was pleasantly surprised, therefore, that Gwyneth hadn't rejected the idea out of hand; indeed, as the conversation progressed, she seemed to grow enthusiastic, as if the proposal corresponded to some previously unacknowledged aspiration of her own.

"I didn't think you'd take to it so quickly", he confessed now.

"Why not? I'd like to give Farquhar a hand."

"That's how I feel, too. It's why I took the job with the *Catholic Truth.*"

Gwyneth nodded approvingly. "You're doing good work there, Arthur. People are sitting up and paying attention."

"To judge from the letters I get and the names they call me."

She laughed and sipped her whiskey sour. "Letters like that are the sign of a healthy newspaper."

He felt encouraged to confide. "For almost the first time since I became a priest, Gwyneth, I feel I'm doing something worthwhile."

"The diocese has a future now. So do you."

"We're catching up with the rest of the Church."

"Soon we may be showing the way."

He was growing positively animated. "God, wouldn't that be something! Wernersburgh out front in the renewal—a few months ago I'd have said no way, but now it's possible."

"Thanks to Farquhar."

"Here's to Farquhar", he exclaimed, raising his Scotch and soda. Touching glasses, they toasted their Bishop.

"How are you and Justin Walsh getting along?"

He shrugged. "I think he's resigned to the situation. And he *is* competent, you know. I'm glad to leave a lot of the crap to him."

"He doesn't fight you?"

"How could he? He'd have to go over my head, and that route leads directly to the Bishop."

She smiled complacently. "When I talked to Farquhar in New Antwerp, the only real doubt I had about him was whether he was tough enough. It sounds like he is."

"He's plenty tough. Nobody can buck him in this diocese now."

"How is he handling the priests?"

Arthur grinned. "We've got three kinds. Some are like me. They couldn't stand Frisch, and they only wish Farquhar had taken over years ago. He doesn't have to 'handle' us—we're rooting for him."

"I'm happy for you, Arthur."

"Thanks." He sipped his drink. "The second group are floaters. Frisch, Farquhar—they don't care who's in charge." His voice was tinged with scorn. "Some people would call them the backbone of the priesthood. I call them spineless."

She laughed. "And the third group?"

"Reactionaries. People like John Caldron. They'd like to fight Farquhar, but they haven't got a leader. Look at how Farquhar eased out Boylan."

"Exiled to Siberia?"

"Before he knew what hit him. That sends a message to guys like my pastor. If Farquhar can take Boylan out of the picture that easily, he can do the same with anybody else. In fact, he's *already* done it with Caldron."

Gwyneth nodded in appreciation. "Farquhar is an idealist who isn't afraid to knock heads together."

"He's the kind of bishop who knows that power is meant to be used. And remember, this is only the beginning. In a couple of years he'll have turned this diocese around a hundred and eighty degrees."

Her eyes were shining. "I'd like to be part of it, Arthur."

"We're the future of the Church, Gwyneth—Farquhar, you, me, and all the others who think as we do. It's been a long time coming, but now it's our turn. Let's make the most of it."

"No turning back."

"None", he declared firmly. "Not ever."

"You actually want to do it?" Fritz Jacoby queried. They were drinking coffee later that night in the living room of the apartment they shared.

"Yes", Gwyneth said without hesitation. "For a year anyway. It's going to be fun."

"Fun", Jacoby mused, picking at his beard. "Catholics have strange ideas of fun."

She bridled. "What's that supposed to mean?"

"You can't leave the Church alone, can you?"

"I don't *want* to leave her alone. Not when there's finally some hope for her."

"Thanks to Farquhar?"

"That's how I see it."

He raised his eyebrows skeptically. "So enjoy."

"It's different for Jews?"

"A Jew hasn't any choice about being a Jew. But a Catholic—you tell me."

"I chose."

He smiled into his coffee cup. "Looks like."

IX

Cramped and dark, the office that Justin had occupied in self-immolation squinted through a small, grimy window onto a gloomy air shaft. The walls were bare except for a 1967 undertaker's calendar featuring garish reproductions of bad religious art, while the cardboard box into which he'd so dramatically thrust his trophies and mementoes sat untouched in a corner, making to those who knew its story a protest more eloquent than rehanging its contents could possibly have done.

Inelegant as it was, this was where he and Kucharski now transacted business. He hadn't formally refused to re-enter his old office—he simply did not go there. The priest took the hint. Whenever need arose, he walked down the hall, knocked at Justin's half-closed door, and waited for a growled "Come in" before entering. He did it again that Monday morning in mid-April and found Justin editing copy.

Helping himself to a straight-backed metal chair, Arthur waited, tapping his fingers on his knee, until the older man reached a break and looked up with a grunt. "I need to talk to you about a story", he explained.

"What is it?"

"Bishop Farquhar is going to name a director of communications."

"What does a director of communications do?"

"Advises the bishop."

"Frisch never looked for that kind of advice."

"That was part of his problem."

Justin snorted. "Who's it going to be?"

"Gwyneth Harley."

Justin's jaw dropped. "You aren't serious. She's the worst enemy the Church has in the media."

Arthur laughed outright. "I know Gwyneth well. She's a committed Catholic."

"You've read what she's written about us over the years?"

"She didn't like Frisch, but that doesn't make her an enemy of the Church. Anyway, cheer up—she's only taking the job for a year. Time enough to get things started."

"Time enough to do a lot of harm."

"The announcement will be next week. Besides the story, I want an interview."

"We don't interview pastors when they're appointed."

"This is different. It's a new position in the diocese, and Gwyneth will be the highest ranking lay person on the chancery staff—and a woman at that. Plus she's a damn good professional with a lot of ideas about the Church and media. It's worth playing up."

"To please Bishop Farquhar?"

"Even if you don't like it, Justin, it's news."

He scowled. "I'll handle it", he said, bending over his work to signify the conversation had ended.

"Of course I look forward to the job", Gwyneth protested. "I wouldn't take it otherwise."

"But only for a year?"

"It's perfectly simple, Justin. I'm happy to give Bishop Farquhar a hand, but I can't make a lifetime of it. The *Globe-Herald* will let me have a year's leave of absence, but that's all.

And the Bishop is pleased to have me on those terms. Everybody's happy."

"Aren't you lucky though?"

"It looks that way."

They faced each other that Thursday across a table in a conference room off the *Globe-Herald's* newsroom. Accusatory and frowning, Justin sat hunched forward in his chair waiting to pounce on error. His cassette recorder stood between them, and occasionally he wrote in a small notebook. Gwyneth regarded him with a mixture of irritation and apprehension. They'd been at it for nearly an hour.

"Is a year really enough time?" he demanded again.

She sighed. "To start something? Sure it is. Basically, I want to define the job—then leave it in good shape for somebody else. Farquhar agrees."

"Most people could define a job in less than a year."

"I'll establish what the job is by *doing* it. I'm not talking about writing a job description."

"What *do* you plan to do?"

Lighting a cigarette, she said, "The job looks in two directions. Inside—toward the diocese, I mean—and outside—toward the media. The problem is bringing the two things together. Media are the environment people live in today. The Church has to learn how to relate to that."

"You're going to do public relations?"

"I'm not a flack."

"You'll be flacking for Farquhar."

"He's already got a good feel for media relations. I'm talking about the rest of the diocesan operation."

"You mean the chancery?"

"To start with."

"So you'll look us over and critique us to the Bishop."

"That's your way of putting it, not mine."

"And does that include the *Catholic Truth?*"

She smiled. "Don't worry, I'm not going near the paper. Arthur Kucharski has that under control."

She was laughing at him. He said furiously, "I suppose that as the diocesan flack, you'll make the *Globe-Herald* one of your priorities."

"No doubt."

"Isn't that awkward? You're only on a year's leave."

"Actually, it has advantages."

"And then—the paper has a history of hostility to the Church."

Gwyneth's eyes strayed to the tape recorder. "What the hell kind of interview is this anyway?"

"Are you suggesting the *Catholic Truth* shouldn't ask hard questions?"

"*Ask* whatever you like. But when you start making speeches, the interview isn't on any more."

"Then let me ask this. Hasn't the *Globe-Herald* got a long record of hostility to the Catholic Church?"

"No."

"A lot of people think so."

"A lot of people are full of crap."

"I want to read you something." He produced a scrap of newsprint from his pocket.

Gwyneth fumed. "Is this show and tell?"

"It won't take a minute. I have here—" he held it up for inspection "—the *Globe-Herald's* editorial on Bishop Frisch's retirement."

"Oh, God."

"Let me read—"

"Must you?"

"—one short passage." He cleared his throat. "We congratulate Bishop Frisch on long service marked by total conviction in the performance of his duties. But this newspaper's differences with him are too well known to gloss over even on this occasion—indeed, we couldn't honestly do that. Peter Frisch has been an articulate and tireless champion of the Catholic Church as it used to be. Unhappily, instead of leading his diocese in the renewal promised by Vatican II, he has been a serious obstacle to that healthy process. We mean no disrespect to an earnest and hardworking churchman in pointing out that the diocese of Wernersburgh is also in line for congratulations as he steps down." Justin gave her a challenging stare. "That isn't hostile?"

"It's a fair assessment of Frisch. As for the Church—I'd call it friendly." Fritz Jacoby had written the editorial; Gwyneth remembered congratulating him at the time.

"Is this an accurate reflection of your views?"

"Entirely."

Justin nodded and made a note. "Of course," he went on, "the *Globe-Herald* and Bishop Frisch tangled over public issues as well as over the running of the diocese."

"Obviously."

"For example, abortion. You people have campaigned for legal abortion for years."

"It's coming, Justin."

"How do you feel about it—personally, I mean?"

Flushing, Gwyneth said, "The law shouldn't get in the way of a woman's choice. If women want abortions, they ought to be able to get them—safe and clean, no back alleys and coat hangers. It's a scandal that women must risk their lives to have them now. If men got pregnant, abortion would have been legalized years ago."

"The Church teaches that abortion is wrong."

"It's another case where a male-dominated Church needs to take a fresh look at an issue."

"Thanks." He turned off the tape recorder and closed his notebook.

"That's all?"

"Haven't we covered everything?"

"I suppose so." She lit another cigarette.

"Something else you want to say?"

"Skip it."

"Then thanks again, Gwyneth." He left almost jauntily.

She sat smoking thoughtfully for a few minutes, then followed. Jacoby was passing by the conference room as she came out.

"How did it go?"

Taking a long drag on the cigarette, she said, "He's got enough to kill me if he has the nerve to use it."

Jacoby looked interested. "Will he?"

"I couldn't say. I'm not sure he knows either."

"Better tell your friend Kucharski. Let him shut Walsh up."

For a moment she considered it, but then she said, "I'd be giving the son of a bitch what he wants; he'd *like* to think we'd ganged up on him. If he embarrasses me, it will cost him plenty. If he doesn't, he'll blame himself. That's an interesting problem for him, Fritz. I think I'll let him sweat it out."

"I have been put on the shelf," Bishop Frisch said, sipping his sherry, "not buried. The difference merits a modest celebration."

There were appreciative chuckles from the others, and Bishop Boylan said, "Hear, hear."

Standing at the sideboard, Justin helped himself to ice from a silver bucket and splashed bourbon into his glass generously. "I hope the celebration isn't *too* modest", he said heartily.

"Trust me, Justin", Bishop Frisch replied. "Our numbers may be reduced, but I hope I've retained some standards of hospitality. And even if *I* haven't, the sisters still cook a damn good meal."

They were gathered, the two bishops, Monsignor Caldron, and Justin, in Frisch's large living room. For many years he'd celebrated the anniversary of his episcopal ordination with a dinner party for close friends and collaborators. This year Justin had the sense of taking part in one of the court functions of a deposed monarch; it was as if he were having drinks with Lear.

"We're lucky you still have the sisters", Caldron commented. He sat feeding voraciously from a platter of hors d'oeuvres on the coffee table.

"My successor has been extremely generous", Frisch said coldly. "A comfortable house arrest, you might say. He *insisted* I keep the residence and the sisters. I can't fault him on that score."

"It must be the only one", Caldron said.

"We mustn't be bitter, Jack", Bishop Boylan cautioned mournfully.

"I'm not bitter, Hugh, only realistic."

"I call your attention, gentlemen," Frisch said, "to the vulnerability of a retired bishop. To dig I am not able, to beg I am ashamed. I owe all this to my successor's generosity."

Justin, resuming his place on the sofa, took in the familiar room. Long and dimly lighted, it was crowded with deep, vastly comfortable chairs and sofas. Large, dark paintings—portraits of former bishops of Wernersburgh for the most part—graced the walls, while the numerous end tables and cabinets overflowed with knickknacks: china figurines, yellowed photographs in gilt frames, Waterford crystal, and much else besides. Wernersburgh's bishops had lived here for nearly sixty years. He couldn't help but agree: it was a handsome gesture on Farquhar's part to let Frisch remain.

But Monsignor Caldron saw it differently. "This wouldn't suit him", he remarked.

"Too old-fashioned?"

"Definitely not his style."

Bishop Boylan said, "How are things going out at St. John's? Are people happy with Ron Lackner's appointment?"

"Lackner is. Otherwise the place is knee-deep in anxiety."

"Most of it warranted", Bishop Frisch remarked.

"You heard he'd lined up this fellow Poirier?"

Boylan sighed. "That word has gotten around."

"Lackner couldn't be more pleased with himself."

Justin said, "Poirier was campaigning for contraception long before *Humanae Vitae* came out, and he's expanded his program since."

"Well, he's ours now", Caldron observed angrily. "Ours and the students. *They're* the ones who will suffer."

Bishop Frisch looked disgusted. "And through them this appointment will go on doing harm for years."

Bishop Boylan said, "I'm sure Ron Lackner doesn't see it that way."

"You can say the same of the man he works for", Frisch said. "No one accuses them of bad will, Hughie. They're like children who've got hold of your watch. They mean no harm, but they're sure to break it."

As the conversation continued, Justin considered his dilemma. Did he dare to write and publish all that Gwyneth Harley had told him? For that matter—did he dare not? Unexpectedly he'd been given a way of striking back against the outrages inflicted on the diocese and those inflicting them. But he was frightened, and the fear angered him at the same time it sapped his energy and resolution.

For years he'd enjoyed absolute security in his work, and that itself had ratified the wisdom of his decision in taking the editorship of the *Catholic Truth.* At the time, quite a few people had questioned his sanity; it had been pleasant to be vindicated.

He'd been thirty-five at the time, a rising luminary at the *Globe-Herald* who knew he wanted something else. It came of being a Catholic, or at least, the kind of Catholic *he* was. Confirmed in the dogmas of his mother's unyielding faith and schooled in their defense by the syllogistic apologetics of the Companions of Christ, Justin, in twentieth-century America, had been formed by the standards of sixteenth-century Spain; quite possibly he was the last campaigner in the Counter Reformation.

That kind of thing makes a difference in how, and especially why, a man does his job. Other people worked for money, satisfaction, prestige, or just to fill the time, but a job for Justin was part of a crusade. Visible to him alone, the banners of chivalry snapped bravely in the wind against a crimson sky, while the silent shouts of legionaries sounded in his ears.

In sum, after ten years of trying to convert the *Globe-Herald,* he had reached the conclusion that he'd have to fight it instead. No use imagining any longer that the paper would oppose the forces of secularism, materialism, hedonism, communism, socialism, and permissiveness that Justin saw rotting the fabric of society; in fact the *Globe-Herald* was well on its way to joining them.

Most readers of Wernersburgh's distinguished, century-old daily considered it a cautious, conservative, expertly edited organ of the Establishment, in whose pages trendiness and moral laxity were about as popular as free advertising. But from the inside Justin saw the *Globe-Herald* becoming a mouthpiece for the godless values and pleasure-seeking life-style he deplored. Early inroads came through the entertainment and cultural sections—movie and book reviews: evidently the arts were prime channels of subversion in these latter days. Soon the same spirit of libertine nihilism began to manifest itself in the editorial columns. Justin was sure the rot had gone deep when the paper declined to endorse Taft and backed Eisenhower instead.

Other straws in the wind abounded. As the organ of Wernersburgh's WASP oligarchy, the *Globe-Herald* traditionally took a cool view of Catholicism. Justin deplored that, but saw it as something he might change. Lately, though, the paper's increasingly liberal editorial policy had put it on a collision course with the Church. As far back as the '30s, the *Globe-Herald* had been outraged by Spanish Catholicism and its ties to Generalissimo Franco. In the '40s it proclaimed itself a foe of aid to parochial schools and began fuming about the Legion of Decency. Whenever opportunity arose, the newspaper took to the ramparts atop the wall of separation between church and state, hinting darkly about the intentions of unnamed ecclesiastics who bore a striking resemblance to the Catholic bishops. And in time, as the first faint signs of a sexual revolution appeared in the land, the *Globe-Herald,* sublimating furiously, discovered the population explosion—an alarming proliferation of little brown and black and yellow people—and blamed it on the Catholic stand on birth control.

It didn't take long for Bishop Frisch to get his back up. Gingerly at first, then openly and with a certain gusto, the Bishop and the paper began squaring off in public. That was an unaccustomed spectacle in Wernersburgh, where clergymen were traditionally treated with the respect otherwise reserved for the dead. But the *Globe-Herald* began taking Frisch seriously as an opponent, referring to him at various times as "backward-looking", "reactionary", and "not a man of the mid-twentieth century". The Bishop, master of a livelier invective, was heard to speak of "that pinko rag in league with the pornographers and the birth controllers." While even Justin found the rhetoric somewhat exaggerated, he had to concede the substance, for by that time he'd arrived at a similar assessment.

It was then, with a crisis of conscience bearing down on him, that the offer of the editorship of the *Catholic Truth* came, unsought and unexpected. One day shortly before Christmas of 1952 Hugh Boylan, the Chancellor, called him at work. Justin knew him well; in years gone by, the young Father Boylan had been one of his mother's protégés, and even after she'd retired he'd visited her frequently—a gesture Justin held much to his credit. Boylan got quickly to the point: Would he be interested in the job? They met next day to discuss it; two days later he saw Bishop Frisch. His appointment was announced between Christmas and New Year's. His main regret then was that neither his mother nor his Uncle Henry had lived to see this turn of events.

"And you, Justin," Bishop Frisch was saying. "I don't know whether you've been the least affected by the transition or the most. You're still where you've always been, doing what you've always done."

He awoke from his reverie with a start. "Not quite", he said. "Kucharski's in charge. But he leaves me pretty much alone. It wouldn't be a bad arrangement if I weren't used to a different one."

"*I* knew I could leave the paper entirely in your hands", Frisch said affectionately. "You never let me down."

Justin blushed. "Thank you."

"I take it that you haven't any real say about what goes in these days?" Monsignor Caldron demanded.

"He decides. I just see that it gets into print."

"Then you won't take it personally if I say your coverage of the mess at Maryheights has been a joke."

"Bishop Farquhar doesn't want to pass judgment."

Frisch frowned. "What does he imagine bishops do?"

"I saw that situation coming", Monsignor Caldron observed tartly. "Those women lost their minds five years ago. The Council drove them mad. It was only a matter of time until they did something like this."

"There are some fine religious at Maryheights", Bishop Boylan protested.

"They have my sympathy. They must be suffering terribly at the hands of the enthusiasts running the show these days." Caldron turned back to Justin. "You have my sympathy, too. The *Catholic Truth* reflects Arthur Kucharski to a tee—superficial, irresponsible, wedded to its own ideas. If I'd had any notion when he was at St. John's that *this* was going to happen, I assure you I'd have done everything in my power to see to it he wasn't ordained."

"The fault is mine", Bishop Frisch said glumly.

"None of us knew what to do with him over the years", Bishop Boylan added. "But none of us could see the future."

"If you'd like refills on your drinks, gentlemen, help yourselves", Frisch said. "I believe the sisters want us to go in to dinner."

He was right—the sisters cooked an excellent meal. Vichysoisse and a salad were followed by a savory dish of fish and tiny shrimps in puff pastry. The Bishop poured an excellent Soave with a liberal hand. Before long Boylan began telling anecdotes about eccentric pastors of the past, and the conversation grew merry. Years ago, he said, there'd been a fierce, elderly German named Kepler in the west end of town, whose browbeaten curates chipped in one winter to send him a cashier's check for a substantial sum, along with an anonymous, admiring note urging him to use it for the Florida vacation he so richly deserved.

"But he wouldn't go", Boylan recalled. "He banked the check and told the boys, 'If somebody gives you money with strings, the first thing you do is cut them.' They never did get the old man out of town."

"I remember Kepler", Bishop Frisch said. "A pastor of the old school."

"Those men did a good job in their time", Monsignor Caldron declared.

"People respected them", Justin added.

"Respect", Frisch mused. "I don't think the clergy are held in respect today. There are exceptions, but by and large, and take us in the aggregate, are priests really *respected?* How does it seem to you, Justin?"

Sipping his wine, Justin said, "A lot of priests *want* people to think of them as just like everybody else, and they've succeeded. Then respect goes. People may have sympathy for a priest they think is just like them, but they don't respect him."

Monsignor Caldron cackled. "Are you speaking of yourself?"

The conversation moved on to other topics, but Justin grew thoughtful. He was no fool: the closer one drew to the clergy, the plainer their faults became. Yet up to now he'd not entirely lost his virginal sense of privilege at being permitted to work with them. Moreover they'd let him edit the *Catholic Truth* as he saw fit. Weren't he and they working for the same cause: to serve the Church? And the paper had flourished under his management, become a lively, often bellicose voice of Catholic triumphalism, much applauded by the clergy.

Throughout the 1950s the *Truth* let the world know, weekly and in forceful terms, that it opposed Communism, opposed secularism, opposed church-state separation, opposed pornography, opposed birth control, opposed a host of ideas and practices warring against the ideal Christendom it was sworn to defend. Justin's was a journalism of negatives—while knowing beyond the shadow of a doubt what the paper was against, you might have found it hard to say what it was for—but he carried it off with style, cramming his pages with a peppery stew of news, features, and vitriolic editorials expressing his integralist view of life and providing the mildly paranoid Catholics of Wernersburgh with a champion against the crusading secularism they now saw rampant in the *Globe-Herald.*

Times change. The Church in 1950 had been a great monolith impregnable to flux, a rock of certainty against the winds and waves of doubt. Little more than a decade later, the Church seemed a dwindling ship on the same seas, tossing in fierce gales of revisionism and dissent. The difference lay in the papacy of John XXIII, a pope of endearing homeliness who appeared at ease with advocates of virtually any philosophy or world view, no matter how obnoxious, and in the explosion into Catholic life of Vatican Council II, a council convened to change the changeless.

Justin struggled loyally to cope with and explain both phenomena, Pope and Council. It wasn't easy. John was picturesque and charming, conceivably a saint, but for Justin's tastes too spontaneous and trusting—even harum-scarum—to occupy the chair of Peter. You never knew what he'd do next, for apparently he operated more by heart than head, a dangerous habit in a pope. As for the Council, although Justin felt obliged to speak well of it in print, he didn't really see the need for it. The Church was perfect as it was, and *ecclesia semper reformanda* was absurd as a slogan and a goal.

As time passed and Bishop Frisch returned from Vatican II's yearly sessions with tales of confusion and intrigue, Justin's uneasiness increased: something was going badly wrong in Rome, and the careful handiwork of centuries was suddenly at risk. Verities he'd have staked his life on were being shunted casually aside, while innovations that Catholics had been taught to reject and scorn were now winning approval: in place of the catholicity of Latin, English in the Mass; in place of Counter

Reformation apologetics that smote the heretic, a breast-beating plea for ecumenical dialogue; in place of hostile contempt for the world, a confession of faults and a request to be allowed to learn and serve. Nothing and no one seemed to escape the undiscriminating benevolence of this madcap Council, except those Catholics who had responded to the Church's repeated exhortations to reject what the Council now embraced and who, in the changed climate of these strange times, found themselves criticized for having done so.

Even worse, once the Council had ended, were its interpreters; ubiquitous discerners of the "spirit" of Vatican II, who in a thousand pulpits, books, and workshops preached open heterodoxy. A demon of madness was trashing the Church. The mildest and most docile of individuals now gabbled revolutionary schemes which they themselves would have rejected with shocked horror not long before. Bizarre liturgies sprang up like toadstools: priests in clown suits, jazz bands, readings from Walt Whitman and Jack Kerouac; exalted rhetoric accompanied dramatic falls from grace; it was a time of speaking in tongues, hysteria, and spreading anarchy. Thus was the stage set for *Humanae Vitae.*

Startling and frightening Justin more than anything yet, a universal snarl rose against Paul VI's reaffirmation of the Church's ancient teaching on birth control. Something powerful and dangerous was on the move; something bent on destroying the Church. Justin knew then what he had to do. Long a defender of the Church against external enemies, the *Catholic Truth* now adopted an equally ferocious line with enemies within, branding as heretics and altogether bad eggs the advocates of dissent and change.

In all of this Justin had the full support of Peter Frisch. Frisch had never trusted Vatican II, and the all-out attack on *Humanae Vitae* settled things for him: renewal had had its day in Wernersburgh; it was time to dig in and defend the faith. "Think of it as war", he told Justin, "because it is. Remember that I'm counting on the *Catholic Truth* to help me hold at least this one diocese together." Justin saw Frisch and himself as heroic figures, standing against a tide of heresy and schism, vilified from without, betrayed from within, but undaunted in championing the faith in its moment of supreme vulnerability. The numbers were against them, but truth was on their side. He counted on winning in the long run.

It couldn't last. Frisch's retirement was approaching. But Justin was stubbornly optimistic: surely the authorities would provide a successor who'd carry on the struggle—meaning, among other things, a renewed mandate to the *Catholic Truth* to keep on hammering the enemy. The one thing he hadn't counted on was that the authorities, when the time came, would be looking the other way; or, if looking in the right direction, simply not liking what they saw in Wernersburgh.

Like Frisch, like Boylan, like Caldron, like many others he could name, Justin by now had the sense of having served with distinction in an unpopular war. He was frightened. He didn't want to lose his job, for he might not find another. He was too old, he'd made too many enemies. What therefore was he to do with the Gwyneth Harley interview? Kucharski, a lazy amateur playing editor, would suspect nothing until it appeared in print. But could Justin risk it? Sheltered by Frisch, he'd been the boldest of orthodox controversialists. But what do you do when you can't hide behind a bishop any more—when in fact *the bishop* may give it to you in the neck? Like many Christians before him, he was learning that it's safer to praise the martyrs than annoy the lions.

Thoughts like these weighed on him as dinner ended and they sauntered back to the living room for brandy and cigars.

"How are you finding your changed circumstances, Hughie?"

Caldron asked Bishop Boylan after they'd sat down. "What's the name of that job the man gave you anyway?"

"Exurban Vicar."

"What the hell is that?"

"I travel around to parishes. I talk to priests. I talk to nuns. I talk to anybody who'll talk to me. I send reports to Bishop Farquhar."

"Saying what?"

"There's a lot of confusion out there."

"And what comes of telling him that?"

Boylan winced. "More confusion."

"I hear Danny Flynn quit the priesthood last week", Frisch remarked, naming a pastor they all knew.

Monsignor Caldron said, "I talked to him before he left."

"I suppose it was a woman?"

"Oh, Danny's looking for one all right. But that isn't what did it. Not to hear him tell it anyway."

"What did he say?"

Caldron looked grave. "That he'd stuck with the Church through thick and thin, defended hard doctrines and insisted on unpopular policies, because he trusted the leadership and knew what was expected of him. But now he can't tell what the leadership has in mind—"

"He's not the only one."

"—and he'd even begun to suspect it doesn't really believe in what he's been defending all these years. Once *that* idea got into his head, it was all over for him with the priesthood. He felt he'd been made a fool of—asked to spend half his life building something and the other half tearing it down. 'Maybe they can find younger men who've specialized in demolition from the start', he told me. 'But I'm confused and humiliated, and I just want out.' "

Frisch said, "That's an awful story."

Rising, Justin went to the table in the corner and helped himself to another brandy. He'd had a lot to drink by now, but it gave him a sense of seeing things more clearly. "I'd like your advice", he told the others, returning to his place. Lucidly and precisely he sketched the situation, even acknowledging his fear. "Frankly," he concluded, "I think the interview might sink the lady's appointment and wake people up to what's going on. But it's risky for me."

Frisch was too disturbed to take it all in at once. "Gwyneth Harley!" he exclaimed. "He's crazy even to consider it."

"He's done more than just consider it, Bishop", Caldron remarked. "Evidently he's well on the way to doing it."

"I know that", Frisch snapped. He was lapsing into a familiar pattern of behavior, as if it were still up to him to take charge, make decisions, give commands. "The question is, what do *we* do? Hughie, what's your opinion?"

Bishop Boylan's kewpie-doll face wore a pained look. "It's dangerous for Justin to say much in print. Perhaps he could tell the Bishop privately what he knows. In fact, I'd recommend that."

Monsignor Caldron appeared disgusted. "Suppose Justin does that, and Farquhar does nothing about it? That's what would happen, if you ask me. And what's Justin to do then—go into print with information that Farquhar himself has already hushed up? That *would* be sticking his neck out."

"He could just leave it up to Bishop Farquhar to decide what's the right thing to do", Boylan said stubbornly.

Caldron regarded him with scorn. "After all, you're *Farquhar's* Auxiliary now, aren't you, Hughie?"

Boylan turned scarlet. "What is that supposed to mean?"

"Calm down, Hughie", Frisch growled. "Jack, that wasn't called for."

"Sorry, Bishop", Caldron said contritely. "Sorry, Hughie. Just slipped out in the heat of battle, so to speak."

"I don't think," Frisch remarked, "we're helping Justin much."

"You are", Justin assured them.

Cigar smoke lay over the coffee table like the after-spew of cannon fire. Through the writhing fumes Bishop Frisch riveted Justin with a stare. "The fact is, I can't tell you what to do", he said sepulchrally. "I haven't the authority any more. Besides, I'm not even sure I know what's right and wrong in this case. Maybe Hughie's right—my successor is bishop now, and you'd best play ball with him, not just to protect yourself but because it's the decent thing to do. But we all know things have gone sour in the diocese, and we all know who's behind it. If you go to him privately with what Harley told you, he *might* ignore it and go right ahead with this appointment. He might even hold it against you for tattling on her. So what about publishing your interview without consulting him? He may act and feel just the same, but at least other people will have been put on notice how things stand. On balance. . . . " But instead of drawing a conclusion, he made a palms-up gesture. "It's your call, Justin."

Justin nodded. "On balance. Exactly what I was thinking myself."

Arthur Kucharski was reading the *Catholic Truth* with growing panic the next Thursday morning when the telephone in his office rang.

Monsignor Dudley said, "The Bishop wants to see you at eleven."

"If it's about this damned interview—"

"Eleven." Dudley repeated. The phone clicked dead.

When Arthur walked into Farquhar's office an hour later, the Bishop was unsmiling. They sat at the desk instead of in the comfortable chairs. As the conversation progressed, Farquhar generally maintained a more-in-sorrow-than-in-anger tone, but anger did break through now and then.

"I wasn't expecting that sort of interview with Gwyneth Harley."

"Neither was I", Arthur confessed.

"But you're the editor."

"Usually I just tell Justin what I want to go in the paper and leave it to him. I mean, if I read every word. . . . "

Farquhar raised his hand in admonition. "You let him outsmart you. This interview will do a lot of harm."

"I guess so", he admitted sheepishly.

Picking up a copy of the *Catholic Truth,* Bishop Farquhar read aloud. " 'The diocese of Wernersburgh's newly appointed director of communications supports legalized abortion and disagrees with opposition to the practice on the part of what she calls a 'male-dominated' Church." I expect the phones to start ringing today and the letters to start coming tomorrow. Tell me . . . does she really feel that way?"

"I never asked."

Farquhar eyed him sorrowfully. "It isn't even the controversy that I most regret. How do you think *I* feel, knowing she thinks like this?"

"Badly, I suppose."

"*Very* badly," the Bishop confirmed. "I don't inquire into what everybody who works for me thinks about everything, and I welcome a diversity of views. But to have ideas like *these* flaunted publicly by someone who's proposing to join my staff, someone who will represent me to others. . . . Why did she do it?"

"I guess Justin must have egged her on."

"And then he wrote an interview that you never read until you saw it in print in the newspaper you edit—a circumstance which I now learn represents your standard procedure." Bishop Farquhar was growing agitated. "Arthur, I must be candid. I am not well pleased."

"Neither am I."

"What shall we do?"

"Well . . . ", he scratched his head. "The trouble is, the interview's in print and the paper is out."

The Bishop shook his head in disgust. "I'll tell you what we shall do, Arthur," he said with exaggerated patience. "First, about Justin Walsh. It saddens me to see he can't be trusted. You must watch him closely. Don't give him any latitude. And tell him there's to be no repetition of *this.*"

"Right."

"As for Gwyneth Harley, she simply can't work for me in these circumstances. Call her and tell her that. Tell her that I'll write her myself. Later."

Arthur winced. "Can't Dudley make the call?"

"She's *your* friend", Farquhar said sternly. "You recommended her. And you edit the newspaper that carried this interview. Consider it a pastoral problem."

"There'll be a stink when it gets out that you wouldn't hire her."

"Better that stink", Farquhar said bluntly, "than this one."

Sighing resignedly, Arthur started to get up. The Bishop motioned him back down.

"Finally, about you. "This isn't my idea of how to edit the *Catholic Truth.*"

"You've been satisfied up to now."

Farquhar ignored that. "I want you to be a working editor, Arthur, not a spectator. That's all."

But Arthur stayed put. "I'm sorry about what happened, of course . . . ", he began.

"Naturally."

"But it isn't fair to put all the blame on me. You and Dudley talked to Gwyneth. As for Walsh, you're the one who told me to handle him with kid gloves, Bishop. I may not look so smart right now, but I'm not the only one."

Bishop Farquhar stared hard at him. "Arthur," he said, "I plucked you out of a situation you were miserable in and gave you a position of trust. I've treated you with consideration. I've offered you my thanks. But your performance in every aspect of this matter has been negligent and stupid. Don't blame me for your failings. I wouldn't welcome that. Is that clear?"

Stunned, Arthur stammered out a yes and stumbled from the office. Retreating to his own, he sat for a while, trying to collect his thoughts, then with a groan dialed Gwyneth.

When she heard about the interview, she was furious. "I knew the bastard would do something like that", she snarled.

"I don't guess by any chance he misrepresented you?"

"Sorry, I can't say he did."

"I've been talking to Bishop Farquhar."

"Oh?"

"Listen, Gwyneth, I feel crappy about this. If there were anything I could do, I would. You know that, don't you?"

"What did Farquhar say, Arthur?"

"He thinks there's going to be trouble."

"Brilliant."

"He doesn't feel he can hire you under the circumstances. There'd be too much criticism."

"In other words, he doesn't like me saying what I think. If I'd kept my mouth shut or lied, it wouldn't make any difference."

"You're overstating it."

"Shit! *Understate* it for me, then."

"There's no way Farquhar can go ahead with the deal now. You know that perfectly well."

"I'm learning."

"Look, I'm really sorry."

"Arthur, you make me sick. You, Farquhar—the whole lot of you. Walsh is the only one of you who has any guts. But you and Farquhar want a revolution without fighting for it."

"That isn't fair."

"I'm too pissed off to be fair. Try me some other time." The phone clicked dead.

Hanging up in disgust, he went down the hall to Justin's office. The editor was smoking his pipe and working on some wire service copy. He glanced up as Kucharski entered but said nothing. Sitting down uninvited, the priest said, "I suppose you're pleased with yourself."

Justin put aside his work and said, "I'm a journalist. I interviewed her. I found out what she thought, and I reported it. That's my job."

"From now on, Justin, everything you work on, every scrap of copy, goes to me before it goes any place else. Got that?"

"That puts kind of a burden on you."

"Spare me your sympathy."

"You're the boss, Father."

"Believe it, Justin. Believe it."

X

Remorseless sunlight smote the courtyard like a fist. Although it was only June, the grass had already turned brown. Standing in a blast of air-conditioning, Vincent stared out the picture window at two small children, a boy and a girl, squabbling listlessly over a Bigwheel in the shallow shadow of the building opposite. It was identical to Megan's building, a long, three-story structure of yellow brick dotted with postage stamp concrete decks. Like Megan's, too—indeed, like all the buildings in Wernersburgh Terrace West—it exuded weary domestic shabbiness, as if in sympathetic interaction with the lives it housed.

The children were turning ugly with heat and boredom. Finally the little boy slapped the little girl, and she went off crying. "Those children don't play together very nicely", Vincent remarked sadly.

Coffee cup in one hand, cigarette in the other, Megan approached the window and took a casual glance. "The Rafferty twins", she observed. "They're little devils." It was Saturday morning, her day off, and she wore a green bathrobe although it was already after ten.

Sighing, Vincent turned away from the window. "How much pain there is—even in families!" He wore gray slacks and a white knit sport shirt, and he looked very young.

Megan laughed. "Oh, Vinnie, what a pain having a family! Come off it anyway. You're too serious for your own good. Are you enjoying your vacation, or does that pain you, too?"

Sitting down and retrieving his own cup from the coffee table, Vincent told her about his summer job at the rectory. "Not that I'm doing much of anything", he added. "Answering the phone and updating the parish files is about the extent of it. But I enjoy being there. I guess I'm looking ahead to when I'm a priest." His eyes shone when he spoke of that.

His sister smiled. "If I didn't like my own job, I'd envy you."

Vincent smiled back. "Is Jon about ready?" He was taking the boy over to the parish for the day; on the way they'd stop for hamburgers at a Roy Rogers.

Megan went up the hall to check. Presently, Vincent heard the sounds of an altercation. He rose and followed her.

Flushed and defiant, the little boy lay on the floor in front of a television set. A Japanese monster movie was on: humanoid robots and an armor-plated dragon were leveling Tokyo. Megan was berating him.

" . . . entirely too much time watching this trash. Your uncle wants to take you out, and you ought to be grateful he does."

"It's just getting good", Jon protested, tears in his eyes.

"That junk?" Megan started angrily toward the TV set while Jonathan got ready to howl.

"That's okay", Vincent intervened from the doorway. "Jon doesn't have to go out with me if he doesn't want to."

"It isn't only you . . . ", Megan began.

"Just let me see the end of the show", Jon begged her crossly. "Uncle Vinnie doesn't mind."

"How do *you* know?"

"I can wait, Megan", he assured her.

Giving up, she left Jon to the monsters and they went back to the living room.

"Sometimes I don't know what to do with him", she confessed, frowning with concern. "He gets glued to that set."

"I guess he has more exciting things to do than sit around a rectory with me."

"I only wish he did. But if he stays home, it will just be television all day."

"He doesn't play with other children?"

"He hardly knows any other kids around here. He's over at mother's all week. I'm afraid he's a solitary little boy."

"That doesn't seem much of a childhood", Vincent said.

She eyed him strangely. "The wages of sin?"

He blushed. "I didn't mean that."

"It's Daddy's line."

"You ought to have more sympathy for him", Vincent protested. "Things are going very badly for him."

"Because he won't accept Farquhar, you mean."

"It isn't a question of just accepting him. After all, they even put somebody else in charge of the paper."

Megan looked queer. "Things like that happen all the time. Daddy's been too sheltered for too long."

"That's a callous thing to say."

"So what's callous? He needs to take a realistic view of his situation. It isn't just Farquhar that's doing him in, it's his fantasies."

"I don't know what you're talking about", Vincent said, offended.

"Daddy imagines he was calling the tune before, but he was just as much under Frisch's thumb as he is under Farquhar's. The difference is that he liked it when Frisch was in charge—given his crazy ideas about religion—and he doesn't like it now that Farquhar is."

"I happen to share many of those crazy ideas", Vincent said stiffly.

Megan's laugh was mocking but affectionate. "I know that, little brother. Don't worry, you have time to outgrow them. I just wish the same was true of Daddy. But maybe it's too late for him."

"You're saying he ought to knuckle under."

"That's what it takes to get along in the Church. Don't they teach you *that* in the seminary?"

"Does it extend to taking orders from Arthur Kucharski?"

She started. "It's . . . I couldn't say."

"Because you can't pretend Dad had to put up with anything like that under Bishop Frisch."

Megan said angrily, "If he can't work for the people in charge now, he'd better just get out."

"At his age? And do what?"

"He's got all those rich friends in the—What do they call it?"

"The Knights of Mount Olivet."

"Let the Knights find him a job."

Vincent said sententiously, "Do you know what I hear as I listen to you? Hostility. A great deal of hostility toward Dad. You haven't got much sympathy for him."

"We've been short on mutual sympathy for years. He doesn't understand what he doesn't like. He doesn't understand his own situation, and God knows he's never understood mine."

"I think he understands it, Megan, but he doesn't accept it. Neither do I."

She glanced at him disgustedly. "But they *do* teach you to be moralistic, don't they?"

"It's your relationship with the Church I mean."

"I haven't got one."

"You have a very unsatisfactory one."

"Vinnie, you're a royal pain in the ass."

"We need to talk about this, Megan", he said earnestly.

"At least have the decency to wait until you're a priest."

"I can, but what about you?"

"Oh, shit!"

"Think of Jon, too."

"Don't lecture me on that subject."

"Megan, why haven't you married?"

She stared at him incredulously. "I've been on the brink dozens of times," she said slowly, "but my screwed-up family scares them off. You religious nuts are a big handicap."

"Don't joke."

"Vinnie, get this through your head. I like my job. I like my life. I don't need the Church in order to feel good about myself, and I don't need a man either."

"I think you've been hurt."

"Brilliant. If you were any more perceptive, you'd have the sense to shut up."

"Your relationship with Dad—"

Abruptly Megan slammed her fist down on the end table, making her empty coffee cup dance in its saucer. "I am sick to death of listening to you, you bastard", she snarled. "Stuff my relationships! You're a prig, Vinnie, and the only amusing thing about you is the cruddy jargon you talk. Now shut up or get out of here."

"What are you two arguing about?"

Jon stood in the doorway staring at them with large eyes. "Terrific!" Megan exclaimed, shooting a killing look at Vincent. "Don't you know not to eavesdrop, Jonathan?"

"I wasn't", the boy protested. "Anyway, I live here, too."

"Your mother and I were arguing", Vincent said, "because we're fond of each other. Brothers and sisters do that sometimes."

Jon seemed unimpressed by the explanation. "My show's over", he said.

"Then it's time for us to be going." Vincent rose.

"I'm not sure you ought to, Jon", Megan said, frowning.

"Aw, Mom."

Suddenly she burst into tears. Leaping up, she rushed across the room and embraced the boy, exclaiming, "You don't want to go with him, do you? Stay here with me. We'll have fun together."

Jon wriggled away in embarrassment. "You said you have to work this afternoon", he reminded her sternly. "And I want to go with Uncle Vinnie."

"To a *rectory?*"

"I get to answer the phone. You *will* let me answer the phone, won't you?" he added anxiously to Vincent.

"Sure. If your mother lets you go."

"Mom . . . ?"

"Go ahead, then", Megan said curtly, rubbing her eyes with the back of her hand. "I need a little peace."

"I hope you get it", Vincent told her.

Mouthing a silent "Go to hell" at him over Jonathan's head, she turned and disappeared up the hall.

The idea for the dinner began, surprisingly enough, with Father Drake. He'd been listening for some time that afternoon to Eleanor explaining her anxieties about Justin. His deteriorating relationship with Kucharski and her sense that she was failing him by doing nothing to help were her major themes. "I see the situation growing worse before my eyes, Father, but I have no idea how to make things better."

Paul Drake squirmed impatiently; it was stuffy in his office, and he'd heard this before. "Have him to dinner", he said shortly.

Eleanor looked confused. "Who?"

"Kucharski, of course."

She considered that doubtfully. "Do you think it will help?"

"From all you tell me, it can hardly hurt."

"I'm sure Justin won't agree."

"Invite Kucharski first, then tell Justin. He can't refuse to come to dinner in his own home, can he?"

"I suppose not. But I'm not sure. . . . "

"Neither am I. You asked what you could do to help. If you have a better idea, do that instead."

Eleanor looked hopeless. "I'm certain I don't have a better idea."

Kucharski sounded baffled when she called him the next day. "It's kind of you, Mrs. Walsh. Have you . . . ah . . . talked to Justin about it?"

"He'll be very pleased to have you, Father."

He surrendered. "I look forward to it."

Predictably, Justin put up a stiffer fight. "I'd rather have dinner with Judas Iscariot", he said.

"Justin, you need to make a greater effort to be accommodating."

"I have no intention of compromising my principles."

"I don't know of any principle that says you can't have dinner with him."

"I suppose, Ellie, you have some halfwit notion that he and I will patch things up over coffee."

"I expect nothing of the kind. But you may learn to be civil to each other. That would be progress."

"It can't hurt, Dad", Vincent volunteered.

Justin looked grimly at him. "You'd be surprised, Vinnie, at what can."

In the end there were the usual last minute complications. Megan phoned at five, said she'd have to work late, and could Jon stay on until she was able to swing by and pick him up? Obviously he could. Justin grumbled, but Eleanor assured him, "He's no trouble, dear."

"*She* is, though. She treats this house like a bus station."

"Bus station?"

"Tramping through at odd hours, with no regard for our wishes or convenience."

Eleanor shook her head but said no more. He'd always been sensitive about advertising Megan's situation to outsiders, and this blustering signaled reluctance to let Arthur Kucharski in on the secret, if secret it was anywhere but in Justin's mind. Still, he did seem to care how the evening went; to that extent, Eleanor was encouraged.

Arthur arrived at seven wearing gray slacks, a seersucker jacket, and a polo shirt, and carrying a bottle of white wine.

"A peace offering, Mrs. Walsh", he explained nervously, handing it over in the hall.

"You don't have to make peace with me, Father."

Justin took the bottle from her and examined it. "We're having roast beef", he announced.

"It doesn't matter, dear," Eleanor told him lightly.

"Unless you care about wine."

It was too hot for the patio, so they sat stiffly in the living room. Jon strolled in while Justin was getting drinks.

"This is my nephew Jonathan, my sister's son", Vincent told Kucharski.

"Pleased to meet you, Jonathan." The priest extended his hand, and the slender, blond boy took it gravely.

"Me too", he replied. The moment had an odd formality about it.

"My sister works at Channel 6", Vincent said. "She's a producer with the 'Evening News'."

"It must be exciting, having your mother in television", Kucharski said to Jonathan.

The boy looked unimpressed. "She's never on the show."

"But still—television!"

"She isn't home much either."

Justin and Eleanor returned bearing drinks, together with a dip and chips. "So you've met Jon, Father", Eleanor said brightly.

"We were discussing television. I hear your daughter is in TV news."

"She loves it. In fact, she's working late tonight. She'll be dropping by later for Jon."

"So there are two journalists in the family", Arthur said to Justin with a grin.

Justin grunted. "Television isn't journalism."

"Everybody watches it."

"Then it's entertainment, not journalism."

Jon was bored. "I'm going to watch a show", he announced.

"Come on, dear", Eleanor said. "Excuse me, Father. I have to get dinner."

Arthur sipped his Scotch and water. "He's a fine boy", he told Justin. "How old is he?"

"Eight."

"Do you enjoy being a grandparent?"

"My wife makes more of it than I do."

Arthur dropped the subject and turned to Vincent. "You've only got one more year before ordination?"

"That's right, Father."

"How do you like St. John's?"

"It's been an excellent experience."

"*I* felt like I was in jail all the time I was there. But you're getting rid of Caldron anyway. Ron Lackner will give the place a shaking up."

"Do you imagine", Justin rumbled dangerously from behind a bourbon on the rocks, "that there is some intrinsic merit in shaking things up?"

"The greatest threat to the Church is stagnation."

Vincent realized that the conversation was going sour. "St.

John's is a good seminary," he said quickly, "but I guess it could be better."

"Lackner's the man to do it. I hear he's got Bruce Poirier lined up as a visiting professor."

Justin started. "*Who?*"

"Bruce Poirier."

"The moral theologian?" He set his glass down firmly. "That man shouldn't be allowed in the diocese."

"Believe me, Justin, seminarians benefit from exposure to ideas."

"Only if they're true."

"Is the truth always that obvious?"

"We have the Church to tell us."

"But somebody has to tell the Church. That's what theologians do."

Justin was unimpressed. "I've heard all this cant about academic freedom from St. Bruno's—*my* old school—and I don't need it from St. John's, too."

"What have you got against St. Bruno's?"

"A total breakdown of orthodoxy and morality. The place has gone into the business of corrupting youth. There was another antiwar demonstration on the campus last week."

"Do you expect the kids to demonstrate in *favor* of Vietnam?"

"The students are dupes of the faculty", Justin announced. "If the Companions of Christ weren't in a state of anarchy themselves, this wouldn't happen. It never happened in *my* day."

"I didn't know we'd been in Vietnam that long."

Eleanor's call rescued them, and they went in to dinner. Justin grudgingly served white wine with the roast beef.

"It doesn't look right", he said, pouring himself a small glass.

"But it tastes fine", Eleanor commented brightly after a sip.

Justin tried his glass and made a face. "We should have had the red."

The conversation struggled on, Justin and the priest wrangling while Eleanor and Vincent tried to act as buffers. Justin had started truculent and grew more so, while Kucharski became sarcastic. The heavy meal lay largely untouched before them as battle lines flowed back and forth across the table.

In response to a chance remark of Justin's, the priest delivered himself on the subject of history. "I suppose it's true that if we don't study it we're condemned to repeat it. But it also works the other way. People who make too much of the past have difficulty living in the present."

"Because the present doesn't measure up very well", Justin said.

"That's sentimental."

"I'm talking about objective standards."

"Frankly, I doubt it."

"You doubt too much." Starting to refill his glass, he stopped abruptly and, muttering "Excuse me", left the room. In a few moments he returned carrying a newly opened bottle of red wine. The others watched with various emotions while he filled his glass to the brim. "Anybody else for red?"

Tight-lipped, Arthur said, "I will."

Justin filled his glass without comment. The priest took a sip and made a face.

Vincent, desperate for something to say, remarked, "I think there's this difference between the Church in the past and the Church now—people used to be pretty tenacious about holding on to the faith."

"How do you explain that?"

"I suppose," the young man hazarded, "because the Church taught them that salvation depended on accepting its doctrine and discipline without reservation."

"As it should be teaching them today", Justin said.

"I think Vinnie's making a different point", Arthur said.

"We've had this tendency to drop out the nuances. Everything black and white, no shades of gray. Is that it, Vinnie?"

"I guess", the young man said doubtfully. "At least . . . salvation and damnation were at stake."

Justin said, "That has always been the authentic belief of the Catholic Church, and it always will be."

"You're more sure of things than the Church is, Justin."

"Certainty about the truth is not a vice."

"Didn't Goldwater say something like that?"

"Aquinas is a model of clarity and sureness of thought."

"And he explains God by saying what he *isn't.*"

Justin scowled. "I suppose it pleases you to say faith isn't rooted in certainty."

Kucharski shrugged. "I don't feel very pleased."

"But to shake others' faith—I find that impossible to forgive. You people are trying to impose your loss of faith on the whole Church."

"Who are we people?"

"You. Farquhar. The whole lot of you. Theologians, bureaucrats, journalists, even bishops now. And what do you all share? Doubt. You're like savages turning your backs on the Sistine Chapel in order to gawk at mud daubings."

A fusillade of hand-claps interrupted him. Megan stood laughing in the hall doorway. "Bravo!" she cried. "You're in rare form, Daddy. I haven't heard anything like that since Fulton Sheen was knocking them dead on TV. You made us watch every week, remember?" Suddenly she stopped and stared. "I didn't know you had company."

Arthur rose as Eleanor, at the far end of the table, said, "Our daughter Megan, Father. Megan, this is Father Arthur Kucharski from the *Catholic Truth.*"

The priest seemed to freeze, while the laughter died out of Megan's eyes like a candle flame being snuffed. Poker-faced, she extended her hand, saying, "I'm pleased to meet you, Father."

Justin and Eleanor were aware of a communication they couldn't read. It passed. The priest shook hands and, mumbling something, subsided back into his place.

"I'd better be getting Jon", Megan said, starting to leave.

"Stay for dessert, dear", Eleanor urged.

"I'm tired. It's been a long day." And with that she was gone.

Eleanor stared after her in puzzlement. "Don't you think", she asked no one in particular, "she seemed a little odd?"

"Megan *is* odd", Justin pronounced.

When Eleanor went to the kitchen a few minutes later to get dessert, Megan and Jon had gone. Apparently they'd left by the back door. Eleanor shook her head, still puzzled, while spooning raspberries over the sherbet.

Dinner tottered to an end. Kucharski had lost his zest for disputation, and even Justin grew subdued. When at last they rose from the table, Eleanor politely suggested going back to the living room for another cup of coffee. To everyone's relief the priest begged off.

"Sorry, Mrs. Walsh. Work to do at home."

"Editorials to write?" Justin taunted.

"Work", Arthur repeated dully, heading for the door.

Standing on the front porch, they watched him walk quickly to his car. Fireflies flashed a staccato code in the twilight, and the raucous chirping of crickets swelled in the humid air, while heat lightning twitched on the horizon like an exposed nerve. The headlights flashed on, and the car pulled away with a sudden screech of tires. Exchanging troubled glances, Vincent and Eleanor followed Justin back into the house.

Upstairs later Eleanor was reading *The Imitation of Christ* in bed when Justin came in from the bathroom in pajamas. An air conditioning unit hummed in the window.

"Are you satisfied?" he said.

She sighed. "I wasn't trying to satisfy myself."

That softened him. "I only meant, how do you think it went?"

"You go out of your way to provoke him, Justin."

"*Me* provoke *him?*"

"I think he's insecure."

"I hope so."

"Justin, your attitude—"

"Don't preach, Ellie. You haven't had to put up with what I have."

She gave it up. "Megan acted strangely", she said after a while.

He frowned at the memory. "Lunatic behavior . . . as usual."

"I had the impression they knew each other."

Justin looked at her more closely. "And didn't want to admit it?"

"Why would that be?"

Annoyed at the turn the conversation had taken, he said brusquely, "Don't make a mystery of it." But after the lights were out he lay in the darkness for a long while watching the glow of distant lightning on the ceiling. Megan. Kucharski. It made a pattern: Megan, Kucharski. Something he couldn't see yet. He believed himself to be a lover of the truth. But were there truths nobody could love? The lightning flickered like a guttering flame; the air conditioner exhaled a steady cold suspiration. Justin fell asleep to troubled dreams.

At eleven-fifteen the phone rang in Megan's apartment just as she'd known it would. She turned down the sound on the late news and answered.

"It's Arthur." He sounded tremulous.

She groaned, as she'd known she would. "Oh, God!"

"You understand, don't you? I had no idea he was *your* father."

"I took that for granted."

"I didn't even know you lived in Wernersburgh any longer. The last time we met, you told me you weren't coming back here."

"We should have left it at that."

There was a long pause. "The boy . . . Jon. . . . "

"What about him?"

Arthur said in a strangled voice, "Is he ours?"

"This is long after the fact", Megan replied coldly. "I think 'mine' comes closer to the truth."

"You have to understand about that, too. I didn't realize you were. . . . " This time he got stuck entirely.

"Let's not prolong this."

"I need to see you, Megan."

"What about? We've both gotten along without setting eyes on each other."

"About Jon, for one thing."

She frowned suspiciously. "What do you mean—'about Jon'?"

He cleared his throat. "After all, I'm his father."

"That's simply a biological accident."

"It takes getting used to."

"Put it out of your mind."

"You know I can't do that."

"I don't know anything about you, and I don't want to."

"I can't blame you for feeling that way. But understand—I simply didn't *know.*"

"You didn't try very hard to find out at the time."

"Let me see you", he pleaded doggedly.

"I don't want you messing in Jon's life or mine."

"I need to work this through. I need your help."

"That was always your line."

"It's the truth."

"I'm tired. I'm going to hang up."

"I'll call another time."

"Don't."

"I have to."

"*You* have to? Never mind me, never mind anybody else. That's always been your way."

"I want to change."

"Then do." Furious, she slammed down the phone, then waited. It didn't ring again. After several minutes Megan reached beside her on the end table for a cigarette. It would be a long time before she slept.

XI

“I don’t even blame your father”, Gwyneth Harley said. “I know where he’s coming from. But gutless wonders like Farquhar and Kucharski bug the hell out of me. One whiff of trouble and they run. They make me sick.”

“I feel the same way, Gwyneth.”

They were in Megan’s crowded, windowless office, its walls a collage of cork boards, planning calendars, and taped messages and memos. Gwyneth sat on a small couch covered in tough yellow plastic, Megan in a director’s chair of navy blue canvas and white-lacquered wood. The two women had known each other casually for several years, but this was the first time they’d talked seriously and at length, and each found the other surprisingly congenial: they despised the same people.

Megan had arranged the meeting to discuss the controversy over Gwyneth’s hiring and abrupt firing and how the “Evening News” might get belatedly into the story. As they talked, however, a larger project began to take shape: a series of reports giving a first-year assessment of Ambrose Farquhar and his impact on Wernersburgh.

“What happened to me”, Gwyneth was saying, “shows how very little difference having Farquhar here makes, despite all his talk about renewal.”

"Of course *some* people believe he's turning the whole diocese upside down."

"Give him credit for a few things, then. A new rector at the seminary—although of course he had to appoint *somebody* to replace Caldron. Changes in the chancery staff—new yes-men in place of old. And what's happened at the *Catholic Truth.* But that's the extent of what *he's* done. Everything else was bound to happen once Frisch stepped down."

Megan leaned back thoughtfully and lighted a cigarette. She wore a blue blazer and jeans. "What", she asked casually, "do you make of Kucharski's role?"

Gwyneth lighted up too and, like Megan, leaned back thoughtfully. "In some ways I'm more disappointed in Arthur than in Farquhar. You know him pretty well?"

"Pretty well."

"I know him *very* well", Gwyneth said emphatically. "Frankly, it's because of him that I've hung in with the Church as long as I have. I kept saying to myself, 'If Arthur Kucharski can put up with the crap, then—who knows?—maybe there's still something good there that will come to the surface if it has the chance.' And to have *him* end up shafting me—that's hard to take!"

"Perhaps he didn't have much choice."

"He had more courage in the Frisch years. At least he didn't knuckle under. You've read his *Catholic Recorder* articles?"

Megan shook her head. "I don't pay much attention to the Catholic thing."

"*You* don't?" Gwyneth looked incredulous. "With *your* father?"

"Maybe that's why."

"I was brought up to take it very seriously." Gwyneth looked at her slyly. "I'll tell you a secret. I went in the convent for a year after high school."

Megan laughed. "You're not the type."

"I found that out. I guess I've been uptight about the Church for a long time."

"Relax."

"*After* your series. . . . Who else are you going to talk to?"

"Just as many people as possible."

"Your father?"

"No", Megan said at once.

"Too risky for him, I suppose. But certainly Arthur?"

Unconsciously she frowned. "I couldn't say yet."

Needling, Gwyneth said, "Do you want to protect him, too?"

Megan was stung. "I have no intention of doing that", she said stiffly.

"This can be a hell of a story, Megan."

"I mean it to be."

"And Arthur in the thick of it! God, how good it will be to see him squirm."

Megan told him on the phone that afternoon, "I'm ready to see you."

"Well. . . . " He sounded unprepared for that.

"A few days ago you were begging to see me."

"I guess I didn't imagine. . . . "

"So that made it safe to ask me."

"That isn't fair, Megan."

"Your tough luck, Arthur. Where will it be and when? You name it, I'm paying."

"You don't have to."

"This is business."

"Business?"

"I'll explain when I see you."

He suggested Palmieri's, a steak house on the edge of town, and they agreed on next Tuesday at eight.

"It will be good to see you again", he said.

"Don't count on it." She hung up quickly, then sat staring at a vacant space several feet before her. When she became aware of the racing of her heart she sprang up from her chair with a curse and hurled a pack of cigarettes at the wall.

For Megan Walsh in the autumn of 1958, the state university was a combination of Parnassaus and Gomorrah. Later she would see it differently, as a relaxed, rather dull campus, but in that trembling moment of her uncertain, young womanhood it seemed to embody everything that fascinated and frightened her. Not only were her professors suave and sophisticated, witty and ironic, as she'd expected them to be, but even her fellow students appeared similarly subtle and worldly wise. Within three years she'd regard the same teachers as drudges and the same students as simple souls; but in those early golden weeks she thought that she was living among giants.

Megan had battled fiercely to go to the university. Her father had chosen Maryheights for her and sung its praises endlessly: it was close to home; her mother was a graduate; it was conducted by the same order of nuns as her high school; most of her friends would go there. And above all it was *Catholic.* For Justin Walsh that was the clinching argument. To give her credit, Eleanor was more open-minded. Maryheights was a good school, and Megan would do well there; but it was, after all, Megan's education, and if she wanted to go elsewhere. . . .

Megan wanted. Urgently. After eight years of parochial school and four in a Catholic girls' academy subjected to the nuns' ferocious piety, she was sick of Catholic education. Almost as sick as she was of being ordered around by her father. The more Justin insisted, the more stubborn she grew. She found she actually enjoyed it.

"You don't realize what you'd lose by going to a non-Catholic college", he told her.

"Daddy, saving my soul doesn't depend on being taught by nuns."

Sensing that she was more than ordinarily dug in, he backpedalled accordingly. Suddenly Megan realized that she was going to win. "Of course, there are other fine Catholic colleges for women besides Maryheights. And I admit . . . there are some advantages to going away to school."

"I'm not going to a nuns' school. I'm not going to a *Catholic* school."

He was growing exasperated. Thrusting out his jaw pugnaciously and leaning forward, red-faced, he demanded, "Then where the devil do you imagine you *are* going?"

Not having dared to dream she might actually escape Maryheights, Megan hadn't yet confronted that question. She blurted the first thing that came into her head: "The state university."

It seemed an inspired choice when, Justin's opposition conquered by her stubbornness and Eleanor's tolerance, she finally arrived there in the fall. Nothing the nuns had taught her had prepared her in the least for the splendid intellectual and social license of the place. Her shyness soon wore off, and she settled down, enjoying the school and the people enormously.

Megan made many friends in that first year while forming no intimate connections. She sampled everything and everybody with enthusiasm, not knowing that what would in some ways be the most remarkable relationship of her life lay just ahead. Older people grow finicky in such matters, picking and choosing not only *among* acquaintances—whom to embrace, whom to reject—but even in their dealings with particular friends: singling out the one or two things they find congenial in particular individuals, while consciously overlooking everything else. The young by contrast are omnivorous, swallowing one another whole with unselective gusto and only later acknowledging the indigestible elements in others. Megan's friendship with Tanya Stein followed that classic pattern.

It was early December of her sophomore year. Megan and some sixty others had just sat through a late afternoon lecture on *The Merchant of Venice.* She left the classroom building in a haze of admiration for the teacher's brilliance and, hardly noticing, fell into step with a red-haired, freckle-faced girl with a sharp nose who'd caught her eye before, but whom she didn't know. Full of enthusiasm, she exclaimed, "I thought that was terrific, didn't you?"

Her companion gave her a sharp glance. Her green eyes were skeptical and humorous. "He doesn't know anything about Jews", she scoffed.

Megan was taken aback: for her the suggestion that a teacher's wisdom was less than total still bordered on heresy; skepticism wouldn't come until later. "Why do you say that?" she demanded.

Shrugging as if to say it wasn't worth arguing about, the other nevertheless answered. "Shylock wasn't looking for revenge. No Jew in his spot would be that stupid. He just lost his temper and made a bad deal. Even then he thought he was safe: Antonio would find the money. When he didn't, Shylock was scared witless. Imagine what would have happened to him if he *had* collected his pound of flesh."

"Why not just forgive the debt?"

"As a Jew he couldn't afford it. His margin of safety depended on sticking to the letter of a bargain and demanding justice. Once he began making exceptions, he'd be done for. Sooner or later they'd tell him the letter of the law didn't apply to him, and not because they wanted to do him favors either."

"Then Portia was helping Shylock as well as Antonio?"

"Shylock *more* than Antonio. What do you do when you

can't afford either to collect your debts or *not* to collect them? Portia gave Shylock a way out. He must have been secretly grateful to her."

"But why 'secretly'?"

The red-haired girl broke into a laugh. "Jews can't talk about these things. It makes them vulnerable."

Megan laughed, too, liking her companion's mix of cleverness and down-to-earth humor. "I'm on my way to the student union for a cup of coffee. Care to join me?"

"Let me buy", the other said, and they crossed the icy campus in the failing daylight, chatting amiably.

Her name was Tanya Stein. Her home was in New Antwerp, where her father had a jewelry store. She was a sophomore too, and planned to major in political science. As far as Megan could recall, Tanya was the first Jew she'd ever known; very soon she was also—and certainly—the first whom Megan had as a best friend.

Early on, she discerned that Tanya was drawn toward gentiles— "Like a moth to a flame", she told herself knowingly—with a curious mixture of hopefulness and fear, a craving for acceptance and the bitterness of anticipated rejection. That idea made her grieve for her friend and feel guilty for the betrayals that she supposed accounted for Tanya's attitude. She made a silent vow: never would Tanya feel betrayed by her, never would she regret their friendship. Events would teach her a valuable lesson: the rashness of guaranteeing what she couldn't control. But for the moment friendship's flame burned ardently. Her sophomore year was, and would always remain, the year of Tanya.

Her new friend was humorous, she was wise, she was spirited and deep. Megan sometimes wondered what Tanya could see in her that she needed or wanted. Perhaps, she decided, it was precisely her appreciation of Tanya. She provided an audience. Later, when her own self-confidence and conscious self-esteem had grown, Megan was amazed at how willing she'd been to cast herself in a self-deprecating role. Yet wasn't there something essentially patronizing in that? *She* would satisfy *Tanya's* need, not the reverse. So powerful an implicit claim to superiority contained the seeds of conflict, but Megan didn't know that then.

One day in early spring, as they were leaving the library, Megan was moved almost to tears by the sight of a glorious sunset flaming in glowing overtones of peach and amber across the western sky. Without preamble she declared, "You are the best friend I've ever had or ever will have."

These were still relatively innocent times, and such professions could be made and received without the sinister assumptions they would provoke a few years later. Tanya smiled. "And you are mine, Megan."

"Look at the sunset!"

Tanya glanced. "Pretty." The yawn that followed reminded Megan that her friend, so sensitive in so many ways, had little appreciation of natural beauty. Tanya held that only what was touched by human genius merited serious attention. She loved paintings, sculpture, music—all the arts of man—but mere scenery left her cold.

They walked slowly across the campus, speaking of the future. Tanya planned to go to law school, then run for the state legislature. Megan, who was studying history, would get her doctorate and be her friend's chief advisor. Their careers would mesh, fuse, be inseparable. Down the road lay Washington, Congress, the Senate: Was a cabinet post for Tanya out of the question? Not at that moment anyway. And Megan with her at every step: nothing could part them.

Stopping at the entrance to her dormitory, Megan said, "Come on up to the room."

Tanya shook her head. "Can't. I have to study." But she lingered, and Megan was disconcerted to see profound sadness in her eyes.

"What's wrong?"

Now Tanya seemed on the verge of crying, as Megan had been a few minutes earlier. "None of it will happen", she said.

"What do you mean?" But Megan knew, and that frightened her: did she think the same thing?

"It isn't going to happen. We won't be able to stay together."

"Of course we will. What can prevent it?"

"*They* will. All the others. You'll see, Megan."

"That's foolish", she chided.

But Tanya was adamant, and murmuring, "It will happen", she slipped off into the dusk, leaving Megan shivering in the suddenly cold air.

When she went home for the summer, the first thing she told her parents was that she planned to visit Tanya in New Antwerp in a few weeks.

"Who's she?" her father asked.

"My best friend at school."

"You remember, Justin", Eleanor prompted. "Megan has written us about her."

"Funny name—Tanya." His eyes narrow shrewdly. "She isn't Jewish by any chance?"

"Of course she is", Megan snaps. "What about it?"

"Don't you know any Catholics there?"

She groans. "I know plenty of Catholics. I've *always* known plenty of Catholics. Just about everybody I *do* know is Catholic. Aren't there one or two people in the world worth knowing who aren't Catholic?"

"Don't exaggerate. . . . You say this girl is your best friend?"

"Why are you grilling me, Daddy?"

"Since you're going to be staying with her, dear," Eleanor

interposes to put Justin's questioning in a benign light, "we want to know a little more about Tanya."

Justin frowns. "Who said—"

"It's obvious, dear", Eleanor tells him mildly but firmly. "It's natural that Megan wants to visit her best friend, just as it's natural that we want to know more about her. We needn't quarrel."

Megan laughs. "You make such good sense, Mother."

Eleanor smiles pleasantly. "When you and your father start in on each other, dear, somebody has to keep things on track."

Justin was far from satisfied. "Tanya Stein", he repeated to himself half aloud, shaking his head. "Tanya *Stein.*" The point wasn't lost on Megan.

Megan's ten days with Tanya in August weren't quite the idyll she'd expected. The Steins, gracious East Europeans, outdid themselves in hospitality, so that Megan felt more at home in their house than she had for years in that of her parents. Tanya, delighted to have her, went out of her way to tell her so. But for all their kindness, Megan found an unexpected and unwelcome third party on the scene: Arthur Kucharski.

She'd met him through Tanya at school, but in the first fervor of their friendship he seemed a marginal, irrelevant figure. Having him turn up now was vexing.

"He's hard to discourage", Tanya said rather defensively after spending a half hour with him on the telephone one evening making arrangements for the three of them to go out together.

"He's chasing you", Megan said with disapproval.

Tanya smiled complacently. "Arthur is harmless."

"He's a pest."

She laughed. "I think he's cute."

Megan saw nothing cute about him. Tall and thin, with limp hair the color of margarine and eyes the palest blue she'd ever seen, Kucharski was infatuated with her friend, and, Megan was irritated to observe, Tanya didn't mind that in the least.

That Saturday night, after seeing a movie, they sat drinking Budweiser in a booth in a bar. Arthur paid for Tanya, Megan paid for herself. The place was crowded and noisy, with a jukebox adding to the din, so that they almost had to shout to be heard. Summer was winding down, and conversation turned naturally to school.

"God, how I hate the thought of going back!" Tanya exclaimed.

Megan is shocked. "I thought you liked the university."

"I've outgrown the place. I mean, I could die of boredom in the next two years." Tanya had taken up smoking that summer; she flicks the ash from her cigarette with a gesture that manages to convey world-weariness.

All this is news to Megan. Is Tanya's sudden disillusionment intended somehow to impress Kucharski?

Apparently oblivious, Arthur sits sipping his beer with one arm draped loosely around Tanya's shoulders. Unconsciously Megan frowns at him, and he smiles back in surprise, even as he says to Tanya, "I wouldn't let you die of boredom."

Megan considers that disgusting. "*I'm* looking forward to school", she says primly.

"Me too", Arthur agrees, as if the remark had been addressed to him. "Did I tell you I'll be writing a column for the *Banner* this year?" He had indeed told them—several times: the *Banner* was the campus daily, and for Kucharski, a journalism major, his column was a topic of singular interest evidently bearing frequent repetition.

"Arthur," Tanya says with a thin smile, "you certainly did tell me, and if you tell me one more time, I am going to positively scream."

"Sorry." He looks abashed.

"Never mind." Reaching up she pats the hand on her shoulder. "I should be patient with you."

These little intimacies are growing increasingly annoying to Megan. Addressing Kucharski directly and brusquely, she says, "You're planning to work for a newspaper when you graduate?"

"Yes. At least . . . I think so." He looks suddenly unsure of himself.

"You can cover my political career," Tanya says, laughing, "while Megan feeds me ideas."

He agrees enthusiastically. Irritated at Tanya for making him part of their future, Megan glances at her watch. "I have to get up for Mass tomorrow", she points out.

"I guess we should be going", Tanya acknowledges. "Arthur, leave a tip."

He does. On the way out he says to Megan, "Need a ride to church?"

"It isn't far from the Steins' house."

"It *is* far", Tanya contradicts. "Let him do it, Megan. He's got a car, and he has nothing else to do."

"We could all go out afterward", he suggests hopefully.

"That would be lovely, Arthur."

"What time should I get you?" he asks Megan.

"I'm going to the ten-thirty Mass", she says coldly.

"I'll be over at ten."

He was. Megan, sitting on the front porch with Tanya, felt a fresh surge of irritation at seeing the old, green Hudson pull up but she got in anyway. Arthur and Tanya chatted for a few minutes, and then he pulled away.

"We'll be early for Mass", he remarks.

"You didn't have to get me."

"I think maybe we'll drive out in the country this afternoon."

"Go without me", Megan says. "I'm just a fifth wheel."

He glances at her in alarm. "Tanya won't go if you don't."

"Try her."

"Come on, Megan, be a sport."

She sighs resignedly. "I never wanted to be a nursemaid."

"But you're her guest, you know, and—"

"I understand the situation perfectly well, Arthur."

They are silent for a while; then he says, "Do you always go to Mass?"

"Every Sunday, naturally."

"I got out of the habit. I just started again last semester."

"You're doing God a big favor."

"I didn't mean it like that."

"Skip it."

"Anyway," he adds, still hurt, "sometimes I think I *would* like to do something special."

"Like what?" she asks without interest.

"I don't know . . . be a priest."

She scowls in his direction. "Tanya would be surprised to hear that."

"It's just this idea I have."

"I know", Megan assures him. "*I* used to want to be a fireman."

Offended again, he protests, "It isn't like that."

I'm being harder on him than he deserves, she admits to herself, but he brings it out in me. She feels relieved when they turn a corner and see their destination, a large Gothic church called St. Agnes's, just a block ahead. More kindly she says, "Who knows, Arthur, maybe you've got a vocation."

He nods, looking serious, and says, "Wouldn't that be a bitch though?"

When her visit ended three days later, Megan was secretly pleased. She'd stayed longer than was wise; Kucharski's presence divided Tanya's loyalties; and, although there'd been no scenes or incidents, she knew her friendship with Tanya had turned just a little sour.

At the train station she says, "Your parents were darlings to have me."

"They're crazy about you", Tanya assures her. But she looks grave. "I wish things weren't so complicated."

"Complicated?"

"I shouldn't talk about it."

"You *should* . . . to me."

"Oh, Megan . . . ", suddenly Tanya is on the brink of tears. "It's Arthur . . . my parents . . . they're terribly upset."

Disappointed and angry at hearing his name, Megan says, "They don't like him?"

"It isn't *him.* It's the other thing."

Light begins to dawn for Megan. "You mean, the Jewish thing?"

"I mean the Christian thing."

"*I'm* a Christian."

"But you aren't—"

"—a man." Megan looks into her friend's eyes. "So it's irrelevant between you and me."

Tearfully Tanya murmurs, "I know."

"It will always be irrelevant . . . between us", she adds for emphasis. "You're my friend. Nothing will change that. Not ever."

They embrace. Boarding the train and taking a window seat, Megan turns at once to wave and goes on waving until they've pulled away from the platform and Tanya is long out of sight. Sitting back, she asks herself: What would she say if she knew he wants to be a priest? Somehow that strikes her as funny, and as the train crawls that long afternoon through rolling farmland beneath an implacable August sun, Megan feels more lighthearted than she's felt in days.

"I don't see how I can possibly appear on a program like that," Arthur said.

"If we can't find anybody to say a good word for Bishop Farquhar," Megan protested, "it's going to be too one-sided."

"You can find plenty besides me."

"I thought you were one of his biggest admirers."

Not at ease with the remark, he said, "He's doing what has to be done."

"Say that on the air."

Seated in a corner of the restaurant sipping drinks before dinner, Megan wore a severe, black suit while Arthur was in blue blazer, a regimental tie, and gray slacks. Tasting his Bloody Mary, he said uncomfortably, "It's the Gwyneth Harley business. I don't want an argument with her."

"I'm not planning a confrontation—you versus Gwyneth. But we do need you for the series, Arthur. Revamping the *Catholic Truth* has been one of Farquhar's great coups." Megan sipped her Campari and soda, and watched him closely. "And of course," she added, "you deserve your share of the credit, too."

"I see what you're getting at. . . . "

"You're needed", she repeated. "It comes with the job."

"I'd like to oblige you, Megan."

"Then do."

"I suppose it would be okay. I mean, as you describe it."

"I've always played square with you, Arthur."

"Of course." He reddened. "I guess the answer is yes."

"Wonderful."

"What about . . . ", he hesitated, "your father?"

"For an interview? No way. He has too much to lose by speaking his mind. Which is the only thing he knows how to do."

He stared down at his glass. "I never dreamed you were Justin Walsh's daughter."

Megan didn't so much as blink. "What difference does that make?"

"I mean, you might think I was pretty insensitive. . . . "

"Your quarrel with him is no business of mine. Let's order."

After they had, Arthur leaned forward and said, "I guess I should be glad about this series because it gives us an opportunity to talk."

She lighted a cigarette, avoiding his eyes. "This is strictly business."

"I don't blame you for being angry at me. But bear in mind my total ignorance about so many things . . . right up to that moment at your parents' when you walked in."

The memory made her laugh. "Did you think I'd come to haunt you?"

He smiled wanly. "When can I see Jon again?"

Her laughter died out. "You've gotten along perfectly well up to now without knowing he existed. Leave it that way."

"But now I *do* know."

"He doesn't need you", Megan said angrily.

"Maybe I need him."

"I don't give a damn what you need, Arthur."

"I suppose I deserve that. But . . . why didn't you *tell* me you were expecting a child?"

Tight-lipped, she said, "You may recall that was just when you announced you'd decided to be a priest."

He stared at her, appalled. "You were saving my vocation?"

She felt confused; this wasn't going as she'd intended. "I wouldn't have married you if you *had* thrown over the priesthood. So why bother telling you? It would only have complicated things for both of us."

"My God!"

"I don't recall that he showed much interest either."

Their steaks arrived. He ate without appetite. She barely picked at hers. Neither spoke. She had a headache. This meeting was a rotten idea. At least they wouldn't have to do it again, now that he'd agreed to be interviewed.

"How have you gotten along?" he asked suddenly, breaking a long silence.

"What does it matter to you?"

"Believe me—if you want me to feel guilty, I do."

In fairness, she had to admit that he did seem subdued. It might even be contrition. But she was wary: he'd always been that way with her, yet beneath surface abjection lay an enormous will to gratification. Not strength of character by a long shot, but it resembled strength in being able to absorb abuse for the sake of what it wanted. Megan said, "How did I get along? I'll tell you then."

It had been hell living at home before Jon was born. Her mother was kind, but there was nothing to be done about Justin. He nagged her: about going to confession (she didn't), about attending Mass (she'd given that up), about naming the child's father (she was adamant), about putting the baby up for adoption (adamant), about straightening out her life—according to *his* notions—and planning for the future (she was doing that urgently, but she didn't share her plans with him, and she knew he would reject them by rote if she did).

"I hated him in those months", she told Arthur. "He doesn't quit. He has this absolutely rigid idea of how everything and everybody ought to be, and he won't rest as long as reality doesn't measure up."

He rubbed his eyes wearily. "I've had to deal with Justin."

"Then you know." Megan lighted another cigarette as coffee came; both of them were smoking heavily. "I had to get the hell out of that house. My sanity depended on it. But I couldn't hope to get a job or make a move until after the baby came. Believe me, I started looking for work the moment I could."

"And you found your present job?"

She laughed harshly. "Do you imagine a dumb kid fresh out of college, with a child on her hands, can walk right into something as good as I've got now? I showed up at the station cold, no experience and no prospects, and they gave me the dirtiest gofer job around because the last person to have it had quit two hours earlier and it took no skill and they knew they could always get somebody else when I quit."

She'd hung onto that job like grim death: it meant escaping from her father's home into a furnished apartment—living room, bedroom, kitchenette—in a seedy old building where the elevator usually didn't work and the halls stank of cooking smells or worse. "It was dirt cheap," she explained, "but even so I could only manage it thanks to my mother."

"She gave you money?"

"A little. On the sly. But mainly she helped by watching Jon. Even that took courage. *He* didn't want it."

"I don't understand."

"If I hadn't been able to work, I couldn't have left home, and if I hadn't left, I'd still have been under his thumb. He was furious at my mother for making it possible for me to go."

"But he accepted it?"

"She doesn't fight him often, but when she does, she usually wins. Because she's right, and he knows it. . . . Anyway, that's pretty much the story. I've worked like a madman at the station, and I've moved up. I could do commercials for the Protestant work ethic. Jon's a delight. I'm just sorry he hasn't got more friends."

The check came, and she paid it. Arthur asked, "Why doesn't he?"

"Think about his schedule—*my* schedule, that is. He practically lives at his grandmother's. He just doesn't see that much of other kids."

"That's kind of rough on him."

"Things could be worse for both of us. We're not complaining."

"And Justin—has he come around?"

"At least he's kind to Jon. I can't ask more of him, considering how he thinks about things."

"I suppose he'll never change."

"Not bloody likely", she said in a cockney accent. Arthur grinned, and she caught herself, afraid of growing too chummy. "I have to go", she added with deliberate coldness.

"When can I see you again?"

Megan looked at him suspiciously. "About the series? I'll call you in a couple of weeks."

"That's not what I meant."

She frowned. "Buzz off, Arthur."

"There's so much catching up to do."

"I don't want to be your pal. What happened back then was between two other people—two dumb kids. It has nothing to do with you and me."

"What about Jon?"

"Crap!" She glared scornfully. "I am not prepared to entertain the notion that, having seen him once, you are now awash in paternal juices."

He didn't raise his eyes. "I'm not certain I can go on", he said in a low voice.

Something in his tone made her uneasy. "Do you mean . . . as a priest?"

He nodded. "This is a weird situation for me. You can't imagine what's been going on in my head since we met."

"Then have the decency not to bug me about it."

"I know you don't owe me a thing, Megan—"

"You're absolutely right."

"—but I need your help in working this through. I can't do it by myself."

" 'I need your help' ", she repeated bitterly. Abruptly she stood up. "That's where I came in."

She turned on her heel and made for the exit, Arthur trailing miserably behind. Catching up with her in the parking lot, he said, "I'll phone you."

"Forget it."

"I don't wish to cause you pain."

"Then for God's sake don't."

"But there's so much we need to resolve."

"We never will. Just shut up, Arthur. Shut up forever." She walked away toward her car in the mild night, leaving him standing alone in the pink glow of a neon sign that overlooked the parking lot. One letter was out, and it read GOOD FOOD GO D CHEER.

It was two o'clock in the morning. Megan sat in her living room, smoking and drinking a beer. Down the hall Jon turned over in bed with a whimper and a rustle of sheets. Relieved at the distraction, she rose and, stubbing out her cigarette, went quietly to his room.

He lay on his back, head turned to the wall. His features were in shadow, but she could see the pulse throbbing in the well of his neck and hear his breath, shallow and rapid. Fascinated, she watched his fine-boned chest rise and fall, rise and fall, fragile as a bird's, enclosing heart and lungs, the very stuff of life, in a delicate embrace bespeaking—what was it, boldness or despair?

The boy stirred, turning his head, and his eyes flickered open, met hers without recognition, then flickered shut again. Deeply moved, she brushed the limp flaxen hair from his forehead. Her fingertips came away moist, and suddenly her son's bodiliness staggered her. Entirely himself, he was also uniquely *hers.* Blessed is the fruit of thy womb, she thought, the words springing up from depths she hadn't explored in years. Damn you, she addressed Kucharski in her mind. But at the same time she conceded bleakly: they look like each other. Fruit of *my* womb . . . but with *his* features, *his* expressions, *his* capacity for being hurt. It was unfair: biology, genetics, the formulae of life, linked them in Jon with an intimacy that made her gasp to think of it. As an instrument for uniting them, the act of love itself paled by comparison. If she and Arthur were to flee to opposite ends of the earth, they couldn't help remaining two in one flesh, this scrap of flesh and bone, their son.

Megan's head swam. Raising a hand to her forehead, she was aware once more of the moisture on her fingertips that, moments before, had formed a damp chaplet on Jon's brow. She felt suffocated, hemmed in. The autonomy she'd cherished was a sham; linkages joined her against her will to other lives on levels at once elemental and decisive: Jon, Arthur—Justin and Eleanor! I am myself, she thought doggedly, I am myself. But she was aware of a mocking, uninvited counterpoint: You are others, others are you.

Turning with an effort from her son's bed, Megan walked weakly, blindly back into the living room and, sitting down, mechanically resumed smoking. Useless now to fight the swarming memories that clamored for her attention. The past was no more her own than the present was.

All their junior year the romance—Megan's scornful word for it—between Tanya and Arthur had been intense. This first proximity to passion unsettled Megan. Tanya was a different person, virtually a stranger at times, distracted and brusque as she pursued something Megan couldn't offer. Bitterly jealous of Kucharski, Megan often found herself furious at Tanya, yet unable to confront her new, disturbing emotions.

Tanya and she roomed together that year, but the arrangement Megan had anticipated with such eagerness was shadowed and spoiled by Kucharski's presence. She sat one night in January watching her friend apply lipstick before meeting him for a date.

"How do I look?" Tanya asks, examining herself critically in the mirror.

"Fine."

"Do you think this color suits me?"

In fact the lipstick is too purplish. "Orange is better with your complexion", she says irritably.

"Arthur likes this."

"He has no taste."

"That isn't true."

"If he does, I've never noticed it."

"Obviously," Tanya says haughtily, "there's a great deal you don't know about him."

"Or care to know."

Something in her tone catches Tanya's attention. Suspiciously she says, "What is *that* supposed to mean?"

Megan hears the challenge and responds. "It's your business of course, Tanya, but a lot of people think this situation is disgusting."

"What situation?"

"Sleeping with him."

There, unspoken for weeks, it's now suddenly out in the open, a surprise to them both. It will be several years before the sexual revolution is proclaimed; sex is still intensely serious. Megan is frightened at what she's said, but it can't be taken back. They both know it's true.

Tanya has grown tense. "Spare me the sermon", she snaps. "You'd do the same if you had the chance."

Megan flushes furiously. "That's a horrible thing to say."

"Jealous", Tanya taunts. "You're only jealous. Too bad the Church won't let *you* —"

Megan starts up, tears of rage in her eyes. "Go to hell, you Jewish slut. Just go to hell!" She rushes from the room, slamming the door behind her.

Two weeks of hostile silence followed, and when communication resumed the relationship was radically altered. Both were grieved at what had happened, but it couldn't be undone.

Realizing that something had happened and that Megan blamed him for it, Kucharski stopped her outside the library one afternoon and insisted on buying her coffee. Megan objected, but secretly she was rather pleased. Why, she couldn't have said.

"You and Tanya had a fight", he informs her. They are sitting in a corner of the huge, noisy cafeteria.

"Why should you care?"

"Tanya takes it out on me."

Megan says deliberately, "You make me sick."

He spreads his hands helplessly. "What can I do about that?"

"Leave her alone."

He pauses to sip his coffee. "Maybe that's not a bad idea."

She looks at him suspiciously, then, sensing he means it, says, "You aren't doing her any favor, Arthur, and as for yourself, I thought you wanted to be a priest."

"That was just an idea I had."

"And now?"

He blushes. "I don't know. . . . "

"Then you see?" Triumphant. "How can you go on like this?"

Uneasy. "If you think it's all up to me. . . . "

The words puzzle her. "Who else?"

"You may have noticed that when Tanya has her mind made up, it isn't that easy to change it."

"That's disgusting", she tells him, echoing her words to Tanya.

"I can't help it." He stares at her earnestly. "I don't want to hurt her."

"You mean you'd break it off if you could?" She is astonished at this revelation.

"It's frightening sometimes, Megan. I mean, she seems so intense. And this fight with you has made her worse."

Megan looks at him with dawning sympathy, suddenly seeing him in a new light. "Break loose, Arthur", she urges, visions of moral regeneration already forming in her mind: she is, after all, her father's daughter. "It isn't right to act this way. Especially if you have a vocation."

"Maybe", he says doubtfully, "if you were to help me. . . . "

This conversation was curiously exhilarating to Megan, giving her a new role that she fancied: preserver of Arthur Kucharski's priestly vocation. Her spiritual nobility pleased her. Without noticing it, she had transferred allegiance from Tanya to him.

Tanya's and Arthur's relationship came slowly apart in the weeks that followed. Megan followed the course of events with quiet satisfaction. There was no trip for her that summer to New Antwerp, but Arthur phoned occasionally with reports from the battlefront. In general, she liked what she heard.

"She's driving me crazy", he tells her bluntly one night in late July.

"Tanya can be terribly demanding."

"Neurotic, you mean."

"She has this sensitivity about being Jewish."

"Yeah, I see that. Sometimes I think *I'm* meant to prove something, too."

"Prove something?"

"That she can be Jewish and still. . . . " He lets the sentence tail off.

She winces. "How dreadful for her—and you."

"I have to pull out of this."

"For your own sake. . . . But you've got to think of her, too."

"I do. But this is no good for either of us."

"When will you tell her?"

"Soon. Before we go back to school."

Megan smiles without knowing it. "Try not to hurt her."

Hanging up the phone in the kitchen, she comes into the front hall, intending to go upstairs. Justin calls to her from the living room: "Who was that?"

"Somebody from school."

"He's phoned before."

Megan takes a few reluctant steps into the room. "He's just a friend. He lives up in New Antwerp. He gets bored."

Lowering his newspaper, her father looks at her over the rim of his reading glasses. "You aren't planning to go up there, are you?"

"Why would I do that?"

"That girl you visited last summer . . . you could invite her here if you wanted to. I don't mind that she's Jewish."

Her smile is glacial. "I think she's too busy to come."

"I hardly know any of your university friends", he complains.

"That's because I go to school away from home."

"Has that really been for the best?"

"Certainly."

"What have you gotten from it that you couldn't have gotten—plus some theology—at Maryheights?"

She has a ready answer. "I've met people I'd never have met at Maryheights."

"Is that an advantage?"

Megan laughs. "It's called education, Daddy", she exclaims, and runs upstairs.

In due course Arthur proved as good as his word: breaking with Tanya in August, he returned to school certain of Megan's approval.

"It was a hard thing to do", he assures her.

"It's best for both of you."

"Sure, but I didn't like hurting her."

"Sometimes", she says, impressed by her wisdom, "you have to hurt people in order to help them."

Tanya was cold and distant. This year Megan shared a room with an affable blonde named Gloria, a history major like herself, and she and Tanya saw little of each other. Their first serious encounter took place at an party in early October.

The night is unseasonably warm, and Tanya is drinking a daiquiri, not her first, alone on the patio. Megan steps out for a breath of air and finds her there. Tanya turns before she can escape back inside, and their eyes meet. "I guess you know Arthur and I broke up", Tanya says abruptly.

"I heard."

"Pleased?"

"I think it's for the best."

"You always know what's for the best, don't you, Megan?"

"Not always."

She tastes her drink. Music and laughter float out to them. "He's all yours now, darling."

Megan starts. "Arthur? You're crazy."

Tanya's smile is pained. "Obviously it's what you've wanted all along."

"It isn't going to happen."

She shrugs. "Wait and see, darling. Wait and see."

Later Tanya's words took on for her the character of a

prophecy. At the time they seemed merely farfetched. Yet soon Arthur began asking her out—no longer to talk about Tanya, but just to talk. To her surprise, she discovered that he had an interesting mind, its idealism curiously counterpointed by irony verging on cynicism. Self-sacrificing and humble one moment, egotistical beyond belief the next, he could accept any rebuke without faltering in his self-esteem. His growing claims upon her were grounded totally and unblushingly in his own need.

And Megan's need met his: the sense that someone else couldn't face life without her. If Arthur had been proud, she'd have ignored him. As it was, his declarations of dependence bound them both fast.

"I don't know how I could have wasted so many years", he tells her one evening in November. They are parked after a movie in a remote corner of the campus, the Hudson's engine idling to keep the heater running.

"Wasted . . . ?"

"Not knowing you, Megan."

She smiles in the darkness and takes a drag on her cigarette. "You do now."

He sighs. "Not entirely." Megan has refused so far to sleep with him. She has long since rejected her father's moral code, but not yet brought herself to violate it in this ultimate particular. With chastity having been set aside, virginity at least remains her unnegotiable position. Hearing in Arthur's tone the bleat of a need unmet, she quickly turns the argument against him.

"What if you become a priest?"

He squirms uneasily. "I'm not even thinking about that."

Smugly she says, "You should."

Over the next several weeks they go on like that, till the time comes when Megan, bored at last with the argument, consents. Why not? A small thing for her by then, to him it matters greatly. The relationship intensifies; both are satisfied, though for different reasons.

One day Tanya stops her on the campus. "I hear you and Arthur are getting along beautifully."

Megan flushes, remembering her disclaimers the last time they met. "We're good friends", she acknowledges grudgingly.

"More than that, I think. Don't imagine I'm jealous. I had a good time with him. You're welcome to yours. There's just one thing. . . . "

"What is it?"

"He's very unstable. Still a child. Don't count on him."

"I don't."

"He'll let you down sooner or later. Be ready for it when it comes."

"Thanks for the advice." Megan begins to move away.

"It was free!" Tanya calls after her, laughing. "I'd do as much for anybody in your spot."

By February Arthur began to act strangely: he is nervous, vague, given to long silences and unexplained outbursts, conversational fits and starts. Megan, however, has worse things to worry her. Finally she works up the courage to see a doctor.

A grandfatherly man, he studies her face with concern after the examination. "Are you married?"

"No."

"Planning to be?"

She manages a thin smile. "You mean I'd better?"

"*He* ought to carry his share of the responsibility."

Fair enough. This isn't how she'd planned marriage, but in the circumstances she is willing to accept it. And after all it appears that she loves Arthur in her way; at least she wishes to make a life for herself protecting him. Not ideal love perhaps, but already she's begun to suspect that love comes in many flavors. They sit one evening over coffee in the student union. He appears apprehensive, and, reserving her own news for the right moment, she says, "Something is bothering you. Tell me."

Frowning, Arthur says, "It doesn't seem quite fair."

Megan smiles indulgently and takes his hand. "Go on."

The anguish in his eyes when he looks at her is frightening. "It's come back."

"What has?"

"The idea . . . Megan, I think I want to be a priest."

She feels nothing special at that moment. It is a problem of locating the appropriate response. Does one laugh, cry, scream? The possibilities are inconveniently numerous. She simply says, "I thought you'd forgotten about that."

"I can't. I have to do it."

"Do you have visions, hear voices telling you to?"

His smile is ghastly. "I don't blame you."

Megan shakes her head, as if waking. To her surprise she is still holding his hand; she drops it, as she might a corpse's. "This is definite?"

"I haven't any choice. I hope you don't mind . . . I'm going into the Wernersburgh seminary."

"Getting out of New Antwerp to avoid Tanya?"

He gestures helplessly.

"Never mind", she adds wildly. "It doesn't matter to me. I'm not going back there anyway." Pushing her chair away from the table, she rises. "So good luck."

He reaches out to her, a groping gesture. "I'd like to explain—"

"You did. Good luck", she repeats, and, turning, walks quickly away.

That was the last time she spoke to him. She felt no further inclination to tell him about the child; she simply didn't want him on those terms. As for the child itself, she never doubted that she would bear him and raise him. Believing like Justin that one should take responsibility for one's actions, she had every intention of doing exactly that.

She met Tanya one afternoon in spring leaving the library, and they naturally fell into step together.

"I hear we have something in common."

"Arthur?" Megan smiles wryly. "Did you know he's going to be a priest?"

"They must be hard up."

"Vocations are difficult to explain."

"Don't try. How do *you* feel?"

"I've learned a lot."

"So did I. Don't trust", Tanya says.

"I'm sorry."

"It's a useful thing to know. What have you learned?"

She considers that seriously. "I'm waiting to find out", she confesses.

The telephone rang next to Megan's chair, startling her. Taking a drag on her latest cigarette, she answered.

"I hope I didn't wake you up."

"You called to see if I was sleeping?"

"It's sheer hell for me." She'd heard that before: *it hurts.* That was the bait he always used. She found to her surprise that knowing that made no particular difference to her.

"What am I supposed to do about it?"

"See me again. Please. I have to work this through. You've got to help me."

"It's late."

"Please see me."

She sighed. "Next Wednesday at eight. The same place."

"Thank God."

"Oh, yes. Be sure to do that." She hung up wearily and stubbed out the cigarette. But whom, she wondered, should *I* be thanking?

XII

"Generally speaking," Ronald Lackner said, "you'll find the students here a docile lot. *Too* docile, in fact. I intend to change that, but I can't do it overnight."

Bruce Poirier nodded. "It takes time to change anything in the Church. A seminary is a good place to start."

Sitting in Lackner's room drinking brandy after dinner, the seminary rector sprawled in an easy chair puffing on a pipe, while the moralist perched on the sofa, a glass in one hand and a large cigar in the other. Small and chubby, his flowing locks surrounding plump cheeks with reddish ringlets and his heavy-framed round glasses sliding constantly to the tip of a snub nose, Poirier resembled a scholarly Pekingese. It was early September; classes would resume in a few days.

"Of course", Lackner continued, "Monsignor Caldron did everything he could to enforce discipline and conformity. The effects aren't easily reversed."

"Perhaps not," Poirier agreed, "but we must try." His voice was incongruously high and reedy. "I appreciate your invitation, Ronald."

Poirier meant it. He'd knocked about enough in the last decade, teaching, lecturing, writing, heavily engaged in the theological wars during and just after the Council. Much time had been spent in Rome during Vatican II; much also on the hustings, preaching what he and others called the spirit of Vatican II in lecture halls and classrooms all across the country. Often in the thick of controversy, he'd nevertheless found time for a steady stream of articles and books—three, in fact, undermining traditional teaching on a variety of moral questions—along with more media interviews than he cared to recall. After all that, he'd frankly welcomed Lackner's invitation to spend a little time at St. John's. He needed a chance to catch his breath, do some reading, and work on the big book on moral theory that the distractions of the last ten years had kept him from. A year or two in this backwater would help.

"What did you think of Bishop Farquhar?" Lackner asked. Poirier had flown in yesterday, and today they'd driven to Wernersburgh to meet the Bishop.

The theologian drew pensively on his cigar. "An excellent example of the younger, post-Vatican II sort of bishop we need more of", he pronounced. "They're transitional men of course—one foot in the past, one in the future—but they deserve encouragement. Very often one can bring them around to one's own way of seeing things."

"I wonder what even a man like Farquhar can make of the sort of priests this seminary has cranked out for years."

"I'm sure he can do nothing with many of them. That's not your worry, Ronald. Concentrate on the priests who *shall* be."

"Some of them are beyond redemption, too", Lackner confessed. "Frisch and Caldron had a policy of poisoning the well." He crushed out his cigarette with an angry gesture and took a swallow of brandy.

"When tempted to discouragement," Poirier replied ponderously, "I remind myself that the years before the Council seem a century ago, yet we're only a decade removed from that time. Think what's happened to the Church since then! There's cause for hope."

They drank to that.

Bruce Poirier came quickly to the conclusion that the students indeed had a great deal to unlearn. It didn't dismay him. He rather enjoyed demolition work.

"Gentlemen," he began his first lecture in his morals seminar, "moral theology typically is a system for turning intuitions into rules. One can't help doing that. It expresses the human urge to find meaning or to invent it where it can't be found. Still, I hope we'll be able here to reverse the process, and work back beyond the rules to the intuitions. In other words, back to the primitive stuff of Christian morality—the prime matter, as it were—in whose authenticity we can trust, whatever doubts we may have about the accretions of the last two millenia."

That seemed to wake them up. The attention of the two dozen young men was now riveted—whether in apprehension, hope, or curiosity he couldn't tell and didn't really care—upon him. A methodical lecturer, he went on with no breaks until almost the end of the period, sketching a plan (or at least a promise) to show up the inadequacies in much that they'd been taught so far. With a few minutes remaining, he stopped, checked his watch, and asked, "Are there any questions?"

A hand shot up. Father Poirier nodded.

"Vinnie Walsh, Father. I believe you said," he consulted the notebook open before him " 'Where people don't naturally find meaning, they invent it.' As that applies to morality, are you saying that subjectivism is right?"

The theologian smiled indulgently. "You're good at putting labels on things, Mr. Walsh. Would you care to say what you mean by 'subjectivism'?"

Vincent blushed. "It's the idea that things are right or wrong according to how I think of them."

Poirier nodded patronizingly. "Acts, of course, not 'things'. Now tell us what you find objectionable in that."

"There's an objective moral order."

"What does that mean?"

"Things are right and wrong in themselves."

"Things?"

"Acts."

"And what is a human act, Mr. Walsh? Where does it take place?"

Vincent hesitated a moment. "In the will", he said.

"In other words, not out there," Poirier pointed toward the ceiling, "but in here." He tapped his forehead. "But if it starts here," he went on tapping, "and takes place here, where else does it get its meaning except—*here?*" He dropped his hand and smiled. "Too simplistic? I'll give you an example. A couple choose to practice contraception. We can agree, I suppose, that the human act isn't the mere physical act of contraception—it's the *choice* to contracept. But that choice can have different meanings. It can express selfishness, in which case it's something less than ideally it should be. It can also express love, in which case it's a good choice. Morally speaking, *we* give meaning to what we do."

The class stirred uneasily. Vincent was about to reply, but the bell rang. Poirier dismissed them, and the room emptied quickly. All except Vinnie. Frowning, he approached the desk where the priest was returning books to his briefcase. Poirier looked up affably and said, "I trust that I didn't scandalize you, Mr. Walsh."

"I've heard that sort of thing before", Vincent said unflinchingly. "It's just the old business about the end justifying the means."

Poirier looked amused. "You didn't quite get my point."

"Maybe not. . . . But I hope you're going to clear all this up next time. I think a lot of the fellows were confused."

"And it's your job to see that they aren't?"

"I thought you might not have realized—"

"I've done a bit of teaching before, Mr. Walsh," Poirier said coldly. "Twenty years' worth, to be precise."

Vincent was not abashed. "Then you understand what I'm talking about."

Annoyed, Poirier glanced at his watch. "You'll be late for your next class, won't you?"

"I hope you don't mind my mentioning this, Father."

"Mind?" the priest repeated. "What is there to mind?"

"Who the devil is Vincent Walsh?"

Lackner gave him an ironic smile. "You've had your first run-in with him?"

"I'm afraid so."

"His father is with the *Catholic Truth.* Justin Walsh—you may have heard of him. He was very close to Bishop Frisch."

"I know the name. And the reputation. Like father, like son?"

"Exactly."

Poirier brooded. "Officious and closed-minded. It's impossible to reach that sort." He shuddered.

The rector nodded. "I'm afraid Vinnie Walsh is determined to fight the renewal."

"You think he'll have to go?"

Lackner shrugged. "I'll welcome your opinion."

The theologian nodded. "Of course", he said reflectively, "there are such things as casualties of renewal."

Vincent had expected trouble with the new regime at St. John's, but he hadn't returned to the seminary spoiling for a fight. Just before leaving home he'd made his attitude clear to Justin.

"I suppose", his father growled at dinner one night, "the Modernists will be dug in when you get back to St. John's."

The young man smiled apprehensively. "Maybe it won't be so bad."

"If it isn't, it will be a refreshing change from everything else that's going on in the diocese."

Casting a reproachful glance at Justin, Eleanor told Vincent, "Don't go back expecting the worst, dear."

"I'm trying to expect the best, Mom."

"Exactly right", Justin affirmed. "No matter how bad the mess out there is, your job is just to get through the next year and get yourself ordained."

Vincent chose not to pursue the obvious question: If the seminary was a mess, and if, further, it reflected conditions in the diocese as a whole, what would the future hold for him as a priest of the diocese of Wernersburgh? Putting that aside, he forced himself to agree with Justin. Ordination was his goal. If that required overlooking many things, then he would do his best to overlook them.

It dawned on him soon, however, that resolutions like that were far easier to make than keep. Expecting radical change, his classmates were—he couldn't help but notice it—looking to him to see how he would handle the new situation. "Father Poirier . . . ", Fred Connery had remarked to him as they strolled the grounds after dinner on their very first evening back, "I guess he's something else."

"We'll find out soon", Vincent said rather grimly.

"He's been in lots of hot water", Connery pursued. "You know he was one of the leaders of the dissent against *Humanae Vitae?* I saw him a lot on TV back then. I never imagined I'd have him as a teacher." Connery, a tall, earnest youth, made a clucking sound to express wonderment.

Vincent said bravely, "I intend to give him the benefit of the doubt. And I also plan to pass his course."

Rounding a corner of the massive gray building, they saw approaching in the mild twilight two younger men whom Vincent didn't immediately place. They were in animated and apparently hilarious conversation, gesticulating and laughing, but as Vincent and Fred drew near they quieted down and passed with demure murmurs of "Hi".

"First-year men?"

Connery nodded. "That's Evans and Maguire."

"They enjoy each other's company."

"So I hear."

Vincent let it ride. Poirier was still on his mind. "Don't expect me to take him on, Fred", he told his companion.

"Nobody *wants* you to, Vinnie. But if he lives up to his reputation . . . well, you can't blame people for wondering what you'll do."

Halting, Vincent looked out over the valley, calm in the fading light, and breathed deeply as if to say he was at peace with the world. "Beautiful, isn't it?"

An occasional car sped in ghostly silence along the distant highway, its headlights probing antennae of light in the dusk. The only sound was the passionate choraling of crickets. Connery said, "Sometimes I think we're awfully isolated here."

"There's a lot I don't mind being isolated *from.*"

In view of all that happened later, Vincent was often to recall the equable mood in which he'd begun the year. Trouble had simply thrust itself on him, in ways he couldn't ignore or escape.

That was especially Father Poirier's doing. The first day's lecture was no fluke but a harbinger of what followed. It wasn't so much that the moralist flatly denied what they'd been taught; he merely suggested alternatives, other ways to think of problems, other principles and conclusions reachable by their means, side by side with the orthodoxies they'd previously learned. One couldn't fairly say of Poirier that he had no standards to propose, but his standards were so broad, so unspecific, that they could be fitted to virtually any behavior, provided only it was performed with good intention. The effect was a profound relativizing: if ultimately the only standard was love, the door was open to almost any loving horror, the only criterion a moral intuition as unique and incommunicable as aesthetic sensibility.

Or so it seemed to Vincent. He had no difficulty accepting a lot the theologian said. He agreed with Poirier that the morality of the New Testament marked a sharp break with the Old. Christian morality had burrowed inward, abandoning the world of ritual, where moral transactions were external, in favor of the psychic sphere where the great dramas of deliberation and choice were enacted in nuanced obscurity. "The Christian view", Poirier announced one day, "makes morality an art form where everyone is a master from the start."

There, inevitably, Vincent parted company with him. Such thinking was unconscionable. Didn't the New Testament itself lay down specific moral norms? To be sure, Poirier replied, but these were culturally conditioned expressions of the only absolute norm: love. Today the relevant question wasn't what that passionate neurotic Paul of Tarsus thought charity to required of *him;* it was what one chose to understand charity as requiring of one in one's own life.

"How we *choose* to understand . . . ?" Vincent repeated one day in class. "Do you mean, Father, that morality isn't concerned with what we choose to do, but with what we choose to believe?"

Poirier gave his small, superior smile. "Really, Mr. Walsh, I believe you're getting the hang of it."

"Then why not choose to believe whatever suits me? If I choose to believe that murder is right, what's to say I'm wrong?"

"Intuition."

"Intuition?" Vincent examined the word suspiciously.

"If it makes you feel happier, consider it the equivalent of what we used to call natural law. Moral philosophers always come down finally to saying there are some things—the most important things of course—that can't be demonstrated because they're self-evident. Let's be candid. All moral choices are rooted in intuition. It's like an apprehension of the aesthetically satisfying. You don't need a syllogism to prove that a Rembrandt portrait is beautiful—you *see* that it is, and a syllogism couldn't prove it anyway. The flash of intuition comes first, and only later do we construct arguments to vindicate it."

Frowning, Vincent hung on doggedly. "Then how do you explain the fact that people disagree about what's good? According to what you say, shouldn't everyone see the same thing?"

"No more than everyone sees beauty in a Rembrandt—or a Rothko, or an African mask. The ideal is to be open to beauty wherever it exists. Or at least to grant to other people their right to see it where they can, even if a particular expression of it doesn't suit one's own taste. Similarly," Poirier stared deliberately at Vincent, "the ideal in morality is to take a lowercase 'c', catholic view and acknowledge that other people are perfectly capable of finding, and have a perfect *right* to find, the good in places where we miss it."

"Then anything at all is permitted."

"It would be better to say that nothing is excluded in principle. In theory the possibility always exists that someone will find good where it hasn't yet been found. We can't dictate other people's moral intuitions, Mr. Walsh, and we sin against freedom when we try."

Vincent's distress was evident. The rest of the class watched anxiously. "But, Father, this is a seminary. We're preparing to be priests, to hear people's confessions and counsel them, answer their questions and give them something to live by. How can what you're saying help me help a woman who wants to know whether it's better to leave a husband who drinks and plays around or stay with him for the sake of their kids?"

The priest gestured impatiently. "How does anything help her? And what do you imagine you have to say to her that will be of assistance? Tell her to do what she pleases—she'll be absolutely right in doing that, whatever it is. But don't think you should play God just because you're a priest. The best answer to people who come to you with questions is that *you* have no answer. Tell them that the answers they find for themselves are the only valid ones. Tell them that's what will please God and keep them out of hell—*if* that's what they want to be told, and usually it is. But for pity's sake, don't tell them that because you're a priest you know something they don't."

With those heated words Father Poirier dismissed the class. Several of the other students glanced apprehensively at Vincent in the hall, as if wishing to speak to him but uncertain what to say. Fred Connery drew him away quickly, and together the two friends walked down the long corridor.

"Lay off him, Vinnie", Fred said in a low, urgent tone. "It's getting tense in there."

Vincent's jaw jutted like his father's. Twin spots of crimson burning like coals in his cheeks, he said furiously, "I'm not looking for a fight, but I'm not going to duck one either. Somebody's got to call him on that stuff."

Stopping, Fred gripped his arm earnestly and swung Vincent

around to face him. "That isn't your job. What do you know about it anyway?"

Vincent shook off his friend's hand. "I know bullshit when I hear it."

"It doesn't bother the other guys."

"They must be sheep. It bothers me plenty."

"Vinnie, I swear to God, you're heading for bad trouble. If you keep pushing him, Poirier can't let it pass."

Vincent rounded on him. "*I* can't let it pass. Stuff your advice, Fred. I don't need it."

"Then get somebody else's advice, you screwball."

"Stuff it", Vincent repeated, striding away angrily.

After that things went rapidly from bad to worse. Righteously angry though he was, Vincent still tried to say no more than he felt he absolutely must; but now Poirier, incensed, took to needling him in class. "Does that way of putting it meet with your approval, Walsh?" he would inquire with mock deference after explaining a point. "Do I satisfy your standards of orthodoxy?" And Vincent, jaw thrust forward, scowled back defiance.

Soon, however, Vincent's attention was distracted by another festering situation. Word had begun to circulate among the students about the two first-year men, Evans and Maguire, whom Vincent and Fred Connery had encountered strolling on the seminary grounds that first evening back at school. Nothing specific was alleged; it was a matter more of sentences left unfinished, tones of voice, eyebrows raised meaningfully. "Evans and Maguire, you know . . . real palsy-walsy, aren't they? . . . I never thought we'd have *that* kind at St. John's."

"What are you driving at?" Vincent demanded of Fred one evening in the student recreation room after suffering a series of such vague hints with mounting impatience.

Fred gave him a glum look. "What do you think?"

"That stinks."

"Sure."

"How come no one has gone to the administration about it?"

"Who can be sure the administration doesn't know?"

"And hasn't done anything?"

Fred smiled cynically. "Maybe Father Poirier is handling the case."

Vincent took it all to prayer and spent as much time as he could in the chapel, asking for enlightenment. He saw no visions, heard no voices, but one thing became unmistakably clear: it was time for him to see Father Drake.

Like many seminarians before him, Vincent had chosen the old priest as his spiritual director. Among the changes instituted by Ronald Lacker, greeting students when they returned to school that year, was a new system under which each was assigned to a director. Father Drake's name wasn't among those designated for such work. Vincent's new man was a young liturgist on the faculty. They'd met once and discussed the merits of various translations of the psalms. He had no intention of repeating the experience.

One rainy, chilly afternoon in October he sought out Drake in his rooms, even more book laden and dowdy than Lackner's. The radiators beneath the streaming windows were groaning as if pained to be chafed back to life. Drake sat in a worn leather armchair, holding his cane in both hands and listening with his peculiar, crooked half-smile while his gaze remained fixed meditatively on the worn scrap of Oriental carpeting at his feet. Sitting opposite, Vincent spoke steadily in a low, earnest tone, all the while searching the old man's face for some sign of what he was thinking. None coming, Vincent persisted with his tale: his clashes with Poirier, the suspicions abroad concerning Evans and Maguire, his growing sense that something had gone deeply wrong at St. John's. Father Drake heard him out in silence and, even when he'd finished, remained impassive. Vincent waited, listening to the hissing and cracking of the radiators and the rattling of the windows in their frames (the wind was rising). Finally he said, "I haven't any more to tell you, Father."

Stirring slightly, Drake gave him an oblique glance. "They've begun to discourage students from seeing me", he remarked.

It caught the young man by surprise. "I know."

"Have you considered the possibility that they know what they're doing? I hear we live in new times. They call it renewal. I may not be the man you need, Vincent."

"I think you are."

"Because of your mother?"

"It's my choice."

"I feel affirmed", Drake said with mild mockery. "Those two you mentioned—what are their names?"

"Evans and Maguire."

"What do you personally know about them?"

"Nothing."

"Then you've merely brought me hearsay?"

"Yes."

Drake nodded. "Keep it to yourself. You've done enough in carrying it this far. Carry it no farther. And try to discourage gossip. I'll discuss the matter with the authorities. But the students shouldn't be whispering among themselves about this sort of thing. Is that clear?"

"Yes, Father."

The old priest blew his nose laboriously. Then: "About Father Poirier—what is it that *really* bothers you?"

"The harm he's doing to the others", Vincent said stoutly. "The confusion he's sowing."

"Do you know that for a fact?"

The question took him by surprise. He said stiffly, "You agree with what he says, Father?"

"Of course not. And do the students?"

"He's confusing them", Vincent repeated.

Drake frowned. "Don't think everything depends on you. If God wants something, he'll make it possible. If it isn't possible, you can be sure he isn't counting on your help."

Blushing, Vincent said, "I'm sorry." The words had stung. Seeking justification, he added, "Leaving *me* aside, aren't there reasons to be concerned about what's happening here?"

"Of course. This represents the new, approved thinking on how to run a seminary. St. John's will soon be a model of its kind. It will be a disaster."

Vincent looked grim. "How do you explain that, Father?"

"The soul is being systematically extracted from the enterprise. The new model is academic, pragmatic, efficient. It even talks a good game of caring and compassion. But it has no soul."

"Do you also agree with me about what Father Poirier is teaching?"

"Yes, I agree, Vincent. Bringing him here was an act of sublime irresponsibility. Are you pleased that I've said it?"

He shook his head. "I don't know what to do about it."

"That again!" Father Drake raised a crooked index finger from the cane head. "I'll tell you what to do—suffer."

"Suffer?"

"What else is a Christian to do about evil? He can flee it, join it, fight it by its own weapons—or suffer it. Suffering is the Christian response."

"That sounds like defeatism", Vincent protested.

Drake made a weary gesture. "Christ was defeated", he said. "So must we be."

"Forgive me, Father, but I'm not sure that's right."

The old man looked at him mildly. "The young never are. I have no other advice, Vincent.... Do you wish to go to confession?"

"Yes."

"Then be so good as to hand me the stole you'll find in the drawer of the table next to you."

Leaving several minutes later, Vincent closed the door behind him, turned to the right, and walked quickly away up the hall. At that moment Ronald Lackner, returning to his rooms, rounded the corner at the other end of the corridor. Squinting in the gloom, he recognized Vincent. Lackner shook his head. Still talking with Drake, he thought. Vincent, my lad, this will never do. We'll have to take you in hand soon, or there may not be room for you in this seminary much longer. With which thought Lackner, whistling, let himself into his apartment and helped himself to a drink.

XIII

"I suppose you're surprised to see me here, Bishop Frisch."

" 'Surprise' doesn't capture the fullness of my emotions, Father Kucharski."

Thudding against the windows of Frisch's study as if hurled with malevolent intent, great drops of rain (the same storm lashing St. John's on its hilltop that afternoon) streamed down the panes like wrathful tears. It was a long, dark, paneled room whose bookcases brimmed to the ceiling with bound volumes of the *Acta Apostolicae Sedis,* the *Annuario Pontificio,* the original Catholic Encyclopedia, the Fathers of the Church, and the approved theologians and spiritual writers.

The Bishop and the priest faced each other in leather armchairs. Frisch's arthritis had been bothering him more than usual that day, and he looked weary and out of sorts. Arthur was damp and disheveled, a puny rivulet of water from hairline to nose suggesting he'd been walking in the rain before braving Frisch; he was in a state of high tension.

"I felt I had to come, though," he went on, oblivious to the Bishop's bad humor. "You ordained me. I've always felt accountable to you for my priesthood."

"I can't deny having ordained you, Father, but one of the small advantages of retirement is that the consequences have been transferred from my shoulders to my successor's. You're accountable to *him.*"

"I want to make my confession to you."

Frisch blinked in surprise. "Frankly, I don't understand. . . . "

"Hear me out."

The Bishop nodded. "There's a stole in the upper drawer of the desk, on the left hand side. You would oblige me by getting it out."

Frisch watched the tall young priest with mingled dislike and apprehension. Over the years they had often enough been uncomfortably aware of each other, but they'd rarely met or spoken. Kucharski's telephoned plea yesterday for a meeting had struck Frisch as extraordinary, and their encounter so far verged on the surreal. Was Kucharski suffering some kind of breakdown? It seemed entirely possible.

Returning with the stole, Arthur handed it over and knelt. Slipping the purple silk around his neck, Frisch felt more in command of the situation. *"In nomine patris et filii . . . "*, he began. "Well?"

"Let me start," Arthur said in a low voice, "by repeating what I just said. I want to confess to *you.* I know where you stand. I know you aren't going to compromise on principle. I don't want cheap absolution, you see."

"How long has it been since your last confession?"

"Three years. I was on retreat . . . an attack of fervor. It passed."

Frisch shook his head in disapproval. "Priests who abandon confession are courting disaster."

Arthur rubbed his eyes with thumb and forefinger. "I have recently learned", he said with an effort, "that before I entered the seminary, I fathered a child."

The Bishop's expression did not change, but he leaned forward in a posture of tentative solicitude. Kucharski the rebellious priest evoked his wrath, but Kucharski the potential penitent called his own priesthood into play. "Go on."

"She didn't tell me about the pregnancy at the time. She wanted to leave me free to become a priest. It's only lately that I've met her again after all this time—her and my son. . . . The woman is Justin Walsh's daughter, Bishop."

Frisch grimaced. "That is an ugly joke", he pronounced.

"It's a fact. Maybe it's also a joke. If so, I didn't make it."

The old man leaned back and let his head rest against the chair. There was a long silence. Frisch recalled himself with an effort. "You had absolutely no knowledge, no suspicion even, before you were ordained?"

"It didn't enter my mind. . . . " But Arthur faltered. "Unless . . . perhaps I *did* suspect at heart. How can I know?"

"You can't. Only God knows perfectly. You should find that a motive for not neglecting penance. Go on."

"The question is, what should I do?"

"What *can* you do?" Frisch asked sharply. "There's no way of undoing this. Work hard at being a good priest."

"You don't understand", Arthur said in a flat voice. "I want to marry her."

Frisch sighed. "Out of guilt?"

"Partly. Also out of love."

"Or lust?"

"I'm human. But I want to be father to my son."

"I have no difficulty", the Bishop said slowly, "in understanding that. At first it's giving up sex that hurts the most, but later it's having given up children. Have you any reason to think, though, that she would marry you now?"

"I can't tell."

"Then my advice stands. You're merely indulging yourself in dreaming of marriage. Be a priest."

"However, I'm free to leave the priesthood."

"It would solve nothing."

"I don't believe I should ever have been a priest." Arthur paused, wiped his forehead with his hand, looked down. Then he brought out painfully, "There was also another girl before Megan. I was involved with her much longer. Finally I got disgusted. I turned to the priesthood in disgust, I think."

Frisch was shocked. "What made you even think of the priesthood in those circumstances?"

"My parents—they're dead now, thank God—they wanted it. I thought about it because they did. I put it out of my mind for a long time, but when things went sour between me and this other girl, it seemed like a good idea again. I thought I'd been converted, but I suppose I was just running away."

"None of this came out when you were preparing to enter the seminary?"

"I confessed it. Should I also have warned you against me? I wanted *in,* and I wasn't so dumb as to spoil my chances by saying more than I had to." Arthur looked apologetic. "I think you ordained me by mistake."

Frisch shook his head like a man absorbing a blow. "But you *were* ordained", he protested, "you *are* a priest. That may reflect some kind of error, yours and others'—even mine, since that's what you evidently want to hear. But acknowledging all that, you remain a priest now."

"I don't have to stay one."

"You can apply for laicization if you wish. You know that. I don't recommend it, Father, because I don't think your prospects of success are good outside the priesthood and because I therefore believe that if there's any hope for you, it's necessary that you stay a priest and concentrate on being a much better one than you've been up to now. I say that to be helpful, even though I do not personally consider you one of the adornments of the presbyterate in this diocese. But I can only express an opinion. It's a matter between you and your Ordinary. Consult him if you disagree with me."

"Of course, it's possible to leave without being laicized", Arthur mused. "In some ways I like that better. If I was ordained by mistake, I wonder if it even took. If not, I can walk away from the priesthood and it won't make any difference—not to God, not to me, not to anybody."

"Put that out of your mind", the Bishop exclaimed vehemently. "How many mistakes do you suppose you can pile on top of one another without suffering the consequences?"

"I'm suffering them now. I want to do something tangible for Megan and my son. Don't you see that I have a duty to them?"

"A higher duty than you comprehend."

"All you have to say is, 'Be a priest.' What does *that* do for Megan and Jon?"

Spares them having to endure you, Frisch thought; but he said, "Either you agree that the most important transactions are spiritual ones, Father, or you abandon faith."

"On that basis", Arthur said righteously, "the Church has blessed injustice and misery for centuries."

Bishop Frisch regarded him sadly. Impossible that he should have guessed all this; yet hadn't he had a duty to probe for problems? Kucharski had been presented for ordination with an equivocal evaluation from Jack Caldron: "Good scholastic record, for a lazy student; intelligent; potential leader; wishes to be ordained. Finds it hard to accept authority; sometimes questioning and rebellious; has difficulty with the discipline of interior life; could feel confined in the routine of priestly work." Unimpressive, but Frisch had seen worse; he accepted Kucharski as a priest of the diocese. But what to do with him—*for* him—now? Arthur's face was pale, sweat trickled into his foolish walrus moustache, and he was glaring defiantly.

"For better or worse," Frisch said, "you *are* a priest now, by the grace of God and your own bad judgment. I tell you what I'd tell any other priest in such circumstances: make the best of it. Do you imagine we're all models of sanctity and zeal—all except you? To judge from your writing—the 'Suburban Priest' for instance, oh yes, I read it with interest if not precisely appreciation, in case you wonder—you have no such illusions about your brother priests. And shall I tell them all to quit? Do mediocre priests make superior laymen? I advise you to stay put and find out what priests do, what they're good for."

"I want to help Megan and Jonathan", Arthur said doggedly.

"Yes, by inflicting yourself on them", Frisch agreed coldly. "But she's gotten along without you for a long time. Why not leave it at that?"

"Because *I* need *them.*"

The Bishop nodded. "That's closer to the truth. *You* need, *you* want. . . . I suppose that's what led you into the priesthood, and now apparently it's tempting you to get out. It's time you were ruled by something besides your own cravings."

"Be ruled by yours instead. . . . Is that what you're telling me?" Kucharski scowled. "You ran this diocese for years as if you owned it, and I guess it's hard to kick the habit. But I don't have to do as you tell me any more."

"I can't imagine, Father", Frisch said drily, "that you were ever terribly scrupulous about that. As for my telling you what to do, I was under the impression that you were making your confession to me."

"Then give me absolution," Kucharski said sullenly, "and let's have it over with."

The Bishop sighed again and shook his head; he was growing tired. "Absolve you of what?"

"My sins, of course."

"But what have you told me? That you had sexual relations

with two girls many years ago. But you said that's long since confessed, didn't you?"

"Yes", Arthur admitted uneasily.

"That you fathered a child and neglected your duty by entering the seminary. But you didn't know about the child, and your behavior toward Megan Walsh, based on what you did know, was arguably best for her."

The priest started to object, but Frisch raised a monitory hand. "Finally, you tell me that you feel a craving to resume that life, and that you're thinking of leaving the priesthood without being laicized. I can caution you against that, as I've done, but I can hardly absolve you unless I know that you've put the idea aside. Nor can I absolve you of anything else, supposing you have something else to tell me, as long as you continue to toy with the notion. That is elementary sacramental theology, Father."

"So you refuse me absolution?"

"You've told me nothing from which I *can* absolve you."

"I see." Taking out a handkerchief, Arthur dabbed his forehead and temples thoughtfully. "Fair enough. I asked for your view, and I got it. I won't take more of your time."

Bishop Frisch had a numbing sense of failure: he ought to have helped this man, and instead he'd driven him away. But what could he do except speak the truth? God help me, he thought, have I denied him absolution wrongfully, or have I only done what must be done if he's ever to turn honestly to you? "Arthur," he said, "what will you do?"

"Whatever I have to do", Arthur answered, rising with a crooked smile. "Whatever the hell that is."

Crouched like supplicants, in the oracle's cave, Megan and Gwyneth sat in the darkened control room before a large television monitor. Above it a bank of small monitors flashed repetitive, alienated images: a game show, a western, color bars, the Pirates at bat against the Orioles in the World Series. Megan's eyes strayed to the western—John Wayne's forbearance was running thin, promising an explosion of retributory violence—but mostly they were fixed on Gwyneth's face.

To all appearances she was reacting well. Occasionally she tossed a comment to Megan, but otherwise she devoured the screen, now smiling, now frowning at what she saw. Just now she was frowning as Dr. Walter Caldron held forth like an angry turkey.

"Where did you find *him?*" Gwyneth asked.

"I've known him since I was a little girl", Megan said. "He's a crony of my father's. *Very* big in the Knights of Mount Olivet."

"Why wasn't he wearing his Council of Trent tee shirt for the interview?"

"The seminary", Doctor Caldron was saying fiercely in reply to a question. "That's one example. St. John's was an admirable institution under Bishop Frisch. It turned out hundreds of loyal, dedicated priests—men who've served this diocese with distinction. And what has Bishop Farquhar done? Brought in a new rector, new faculty—radicals and dissenters, you understand. The place is in turmoil, the students are hopelessly confused. Tragic! And it didn't have to happen. It *wouldn't* have happened, if the Bishop hadn't caused it."

Then it was Ronald Lackner's turn. Squinting into the sun on the front lawn outside St. John's, Lackner looked like a man trying to look at ease.

"... time for a change", he was saying. "The seminary was preparing priests for the pre-Vatican II Church, but that isn't today's Church. We need priests for the Church of 1971."

"What changes have you introduced since taking over?"

"Some faculty changes, of course—any school needs new

blood, new ideas, now and then. But we're really aiming at a new spirit."

"Is Mass attendance compulsory?"

"I wouldn't *force* anybody to attend, not even a seminarian", Lackner said. "Maybe least of all a seminarian. We're forming open-minded, self-directed priests. You can't do that by regimentation."

"He's very credible", Gwyneth remarked.

They'd managed to corner a seminarian, a gawky youth who stared earnestly into the camera through aviator's glasses. A touch football game was underway in the background. "The students are happy here", he said. "St. John's is a nice place. I'm lucky to be here."

"Some people", pronounced the interviewer, a square-jawed Channel 6 veteran named Max Riemer, "say the seminary has gone downhill. What do you think?"

The young man looked embarrassed. "Well, I don't know. I mean, things change. It's still a nice place. Maybe nicer than it was. I mean, I'm really looking forward to being, you know, a priest. St. John's is pretty nice and all for that."

Gwyneth groaned.

Megan shrugged. "It's the only footage of a seminarian we have."

Hugh Boylan's cherubic face filled the screen. " . . . a change of course, going from Bishop Frisch to Bishop Farquhar. But I don't ask questions. A loyal Catholic doesn't. We take the bishop whom the Holy Father sends us in his wisdom."

"But having worked for both," Max Riemer insisted, "you're well situated to see the differences between them. Wasn't Bishop Frisch an ultraconservative?"

"I don't know about that", Boylan said. "He was very loyal to the Church."

"And Bishop Farquhar isn't?"

"Of course he is. Definitely. There's no question about it."

"Then the difference must be in their styles. Is that what you're saying, Bishop?"

Boylan appeared relieved at being shown a way out. "That's it", he agreed. "Bishop Farquhar is a very outgoing man. He's interested in seeing what can be changed."

"In the Catholic Church, how much *can* be changed?" Reimer, seated now in a studio, was bridging to the next interview. Looking earnestly into the camera, he said, "There are those who say it isn't the Ecumenical Council that's shaking up Wernersburgh, but only Bishop Farquhar. We asked parishioners outside Holy Comforter cathedral after Sunday Mass what *they* thought."

"I wish they'd bring back Latin", an elderly woman said morosely.

"This new bishop is okay with me", a young man announced jauntily. "I mean, the Church has been hassling people about birth control for years, but like now, you know, we don't hear so much about it. That's progress."

"Change?" a black woman repeated, open eyed. "Lord, why *do* they keep talking about change? I didn't join the Catholic Church so they could change it, and I don't think all this monkeying around makes Jesus happy either."

"What kind of monkeying around?"

"You listen to the sermons", she said. " 'Love, love, love'—that's all they got to say any more."

"Didn't Jesus say a lot about love?"

The woman frowned. "Had plenty to say about sin, too. If you want to talk about love, you *better* talk about sin, else you're going to have some kind of trouble on your hands. Now, Jesus knew that, but these priests—no way!"

Gwyneth said, "Not bad."

"We have with us in the studio", Reimer was saying, "the

former rector of St. John's Seminary, Monsignor John Caldron. We've asked him to shed some light on this question of continuity and change in the Church, and whether, as certain people claim, the diocese of Wernersburgh has come down too heavily on the side of change lately. What's your view of it, Monsignor?"

Smiling like a crocodile, Monsignor Caldron said, "A bit too far, a bit too fast. Of course I deeply respect Bishop Farquhar, but I'm afraid the diocese wasn't ready for him. This was a *very* stable place for years."

"What changes has he made?"

"Of course, there have been changes in personnel. . . . "

"One involved you."

"Obviously. And others as well. The diocesan paper is an example. But the biggest changes, I think, have been out there in the parishes."

"What's happened?"

"Some people think anything goes now. Not that it's the Bishop's fault, but he does like changes. Now every parish is doing what suits it, and in some the people are at each others' throats. People can't handle too much change. It's beginning to show."

"In other words, the Bishop ought to run a tighter ship?"

"Oh, I wouldn't presume to give him advice", Caldron said with relish. "But ships have been known to sink. Even with the *best* of captains at the helm."

Gwyneth shook her head. "Tough old bastard. Why let him run his mouth, Megan?"

"It's hard to find a priest who'll talk against Farquhar in public. They're afraid of him."

Oscar Dudley was being interviewed in his office. Round-faced and content with himself, he was the embodiment of bureaucracy certain not only that it ruled the world but also that the world was better off because of it.

"Bishop Farquhar is a superb communicator", he was saying. "Intelligent, articulate, open. It's a joy to work for him."

"However, Monsignor," Riemer said, "some say it's no joy having him in charge. They fault him as a communicator. They claim they get mixed signals from the chancery—people hardly know what he has in mind, where he wants the diocese to go. Any truth to that?"

Dudley smiled primly. "Give me an example."

"The Gwyneth Harley case." (In the control room, Gwyneth caught her breath.)

Monsignor Dudley frowned. "We were given bad advice."

"Then there's the *Catholic Truth.* People say it's turned around a hundred and eighty degrees in a year, extreme right to extreme left. Leaves them wondering what 'Catholic truth' is."

"The Bishop wants a newspaper that contributes to renewal."

"Maybe", Riemer said, assuming a reflective air, "when the Bishop speaks of renewal, people don't know what he's talking about."

"Give us time", Dudley said irritably. "They will."

Now it was Gwyneth's turn. Sitting in one of the *Globe-Herald* conference rooms, she looked sure of herself and angry. (She watched the screen intently during this segment, while Megan watched her just as closely.) "That's right," she was telling Riemer, "Farquhar pulled the job out from under me as soon as he got some flak. Not a classy performance."

"What conclusion do you draw?"

"The next time a bishop offers me a job, I should get it in writing."

Megan snickered.

" . . . want my serious opinion," Gwyneth on the screen was saying, "the whole episode tells a lot about Bishop Farquhar and his style."

"How would you define that?"

"He has vision; he has imagination; he knows what needs doing to bring Wernersburgh into the twentieth century. But he lacks determination. He backs down when he's challenged. That doesn't make for firm leadership."

Arthur Kucharski's moustached face flashed on the screen. He looked tired and tense. The interview had taken place in his office at the chancery; behind him on the wall hung a photograph, apparently autographed, of Bishop Farquhar.

"He doesn't believe in censorship", Kucharski was saying. "He wants a lively newspaper open to different points of view. He lets me publish what I want."

"Suppose you wanted to publish criticism of the Bishop?"

Kucharski gave the sickly smile of a man who realizes he's stepped into dog mess. "That would never occur to me."

"It's widely felt", Riemer said, "that one of the most notable changes in the last year has been the change in the *Catholic Truth.* It's gone from ultraconservative to very liberal. But the critics say it's no more open than it was. The ideology has changed, but it's as closed-minded as ever. Is that fair?"

"Look, I have a free hand around here." Kucharski gestured. "Farquhar doesn't tell me what to print. I mean, I'm the editor and I do the editing."

"You agree with the Bishop about most things?"

Arthur looked suspicious. "*Most* things."

"Maybe that's the problem", Riemer said firmly in conclusion.

Gwyneth chuckled. "That was nasty."

Megan looked uncomfortable. "Farquhar prides himself on being open to new ideas. We had to probe that", she said defensively.

"And embarrassed Arthur doing it." Gwyneth grinned. "Great!"

Other segments followed. Several priests defended the Bishop. Lay people volunteered opinions pro and con. Scenes of an experimental Mass in a suburban parish followed: a woman in flowing robes swayed up the center aisle in liturgical dance, to the accompaniment of "Lucy in the Sky with Diamonds", the congregation tore chunks from loaves of French bread and quaffed wine from crystal goblets at communion, then were handed balloons to carry back to the pews. Neither depraved nor edifying, it was a performance that no one, having seen it once, would much care to see again.

A long interview with Bishop Farquhar brought the series to a conclusion. Looking boyish and earnest, he sat at his desk fielding questions with a pained smile.

" . . . not happy with all the changes in the diocese," he was saying, "but that's inevitable. It had been a long time since *anything* changed in Wernersburgh. Some people had grown suspicious of change."

"You think Bishop Frisch let the diocese stagnate?"

Farquhar winced. "I have great respect for Bishop Frisch. He was in charge here for a long time, and he ran the diocese well. But, by the time I arrived, some changes were definitely needed."

"Such as?"

"Vatican II called for the renewal of the Church. I want that in Wernersburgh."

"What specific areas have you been concentrating on?"

"I'm proud of what's been accomplished at St. John Vianney's. I hope to turn our seminary into a model, and I think we have the team to do that. How we train our priests is crucial to the future of the Church."

"Some people say the teaching at the seminary isn't orthodox any more."

"This constant harping on what's 'orthodox'", Farquhar said irritably, "is not a healthy sign. There are people who want to use what they call orthodoxy to block any change they don't like. And it pains me to point out that it's presumptuous for Catholics to lecture their bishops on what's orthodox and what isn't."

"Where else do you think you've been successful in bringing about renewal?"

Bishop Farquhar said promptly, "The *Catholic Truth* isn't what it used to be."

Max Riemer smiled patronizingly. "Some Catholics would say, that's become the motto of the diocese. Whereas others feel you haven't moved far enough and fast enough, or you have backed off when challenged. "What's your long range vision for the Church, Bishop? If you had your druthers, what would you really hope to accomplish?"

"I want to turn this local church into a real Christian community. I want innovation and ongoing renewal to become normal elements of our life together as a pilgrim people. I want the differences that divide us to become creative catalysts for the dialogue that leads to change. I—"

"How willing to change are *you?*"

Farquhar blinked. "I . . . change is essential. Isn't that what renewal is all about?"

"Thank you, Bishop Farquhar", Riemer said crisply, "for sharing your thoughts with us."

"Now", Megan told Gwyneth, "comes Max's summing-up."

Riemer, looking stalwart, stood on the cathedral steps, staring into the camera like a physician delivering bad news to a patient. "A year ago," he intoned liturgically, "Bishop Ambrose Farquhar was chosen by the Pope to head the diocese of Wernersburgh. Since then the changes in the lives of Catholics here have been numerous and controversial. Nuns have given up control of a college they ran for many years. People have come and gone in the chancery. The seminary has been shaken up, reoriented. The Catholic newspaper bears no resemblance to its former self. And out in the parishes the word has gone around that avant-garde liturgies are acceptable, perhaps even encouraged. For Bishop Farquhar wants to renew the Church, and, practically speaking, renewal seems to mean change.

"Not everybody likes it. In the last year the diocese has often been in turmoil and tension. A few people, mainly those who work for him, say the Bishop is doing just the right thing. Others think he should be moving farther faster. And others—a vocal, if not large group—think his policies have been a disaster and openly question his judgment, if not his orthodoxy. They believe the diocese's golden days ended a year ago, when Bishop Peter Frisch retired.

"We tried to talk to Frisch to get his view, but he declined. There's a strong tradition in the Church that bishops don't second-guess their successors. At least not in public. We regret not being able to interview Bishop Frisch, but, considering the readiness of others to discuss the situation, it's likely that his viewpoint is represented somewhere in all we've heard. For if one thing is true about the diocese of Wernersburgh these days, it's that people aren't shy about speaking their minds.

"Where is the Church headed, and how does the Bishop see the future? That isn't easy to find out. When he talks about renewal, he seems to be endorsing a process, with no clear notion of what it leads to. Which may account for some of the apparent contradictions in his record. He's an open-minded man who dismissed his newly hired communications director for her views on abortion; a believer in dialogue who's said to be isolated, hard to reach, and possibly out of touch; a compassionate individual who's been cold-blooded about taking the old away from people and making them accept the new. Few Catholics in Wernersburgh are indifferent to Bishop Farquhar, but very few seem certain what he's up to, and few, frankly, appear to trust him much.

"What's happening in Wernersburgh may be part of the larger picture of what's happening everywhere in the Catholic Church today. Change, controversy, turmoil, tension—renewal. Once Wernersburgh lagged behind, but under Ambrose Farquhar that's changed. Give the man credit. He has his eye on the future. But in a year of trying, he and the people he wants to lead haven't been able to agree on what that future ought to be. Good night."

The camera lingered on Riemer's solemn face until the screen went blank.

"Well?" Megan asked.

"If I were Farquhar, I wouldn't be pleased." Gwyneth smiled complacently.

"Were we fair?"

"Sure. Everybody has his say. People can draw their own conclusions."

"What about Kucharski?" Megan asked uneasily. "He doesn't come off very well, does he?"

"Weak, defensive. But that's Arthur."

Megan looked troubled. "It's just as you said, we wanted to let him and the rest speak for themselves."

"And they did. You've got a bombshell here, Megan. It's going to blow the diocese wide open."

Gwyneth's choice of metaphors was vulgar, Megan decided as she drove to her parents'. It had something to do with the trade. Journalism was coarsening: superficial glances passed for penetrating insights; cliches took the place of wit. Gwyneth depressed her—not just as a warning of what she might become, but as a reflection of what, in essence, she already was. And if Gwyneth's example weren't bad enough, there was always her father's, confronting her with the epitome of self-righteous journalism—she could become equally self-righteous, if she wasn't careful.

Rain had begun toward sundown, slowing the rush hour traffic to a turgid ooze. Waiting impatiently for the cars ahead to move while the windshield wipers beat out their monotonous rhythm, Megan smoked steadily. Gwyneth's words of praise had made her anxious.

Professionally speaking, of course, the series was a solid piece of work. The station management had already signaled appreciation by deciding to run it for five successive weekdays on both the early and late evening local news. Her colleagues were looking at her with fresh respect. Megan Walsh, news director? It could happen.

So what was bugging her? "Blockbuster", "bombshell", "blow the diocese wide open"—Megan's ambition craved something nobler than tawdry success.

But there was more to it than that. She was worried about the effect the series might have. Suppose it turned people against Farquhar? Who were she and Channel 6 to pronounce judgment on him? Who gave *anyone* that right? She didn't even know the man, had no settled opinion of him. Yet journalists made judgments all the time—true or false, important or trivial, good or bad—and these formed a kind of moral placenta through which harsh and intractable shards of actuality were strained into a pure distillate that nourished the public's presumably embryonic conscience. That made journalists rather godlike, didn't it? And having criticized others for playing God, Megan didn't care for the thought that she'd now assumed the role.

What *had* she meant to do in the series? Tell an honest story, she supposed . . . at least, as much of one as could be told in five segments under five minutes each. That, depending on how you looked at it, compelled the journalist either to get immediately to the heart of the story (a virtue) or to reduce complexity to comic book terms (an unspeakable vice). Had she then merely settled for a "professional" job of lively reporting, skewering a few vulnerable souls with leading questions and selective editing?

Even Max Riemer, a hack at heart, had voiced dismay at the questions she was feeding him (though he'd settled down when it became clear that they produced effective television journalism). "Jesus, Megan," he'd protested, "I don't feel comfortable cutting people up on the air."

"It's the name of the game, Max."

"Not *my* game, dear one. The viewers aren't used to seeing friendly Max play tough guy."

"We're trying to dig out the truth", Megan said irritably. "Or do you just want to do a puff piece for Farquhar?"

He shrugged. "Have it your way, kid. Maybe the public will like seeing another side to me. But I'm not keen on fronting for a producer who's working off a grudge."

She'd bridled at the time, of course, but was it true? And if so, toward whom did she carry a grudge? Farquhar was the focal point—the target, some would say—but that was unavoidable: if you were going to profile a bishop's first year on the job, on whom else would you concentrate? Still, she might easily have treated him more gently, put him in a better light. Admit it then: she was angry at this man she'd never met, to the extent of dragging his reputation through the mud twice nightly for five nights running. It was only returning to him what he'd done to others (Gwyneth and her father came to mind) only giving him a taste of his own medicine.

How odd, Megan thought sourly, that I should become Daddy's avenger. But fair's fair: that bloody newspaper was his life, and Farquhar not only took it away from him, he humiliated him in the process. Let him be humiliated, too!

Of course, humiliating Farquhar in the matter of the newspaper also meant humiliating Arthur. God, doesn't he have it coming though? Arthur went tramping recklessly through other people's lives, seeking his pleasure without regard for anybody else. The series was a chance to pay him back. Finally he had to accept responsibility for something that wasn't turning out well. Let him share the experience of being disappointed by dreams that *do* come true.

Even as she thought it, Megan was aware of her familiar ambivalence toward Kucharski. She'd always been responsive to his fecklessness, his disorder, his weakness and confusion; the infantile selfishness of the man called out to some maternal capacity for indulgence. Arthur's wants were a vacuum she felt drawn to fill, as much now as ever.

As much now: Megan froze at that, and almost rammed the car in front of her as it braked for a stop sign. "As much now", she repeated, half aloud. His importunings still worked on her, and for the same reasons. Only now, he wanted her to marry him. Could she seriously mean to say yes?

Furious horns bleated behind her. Megan, awakened with a start and gunned the little car through the intersection. Damn Arthur Kucharski! It had always been this way: Arthur insisting that she concern herself with him instead of what was properly hers. Yet wasn't that what she wanted him to do? Wasn't it precisely their interlocking needs that made them a match? Storybook romances were fantasies. In the real world, two people's needs flowed so thoroughly together that, in the end, there was no separating them and no saying who gave and who received. That was how it was with her and Arthur.

At first the realization numbed her, and then she felt a fierce resentment, not just against Kucharski, but against God. All right, she thought, Arthur and I might have married years ago. But don't pretend you told us, and we disobeyed. You let him think *you* wanted him. Okay, he was rationalizing about becoming a priest, but at least you let him get away with it. Do you know what that looks like to me? It looks as if you *did* want him, or at least you wanted to mess us up. I don't know which, but it really doesn't matter to me. Even if people cared to do your will, they couldn't, because you can't be bothered to tell them what it is. Now do you wonder why so few even try?

Look at the extremes in this diocese, Megan thought: from Ambrose Farquhar to my father. And each of them imagines that he does your will—which, if true, could only mean that you can't make up your mind, you want contradictory things, and, since it isn't true, can only mean you don't really care. Is that the secret—you are indifferent? God isn't dead, he's merely lost interest?

Megan shook her head violently. This wasn't what she needed to think about. Her problem was what to *do.* It struck her suddenly that she was on her way to see her mother. Eleanor's religiosity was off-putting, but beneath it lay reliable instincts. Megan laughed aloud. She would confide in her mother. Daughters had done that from time immemorial. The wisdom of the ages. God had nothing to tell her; perhaps her mother did.

"Not for anything in the world or for the love of any created thing", Eleanor read, "is evil to be done. But sometimes, for the need and comfort of our neighbor, a good deed may be deferred or turned into another good deed. Thereby the good deed is not destroyed, but is changed into better."

How helpful if they all, Justin and Bishop Farquhar and all the rest, would read that and take it to heart. The *Imitation* was out of vogue, she'd heard priests disparage it and even warn against its use, but she found it full of common sense. As here: the trouble in the diocese was that nobody would defer or put aside what he judged a good deed, in favor of another better suited to his neighbor's need. Hence conflict; hence also—a point the *Imitation* itself might well have made—even the good deeds that were done tended to become the evil that ought never to be done. If only they would *see:* goodness, happiness, fulfillment lay in *not* seeking one's own will, and most especially not under the guise of seeking God's.

Turning back a page, she considered another passage in the little book: "Many persons, through a secret love that they have for themselves, work indiscreetly according to their own will and not according to the will of God, yet they do not know it" (which was extremely fortunate; not knowing was one of his greatest favors, it excused so much). "But if you cling more to your own will or to your own reason than to the humble obedience of Jesus Christ, it will be long before you are a man illumined by grace."

She sat at the desk in Justin's study. The hard rain rattled against the windows. Downstairs Jonathan, fed and sleepy, was watching television. Eleanor, waiting for Megan to arrive and knowing Justin would be late (he was putting the paper to bed at the printer's), had stolen a few moments, as she often did in the course of a day, to open her mind to God. Frequently, she had the experience of commencing one of these sessions in one frame of mind—with a question, a problem, a complaint—and ending in another: the question answered, the difficulty resolved. Then she had no doubt that God had spoken to her.

That seemed exceptionally generous of him, considering how much she still clung to her own will. Father Drake had told her often that no one should trust himself, and her experience supported that. Even her best motives she found to be shot through with self-seeking, like good water clouded by silt. It took time to know oneself. Which was why, disinclination aside, so few people made the effort. For her part Eleanor was sure she'd only scratched the surface.

And what of the others? What of Justin? Self-knowledge was conspicuously not his line. (She smiled fondly at the thought.) He could afford to be oblivious because he was basically sound—capable of blunders, but no more capable than a child of true malice. His rhetoric was fierce, but with him aggressiveness and vengefulness went no deeper than that—rhetoric. Justin found it hard to forgive those who hurt him, but even harder to hurt them in return. You'll agree, won't you, she thought, pausing to address her invisible interlocutor directly, that he should be rewarded for that? Oh yes—I, too, wish he were more forgiving; but see how he holds back from injuring even those he won't forgive: surely that must count for a great deal? Surely it matters that, although she broke his heart, he hasn't tried to break Megan's?

Megan was a more troubling case. Unlike her father, she practiced introspection, understood what drove her. Great fears and great hopes alike were warranted with such people; it was certain they'd live up to one or the other. Megan frightened Eleanor in a way Justin didn't, couldn't, begin to match.

It was clear that lately she'd been carrying some great burden; Eleanor knew her daughter too well to miss the telltale signs—the perpetual frown, the heavy smoking, the abstracted air, as if she were grappling with an intractable question. Was it something about this television series on the diocese? Something else? Eleanor could only wait, confident Megan would tell her in her own good time and way. But that was also a hard thing about having children grow up: loving them so much, wanting still to know every corner of their lives as you had when they were small, you had to settle instead for the occasional scraps of information they grudgingly conceded, as if afraid that telling too much would make them again as dependent as they'd been at five and six—which left so much untold, unfilled in. Whole mysterious continents in their lives were as frustratingly blank to a parent as the vacant white spaces signifying unexplored regions on an old map.

Almost unconsciously, she turned the pages of the little book until she found what she wanted. "We might have much peace if we would not meddle with other men's sayings and doings that do not concern us." Yes, of course that was true; but did it apply in this case? "do not concern us"—and is Megan's life no concern of mine? But it is my concern—you know that perfectly well—and I can't believe you want it otherwise. Unless of course your point is that she's more your child than mine, that you understand her perfectly even though I don't, that you know exactly what she needs and how to provide it, and the only thing you wish of me in her regard is to admit I can't begin to match your mothering of her. And if that's it, it's asking a lot, you know—to spend half a lifetime learning to do something and the other half unlearning it. It's hard to become a parent, but even harder to stop being one when you have the habit.

And even if I didn't worry about Megan, Eleanor thought, there would still be Vinnie. Something was happening there, too, and although she didn't know the details, it troubled her. He'd been anxious and tense during his last few calls home, evidently holding back something that he didn't care to talk about. Changes at the seminary—no doubt that was it. Justin was always fulminating against what was going on out there, whatever that might be, and even Father Drake dropped hints of untoward happenings. But what did all that have to do with Vinnie? He was only half a year away from ordination. Soon after the first of the year he'd be a deacon. They could stand St. John's on its head, and it would make no real difference to him in the few months that remained. Then what was troubling him? She prayed for serenity, abnegation, detachment. But as with Megan, so with Vinnie, her ignorance of his situation and incapacity for rendering help only inflamed her concern.

She found it hard to surrender her will to God's, not just the doing of it—though God knows that was difficult enough, next to impossible if the truth were told—but even in principle the exercise seemed risky, for it could become a mask for idleness, torpor, sheer spiritual sloth. Embracing God's will could turn out to mean doing nothing at all, relaxing in a sanctimonious glow of Quietist self-congratulation. Precisely the attraction that held for her caused Eleanor to feel especially troubled, lest in some way she neglect her duty to Megan, Vinnie, or Justin. God, she prayed, if there is something I can do, help me know what it is and do it. Don't let me shirk my duty on the excuse that I'm putting my will aside.

The door opened. It was Megan, raincoated and dripping. Eleanor smiled. "I didn't hear the front door. Come in."

Megan glanced disgustedly at the book open near her mother's hand. "Too lost in your prayers, I suppose. What's this one, Mother?" Tossing her coat over a chair, she picked up the *Imitation* and flipped the pages. "'... if he can come to a perfect and full contempt and despising of himself, then he will have a full abundance of rest and peace in joy everlasting, according to the measure of his gift.' Is that *all* it takes? Despise yourself and be at peace? There must be a lot of peaceful people in the world."

"It means, despise yourself *and* cling to God", Eleanor said.

"There's always a catch." Megan dropped the book on the desk. "Daddy's late?"

"I don't expect him until eight."

"Good. I need to talk."

Megan looked determined, almost grim. Eleanor felt mingled fear and elation in the certainty that her prayer was being answered. "Of course", she said quietly.

"Jon's good for hours with the tube", Megan observed. She took an ashtray from the desk and, settling into the rocking chair that Justin used, lit a cigarette. Frowning at the amber glass receptacle, Megan said, "I gave this to Daddy for his birthday when I was in the sixth grade. Does he still use it?"

"Of course."

"I wonder sometimes what it would take really to please him." Her manner was speculative, detached.

"It would please your father if you were reconciled with the Church. It would please me, too." Ought she to speak of herself? God grant me the right words, she thought.

Megan smiled but at least she didn't laugh: laughter would have been more than Eleanor could have borne just then. "I'm afraid I can't give you that. I've made Jon a Catholic. You have to settle for that."

"Megan, I've never understood . . . " Eleanor spread her hands in bafflement. "Don't you *believe?*"

"Every word of it. And I find it offensive."

"How can you say that?"

" 'God is love.' Very well. Only there seems to have been an exception in my case—mine, and several billion others. Did God love the Jews at Auschwitz?"

"He must have."

She crushed out the cigarette and lit another. "Then I'd rather not be loved like that. But that's an extreme case. Take mine then. I'm supposed to love God because he loves me, but I don't see the evidence for it. Maybe somehow it's true—I can't absolutely prove otherwise—but if I can't *see* the truth of it, how am I supposed to respond? 'As far as I can tell, God despises me, but I love him just the same'? I couldn't say that with a straight face. I *don't* love God, because even if by some chance he loves me, he's neglected to let me know. Sorry, Mother. I don't mean to offend you."

"You don't." Oddly, that was true. The words were those of a hurt and angry child, but they lacked malice. She found that hopeful.

"Anyway," Megan was saying, "I've done my bit for God—Jon, I mean. Won't God give me Brownie points for that?"

"There's a great deal else that Jon needs."

"He's getting older of course", Megan acknowledged ruefully. "Birthday in a couple of weeks, you remember?"

"Yes. Shall we have the party here?"

"If you aren't tired of us."

"You know I'm not."

"In fact, you want what you think is best for us, don't you? A husband for me, a father for Jonathan. That would take care of everything."

"It would take care of a great deal, if he were the right person."

"Define 'right'."

Eleanor smiled gently. "Someone you love."

Megan gave her an ironic look. "I doubt that I can pull that off. But you may get part of your wish anyway."

Eleanor stared incredulously. "What do you mean?"

"You can almost hear the wedding bells, can't you?"

"I don't care about all that."

"Sorry. Nerves." Again she went through the ritual of crushing one cigarette and lighting another; the lighter's flame wavered as Megan held it to her face. Eleanor waited in silence. After a while, Megan said in a low voice, "Would you like to know who Jon's father is?"

Eleanor drew in her breath sharply. "If you've decided that it's for the best."

"You won't tell *him?*"

"No."

"Arthur Kucharski."

Eleanor was conscious of the muted thudding of rain against the windows, the faint whirring of the electric clock on Justin's desk, the creak of the rocking chair in which her daughter, not looking at her, sat smoking furiously.

"Did you hear me?" Megan demanded in vexation.

"Yes."

"What do you make of that?" She laughed harshly. "I have to hand it to God—he's a terrific joker. Does your book cover that?"

Eleanor put her finger tips to her temples. "Please . . . I'm trying to take this in."

More gently, Megan said, "Arthur isn't the devil. He didn't know when I got pregnant. I was planning to tell him, but he beat me to it—announced he was going in the priesthood, I mean."

"So you didn't tell him at all."

"I didn't want to compete with God."

Eleanor extended her hand.

Ignoring it, Megan went on quickly. "And of course Arthur hadn't any idea that Daddy was my father. I never told him that either. When he took the job at the *Catholic Truth* we hadn't seen each other in eight years, and I suppose he'd almost forgotten I existed. He certainly had every reason to *want* to forget. He never dreamed there was a connection between Justin Walsh and me."

"And what did you know of *him?*"

"I've followed Arthur's career for a long time, but it never occurred to me that he'd end up editing the newspaper. Bishop Farquhar is full of surprises."

"When did he find out?"

"At that awful dinner party of yours. Why did you arrange something so dreadful, Mother?"

"I thought it might make a difference between your father and . . . Arthur."

"Well, it's done *that,* hasn't it?"

Eleanor shook her head. "It must have been a shock for him."

"How like you—sympathy to spare for everybody. Even for the man who walked out on your pregnant daughter and made life miserable for your husband."

"You said yourself that he didn't know."

"And if he *had,* would he have done the gallant thing?" Megan shrugged. "Maybe so, maybe not."

"What does he want to do now?"

"Marry me."

"And you?"

"Perhaps I want to marry him."

"For Jon's sake?"

"And Arthur's. And mine. . . . What do you think?"

"How do you feel toward him?"

Megan looked at her obliquely. "The very idea doesn't offend you?"

"Because he's a priest? Do me credit, Megan, just because I pray, it doesn't follow that I'm simple-minded. Perhaps his obligation to you and Jon comes before his obligation to the priesthood. It isn't for me to say. But if you did marry. . . ." Eleanor didn't attempt to finish but let it indicate her willingness to accept the possibility.

"What about Daddy?"

"He'd take it hard at first. But ultimately? I can't tell you."

"Take what?" Jonathan asked, confronting them from the doorway.

Megan sprang up. "How long have you been there?" she demanded.

The boy was frightened by her vehemence. "I don't know. I want to leave. I'm getting tired." He yawned, as if to demonstrate the truth of what he said.

Megan tousled his blond hair in relief. "We'd better be going", she told her mother.

Eleanor nodded. Following them down the stairs to the front hall, she said, "I'll think about what we discussed. It's hard to take in at first."

"But in principle . . . ?"

Eleanor paused on the bottom step, frowning. "In principle . . . " she repeated. "I believe in setting right what's been set wrong. But not by doing worse. In this case . . . it's hard for me to say."

Megan's grin was slightly malicious. "And your book doesn't shed any light on the question?"

" 'Wherefore, it is a vain thing to trust in man' ", Eleanor quoted from memory, " 'for the certain trust and help of righteous men is only in You.' What other light would you expect?"

XIV

Whispering like a conspirator, the wind hissed around the window frames of Ronald Lackner's room and rattled the panes. Lackner and Poirier ignored it. It was Monday night: they were absorbed in the first segment of the series.

"St. John's was an admirable institution under Bishop Frisch", Doctor Caldron was saying on the screen. The set was badly adjusted; he looked green.

"Who's that old bird?" asked Poirier.

"Walter Caldron. Cardiologist. He's Jack Caldron's brother and a big conservative pain in the ass."

". . . men who've served this diocese with distinction. And what has Bishop Farquhar done with St. John's? Brought in a new rector, new faculty—radicals and dissenters, you understand."

Poirier said, "He's not just pretending to be angry, is he?"

"I'm sure he's furious."

Now Lackner himself appeared on the screen, the seminary looming behind him.

"You don't look very happy, Ronald."

"I wasn't. That man Riemer *wanted* to put me on the defensive."

". . . more intellectual openness," Lackner's image was saying, "more recognition that truth is large and complex, and nobody's got it all."

"Excellent", Poirier murmured.

Presently Riemer was on the screen. "St. John's is only one example of the change that has swept the diocese of Wernersburgh since Ambrose Farquhar arrived. Some like it, some consider it a disaster, many believe it's too early to draw conclusions. We'll be looking at other elements in the growing controversy between liberals and conservatives throughout the week as we continue this series on 'The Church Today: Renewal or Collapse?' "

A beer commercial came on. Lackner rose and turned off the set. "Well?"

"They treated you more gently than I expected."

"You're jaded, Bruce. By local standards that was inflammatory."

The moral theologian smiled patronizingly. "The locals inflame easily."

The telephone rang. Father Lackner answered. "Yes, Bishop", he said, giving Poirier a meaningful glance. "Yes, Bruce Poirier and I were watching it. . . . Mixed feelings? That's just how we saw it."

Poirier shook his head with owlish disapproval. He'd come to Wernersburgh for a rest, and here was another controversy instead. It was reduced of course to the local scale; and yet, people here seemed to relish combat, as if, long denied the joys of internecine warfare while Catholics elsewhere were going at it with unprecedented fury, they wanted now to make up for lost time. Poirier had tilted with Ottaviani, served as second to Küng: Wernersburgh's quarrels were trifling by comparison, but there was no doubting their bloodthirstiness.

" . . . appreciate your support", Lackner was telling the Bishop on the phone. "I don't believe we came off badly. Of course I regret all that talk of controversy in the diocese. I suppose they felt they had to make a show."

He paused, listened, grimaced. "Yes, Vincent Walsh. It's kind of you to see him, Bishop. Painful situation. No capacity for renewal. Sad in one so young. . . . Certainly. The father's influence. *Very* strong. I hate to recommend dismissal this late in the game, but it's inconceivable that he should be a priest of this diocese as things stand now. If you think differently, of course. . . . "

Lackner listened, satisfied with what he was hearing. "It's good of you to say that, Bishop. And good of you to call. We can count on having you out here again soon? . . . Excellent. Good night." Hanging up, he refilled and lighted his pipe, and came whistling back to Poirier.

"The Walsh case . . . " Poirier said.

"Farquhar's seeing him next week. That should be the end of it."

The theologian nodded. "He'd never fit in under Farquhar."

"This trouble about Evans and Maguire was the last straw. Not that I would have let them stay. But Vincent is telling people Paul Drake had to prod me to act."

"Ugly."

"At least it's over now", Lackner said. "Or it will be once Bishop Farquhar sees him."

"We take the bishop whom the Holy Father sends us in his wisdom, and that's it", Bishop Boylan was pronouncing from the television screen. "Otherwise you're second-guessing the Holy Spirit."

"Hughie," Bishop Frisch advised him drily, "you allow too little room for the human factor."

They were seated before the large set in Frisch's study. Boylan's attention was riveted to the screen. "I hated every moment of the interview", he said without turning his eyes away.

"With good reason, apparently."

Now the camera was on the angry black woman on the steps of the cathedral. ". . . don't think all this monkeying around makes Jesus happy either."

"Spoken like an orthodox theologian, madam", Frisch observed.

Boylan said, "It's a cheap shot at Farquhar to invite people to sound off like that."

Frisch glanced at him in surprise, but all he said was, "Here's Jack Caldron now. I expect that *he'll* be fair."

"A bit too far, a bit too fast", Monsignor Caldron was telling Max Riemer with a saturnine smile. ". . . a very stable place for years."

Frisch sipped his Scotch and soda. "I'd call that a fair assessment, wouldn't you?"

"What good does it do?"

". . . ships have been known to sink . . . even with the *best* of captains. . . . "

"I can't believe it helps", Boylan repeated.

"It's over. Turn the television off and freshen your drink."

Boylan did both. Frisch watched him curiously. "Well?"

"It's bound to stir things up."

"Things *are* stirred up. More men leaving the priesthood than you can shake a stick at . . . the religious up in arms. And aren't several parishes ready to blow sky-high?"

The auxiliary bishop sighed. "Conservative pastor feuding with liberal associates at St. Martha's; people demanding changes and priests resisting them at St. Bartholomew's; priests demanding and people resisting at St. Luke's; and at St. Dorothy's, the sisters in the school are threatening a strike if they don't get a better contract from the parish council."

"And you think such things should be passed over in silence, Hughie?"

"Poor Ambrose!"

"Your loyalty is commendable, considering how he's treated you."

Bishop Boylan smiled almost shyly. "I'm getting Bridge City", he said, naming a rural diocese in the middle of the state, whose bishop had retired two months earlier.

Frisch's eyes widened, then he grinned. "Congratulations, Hughie. I wish I could have done as much for you."

"You aimed too high. At Wernersburgh, I mean."

"And Farquhar got you Bridge City?"

"He supported me with Archbishop Gatti. And Gatti sold the Apostolic Delegate."

Frisch nodded. He said, still smiling. "They bought you off."

Boylan winced. "I wish you hadn't said that, Peter."

"Another link with the past severed. A link with me. Another step toward making the diocese entirely his—and look at the results! Look at this wretched television series. Look at the defections! Two more priests last month!"

Boylan nodded sadly. "Len Haggerty and Harry Metz."

"Haggerty ordained ten years, Metz a twenty-year man. What's the total in the last year?"

"Seventeen."

"That's a hemorrhage for Wernersburgh."

"It's happening everywhere."

"Haggerty and Metz didn't quit when *I* was in charge—few priests did—and they wouldn't quit now, if the diocese were being run on sound principles."

Bishop Boylan shook his head in discouragement. "We can't tell."

But Frisch wasn't listening. "Farquhar's idea of renewal has bewildered the priests of this diocese", he declaimed. "The goals are uncertain and the future is unknowable. Before, a priest's job was to keep people out of hell and get them into heaven. Now his highest duty is to attend an endless parish council meeting. No wonder they quit!"

Boylan didn't answer for a long time, and when he did it was only to say, "I'm sorry."

Morosely, Frisch rattled the ice in the bottom of his glass. "Enjoy Bridge City, Hughie. You deserve it. You'll do well there. But promise me you won't make it another Wernersburgh according to the Farquhar model."

"I don't think you're going to like your interview", Megan said.

"I didn't at the time", Arthur replied. "Why should I now?"

They were watching the news in Megan's office. It was Wednesday. Max Riemer was speaking into the camera.

". . . a year of change and controversy . . . a microcosm of the Catholic Church everywhere, struggling to find, or retain, its identity . . . closest collaborator is Monsignor Oscar Dudley, the Vicar General of the diocese. We asked him if he thought the Bishop is getting his message across—and what that message is."

"I'm sick of Dudley", Arthur volunteered.

" . . . intelligent, articulate, open. It's a joy to work for him", Dudley was saying.

Megan asked, "Isn't that your line, too?"

"Sure, but Oscar's the king of the ass kissers."

The interview continued; Arthur brightened as Monsignor Dudley faltered and grew irritated. When it was over he applauded. "You nailed him!"

Now Gwyneth was on. Arthur frowned. "The woman scorned?"

"Don't you think she got a raw deal?"

"From your father."

"*He* was the only one of you with the brains and the guts to do his job!"

" . . . vision . . . imagination . . . knows what needs doing", Gwyneth was saying. "But he lacks determination. He backs down when he's challenged. That doesn't make for firm leadership."

Arthur said, "She's on target."

"You're next", Megan warned him.

When it was over, he leaned back and lighted a cigarette. "Couldn't you have skipped that?"

"You and the paper have been a big part of Bishop Farquhar's first year."

"I made an ass of myself."

Megan shrugged. "If anybody remembers anything from this series, it will concern Farquhar."

He looked curiously at her. "Are you really out to get him", he asked, "on account of Justin?"

Rising, Megan turned off the television set. "On account of the truth. A year ago Farquhar was the great white hope. He's changed a lot of things since then, but people disagree on whether it's for the better. . . . Come on, I'll take you to dinner, Father."

They drove in separate cars to Palmieri's. It was crowded, but they got a corner table. Over drinks she said bluntly, "Arthur, you need to know this. I told my mother."

He blinked. "Told her . . . ?"

"Everything."

"My God! Why?"

She looked disgusted. "Did you want to keep it our secret? Something to wink about when we meet?"

"You took me by surprise. Megan, really . . . why *did* you tell her?"

"I wanted her advice."

He took it in carefully. "About what I'd asked?"

"What the hell else?"

"And . . . what did she advise?"

She laughed shortly. "Give me a cigarette." She exhaled smoke slowly. "My mother's a surprising woman," she said. "I mean, she has this rather simple-minded religiosity, but she can be pretty realistic about things."

"About us, for example?"

"She could see it."

"Then that only leaves you."

"You forget my father", she said, glancing at him ironically.

Arthur shook his head. "If we need *his* approval, we'd better stick to winking at each other on the sly."

"Scratch him then."

"Then that *does* leave only you."

She smiled vaguely. "No ring, Arthur?"

"I left it at the rectory", he said quietly.

At a table on the far side of the long, crowded room sat Doctor Walter Caldron and Judge Stanley Gorman. Toying with a whiskey sour, Caldron watched Megan and Arthur with disapproval.

"That's Justin Walsh's daughter."

Gorman glanced in the direction indicated. "Which one?"

"The thin dark girl with the priest."

"I don't see any priest."

"The fellow with the moustache and the blue blazer. They're at the table in the corner."

"Who is he?"

"Arthur Kucharski. The editor of the *Catholic Truth.*"

Gorman looked puzzled. "What are he and . . . what's *her* name?"

"Megan. I don't know what they're doing together. It's a good question, Stanley."

Gorman studied the couple curiously for several moments. "They look awfully intense."

"Don't they though?"

"I don't approve of priests wearing civilian clothes in restaurants."

"It usually means they're up to no good", Doctor Caldron said.

The judge sampled his Scotch and soda. "About this new publication, Walter. . . . "

"The response of the people I've talked to has been very positive."

"You have the money?"

"Enough to start, provided you and a few others put in a good word for the project."

"You understand—I don't want to get involved publicly."

"Of course."

"And I can't support an attack on Bishop Farquhar, even if I do disagree with him about many things."

Caldron smiled. "We're merely speaking of an alternative source of news and commentary. We've lost the *Catholic Truth,* you know."

"Have you spoken to Justin yet?"

"I want to be sure I have an offer to make him."

"That's only fair." Judge Gorman nodded. "As far as I'm concerned . . . I suppose you can count on my support."

"Good."

"Do you think Justin will accept?"

Doctor Caldron glanced again in Arthur Kucharski's direction. "I imagine he'll leap at the opportunity."

Chorus upon chorus of "Amazing Grace" swelled through the church as the priests broke loaves of French bread at the front of the sanctuary and delivered the consecrated shards into the hands of communicants. Each, having received his portion, moved off, right or left as the Spirit prompted, to quaff consecrated wine from one of the glasses on the tables to either side. As the communicants returned to their pews, ushers handed out gas-filled balloons, until soon the cavernous nave was a sea of bobbing, bright-hued globes, upon which the cameras dwelt lovingly. At what effect had the liturgical planners aimed: celebratory? But the result was merely self-conscious, like a touchy-feely sensitivity exercise that is meant to break down barriers but which leaves its victims fuming and defensive behind uneasy smiles.

Justin watched with mounting fury. "Scandalous", he told Eleanor. "An outrage!"

"I don't know, dear—it's just a little silly."

"A *silly* Mass!" He glared at her. "God help us if we've come to that." Setting his jaw with angry rectitude, he turned back to the television set to soak up further aggravation.

Standing at the rear of the balloon-filled church, his back to the sanctuary, Max Riemer was speaking into a hand-held microphone. "Holy Angels is like this every Sunday", he explained. "The creative liturgies of this parish have become the talk of the diocese of Wernersburgh. A lot of people think they're fun and say they've made the Mass more meaningful. But not everybody feels that way." He turned to an elderly, gaunt man standing glumly beside him. "Your name, sir?"

"Fred Haussner."

"You're a parishioner?"

"All my life."

"What do you think of this way of having Mass?"

Stolid, phlegmatic, expressionless, regarding Riemer steadily through steel-rimmed glasses, Mr. Haussner pronounced, "For the birds."

"Young people like it, don't they?"

"Young people like the circus, too. That's no reason to have a circus in church."

Strains of "Amazing Grace" soared heavenward, and Fred Haussner's visage faded from the screen. Seated in a studio, Riemer faced the camera and said, "Mixed reactions greet balloon liturgies and other changes in the diocese. Few Catholics are indifferent to what's going on. Tomorrow we'll talk with the man whom most people credit—or blame—for what's happened, Bishop Ambrose Farquhar, as we conclude our exploration of the changing Catholic Church. Good night."

Justin switched it off. "Farquhar tomorrow", he repeated with relish. "I wouldn't miss that for anything."

Eleanor, already in bed, yawned now. "I'm sure it will be very interesting."

"Say what you will", he announced pugnaciously, "these snippets on television call attention to matters that wouldn't have gotten as much attention otherwise."

"I can't help feeling sorry for Bishop Farquhar."

"You're being sentimental, Ellie. This is war."

"I hate to hear you say that, Justin."

But he wasn't listening. "What I don't understand", he said musingly, "is how this series can be Megan's work. I expected a pro-Farquhar slant from her."

"Perhaps she's more sympathetic to your point of view than you imagine."

Unbuttoning his shirt, he scoffed. "She has no sympathy for me or anything I believe in. Look at how she lives—estranged from the Church, flaunting the fact that that she isn't married even though she has a child. . . . "

"Suppose things changed, Justin?"

Standing in his undershirt in the middle of the room, he gave her a suspicious look. "Changed how?"

Eleanor blushed. "If Megan's situation changed, would your attitude toward her change? Hypothetically, I mean."

"I haven't the faintest idea what you're talking about."

"Supposing she were married?"

He stared hard at her. "*Is* she getting married?"

"She's a young woman. It's reasonable to think that some day. . . ."

The spell was broken. "Some day my prince will come", he snorted, and vanished into the bathroom.

He returned a few minutes later wearing brown striped pajamas. Eleanor was reading *The Introduction to the Devout Life.* Turning down the covers on his side of the bed, he said, "I suppose you'd tell me, wouldn't you, Ellie?"

"Dear . . . ?"

"If Megan were seriously considering something like that."

She closed her eyes. "I'd tell you whatever I could."

Again he paused. She did not open her eyes. "Good", he said at last, getting into bed and reaching for the light.

But doubt had entered his mind like a grain of sand that penetrates an oyster's shell, and while he lay awake in the darkened room unfamiliar secretions laved it, beginning the process by which in time it might become a dark pearl of suspicion.

Friday night revelers speeding to and from Wernersburgh's few downtown night spots ignored the lights burning late in the third-floor front window of the cathedral rectory; they wouldn't have cared to get involved anyway. Ambrose Farquhar's passion was a solitary affair.

The Bishop had skipped the early evening news. He'd had a meeting at the chancery and, more to the point, he wanted to be sure of watching this segment of the series by himself. Reaching his room, he'd read his breviary for a while and prayed: it was a strange fact that lately, despite all the pressure, he'd begun to feel more drawn to prayer than he had for years.

As time passed, nevertheless, he grew increasingly distracted. The clock's hands seemed barely to be creeping toward eleven. Finally he'd given up and turned on the television set, hoping to lose himself in mindlessness. It hadn't worked; he began to feel almost physically ill with suspense.

Throughout the week his spirits had been plummeting. Having courted journalists, he felt betrayed by Channel 6's depiction of a badly led diocese in disarray. Perhaps most painful, he wasn't sure whether it was the distortion he resented or the truth.

He was baffled. Weren't his good motives clear to everyone? Hadn't he broadcast his intentions from the first day he'd arrived in Wernersburgh? Didn't people know how badly they'd been treated before and how grateful they should be for the *aggiornamento* he brought with him?

He hadn't expected so many abrupt and alarming signs of collapse either: the frightening wave of defections by priests, the eccentric liturgies, the indications that even as diehard conservatives fought the renewal, lunatic liberals were pushing it further than he'd expected or could accept. Something like this had happened in New Antwerp, too, of course, but in compact Wernersburgh it had the impact of a disaster by implosion.

And here it all had been this week, capsulized, reduced to comic-strip terms and compressed into the physical dimensions of a nineteen inch screen and the temporal ones of a pair of homilies, to feed the passions of his angry flock. Tonight it was his turn. When the segment finally came on the screen around eleven-fifteen, Bishop Farquhar watched, appalled by something that was even worse than he'd feared.

" . . . a long time since *anything* changed in Wernersburgh", he heard himself saying. "Some people had grown suspicious of change."

Riemer shot back, "You think Bishop Frisch let the diocese stagnate?"

(Of course he did; stagnation had been Frisch's whole policy. Farquhar groaned. Why had he let himself to be trapped? It came of his naive readiness to speak his mind, confident he'd be understood benignly. That had been his mistake all year, and he asked himself: Will I never learn?)

". . . Vatican II . . . renewal of the Church. I want that to happen in Wernersburgh."

(That was all right—wasn't it? It was true that invoking the Council infuriated certain Catholics, but weren't they hopeless reactionaries who couldn't be allowed to block change? But what *was* this renewal of which he spoke so often and so confidently, for whose sake he'd set in motion so much turmoil? Did it have a specific content? It suddenly struck him that he didn't know.)

". . . harping on what's 'orthodox' ", the boyish, rather smug face on the screen was now pronouncing, "is not a healthy sign."

(That was sure to be misunderstood. Some people in the diocese regarded him as at least a material heretic if not yet a formal one. He'd dismissed that up to now; but *should* he? He recalled what one of his seminary professors had said one day many years ago, shocking twenty innocent seminarians: "A bishop, gentlemen, would do better to commit murder than teach false doctrine or permit it to be taught.")

"What's your long-range vision for the Church, Bishop? If you had your druthers, what would you really hope to accomplish?"

". . . a real Christian community . . . innovation and ongoing renewal . . . our life together as a pilgrim people . . . creative catalysts for the dialogue that leads to change. I. . . . "

"How willing to change are *you?*"

(That was unfair. Had they any idea of how far Ambrose Farquhar had come, how much he'd already changed? He'd been a bright conformist in the seminary. It was Archbishop Gatti who'd picked him up, encouraged him to flower, given him room to grow. And he had—couldn't they see that?—he emphatically had! Why bait him? Wasn't he bishop here, and couldn't he do as he pleased—change what he pleased? He couldn't see what Riemer had been driving at, and took the question now, as he had then, merely as a dirty dig.)

Now Riemer was alone. Bishop Farquhar listened appalled as the words of the indictment spilled out. " . . . changes in the lives of Catholics have been numerous and controversial . . . turmoil and tension . . . openly question his judgment, if not his orthodoxy." Farquhar writhed. All this was being said of him, not only on this wretched television series, but in the diocese at large.

"Where is the Church here headed, and how does the Bishop see the future? . . . a process, with no clear notion of what it leads to . . . isolated, hard to reach, and possibly out of touch. . . . " The phrases fell like hammer blows. Bishop Farquhar wiped a damp film from his forehead with a trembling hand; there was a conclusion yet to come: " . . . part of the larger picture of what's happening everywhere in the Catholic Church today . . . He has his eye on the future. But in a year of trying, he and the people he wants to lead haven't been able to agree on what that future ought to be. Good night."

It was over. Numbly the Bishop rose and turned off the set. Resuming his seat, he sat staring but not seeing. The phone next to him rang. He answered it. It was Dudley. The Vicar General seemed at once outraged and solicitous. Farquhar let him run on.

" . . . absolute scandal. Character assassination under the guise of objective journalism. We should protest in the strongest terms. I'll get Kucharski jacked up to write an editorial for the *Catholic Truth.* And I think a letter from the diocesan attorneys to the station manager is in order."

"But, Oscar," Bishop Farquhar said dully, "the harm has been done."

"People will recognize this for the shoddy attack it is. They'll be waiting for our response. And believe me, this two-bit television station will give us all the time we need for one. The lawyers will see to that."

Farquhar was hardly listening. "I don't understand what's behind it", he said dazedly.

"No? I do."

"What do you mean?"

"Justin Walsh's daughter is a producer at Channel 6. She was responsible for this. Does that suggest anything?"

"Justin . . . ?"

"I can't prove it. Perhaps he never said a word to her. But it all hangs together, doesn't it? Father and daughter must think very much alike . . . and son, too, from everything I hear."

"Son?"

"You're seeing Vincent Walsh next Tuesday", Monsignor Dudley reminded him.

"I can't prejudge him."

"Certainly not. But you can't be naive either."

"We'll talk tomorrow."

He hung up, but Dudley's words stayed with him. Was Justin Walsh behind all this? Rationally, Bishop Farquhar rejected that. Yet the explanation had the virtue of simplicity. Walsh's daughter had produced this miserable series. Now the son was to see him about his future at the seminary. Farquhar nodded slowly. He wasn't a vicious man, consciously hurting others wasn't his style. But Dudley was right: people would be waiting to see how he'd respond to this attack. Mildness would only invite more trouble; therefore he must be firm. Did the Walshes wish to challenge his authority? He meant them no injury but he could hardly tolerate that, and evidently the time had come to make that clear.

XV

"Think it over, Justin. You won't get a better offer."

"I don't know if I should be grateful for your consideration, Walter, or resentful at your candor."

Smiling thinly, Doctor Caldron sipped his decaffeinated coffee. "Both."

They sat over the remains of dinner in the Board Room of the Sasser Hotel, a cavernous, dark-paneled place where black waiters, none younger than sixty, presided with a baronial air. The menu featured prime rib, steak, and seafood. No salad bar sullied the Board Room, nor would one ever. Here drinks were large and conversations companionable but serious; one wouldn't have been surprised to hear the gentleman at the next table exclaim, "Bully!"

Justin, smoking his pipe and sipping coffee, was still taking in the extraordinary proposal Caldron had just made him. Could anything that good really come his way these days?

"The money, Walter . . . ?"

"It's committed for the first year. You needn't worry about that." Caldron straightened his bow tie. "Check our figures."

"I will. Including the editor's salary."

"Less than you're making now, of course. It can't be helped. If we had more to offer you, we'd offer it. However, we don't." The doctor frowned at having to make that admission.

"And the money runs out in a year?"

"The *seed* money. More will come in. The assumption is that your newsletter will be approaching self-sufficiency after a year and be totally there after two."

"Suppose it isn't?"

"I couldn't promise you any further subsidies."

I'd be out on the street looking for work at fifty-eight, Justin reflected uneasily. "How badly do you and the others want me involved in this project, Walter?"

"If you aren't editor, we won't go ahead."

Caldron had said that before, but Justin didn't mind hearing it again. Relighting his pipe amid clouds of smoke, he muttered modestly, "Lots of people could edit a newsletter for you."

"Your name counts for something in Wernersburgh. We have an excellent chance of succeeding if you're editor. If not—" Caldron made a throat-slashing gesture with his index finger.

"How much authority will I have?"

"Total."

"And you really see this becoming a national publication?"

"Wernersburgh isn't the only diocese suffering this way. The rot in the Church is universal. There must be a national audience looking for a Catholic publication that's not afraid to speak the truth."

"But that's an audience I have to find."

"Others are willing to put up the money so that you can look for it."

Justin laughed. "I like the way you doctors reduce everything to money."

Caldron wasn't offended. "It's how we concretize matters of life and death", he said.

Justin grew serious. "Understand that I'm not keen on fighting Farquhar in public." Nor, he knew as he said it, did he exactly dislike the idea; it was new, frightening, not unappealing. His feelings would take some sorting out.

"Of course not." Caldron nodded sympathetically. "You learned loyalty under Frisch."

Something in his tone made Justin suspicious. "You object to that?"

"Farquhar isn't Frisch."

"I've noticed."

"Besides," Caldron pursued cheerily, "it isn't a question of opposing Farquhar. We simply want honest reporting of what's happening in the Church. Let the chips fall where they may."

"You know where they'll fall."

"Of course. . . . Would you like a drink?"

Justin ordered brandy. Caldron had more decaffeinated coffee. Each sat musing until Justin, rousing himself, said, "I'll let you know."

"Take your time. But not *too* much time. The money is committed but not forever. We need a decision."

"You'll have one."

"You won't get a better offer, Justin."

"You told me that, Walter."

Leaning back, Doctor Caldron applied his napkin meticulously to his lips. "I saw your daughter last week", he said.

"Where?"

"Palmieri's. It stuck in my mind. She was with Kucharski. That seems strange."

Justin felt something click into place in his mind. Suddenly he was unpleasantly excited. "Kucharski", he repeated, dwelling on the syllables.

"I imagine it had something to do with that television series."

Kucharski.

" . . . a very helpful contribution, incidentally. Congratulate Megan for me."

Kucharski.

" . . . didn't come off very well, did he? Maybe he wanted to lodge a complaint. They seemed intent on *something.*"

Obvious.

" . . . never be entirely comfortable with the sight of a priest in civilian clothes sitting in a restaurant with a woman. If the fellow isn't trying to avoid recognition, why isn't he in clericals? It starts you wondering."

Kucharski. That certainly was the answer. But could he be equally sure of the question?

"Walter," Justin said, "you have given me a great deal to think about."

Useful as he found Oscar Dudley, Bishop Farquhar sometimes would have been happier if he'd been Vicar General of the far side of the moon. Not only was he usually right, he usually managed to call attention to the fact. There were some things the Bishop would have found easier to bear without Dudley's raised eyebrows and faint shakings of the head to remind him that, if he'd heeded Oscar Dudley earlier, he wouldn't *have* to bear them now.

The interview with Vincent Walsh was a case in point. "You don't have to see him, Bishop", Monsignor Dudley had said.

"I know I don't *have* to, Oscar," the Bishop answered patiently, "but he wants to see me, and I believe a bishop should be accessible to his seminarians."

The Vicar General looked skeptical. "This one is a trouble-maker. You should let Ron Lackner handle him."

"He's just a few months from ordination," Farquhar protested. "A few weeks from the diaconate. If there's a problem, let's find out what it is and take corrective action."

Dudley shrugged. "I'll schedule him week after next, Tues-day at eleven. If you think you have to. . . . "

That was before the disastrous week of the television series. For Farquhar it had become an emotional chasm sharply dividing his career in Wernersburgh into two distinct phases: the first year, marked by primal innocence, and all that was to come, indelibly scarred, he now was certain, by the knowledge gained by bitter experience. He wanted not to prejudge Vincent Walsh, but Vincent already had several strikes against him: brother of the woman whom Dudley blamed for the series on Channel 6 and son of Justin Walsh—begetter of troublesome offspring as well as multiple griefs for trusting bishops. And wasn't the assessment Lackner gave him too emphatically offputting: "Hopelessly right wing"? The Bishop wanted to remain open-minded, but as the time for the interview approached that wasn't easy.

At five minutes past eleven on Tuesday morning he checked the quartz clock on his desk, checked the digital watch on his wrist, laid aside his correspondence with a sigh, and buzzed his secretary. "Send him in."

A stocky young man with coarse, blunt features, unruly black hair, and a schoolgirl's complexion burst with animal energy into the office. His resemblance to his father was disturbing. Rising, the Bishop shook Vincent's hand, then resumed his place behind the desk without suggesting that they move to the sofa and chairs at the end of the room.

"What can I do for you, Vincent?" he asked.

"It's about what's happening at St. John's, Your Excellency."

Bishop Farquhar said resignedly, "I'll bite. What *is* happening?"

"I can accept change", Vincent said. "And I have nothing personal against Father Lackner."

The Bishop smiled faintly. "Don't protest too much", he cautioned.

"It's the *way* things have changed", Vincent said earnestly. "I wouldn't bother you, Your Excellency, but it's become a problem of conscience for me."

"Give me an example."

"Father Poirier's morals course."

"Bruce Poirier is a scholar with an international reputation."

The young man didn't falter. "He teaches subjectivism and relativism. He systematically undermines the Church's doctrine. I believe he's a Modernist at heart. My father has told me. . . . "

"Please." Farquhar raised his hand to halt the flow of words. "I know more about Poirier than you can tell me. What else is on your mind?"

"Two men were dismissed recently."

"I'm aware of that."

"Do you know the reason? Unnatural vice." He said it in a whisper.

Bishop Farquhar frowned. "It's not the first time in history, you know. A seminary isn't a hothouse. The point is that they *were* dismissed when the situation came to light." Pausing, he stared hard at Vincent. "Or isn't that enough for you?"

"It was because of me that the administration heard about the problem."

"Then I congratulate you on having done your duty," Bishop Farquhar said, "however painful it may have been."

"I'm resented for it. Father Lackner would have been happier if I'd kept silent."

"I don't suppose he was overjoyed at getting the bad news. But he acted on it, didn't he?"

"He had to be pushed."

Farquhar was growing impatient. "Come, come, Vincent. You're hypercritical. Shall I chastise Lackner for not being grateful enough to suit you?"

The young man's jaw had begun to jut, just as his father's

did when he was crossed. "I believe you're making fun of me, Your Excellency."

"I'm trying to make sense of your story. Is there more?"

"Father Lackner has changed the system of spiritual directors?"

"In what way?"

"We have assigned directors now."

"And I suppose you don't care for yours. Have you considered that might be a good discipline for you?"

Vincent said, "I see my old director."

"Then what are you complaining of?"

"It's the idea of *assigning* directors. I think it's meant to introduce a new element of control. The aim is to make us fit a pattern."

Bishop Farquhar said firmly, "I *hope* so. A seminary is a special kind of educational institution. The program reaches areas of a man's life that ordinary schools don't touch. We have a model of the priesthood in view, and we want St. John's to produce priests who correspond to it. You *do* understand that, don't you?"

"Yes."

Farquhar leaned back. "Why is it that, of all the men out there, you're the only one who's come in to complain?"

"Some like what's going on. Others are afraid to speak up."

"Try this instead: they don't *have* the same complaints. It's not as if dissension were sweeping St. John's. It's peculiar to you."

The young man regarded him with a pained expression. "Do you suppose I invented all this?"

"Not at all. But what you've told me comes filtered through your own notions of how things should be. Shall I tell you how *I* see it?"

Vincent nodded dumbly.

"When I came to Wernersburgh, I found a seminary very

much like the one I'd attended twenty-five years ago! It was fine for the preconciliar Church, everything was cut and dried, and all a priest had to do was learn the rules. But the Church is more complicated than that today. A lot more interesting, too. We need priests who can deal with the ambiguity of change and renewal. Therefore we need a different kind of seminary. You follow me?"

"Yes."

"Monsignor Caldron had to go, and when he did, I gave the rector's job to Father Lackner because he was the best man for it. You don't agree, but that's your problem, not Lackner's—or mine."

Later Bishop Farquhar would regret his self-indulgence, but now he was enjoying giving vent to his pent-up feelings. At this moment Vincent Walsh stood for all his critics and tormentors, usually beyond his reach but for once very much within it.

"Poirier? A distinguished scholar. Your criticism merely exposes the stifling narrowness of your education. You've been trained in integrism. It's not an attractive trait in a young man—to be frightened by new ideas, I mean—nor is it acceptable in a priest in today's Church."

Vincent winced. Farquhar ignored that and went on.

"The other things you complain of are trifles. You don't like this, you don't care for that, things aren't being handled as you'd prefer. Shall I turn St. John's on its ear to suit you? You remind me of your father, Vincent. You're not content unless you're dictating to others. Are you surprised at my lack of sympathy? Frankly, I'm surprised at yours!"

Vincent had turned scarlet. Tight-lipped, he said, "Do you want me to leave the seminary, Your Excellency?"

The Bishop sighed. "I'm sure this is painful for you. It's painful for me, too. But look at it this way—your problem isn't simply with the seminary. If that were all, you could hang on until ordination, then put the place behind you. But the real issue is more serious. Do you want to be one of *my* priests?"

"And", said Vincent, "do *you* want me as one?"

Farquhar said, "Precisely."

The young man rose. "May I have time to think about it, to pray . . . ?"

"All the time you need." The Bishop also rose, ushering him out. "Take all the time you need."

The door closed after the young man. Farquhar remained standing in the middle of the room. He could have wept with anger and frustration. He wished these people only the best, wanted nothing so much as to lay down his life for them, and they fought him at every turn. Vincent Walsh one of *his* priests? It was laughable; but just then the Bishop felt more like crying.

XVI

The long, dim corridor was illuminated only by a faint, dusky glow, hardly more than a luminous gloom, from half-moon windows high up in the wall to his right. On his left the wall was smooth and bare, windowless and without any form of decoration.

Far ahead, Megan was walking rapidly away, giving no sign that she was aware of his presence. It was urgent that he catch her, but his legs were leaden, his feet glued to the floor, so that each step cost him an enormous effort even as the distance between him and his daughter grew. He tried to cry out to her, but no sound came except the thudding of his panic-stricken heart.

At the end of the hall stood a heavy door of richly carved wood. She mustn't reach that door without him—but she did! Megan threw it open, and there stood Kucharski, in black suit and Roman collar. He writhed at the sight. Kucharski took her hand and drew her through the doorway. Gasping, spent, he reached the door only to have it shut in his face.

He began to cry, and while he cried he fumbled with the knob. "Thou shalt not", Uncle Henry said, standing fully vested and frowning beside him. He tried to speak but could only move his lips in soundless frustration. "Love your enemies", his mother commanded him, joining Uncle Henry. "Do good to those who persecute you." She knelt for her brother's blessing, which he gave with a magisterial gesture that, more than anything else, pierced him to the heart, causing tears to leap hotly into his eyes, tears of anger, tears of pain. . . .

Waking with a start, Justin sat bolt up in bed. Gritty light was seeping around the edges of the window shades. Eleanor slept peacefully beside him. Falling back on the pillow with a stifled groan, he rubbed the tears from his eyes with his knuckles. Megan and Kucharski. It was incredible. Therefore it must be true.

This was Jonathan's birthday, and Eleanor had invited Megan and the boy to dinner. It was Justin's chance to confront his daughter. What shall I say? he asked himself, wincing. "Tell me, Megan, is my grandson Arthur Kucharski's bastard?" Clenching his fists, Justin propelled himself out of bed.

While he shaved, he studied his face in the medicine chest mirror. His hair had been prematurely white for a long time, but his beard had remained black until the last few years. Now the bristles were like white spikes sown thickly across cheeks, chin, and neck. I'm getting old, he thought, blanketing the evidence with lather. A bewildered old man who can't understand so many things, can't cope. Farquhar's right: my time has passed. . . . Justin scowled at himself. Where did these morbid thoughts come from? He had jobs to do, missions to perform. There was Megan to be saved, Caldron's offer of an editorship. He was still in the thick of things, a force to be reckoned with in his family and in the diocese. Don't play *their* game by thinking of yourself as old, he told himself, furiously chafing his face dry with a towel.

When he came downstairs, Eleanor, wearing a green bathrobe, was stirring scrambled eggs at the stove. Later, after he'd left for work, she would go to Mass. "Did you sleep well, dear?"

"Fine", he said, remembering his dream uneasily. He sat in the breakfast nook scanning the *Globe-Herald.* The paper contained the daily ration of actual and threatened calamities: "New Violence in the Middle East", "Harsh Words from the Kremlin", "Market Down", "Husband Stabs Wife and Boy Friend". Under the weather forecast ("Cloudy with chance of late afternoon thunder showers") there was a thought for the day: "God loves a cheerful giver."

Eleanor sat across from him while he ate his eggs and toast. "Megan and Jon are coming over tonight."

"I remembered. Did you get him a present?"

"A model airplane kit and a wallet."

He sniffed. "You know I like the boy to have things that remind him he's a Catholic."

"I'll leave that to you, dear." Smiling, she took a sip of coffee and added, "It's hard to imagine he's nine."

Justin let that pass. "Ellie," he said, watching her carefully, "have you noticed anything strange about Megan?"

A shadow flickered across her face, and at that moment it was clear that she knew it all. And hadn't told *him.* He set that aside for another time.

"Strange in what way?" Eleanor asked.

"Distracted. Secretive. As if something were weighing on her mind."

Eleanor shook her head. "I haven't noticed that."

"You two are very close."

She changed the subject. "Have you thought more about Walter Caldron's offer?"

"A lot. The longer I think, the more attractive it becomes."

"If only it had more security."

"People are obsessed with security", Justin declaimed. "It's a delusion. Life is intrinsically risky—without faith." Spreading marmalade on his toast, he gave Eleanor a careful, covert look.

"Walter said he saw Megan and Kucharski having dinner last week. What do you make of that?"

Eleanor's expression was vague, but her cheeks were flushed. "I suppose it had something to do with her job."

"Undoubtedly."

It didn't surprise him that Ellie was in on it. She'd always been much closer to Megan than he, known things about Megan's life that Megan concealed from him. But I always catch up eventually, he told himself. And I've caught up this time, too. Finishing breakfast in silence, he left for work.

He thought of Kucharski as he drove. Surely there'd been a discernible change in the priest's attitude toward him lately? Formerly Kucharski had sought him out at least now and then, asked his opinion about one thing or another, as if still hoping their soured relationship might improve; but now he seemed to be going out of his way to avoid Justin, communicating mainly by written notes and speaking as seldom and as briefly as possible.

Justin had put it down to the final collapse of their relationship: Kucharski had abandoned even the pretense of friendliness. But now he saw it in a different and more sinister light. Wasn't this the behavior of a guilty man who wished to avoid his victim? He gripped the steering wheel grimly. It came over him that on one level he didn't want certainty while on another he had no choice in the matter: truth ought always to be pursued, action ought always to be based on apprehended truth. The adages he'd learned thirty-five years earlier from the Companions of Christ remained controlling principles of his conscious life.

When he got to work he found Ferdy Ruffin waiting for him. Morose as always, he sat in Justin's tiny office sipping coffee from a smiley-face mug and toying with a dead cigar. His retirement, still some months away, was gnawing at him.

Ferdy had declared for years that he was living for the day when he could clean out his desk and say goodbye to his job, but as the time drew near he'd begun to have second thoughts. A widower, childless, he glimpsed loneliness stalking him in earnest. Justin glimpsed it too, but had no idea how to help Ferdy escape.

"I tell you," Ferdy was saying that morning, "there isn't much there when I go home to the apartment. And having no place else to go scares me. You're lucky, Justin, having family."

The irony of that was more than Justin cared to bear. He said, "You know you'll always be welcome at the *Catholic Truth,* Ferdy."

"Sure. For the first ten minutes after I retire. Then nobody will want me hanging around. 'Take your gold watch and beat it.' You know that's how it is."

"Maybe we can work out some kind of part-time arrangement for you."

"With *him?*" Ferdy made a face in the direction of Kucharski's office. "I can't clear out too soon to suit him."

Justin felt strangled. "He isn't crazy about either of us."

"And I've had it with *him.* As a matter of fact, he's probably doing more than anybody to help me with my retirement. It's going to kill me, but that's an improvement over working for him."

At noon Justin walked across the street to Mass at the cathedral. It was a fine, warm day, one of the last of Indian Summer, and before entering the church he stood for several moments on the steps in the sun, looking back at the chancery and ignoring the two street people who skulked near him reaching for a handout. That building had been the center of his life so long and in so many ways: could he really see it as it was? A dumpy office building with a stained gray facade and small windows. Second floor front: the Bishop's office. Shades drawn as usual. Was Farquhar there now? He'd almost always known just where Bishop Frisch was and what he was doing, and earlier his mother had kept him constantly posted on Bishop Weiss's comings and goings. But now he had little or no notion of the Bishop's schedule. Fifth floor front: Kucharski's office, formerly his own. He'd watched the world from there for twenty years. Now his office overlooked an airshaft. Frowning, he turned away and, ignoring the panhandlers, went into the cathedral.

Mass had begun. The congregation was the usual motley assortment. Bag ladies mumbled in the side aisles and a sprinkling of drunks and psychotics dotted the pews, exotic blooms amid a drab crop of office workers. Justin knelt in a pew near the front of the church, before the Blessed Sacrament chapel, and turned his attention to the main altar.

He started. The celebrant was Farquhar. Nothing strange about that—after all, the Bishop lived here—but Justin was disconcerted anyway. He thought of leaving, then set the idea aside. Mass was Mass, no matter who said it. I have as much right to hear this Mass, he thought, as he does to say it. He stayed.

A year ago he'd seen Farquhar offer Mass in this cathedral at his installation ceremony. Then the church had been filled and blazing with light. Now it was dark and sparsely populated. There seemed to be a lesson in that. The thought pleased Justin.

The gospel was from the Sermon on the Mount. Justin rose with the office workers and the bag ladies (the drunks and lunatics tended to keep their seats) as Bishop Farquhar ascended the pulpit and read:

"If you want to avoid judgment, stop passing judgment. Your verdict on others will be the verdict passed on you. The measure with which you measure will be used to measure you. Why look at the speck in your brother's eye when you miss the plank in your own? How can you say to your brother, 'Let me take that speck out of your eye', while all the time the plank remains in your own? You hypocrite! Remove the plank from your own eye first; then you will see clearly to take the speck from your brother's eye."

Justin nodded assent. Let Farquhar take that to heart. But he was hardly likely to. Farquhar knew how to preach; there was no evidence that he knew how to listen.

When the reading of the gospel was over, Justin was ready for the Mass to go on. Instead, to his annoyance, Farquhar lingered in the pulpit. Weekday sermons had come in with other changes in the liturgy. One more bad idea, in Justin's view. Most priests did well to scrape together a single passable sermon in a week; daily preaching only called attention to the fatuousness of the preachers. Another case of renewal gone awry.

"These words", the Bishop began earnestly, "apply to us all. But they are not *easy* to act upon. Our Lord uses the metaphor of seeing—physical sight—to refer to our capacity for being honest with ourselves. When sight is blinded, when there is a 'plank' in my eye, then I'm least able to 'see' either the truth about my brother or the truth about me.

"A self-righteous man suffers spiritual blindness, and that's a perilous condition to be in. By definition, he is sick. But by definition also, he doesn't *know* he's sick. Without exaggeration, the prognosis for him is desperate."

Apply that to yourself, Justin thought. It would make a big difference to this diocese.

"But this is the condition, more or less, of every one of us. Where we are concerned, none of us sees clearly. Pride and smugness blind us. We have to remove the plank."

The Bishop was not aware of Justin's presence, but Justin could see him perfectly; perhaps never before had he observed

Farquhar so carefully. How young he looked! His green chasuble and the small purplish zucchetto perched on the back of his head suggested office, authority, the weight of age, but his boyish appearance canceled out their effect. Justin felt old, and he passed his hand wearily over his eyes. Even age was on Farquhar's side. The future of the Church lay in the hands of this youthful, earnest, uncomprehending man, while he, Justin, had been brushed aside.

"To see ourselves as we really are", Bishop Farquhar was concluding, "is the work of a lifetime. We can't begin too soon, for the chances are that we won't have finished by the time we die.

"Most of us sail through life on an ocean of self-love, borne along by self-deception. Unless we learn honesty—and it doesn't come easily—we face the risk of shipwreck. Let us pray then for the grace to be honest with ourselves, and stop passing judgment upon others. 'If you want to avoid judgment, stop passing judgment.' The Lord couldn't have put it more clearly than he did."

Bishop Farquhar inclined his head in silence for a moment, then turned away and went back to the altar. Standing with the rest for the prayers of petition, Justin suddenly found words ringing in his mind: Megan, Kucharski. Clenching his teeth, he shook his head furiously. Time enough for that later; he knew now what he must do, but there was a possibility that he might lose his nerve, settle for ignorance, if he thought too much about it.

The consecration came. First the host, then the chalice, were lifted by Bishop Farquhar into a slanting shaft of sunlight that seemed to vault heavenward from the altar. The congregation collectively breathed a silent sigh. Justin watched stolidly: he was there to receive the benefits of the Mass, not contribute anything. At Communion time he strode up the middle aisle, feeling that the only really meaningful moment of the Mass had come. As he approached the sanctuary he observed that some of those in line in front of him were extending their hands to receive the Host and Bishop Farquhar was obliging. Another symptom of decay. When his turn came, he opened his mouth wide and shot out his tongue, hoping the other man would feel rebuked. "The Body of Christ", the Bishop announced. "Amen", Justin affirmed, searching Farquhar's face for signs of guilt. Seeing none, he returned disappointed to his pew.

Mass over, Justin left the cathedral and headed for the Venerable Bede Booke Stalle. He'd decided midmorning what to give Jonathan—a copy of the Baltimore Catechism. Since the boy wasn't in parochial school and Megan plainly wasn't doing much about his religious education, it followed that he was woefully ignorant of matters religious. The Catechism might help remedy that, especially if, as Justin intended, he himself questioned Jonathan regularly on his progress in the book. After all, this was *his* grandson.

Rounding the corner, Justin drew near the Booke Stalle. It was Wernersburgh's only Catholic book store, and over the past thirty years it had been the source from which he'd stocked his own shelves with Newman, Chesterton, Belloc, and Knox, Maritain and Gilson, Pegis and Péguy, Sheed and Sheen, Faber and Feeney, Goodier and Prat, as well as classics by Augustine and Aquinas, de Sales and Loyola, Teresa of Avila and Thérèse of Lisieux, and contemporaries like the early Graham Greene and the late Evelyn Waugh. His mother, naturally, had introduced him to the Booke Stalle, and he turned there now with confidence: there the wholesome nutrient of Catholic doctrine was set out in abundance; there the intellectual corrective for Jonathan's religious ignorance—the stalwart Catechism, efficacious tool in forming generations of

Catholic youth—lay at hand, still fit to shape enlightened minds and sound morals.

Approaching the Booke Stalle at a brisk pace, Justin saw something in the front window that made him slow his pace, halt, stare, come on again at a tentative shuffle, and finally stand stock still in contemplation. The Booke Stalle's displays tended to range between the staid and the dull: a multivolume edition of the Summa Theologica perhaps or a new all-purpose book of devotions (stations of the cross, benediction, Forty Hours) or samples of the latest daily missal (in former days, at least: now daily missals had all but vanished, the Council having so complexified the liturgy that even regular Mass-goers couldn't guess what combination of texts selected by what principle of liturgical high gnosticism would greet them on any particular day). Now, however, it was no display of books that graced the Booke Stalle window but a banner. Justin gaped in astonishment.

Upon a beige field bordered in scarlet crosses and dotted with small gold alphas and omegas stood a turkey: a gorgeous creature, cunningly wrought in black and brown and orange and white, his tail fanned like the vaunting boast of turkeydom itself, his wattle a crimson flame, his plumage an artist's palette, his feet huge brazen claws. The banner presented a head-on view of the turkey, but the creature's own head was cocked sharply to the left, so that he confronted the beholder with a single eye, a large rhinestone glittering with singleminded mad brilliance amid the riot of color. Above him in large orange letters of an elegant script were the words "Give Thanks!"

Justin stared at the turkey. The turkey stared at Justin. An idea gripped him with obsessive force: this was an *idol.* One day it would be hung on a sanctuary wall or draped over an altar or lectern, it's mad eye glittering hypnotically at a congregation during Mass. Justin had never seen an idol before, and he'd more or less supposed such things had vanished from the earth. And here was one, in broad daylight, around the corner from the cathedral, in the front window of the Venerable Bede Booke Stalle. Feeling light-headed, he turned away with an effort from the turkey's glittering eye, and stumbled blindly into the shadowy groves of the Booke Stalle, which lay one step down from street level.

Justin paused near the entrance, calming himself and adjusting to the gloom. Then he began to browse. A table of books near the door caught his eye and he turned there first, then recoiled. Nervously he moved to another table, and again stepped back quickly, as if he'd found a cobra coiled among its volumes. The next table, and the next, and so on down the aisle. Frowning, starting to mutter, Justin moved from display to display on a bizarre pilgrimage.

It was true, he hadn't been in the Booke Stalle for several months, but how could *this* have happened in the interval? Justin felt like weeping with rage. Suddenly—overnight, as he saw it—the Venerable Bede Booke Stalle was crammed with postconciliar works. Sociology, spirituality and psychology seemed to predominate, but there were also strange hybrids: theological psychology, sociological spirituality, psychological sociology, theological spirituality, and psychosociological spiritual theology. In one section of the room books by northern Europeans with guttural names flourished like a sea of mushrooms sprung from Hegel's grave. Hunkered down in another quarter was a platoon of liberation theologians, swarthy guerrilla prophets of St. Marx. A shelf in one corner was devoted to what, at first glance (Justin was too embarrassed to take a second), appeared to be Christian sex manuals. Adjoining these, by accident or irony, were books arguing the case against clerical celibacy and the Church's teaching on birth control. Wandering about the store, Justin felt as appalled as a man stumbling onto a battlefield the day after a heavy engagement.

"Hello, Mr. Walsh."

Turning, he confronted the mild gaze of Hazel Weber, the Booke Stalle's proprietor. "Miss Weber. . . . " He stopped, too confused to speak.

She was a small, neat, gray-haired woman in her sixties. Justin had known her for a quarter century, and shared with her an enthusiasm for books and authors that, if narrow, was at least sincere. She seemed to have aged, and he thought she looked embarrassed. "You haven't been in lately", she said with gentle reproach.

"So much has changed . . . ", he gestured about him.

She laughed nervously. "I've been housecleaning."

"Why?"

"You know how dependent I am on the clergy, and these are the books they want to read now." Miss Weber gave him a strange look, as if to say, What would *you* have done?

"They read *this?*" Picking up a volume at random, he scanned the title: *Why Not Christian Atheism?* He dropped it like hot coals and demanded, "*This* is what they read?"

"I don't mean I'm doing a land-office business. But the books I used to carry—*nobody* wanted them any more, Mr. Walsh."

"*I* wanted them, Miss Weber", he said stiffly. "*You* wanted them."

She shrugged helplessly. "That's only two. I couldn't stay in business that way. And," she brightened, as if thinking the news might cheer him up "Bishop Farquhar is very pleased with the Booke Stalle now."

Justin nodded grimly. "I'm sure he is."

"He comes in often. He's a good customer, and he recommends the Booke Stalle to others."

"That accounts for a lot."

"I remember his saying to me once, months back, 'Miss Weber, your establishment can be a very important instrument of renewal. But it won't happen this way'—that was when I still had my old stock. 'You need new titles, new authors, new thinking, the best the Church has to offer today.' Of course I wanted to please the Bishop, and my sales were way off anyway. So I made the change. The Booke Stalle has been renewed." She tried to sound jaunty, but her effort was pathetic to Justin's ears.

"That—" He cleared his throat. "That object in the window?"

Miss Weber brightened again. "The banner? Isn't it a beauty, though?"

"Do you sell many?"

"Banners are very popular. People like them in the liturgy. I think it's because things have started to loosen up in the diocese, if you know what I mean."

"I do."

"Somehow" she said, eyeing him timidly, "I suspect you don't care for banners, Mr. Walsh."

"Certainly not."

"We must move with the times, you know."

"But", he objected, *"turkeys?"*

"You're not a banner person."

Setting his jaw, Justin said, "I'm looking for a gift for my grandson. A copy of the Baltimore Catechism."

Another man had entered the store and was scanning the books near the front window. Miss Weber gave Justin an odd look. "I don't carry that any more."

"You don't carry the Baltimore Catechism?"

"I have the *Dutch* Catechism", she suggested hopefully.

"You must be joking!"

Blushing, Miss Weber glanced over her shoulder to make sure that her other customer was occupied and out of earshot.

Then, stepping closer and lowering her voice, she said in a near whisper, "I think, Mr. Walsh, for you—well, there may be a few copies in the back."

Making an effort, Justin said evenly, "I'd like to have one, please."

"Let me see." She darted into the rear of the store. Justin waited. Miss Weber reappeared in a few moments, a small gray paperback in her hand. "Here", she said, extending it quickly for his inspection; the book was very dusty. He started to reach for it, but Miss Weber was already popping it into an anonymous paper bag.

Justin paid in silence. When she brought his change, he asked, "What's wrong with the Baltimore Catechism, Miss Weber?"

Her blue eyes clouded. "I couldn't say. Times have changed, I suppose."

"Yes."

"It's important to keep up with the times, Mr. Walsh. That's my motto these days."

Justin surveyed the Booke Stalle as he would have done a bawdy house. "So they have."

"Come again soon", she urged him with impersonal good cheer, moving toward her other customer. "Come back soon."

"Yes." He nodded. "I will." But he knew he wouldn't. Leaving the Booke Stalle with a last look behind for old times' sake, he stood squinting for a moment in the sunlight, then, shooting an angry glance over his shoulder at the turkey rampant in the window, strode away clutching the Baltimore Catechism as if somebody might try to take it from him.

All that afternoon he couldn't get Megan and Kucharski out of his mind. Passing the priest in the hall once, he nodded, while the question hammered at his consciousness: *Are* you Jon's father?

He was packing up to leave at five when Ferdy stuck his head in the door.

"Heading home?"

Justin nodded. "We're having my grandson's birthday dinner."

"How I envy you, Justin—family to go home to."

Justin gave him a queer look. "Sometimes, Ferdy, *I* envy *you.*"

Driving home, he knew he'd have to confront Megan. However bad the truth might be, it couldn't be worse than what he already suspected. And supposing he were wrong? Megan would be furious; but considering what she'd done to earn his suspicion, that needn't deter him. Indignation, he reflected, is a luxury she's not entitled to.

Eleanor was getting dinner. She came out to greet him in the front hall, leaving Jonathan watching television in the kitchen, and led him into the dining room, where a gloriously frosted cake with the words "Happy Birthday, Jon" in pink icing stood in the center of the table. Justin regarded it with mixed emotions while Eleanor took his arm. "Aren't you going to compliment me?"

"Very nice", he said, turning away.

She eyed him sympathetically. "I know how Jon's birthday affects you. . . ."

"Do you, Ellie?"

"I feel the same way. But that's *our* problem, isn't it? He's a dear little boy. Nothing that happened changes that."

Justin smiled wryly. "You tell me that every year."

"Do I?" Eleanor laughed. "I'm sorry. What did you buy him?"

He produced the Baltimore Catechism from his coat pocket and handed it to her. Uncertainly she said, "That's very nice, dear."

"Not *nice*—essential to his religious education." He went upstairs to get ready for dinner.

Megan arrived around seven, and they sat down to eat almost immediately. Friday abstinence had long since vanished in the Church at large, but Eleanor still served fish in deference to Justin.

Jon made a face at the slab of cod on his plate. "How come fish?" he asked.

Megan grinned. "Your grandfather would feel guilty otherwise."

"That isn't true", Justin said heavily. Addressing Jonathan, he asked, "Do you know what abstinence is?"

The boy frowned over the word. "Not getting drunk?"

Justin cleared his throat loudly; Megan suppressed a giggle. Jon looked confidently around the table, aware that he'd scored.

"That's part of it, dear", Eleanor said, smiling gently. "*I* think the fish is very good."

"It's delicious, Mother."

"Abstinence", Justin informed his grandson, "refers to not eating meat."

"You mean like a vegetarian, Grandad?"

"*Like* a vegetarian," Justin conceded. "However, I'm speaking of a Catholic practice. We used not to eat meat on Fridays."

"Jews don't eat pork."

"I'm aware of that. But for us, abstinence is a form of mortification and penance."

Jon looked blank. Megan explained, "He means giving up something you like."

"Why?"

She shrugged. "Who knows?"

Justin turned red. "There are excellent reasons", he began, "for mortification and penance."

"But not at a birthday party", Eleanor interrupted, catching his eye.

Justin subsided, and dinner moved on. At dessert time Eleanor got chocolate ice cream from the kitchen while Megan lighted the cake's nine candles and Justin darkened the dining room lights. Then they sang "Happy Birthday", Jonathan leaning forward toward the cake and frowning intently in the flickering candlelight. Justin was startled to glimpse something alien yet familiar in his features and expression. He looks like his father, he thought. The boy blew mightily, and the candles flickered and went out. The instant passed. Reaching behind him to the wall switch, Justin turned on the lights while Eleanor and Megan applauded.

After ice cream and cake Eleanor presented the new wallet and the model airplane kit. Jon was pleased with both. Portentously, Justin announced, "I have something for you, too."

The boy flashed a shy, pleased smile. Justin left the table, got the catechism from the front hall, and, returning, presented it with a flourish. "This comes with my special good wishes, Jon. I hope you'll study it and benefit from it for years to come."

Jonathan examined the drab little book doubtfully. "What is it?"

"A famous textbook of the Catholic faith."

"It's the literary equivalent of fish on Friday", Megan explained.

The boy looked uncertainly from his grandfather to his mother, trying to tell who was serious and who joking—and what the joke was. Eleanor came to his rescue.

"It's a summary of what Catholics believe, dear."

"*Used* to believe", Megan corrected.

Justin turned red again. "Faithful Catholics believe it", he said. "The others aren't Catholics."

"Have it your way, Daddy."

"My hope for you, Jon," Justin said, "is that you will learn the contents of this book from cover to cover. Generations of

Catholics have memorized its questions and answers. *I* did at your age."

"Memorize?" Jonathan wrinkled his nose in disgust.

Megan shook her head; Justin ignored her. "Why not?" he demanded. "What better way to learn what's there? I'll tell you what," he added jovially, "for every question and answer you can prove to me you know by heart, I'll give you a quarter."

Jonathan checked the catechism and did some quick mental calculations; his eyes widened. "That's a lot of money", he said appreciatively.

"You'll come out doubly ahead."

Megan went on shaking her head. "Do you really imagine that memorizing words helps, Daddy? Suppose you know the words, do you know the meaning?"

"Children should be taught according to their capacity for learning."

"Children aren't parrots."

"Obviously you *discuss* the catechism with the child," he said angrily. "Or rather you'd discuss it with him *if* you taught it to him. You don't, of course."

"Justin, Megan—" Eleanor said reprovingly. "We're having a party."

"Sorry, Mother. . . . Anyway it was a lovely dinner. Thanks."

They got up from the table and cleared the dishes. Eleanor and Jon went into the living room to play Scrabble. Megan was starting to follow when Justin stopped her. "I'd like to speak with you."

She grinned. "Mother will be upset if we start fighting again."

"I don't wish to fight." He gestured upstairs. "After you."

They went to the study, her old bedroom. Sitting at the desk, Megan lighted a cigarette. Justin, taking the rocking chair, observed her while he lighted his pipe: cocky, argumentative, edgy. There's never been any peace in her, he thought. Does she suspect what's coming? Probably not. Should I let it drop? But then *I* will be without peace.

"I liked your series on the diocese", he said.

Looking surprised, she said, "We've gotten a lot of reaction to it."

"Favorable or unfavorable?"

"Both. People who like Bishop Farquhar have been screaming, but people who hate him were pleased. I guess I know which camp you're in."

"Have you heard anything from the chancery?"

"I had a call from your friend Dudley. He said we'd been unfair."

"Oscar Dudley has done as much as anybody to ruin this diocese."

"Farquhar relies on him a lot?"

"Too much." Justin sighed. "But maybe it doesn't matter. He might have done just as badly if he'd never met Dudley."

"You really do have a low opinion of him, don't you?"

"Don't *you?* That's how your series looked."

"We were only trying to tell the story, Daddy."

Justin puffed silently on his pipe for several moments. Then he said, "I believe you know Arthur Kucharski."

She didn't flinch. "I met him here—remember?—at that dreadful dinner party Mother arranged."

"Did he say it was dreadful?"

"Mother did. . . . What's this all about?"

"You were seen having dinner with him last week."

"That sounds like a spy movie. Who saw me?"

"Walter Caldron."

"Oh, him!" Megan laughed. "What a Neanderthal he is. I felt sorry for Bishop Farquhar while we were talking to him."

"Nevertheless," Justin said drily, "his eyesight is perfectly good. He saw you and Kucharski together."

"What of it?"

"I didn't know you and he were well acquainted."

"You meet a lot of people in my job."

"Have you known him a long time?"

She hesitated. "I told you—I met him here last summer."

"It's my impression that you've been acquainted a good deal longer than that."

"I don't appreciate this, Daddy."

"How long *have* you known Kucharski?"

"I really don't remember."

"Perhaps you met him at the university?"

"Maybe so."

Justin paused. His pipe had gone out. Raising a match to relight it, he noticed that his hand was shaking. So did she.

"You're getting excited", she taunted.

"I'll be honest with you, Megan", he said slowly, trying to keep his voice level. "I have a suspicion. I've had it for some time, and it won't go away. Call it a hunch, but as time passes, it grows on me. And things keep happening that lend support to it."

She looked disgusted. "You're right", she said. "I met Arthur at the university. You remember Tanya Stein? Arthur was her boy friend."

"Tanya Stein's boy friend?" He tested it for credibility.

"For a long time. They split up in our senior year."

He was silent. Finally he said, "And then?"

Megan bit her knuckle. "You're a good reporter", she acknowledged, not looking at him. "You know how to dig."

Barely loud enough to be heard, he said, "Then it's true."

She took a deep breath and said with an effort, "That Arthur is Jon's father? Yes."

Ever so quietly he said between clenched teeth, "Dirty bitch."

Eleanor and Jonathan were playing Scrabble quietly in the living room when the door to Justin's study slammed and Megan came running down the stairs. She charged into the living room looking pale and furious. "Come on, Jon, we have to leave."

"We're playing a game", he protested.

"It's late. Get your coat." Plainly she meant it. The boy went reluctantly to the hall for his coat.

"Thanks for the party, Mother", Megan said distractedly.

"What happened?"

She gave Eleanor an odd look. "Let *him* tell you."

Jon came back wearing his windbreaker and carrying the wallet and the airplane kit. "Thanks for the presents, Grandma", he said, kissing her.

"Happy birthday, dear."

"I'll call you", Megan told her. They left hurriedly. After they'd gone, Eleanor noticed the Baltimore Catechism on the hall table. Her lips forming the words "Oh, dear", she picked it up and carried it back into the living room.

So Justin knows now, she thought. How is he taking it? Badly, no doubt. Really, that it should be Arthur Kucharski was almost more than Justin should have to bear. Why, she asked God, *do* you do these things? Why burden the already troubled, aggravate the already angered, puzzle the already blind? I suppose you want Justin to learn something—patience, humility, tolerance, how to forgive—but in that case you must help him. And help me to help him.

The upstairs door opened, and Justin came thudding down the steps with an audibly angry tread. Sighing, Eleanor composed herself on the sofa.

Red-faced, obviously furious, yet struggling to control his temper, he stalked in with an accusing glare. "I suppose you've known all about this for a long time?"

"Not *very* long."

"Why didn't you tell me?"

She spread her hands. "Because Megan asked me not to. Because I had no right to. Because it wouldn't have helped."

"How do *you* know that?"

In a low voice she said, "Does it help you now?"

He started to answer, but the Baltimore Catechism which she'd set on the coffee table caught his eye. He snatched it up, then threw it down again with a curse. "Typical", he snarled.

"Don't torture yourself, Justin."

"I needn't lift a finger. It's all done for me. Do you know what she said just now?"

Eleanor shook her head.

"If I go to Farquhar about this, she won't be responsible for the consequences. She was *threatening* me—Megan threatening me!"

Eleanor was dumbfounded. "Go to Farquhar?" she repeated. "Why would you?"

His look was incredulous in return. "Don't you imagine a bishop—even one like Farquhar—needs to know something like this about one of his priests?"

"But you'd be destroying Kucharski", she protested, adding faintly, "and perhaps Megan, too."

Justin shrugged it off. "Don't exaggerate", he told her sulkily. "Let them adjust. *I've* had to. Anyway, it's merely something I'm considering."

You'll drive her into his arms, Eleanor wanted to say. But she was afraid; the idea of Megan's marrying Arthur Kucharski might be more than he could handle just now. Instead she said, "All this happened so long ago . . . before he even *was* a priest."

He looked at her in disbelief. "Are you making excuses for him?"

"Justin, what good would it do for you to do *anything* now? Why not leave them alone? They have enough problems."

"And I suppose they deserve my sympathy", he said scornfully. "Well, don't expect that. Don't expect anything positive from me as far as Megan and her priest are concerned. You can pray for them, Ellie, and you can hear out Megan's confidences, too, since you and she enjoy that sort of thing. But don't expect anything from me except what they deserve—whatever I can give them back for what they've done to me."

"Justin, don't do something you'll regret."

He sneered. "Do you take me for a fool?"

The telephone in the front hall rang. Justin hesitated, then went to answer it. Eleanor could hear his side of the conversation plainly.

"Vinnie, is it you?"

Thank God, she thought: Vincent will settle him down.

"How are things going with you?" Silence for several moments. Then he said impatiently, "Don't be stupid. Cough it up and let me have it. Don't play games with me."

Again silence. Then: "Lackner told you *that?* He ought to be removed from office. . . . Farquhar! When? Why didn't you tell me?"

Eleanor was growing apprehensive. Whatever Vinnie was saying, it was long and complicated. Justin didn't need more bad news, not right now. She started to pray.

" . . . yes, that's exactly what he'd say. I could have predicted it. He sent you back to Lackner. What happened then? . . . Get to the point."

Now came the longest silence of all. Eleanor sat bolt upright, fists clenched in her lap. Suddenly Justin groaned, then groaned again. A terrible sound, the noise of a wounded animal. Leaping up, she rushed into the hall. He was leaning ashen-faced against the wall. She extended her hands to him, but he turned away.

"When?" he said hoarsely into the phone. He nodded at the answer. "We'll . . . see you then." Slowly he hung up the instrument.

"Justin, what is it?"

He seemed not to see her. "They've told him to leave."

"You mean—the seminary?"

He nodded. "He's been ordered out. He'll be home Sunday."

She was bewildered. "Why? What happened?"

Turning away, he began slowly, methodically to beat his fist on the wall. "Farquhar", he said between blows. "Farquhar . . . Farquhar."

Reaching the apartment a little before nine, Megan sent Jonathan to bed as quickly as she could and called Arthur.

"You'd better come over", she told him. "We have to talk."

"What's wrong?"

"He knows."

"Justin?"

"Who the hell else?" She hung up.

Lighting a cigarette, Megan tried to collect her thoughts. This was all happening too fast. She needed time to think, and now time was running out. *He* had seen to that.

What should she say to Arthur? "We've got to stop seeing each other?" Now it wouldn't matter if they did; *he* would still go to Farquhar with what he knew. There was no preventing him. It was too late.

And Arthur? Nothing had really changed since the university. She regarded him as vulnerable, she didn't want to see him hurt. Hadn't she known it was so from the moment she'd stumbled on him in her parents' dining room last summer?

Hadn't Tanya told her it would be like this? His vulnerability and need made the same old claims on her. Was this what they called love—a sense of someone else's dependence? If so, she must love him.

They'd been delaying a decision on their next move for several weeks, but Justin's threat forced their hand. Once he sees the Bishop, Megan told herself, Arthur's finished here—no more editorship, no more nothing. Farquhar will find him the most miserable hole in the most remote corner of the diocese, and let him rot there for the next twenty years. Any bishop would do the same.

So her options were reduced to one. And Jon? They keep telling me he needs a father. I used to think not, but now—maybe so. He seems to like Arthur well enough, too. Why not like him as a father? It was no more bizarre than other couplings and uncouplings she knew of, and the kids didn't seem to be hurting.

The buzzer rang. She went to let him in. He was wearing his blue blazer and a polo shirt. Brushing past her, he went into the living room, demanding agitatedly, "How did he find out?"

Megan followed. "Do you want something—coffee, a drink?"

"A glass of ice water."

"At least sit down while I get it."

He did. Megan went into the kitchen and carefully got him his water, making it a point to refill the ice tray and return it to the freezer: she wanted to be calm for this. Going back to the living room, she handed him the glass and lighted another cigarette while he gulped noisily.

"You'll get a stomachache", she said.

"How did he find out?"

"A little bit here, a little bit there. Somebody saw us at dinner. I suppose we've both been acting funny, too. He's a bright man, you know."

"Oh, sure."

"You underrate him. That's the trouble with priests—patronizing."

"I'm not", he protested weakly.

"And you get into trouble that way", she persisted, annoyed. "You don't know whom you're really up against."

"What are we going to do now?"

"What's *he* going to do? Tell Farquhar, I think."

He froze. "About us? That isn't fair."

Megan eyed him coldly. "In the circumstances you haven't got much room to criticize him."

"I forgot how protective of him you are."

"He's been hurt, too."

He wasn't listening. "Damn, what rotten luck!" He gnawed his thumbnail, looking sorry for himself.

Megan saw him without illusions: a weak man . . . *my* bad luck. "Were you serious about getting married or just talking because you thought it was your duty?"

"I wouldn't say that just on account of duty."

Megan smiled thinly. "We can't stay in Wernersburgh."

"I agree."

"A man I used to work with at Channel 6 is news director at a station in Chicago. He told me once that he'd hire me at the drop of a hat. Shall we try Chicago?"

"Why not?"

"We should move fast. If I can square it with the station- . . . what about the middle of next week?"

"Swell."

She paused and pressed her palms to her temples. "This is crazy."

"It's a crazy world."

Jonathan demanded, "What are you two talking about?"

Pajama-clad, eyes glazed with sleep, he confronted them

resentfully from the hall doorway, brushing back his blond hair from his forehead with an impatient gesture. Megan was suddenly conscious of how tall he was growing and of the adult features—high cheekbones, a broad nose, a long upper lip—already visible behind the features of a child. My God, she thought, he'll look like Arthur; his genes will announce the truth even if we don't.

"You're supposed to be asleep", she said automatically.

"You guys are making too much noise."

Arthur said, "Happy birthday, Jon. Sorry I forgot to bring your present."

"What is it?"

Arthur blushed. "What would you like?"

Megan told the boy, "Go back to bed now."

He ignored that. Stepping into the room, he asked, "What's Father Kucharski doing here?"

"I'm visiting?"

At that instant it all fell into place for Megan. She said, "Actually, Jon, we're planning a trip."

He looked doubtful. "Who?"

"You, me . . . Arthur."

He measured Kucharski skeptically. "He's a priest."

Arthur gave a pained smile. "Priests go on trips, too."

"With regular people?"

"Why not?"

Obviously the boy regarded that as unworthy of a reply. "What about school?"

Megan was beginning to feel slightly desperate. "Thanksgiving is coming. You'll be out of school."

"We always go to Grandma's and Grandad's for Thanksgiving."

"It won't hurt to skip it once."

Jonathan knew better. "Grandad won't like it", he warned.

Arthur spoke up. "We're going to Chicago. Have you been there?"

The idea was novel enough to command his interest. "No", Jon acknowledged.

"How would you like to go to a Bears' game?"

"Can you get tickets?"

He scarcely hesitated. "Sure. I've got a friend."

"I'd like that", the boy admittedly shyly.

Megan let out the breath she'd been holding. "We'll talk about it more in the morning. Now get back to bed, fella. It's late."

Glad to comply as sleep overcame him, Jonathan only turned at the doorway to ask Kucharski, "Can you really get tickets?"

"Sure."

The boy accepted it gravely and disappeared up the hall. When they heard the door to his bedroom close, Megan demanded in an angry whisper, "Where the hell are you going to get football tickets?"

"Your friend . . . ?"

"Oh sure. 'Jerry, give me a job and three tickets to the next Bears' game.' "

"We'll think of something."

"You shouldn't lie to him."

He passed his hand wearily over his eyes. "I'm trying to get to where I won't have to. Help me."

Megan, beyond illusion, regarded him steadily. What are we doing, she asked herself, resuming an interrupted relationship or gambling that eventually there will be some kind of relationship? Anybody else would say we're crazy. But you've thrown us together, and left us hardly any choice. Thy will be done? Isn't it always, whether we like it or not? I hope it makes you happy.

"Help you?" she repeated. "Of course. Isn't that what

you've always believed God put me on this earth to do, Arthur?"

"Justin, revenge won't help you or Vinnie or anyone." It was very late. They lay side by side in the darkness.

"It won't be revenge."

"Don't go to Bishop Farquhar. Leave him alone."

"He needs to know."

"It isn't going to help."

"Keeping silent isn't going to help."

"You have no right to tell him."

"It's my duty."

"You may hurt Megan."

"Megan has hurt me."

"Then it's revenge after all."

"Duty."

"How can I persuade you, Justin?"

"There is no way."

XVII

"The Bishop's very busy, Justin. Whatever it is, it will have to wait until tomorrow."

"No. Today."

He sat down across the desk from Monsignor Dudley and folded his arms, as if to say it would take physical violence to move him.

The Vicar General leaned back and, removing his glasses, polished them irritably with a crisp handkerchief. His plump face looked unformed, fetal. Returning the glasses to his nose, he confronted Justin with a sigh.

"Tomorrow."

"Today."

"Justin, I realize that you've worked here a long time—"

"Twelve years before you even came on board, Monsignor."

"—but that doesn't permit you to make outrageous demands."

"Is it outrageous to want to see Bishop Farquhar?"

"What do you want to see him about anyway?"

"That's my business. And Kucharski's."

Monsignor Dudley frowned. "Frankly, Justin, people are getting tired of hearing that you can't get along with him."

"Then tell Kucharski to stop talking about it."

"No!" Suddenly Dudley brought his fist down on the desk. "The problem is you."

"I'm sure you'd get rid of me if you could, Monsignor. Anyway, when do I see the Bishop?"

"I told you."

"Ask him", Justin commanded.

Monsignor Dudley hesitated, then with an angry shrug picked up the phone and dialed. "Bishop, I'm sorry to disturb you. Justin Walsh is demanding to see you today." The Vicar General listened. "Thank you." Hanging up, he told Justin brusquely, "Four-thirty."

Justin rose. "That wasn't so hard, was it?"

"Don't press your luck."

Back upstairs, he learned from Nancy that Kucharski had phoned in sick. That happened often enough; Kucharski didn't push himself, considering spotty attendance one of his prerogatives as editor. Mondays were especially vulnerable. Justin gave Nancy a wink. "He probably exhausted himself doing pastoral work over the week end."

"Long hours in the confessional."

"Riding to his far-flung missions."

"Spending himself selflessly for his people."

They laughed. "I guess the paper will come out somehow", Justin said and went down the hall to his office.

The day dragged by. Justin edited wire copy, wrote headlines, made a few phone calls to check facts, and composed several simple stories of his own. He could have done it in his sleep after all these years, and lately he very nearly had. The old days were full of gusto and passion, putting out each issue was an adventure. Now the *Catholic Truth* was a dismal boiler plate—routine canned news wrapped around liberal columnists whom Kucharski had installed, plus the priest's own wordy editorials. He'd managed to make the paper simultaneously strident and dull; as with an angry man of limited conversational gifts, one didn't so much read the *Catholic Truth* these days as listen to it sputter.

And there, thought Justin as he worked, stands Walter Caldron's offer. I'll take it, once this is settled between Kucharski and me. Farquhar may get rid of him as editor, but he won't be giving the job back to me; in fact, he'll want me out, too. Didn't Dudley say as much? Dudley is an officious ass and a sneak besides, but he knows Farquhar's mind. He should, he runs it.

It's the same everywhere in the diocese now. Farquhar's formula for renewal. Look at what he's done to St. John's. Look at what he's done to Vinnie! Yes, Vinnie may be able to find another bishop to take him in as seminarian and priest, but he'll never be a priest in Wernersburgh, that's certain. A good thing in a way. It frees me to tell Farquhar what I think of him. Let him hear the truth for once: it will do him good.

The truth about Arthur Kucharski. What will Farquhar make of *that*? Exemplary priest, apt choice as editor of the *Catholic Truth*! Farquhar needs to grow up, stop living in his dream world. My news should open his eyes. Bishops can't afford to be fools; it's a favor to Farquhar to help him stop being one.

But Eleanor's attitude remained a mystery that he pondered petulantly and at length during that endless day, while he worked with half a mind at familiar tasks and repeatedly checked his watch, cursing time's slow plod toward four-thirty. Ellie says I'll be doing something awfully wrong in telling Farquhar what I know about Kucharski. Can't she see it's my *duty*? Seeking revenge? I don't expect it to help *me* in any way; as a matter of fact, I'll probably be out of a job when it's over. But I'll have done what I can for the diocese. And even for Kucharski. He can't do what he's done and get off scot-free. I may be helping him save his soul. Ellie can call that revenge if she wants, but it doesn't look like it to me. Anyway there's no telling what Farquhar will do about it; maybe he'll leave Kucharski in his job and make him rector of the cathedral, too! But even Farquhar should be able to see that Kucharski isn't fit to stay where he is. I may lose my job, but it will be worth it if it costs Kucharski his.

Justin was eating at his desk shortly after noon when the telephone rang. It was Walter Caldron.

"Did I catch you at a bad time?"

Swallowing a mouthful of hard-boiled egg, Justin reached instinctively for a ballpoint pen to take notes. "No. What's up?"

"Good news. Merely on the strength of your name, I have another five thousand dollars in pledges. You're a selling point, Justin. People are delighted when they learn that you're in this."

Justin grinned. "I guess I'm a known quantity."

"You're admired for what you did with the *Catholic Truth.* And there's plenty of sympathy for you now."

"I appreciate that."

"My brother is getting the same reaction among priests—the sound ones, anyway. People are ready for a new publication with you in charge."

"I appreciate that", Justin repeated. He did, too. Walter might be laying it on a little thick, but he didn't mind. Flattery tastes good when you haven't had any for a long time.

"I'm not putting pressure on you", Doctor Caldron went on carefully. "I know you're still considering our offer. But things are moving on this end. The project is viable, *if* we can count on you."

"I won't keep you waiting much longer."

"I look forward to hearing from you. And, Justin," Doctor Caldron's cackle was like a piece of machinery in bad repair, "give my best to the Bishop." He hung up laughing.

Justin leaned back complacently. It *could* work, and he was the man to make it. Would the new publication divide the diocese? If so, that was because any sane voice would be divisive under the present reign of lunacy. That was no excuse for abandoning the field to dissent and disloyalty.

Around two-thirty Ferdy dropped in with a couple of completed stories and stayed to talk.

"Hear any more from our leader?" he asked, lighting his cigar stub.

"Just the message this morning that he wouldn't be in today."

"For somebody who wanted to be editor, he isn't very keen on the job."

"Kucharski's fickle. Most people are."

"You weren't, Justin. You put your heart into editing this damn paper for twenty years."

"Yes." He ran his fingers through his bristly shock of white hair. "That was my mistake."

"Live and learn." Ferdy eyed him clinically. "I'm surprised you've stuck it out. With retirement staring me in the face, I haven't got a choice. But you do."

"Jobs don't grow on trees. Especially after twenty years."

"Wouldn't *anything* be better than this?"

"Maybe."

Ferdy patted his bald head reflectively. "I can't believe the Bishop knew what he was getting when he brought Kucharski in."

Justin nodded slowly. "Maybe not."

"Not that Farquhar isn't crazy, too. Look at what he's done to the diocese."

"I've noticed."

"I keep asking myself, how do things like this happen? Don't the people who run the Church care?"

Justin had often asked himself the same. He said, "They don't know what's happening."

"I guess Wernersburgh doesn't look very big from Rome. But why should we have to suffer for that? It doesn't seem fair."

Justin thought of the newsletter he'd soon be editing, a voice of protest raised against all the harm that had been done. "Maybe we have to suffer," he said, "but it needn't be in silence."

He sat considering that after Ferdy left. We've been trained to put up with any nonsense the clergy choose to perpetrate, he thought, and as for a *bishop*—when I was growing up, the bishop was one step short of God. But when does even loyalty become irresponsible? Doesn't loyalty to the Church come first?

His mother would have been shocked. She'd have seen what he was doing as treason. But you don't understand, he argued silently: things have changed. Farquhar isn't Cornelius Weiss or Peter Frisch. To defend what they stood for, I must oppose Farquhar. He forced it on me. Blame him, not me.

He checked his watch at frequent intervals. Three. Three-fifteen. Outside his window the shadows had moved from one wall of the air shaft to another, and now the small scrap of sunlight discernible from where he sat was scrambling up the bricks toward the roof, as if fleeing the gloom that rose inexorably below it like dark liquid filling a tube. Justin lighted and relighted his pipe. Three-twenty. Three-twenty-five.

Megan says I'll destroy Kucharski by telling Farquhar. That's crap. What Farquhar does is Farquhar's doing, not mine. And what does she mean by "destroy him" anyway? At worst, Kucharski will lose his job as editor, that's all. I didn't notice Megan grieving when I lost the same job, and the job meant a hell of a lot more to me than it does to Kucharski.

Let Farquhar decide what kind of priests he really wants in this diocese: that's the issue. Not Vinnie; then is Kucharski with a bastard son in tow what he has in mind? Farquhar should explain where that fits into his precious renewal.

Justin looked again at his watch. Three-forty. The phone rang. It was Eleanor.

"Something has happened, Justin."

He could tell it was something he wouldn't like. "My God, what now?"

"Megan is leaving with Arthur."

"Leaving?"

"They're going to Chicago. They'll be married. They're taking Jon."

"I. . . ." His mind seemed to stumble, catch itself, look about bewildered. What she was saying made no sense at all. He felt as if he were watching with detachment while he went mad. "That can't be."

"She called as they were leaving her apartment. They've gone."

He tested it as if it were a bizarre object she'd handed him without explaining its use. "Chicago, you said?"

"Megan believes she can get a job."

"Why are they doing this?"

There was a long pause. Then Eleanor said, "You convinced her, Justin."

"*I* did?"

"You told her you were going to see Bishop Farquhar. She thought that would hurt Arthur. He'd asked her before to marry him, and perhaps she would have done it anyway. But when you said that to her, it settled matters."

"She said that?"

"I'm sorry, Justin."

Now that she'd explained it, he couldn't help but see its truth. Of course Megan would respond like this. He hadn't known of Kucharski's importuning, the proposal of marriage on the table, so to speak, but wasn't it exactly what he'd feared? He had no right to be surprised.

"They've gone?"

"Yes."

"And taken Jon?"

"Of course."

"I didn't expect this", he said helplessly.

"Justin, have you seen the Bishop yet?"

"I have an appointment at four-thirty."

"Will you keep it now?"

He shook his head, trying to clear his mind. "Of course."

"I wish. . . . "

"Yes?"

"Nothing. Do what you think you must."

She hung up. That, too, shocked him: for once she hadn't preached love and forgiveness. Did even Ellie crave revenge? Swiveling about in his chair, he stared into the air shaft and waited to feel something.

Time passed. The scrap of sunlight had vanished, leaving the shaft in shadow. The fluorescent light in the ceiling hummed and crackled, flickering occasionally. Peck-a-peck, peck-a-peck went Nancy's typewriter up the hall. Somebody was whistling. A telephone rang far away. Automatically he checked his watch. Four o'clock. There was something he must do soon. He tried to think.

Suddenly emotion hit him in a great surge, and he doubled over. But, my God—what news to carry! Megan married to that priest. He'd never know another moment in his life with such shame. Even her pregnancy had been a small thing by comparison, something comprehensible and commonplace. Undoubtedly people had snickered behind his back—"The defender of the faith's daughter got herself knocked up"—but they hadn't snickered long, for such things happened all the time. But to run off with the priest who was her child's father, to marry the priest, for them to live together as husband and wife: that was something people wouldn't forget. "Remember Justin Walsh? Edited the *Catholic Truth* for years. More Catholic than the Pope, that man. And this ultraorthodox super-Catholic's daughter married a priest. The fellow got her pregnant years earlier, and they finally decided to fix things up. If you can call it that. They're living in Chicago. Justin? You don't hear much of him these days. He preached a lot of sermons once, but I guess he knows people would only laugh if he pulled that now."

Especially, he thought, they'd laugh if they knew I drove her into it. Words that Megan had spoken last Friday night came into his mind: "You are an unforgiving bigot." Just so. And he'd never noticed it. An honest man, a champion of truth, a man of principle for whom compromise was anathema—that was how he'd seen himself. And all the time his wintry rectitude was causing him to cultivate grudges as another man might virtues. If God had a fault, he'd reasoned, it lay in being too ready to forgive; he'd therefore done his best to shield God from the consequences of such foolish fondness by himself forgiving no one. Megan had it exactly right: an unforgiving bigot.

Four-fifteen. Rising wearily, he stood staring into the dingy air shaft. What shall I say to Farquhar? I want to hurt him. Truth hurts. "The truth hurts, Justin", my mother used to tell me. "Tell the truth and shame the devil." But wasn't even the devil pleased to hear truth used as a club? God help me, Justin thought: for twenty years I've used the truth to settle scores.

Leaving the window reluctantly, he went out of the office. Ferdy, coming up the hall, met him at the elevator.

"Are you all right, Justin?"

He grunted.

"You look pale." He eyed Justin with concern.

"I'm going to see Farquhar", he said mechanically. "About Kucharski."

Ferdy looked anxious. "Kind of risky, isn't it?"

"Telling the truth? Sure. If you've got anything to lose. I don't." He turned away.

"Justin. . . . "

"I *don't,* Ferdy", he said ferociously, and boarded the elevator.

On the second floor he stuck his head in the door of Monsignor Dudley's office. "Is he free now?"

Dudley looked up coldly from the papers on his desk. "Don't be longer than you must."

Justin lingered. "Have you heard anything?"

The Vicar General frowned. "What are you talking about?"

Then the news *was* his to break. Abandoning Dudley without a second thought, he went up the hall to the Bishop's office.

Daylight was failing, but the only other light in the room came from the thick-shaded lamp on the desk, where numerous files, ledgers, and loose papers were spread out helter-skelter. Farquhar was bent over the mess in close concentration, but he looked up as Justin entered and gestured to the chair across from him. "Sit down."

Justin took the indicated seat. He wants to keep this short and businesslike, he thought. That's fine.

"Why did you want to see me, Justin?"

He sounded weary. Looking beyond the pool of light, Justin was startled by his appearance. There was nothing animated now in the broad, boyish face. Dark half-moons lay below Farquhar's eyes and hollows slashed his cheeks. Two vertical lines were etched between his eyebrows, giving him an anxious frown. Twelve months ago he'd looked much younger than his years; now he looked much older.

"You're busy", Justin said irrelevantly.

The Bishop smiled faintly. "I have a meeting with the diocesan finance committee tomorrow. We face some rather large decisions."

"Such as?"

Farquhar's look expressed mild surprise at the question, but he answered anyway. "Can the diocese go on subsidizing five elementary schools and two high schools downtown? That costs half a million dollars a year. And in view of other demands. . . . "

"How are revenues holding up?"

The Bishop shrugged. "So-so. Collections are down. The pastors say they're hurting."

"People talk a lot about the inner city though."

"I can't run seven schools on talk. One religious community has already told me it will have three fewer nuns to staff its school next year. That means three more lay teachers' salaries. And I expect to hear the same story from the others. Where is the money to come from?"

"What will you do?"

"Close a school, I suppose, or merge a couple. I'll be criticized. The diocesan school board must be consulted, but first the finance committee. A bishop's main job these days is chairing meetings." The dark stone in his heavy ring gleamed dully as he massaged the bridge of his broad nose with thumb and forefinger. "I suppose you want to see me about your son?"

"Partly."

"I'll be direct with you, Justin. I fully support Lackner's decision. There won't be any reconsideration."

"I didn't think so."

"Vincent may make a good priest. But not in this diocese."

"Why?"

"Because", Bishop Farquhar explained patiently, "that would

mean becoming one of *my* priests. He'll be happier somewhere else. There's nothing remarkable about looking for a bishop you can live with. As a matter of fact," he paused, regarding Justin thoughtfully.

"What?"

"Keep it to yourself, but Bishop Boylan is getting Bridge City. I imagine he'd be delighted to have Vincent."

Justin experienced a small twitch of hope. He even felt grateful to Farquhar. "It ought to work", he acknowledged. "We'd counted on Wernersburgh, but you're right—that's impossible."

"And I've solved your problem?" The Bishop started to rise, as if to see him out.

Justin laughed; Farquhar looked startled. "Let's try another problem", Justin said. "My daughter."

Frowning, the Bishop resumed his seat. "The television producer? I've heard she was responsible for that series on the diocese."

"I think so."

"It was a rotten job", Farquhar said angrily. "Tell her so for me."

"I never thought highly of her work before," Justin said, "but that series was good reporting."

"It was sensationalism!"

"The diocese is in awful shape."

"Every diocese has problems", Farquhar protested, adding with an exasperated gesture at the records on his desk, "This is typical."

"I was thinking of what you call renewal."

"Naturally renewal is difficult for people who fear change. But for that television series to take the side of the most reactionary element. . . . " He gave Justin a suspicious look. "I suppose you had a hand in it."

Justin shook his head. "Megan doesn't ask my opinion. About her work or anything else."

Something in the way he said it seemed to catch the Bishop's attention. "No?"

"We haven't been close for a long time. Not since she got pregnant in her senior year at the university."

"I'm sorry. I suppose that was hard on you."

Justin swallowed. This wasn't coming easily, but he had to go on now. "She's an unusual person in many ways. She has a lot of determination. She doesn't ask favors."

"Did she keep the child?"

"Of course. Megan takes responsibility—even for her mistakes."

"Very commendable of her."

"She started at the bottom at Channel 6 and worked her way up to where she is today."

"You're proud of her then."

"I respect her good qualities. She has plenty of bad."

"We all have a lot of both."

"No. Some have only bad." He was silent. It was growing darker in the room.

Bishop Farquhar's phone rang. Lifting the receiver, he said, "Busy", and hung up. He waited for Justin to speak.

"Why did you choose Kucharski to edit the *Catholic Truth*?"

"I wanted a break with the past."

"You can break with it," Justin said, "but you can't abolish it."

"It's part of the renewal", the Bishop insisted. "I know you've had trouble adjusting to him, but. . . . "

"He's my grandson's father."

Farquhar froze. "What did you say?"

"Megan and he were at the university together. That was before he entered the seminary, of course. It was he . . . she wouldn't tell me then or since, and I've only recently found out. Apparently she didn't tell him either . . . about the pregnancy, I mean. That's like Megan. She wouldn't have wanted him on those terms."

Farquhar was staring fixedly at him. "I don't believe all that."

"I'd be crazy to invent it," Justin replied, "just as you'd have been crazy to send him to the *Catholic Truth* if you'd known. And neither of us is quite *that* crazy."

The Bishop leaned across the desk. He was pale. "You have made", he said, "a grave accusation against one of my priests. I can't ignore it, and I certainly can't take it at face value. Do you mean to let it stand? Because if you do, I shall have to take this up with Kucharski."

"Suppose", Justin said, "that it's true. Will you beg my forgiveness?"

"That's what you want most, isn't it?"

"It was." He passed his hand wearily across his eyes. "Not now." He looked past Farquhar to the double window. Sunset had burst across the heavens, slashing the sky over the cathedral with layers of gold and vermilion. The contrast with the thickening gloom in the office was striking. God help me, Justin thought: what *do* I want? "You'll have trouble reaching Kucharski", he said. "He and my daughter left today for Chicago. Apparently they plan to be married."

Farquhar was speechless. Justin gave him a look that approached sympathy. "I know, it's hard to take in. I learned about it just before I came down here. I'd planned to tell you about them. They knew that, so they took the next logical step."

"You're saying. . . . "

"I'm responsible for what's happened."

After a moment's silence, Farquhar rose and went to the

window. His figure was a dark mass against the sunset. Without turning he said, "It's their responsibility. Don't torture yourself."

"Oh, I'm sure there's plenty of blame for everyone", Justin said. "You, for example."

"I reject that. I triggered a coincidence. Nothing more." The Bishop did not turn around.

"Not moral guilt", Justin said. "But responsibility of a sort."

"What will you do?"

"I resign. Effective immediately. Sorry if that's abrupt, but I can't come here ever again."

Farquhar faced him now. "And where will you go?"

"I had a job offer, but I won't be taking it. It wouldn't interest me any more." I'll have to call Walter, he thought, feeling nothing. A shame to disappoint him, but I've had enough of revenge.

Bishop Farquhar returned to the desk and sat down. He looked exhausted. "Perhaps Bishop Boylan needs an editor."

Justin considered that. The Bridge City *Catholic Trumpet,* edited by a burned-out monsignor, was as feeble a rag as the *Catholic Truth* had been when he'd taken it over. But now he didn't want to be in charge of anything. That craving had slipped away in the course of this very day. "It's a possibility", he said slowly. "Not editor though. I'll speak to him about it." He paused, then added thoughtfully, "You must be pleased to be getting rid of Boylan."

Bishop Farquhar looked pained. "Why put it like that?" he protested. "He deserves his own diocese. Why make me out to be a villain just because he's leaving?"

"The point is", Justin said, "there isn't room in Wernersburgh for Boylan. Or for me."

"But I wanted it to work out for you at the *Catholic Truth*", Farquhar said dully.

"It never could have. Even without Kucharski. *I'd* have seen to that—even if you didn't. Don't you understand? I honestly don't believe in what you're doing. I think you're tearing down the Church here. And you couldn't persuade me, buy me off, or intimidate me into thinking otherwise."

"You're fighting renewal." Farquhar sounded like a man arguing by rote. The sunset had all but vanished and night was falling. The heaps of files and ledgers on the desk resembled battlements battered in a siege. Justin rose; it was time to go.

"Renewal," he said, "what is that? Abandon the old and replace it with the new? But what makes the new any better? Your renewal doesn't go deep enough, Bishop. We needed conversion, and all we got was change."

XVIII

One Monday in the middle of February, Eleanor borrowed a friend's car and drove out to St. John Vianney's to see Father Drake. The weather was changing. A wind from the west scattered the clouds that had blanketed heaven and earth for weeks, while newly liberated sunlight splashed the stubbled, snow-dusted fields with unaccustomed warmth. Quite suddenly, the question of spring had arisen.

Parking down the hill from the massive seminary, Eleanor got out, then paused, gulping intoxicating draughts of startlingly pure air. Mile upon mile of countryside fell away at her feet, a crazy quilt of fields, woods, streams, and little roads, stretching to an immeasurably far horizon. Having hidden itself for a moment behind a scrap of cloud, the sun came rioting out like a brazen beast, blinding her just as a gust of wind roared in her ears. Giddy, crossing herself, she smiled in delight and climbed the hill.

Classes were in session, and, although she saw no one, Eleanor sensed intense activity all around her as she approached the building. Letting herself in through the heavy front doors, she descended to the lower level and followed a long corridor straight back to the archives.

Father Drake was waiting for her. He seemed more insubstantial each time they met, his features thinner and more sharply defined, the skin over his temples stretching ever tauter, almost transparent. The tremor in his hands was noticeable whenever one or the other strayed from the cane that, for the most part, he clutched firmly before him, as if otherwise those age-flecked dry hands might flutter away like dead leaves. Coming upon him suddenly like this, after several weeks' absence, Eleanor felt the accumulating evidence of his frailty with special poignancy. Was the time near when Drake himself would become an item in his archives, a precious manuscript in a neglected file?

But meanwhile he'd plainly determined to keep up the customs of their friendship, a circumstance that brought tears to Eleanor's eyes. A cup of tea steamed on his desk, while the kettle whistled on the hot plate in the corner. "Help yourself, my dear", he invited. "You need warming up today."

Removing her coat, she busied herself with cup and saucer. "The weather's broken", she told him, pouring boiling water over tea. "It's glorious outside."

"St. Valentine's day", he pointed out. "It's always been my personal festival of hope that winter may end."

"Today one could believe it will." Balancing a teacup, she took her place opposite him. "Winter *is* ending." The radiator knocked loudly, subterranean sound of a benevolent giant mumbling in his dreams. She beamed at Father Drake and sipped her tea.

"How is Justin?" he asked.

"He'll start his new job with the paper in Bridge City when Bishop Boylan goes there next month. In fact, he's already driving over several days a week to help out."

"The editorship?"

"He won't consider that. He says it wouldn't be fair to the priest who's editor now. But Bishop Boylan says the man would welcome the opportunity to step down."

"Justin doesn't want the responsibility."

"Of making judgments. No."

"That will pass. But it's best for now."

She nodded. "I think so, too. Look at his refusal of the Caldrons' offer."

"It would have destroyed him to accept."

"Of course. But for *Justin* to see that . . . he's come very far."

"It sounds as if you have much to be grateful for."

"So much", she acknowledged. Tears started up in her eyes again, and, brushing them away with the back of her hand, she laughed at her own foolishness. "Vincent is so happy, and Justin is happy for him."

"Boylan will get a good priest," Drake said matter-of-factly, "and the delay won't do Vincent any harm."

"Of course." Eleanor nodded, but a slight frown knitted her forehead. "Although I still don't understand Bishop Farquhar's attitude entirely. If he thought Vincent was suited to be a priest, why couldn't he be a priest for Wernersburgh?"

The old man readjusted the angle of his cane. "I scarcely know Bishop Farquhar, but I suspect he's an honest man. It's an honest man's solution. Vincent couldn't be a priest for Wernersburgh, because Wernersburgh is *his* now, you understand. But it doesn't follow that Vincent can't be a priest somewhere else."

"It seems strange."

"It *is.* Do we have one Church or many? Frisch's church, Farquhar's church, Boylan's church, as many little churches as there are bishops—"

"—or Catholics."

"Or Catholics. That is the logical conclusion, isn't it? But I'm glad that it's working out for Vincent." Father Drake paused, carefully sipping his tea. "Any word from Megan yet?"

Proudly Eleanor reached into her purse. "I've had a letter", she said, handing it over. The priest took the sheets of paper in silence and read.

Dear St. Eleanor,

Greetings from Sin City North. Your God is full of surprises. I'd heard he broils the wicked for their crimes, but for the last two months he's done no worse than freeze our tails beside this frozen lake.

That's the least of the surprises. Do I dare to say we're happy, and our happiness seems the result of somebody else's willing it? Have it your way, Mother, I do! Nothing dramatic, of course, no lights and consolations. It's a combination of small things going right when they could easily have gone wrong. If I had a shorter memory, I could almost manage to be grateful. As it is, I keep asking: Why did you *wait* so long?

Jon is thriving. He likes his new school—he's even made some friends—and he's taken to the idea of having a father. Apparently it doesn't phase him that Arthur was a priest. Children accept things they haven't learned are unacceptable. Of course he misses you, but I tell him you'll be visiting soon. You wouldn't make a liar of me, would you?

I suppose Arthur's also doing well in his own way. No regular job yet, but the important thing is that he goes on looking. It would be easy for him—very much in character, I mean—to relax and turn the entire burden over to me. I believe he doesn't want to do that this time, thinks it would be a bad example for Jon, and so he's plugging away, looking for work and clerking part-time in a drug store. For Arthur, that's industrious.

Speaking of jobs, things have gone most undeservedly smoothly for me. Your God slipped up a little in this case, since Jerry Wirtz is too plainly an angel in disguise. I do essentially what I did at Channel 6, but do it with a larger and more professional outfit.

The only trouble (and I wouldn't breathe a word of this to anyone but you, and probably shouldn't admit it to myself) is that I've lost my zest for what I do. The news business can't come close enough to the truth to suit me any more. What could? Am I groping toward another vocation, sainted one, and if so, what might it be? Does Francis de Sales say anything about hacks who'd like to be thoroughbreds?

You're wondering, however, about Arthur and me. Same here. It's hard to describe our relationship in conventional terms, or even nonconventional ones for that matter. Love? More and more I wonder what that means: I wouldn't stoop to the evasion of calling anything by that name. (God is love? Then God is nothing in my book, but *that* will come as no surprise to you.) Not love but hatred? That's no closer to the mark. Arthur doesn't hate me, and I . . . I think I hated him once, but I'm sure I don't any more. I don't see how it's possible to hate any human being whom you truly know. Hatred must only be fear of the unfamiliar; something like what happens when an animal catches a strange scent. Once you know the smell, you stop being afraid—and hating.

Call it dependency then. I can't think of a more neutral name. We need each other. Maybe that's my biggest breakthrough—to acknowledge need, I mean. Do you approve? There was a time when I'd have resisted the very suggestion that I needed someone else, and even now I feel a certain contempt for myself in admitting it. But at least—you see how accommodating I've become—it strikes me as a very *Christian* thing to do, needing another. They say God doesn't need us, but then why does he create us? Out of love? But wouldn't that be the key to the whole thing—God creates because he *needs* to express his love? (Why are theologians so afraid to let God look even the least bit attractive?)

I sit here writing at the dinette table, glancing now and then out the window of this rather seedy apartment we rent. Jon is playing at a friend's upstairs. Arthur has gone to the grocery (he does try to make himself useful, you see). It's close to sunset, and three blocks away, just visible beyond another apartment house, the Lake stretches into gray infinity as if all the world beyond a certain point were Lake and Lake and nothing else but Lake. It's supposed to snow. It is easier to believe that it will snow than that it will not, since here it always snows. I feel warm and sleepy. It's my day off.

What do I depend on Arthur for? But we both know the answer: I depend on him to need me. Relationships are tricks with mirrors: one plane within another plane within another . . . on and on. Which is the reality?—Or is the *whole thing* reality? I favor the latter view. I need Arthur because he needs me because I need him because . . . the entire system is the relationship. Why evade it or deny it or apologize for it? Like everything else, it's your God's doing and not mine.

I keep circling around him, don't I? But don't worry, I'm not obsessed with God, it's writing you that brings it out in me. I know that nothing that leaves him out of account satisfies you as an explanation for anything, so I introduce him to oblige you. I repeat: I have become very accommodating lately.

Anyway, I don't mind explaining things by God. I merely point out that it makes him to blame for a lot of things I should think you'd rather not hang on him. We've done well for these two months—Jon, Arthur, and I—but we did quite badly before, and may do badly again. If God is the explanation for everything, I can't help but be suspicious of him.

They say God writes straight with crooked lines, but I once heard a variation that I like better: God writes with a piano leg, to make it clear that he's the one doing the writing. At least that gives us a small, inglorious role—God's inadequate writing instruments—in the master plan. I think it means he uses us to write our own stories, but we no more know what the ending will be than a pen—or a piano leg—would. I don't *like* that, but I can understand it.

I want to ask you to do something for me about Daddy, but now that the time has come, I can't think of anything more to ask than: explain me to him. And you've always done that anyway, haven't you? Or tried at least, since I don't know who can explain *anything* to him when he resists it, as he obviously does in my case and many others. But if you find a way, you might tell him that—even though he may not believe it—I've never really meant to hurt and confound him. I've only tried to live my life as it was given to me. And if it hasn't been what he'd have chosen for me, neither has it been exactly what I'd have chosen for myself. God again—and Daddy must make allowances for him, just like the rest of us.

But I don't mean to lecture him through you. I'm sorry for all his pain, and especially for the part of it I've caused. I hope it's begun to subside. I hope he's started to forgive me—again. I even dare to hope that some day he will understand me.

Who am I though to wish understanding to someone else? Night and snow are closing in. The visibility here is minimal. If it pleases you to know that I have faith, then know that I have this much: he gets his way.

Don't hold your breath waiting for more.

Love from your faithful piano leg,
Megan

Father Drake folded the letter carefully and handed it back to Eleanor with a smile. "Did you share this with Justin?"

"I offered, but he'll only hear about her from me. He says I put her in a benign light for him."

"I'm sure you must."

For a moment Eleanor faltered. "But what they did . . . it wasn't right, was it?"

"No", Drake acknowledged, "and God doesn't repeal our pasts. He only wants to carry us into the future if we allow him. . . . Perhaps now they've finally begun to allow him."

"Then it's strange, isn't it . . . ?"

"What?"

"Isn't it possible that everything that's happened is better for

Megan and Arthur? For Jon? For Vincent? Even for Justin? And if for them, why not for others, too?"

"Bishop Farquhar's renewal has been a *felix culpa?*"

She laughed. "I know it sounds foolish. Still . . . *omnia in bonum.*"

"There's nothing foolish about that. Except that one seldom sees *how* it works."

"Then perhaps we're more fortunate than most people." She leaned back, eyes fixed on the high ceiling, forming her thoughts while the radiator hissed and rumbled. "I wouldn't be surprised if we were. To see . . . oh, imperfectly, of course, but still . . . to glimpse how everything *does* work together. Is there anything to that, Father?"

And he also paused, letting the question hang in the motefilled air, which a ray of sunlight now pierced with the acuity of a two-edged sword. The moment seemed to cry out for deliverance of the truth, but it passed quickly, as such moments generally do, with the truth either undelivered or, perhaps, too plain to both of them to need speaking.

"Everything, my dear", he merely said. "Everything."